Rose Gray

Rose Gray

Tansy Chapman

RESOURCE *Publications* · Eugene, Oregon

ROSE GRAY

Resource Publications
An Imprint of Wipf and Stock Publishers
199 W. 8th Ave., Suite 3
Eugene, OR 97401

www.wipfandstock.com

PAPERBACK ISBN: 978-1-7252-6531-8
HARDCOVER ISBN: 978-1-7252-6514-1
EBOOK ISBN: 978-1-7252-6521-9

Manufactured in the U.S.A.   06/03/20

For my beloved grandchildren:
Daniel, Andy, Mae, Auden, Tessa and Nicholas,
who give me hope for the Future.

Acknowledgements

THIS NOVEL WOULD NEVER have been completed without encouragement, over the years, from my gifted writing teacher, Charlotte Gullick, who had faith in the emergence of my main character, Rose, while pushing me, long distance, after she moved to Texas, to revise, revise, revise.

I also want to thank Molly Dwyer, author and teacher, who has helped me in countless ways to keep going, when I might so easily have given up.

Consistent inspiration has come from my writing groups. Until I semi-retired, I wrote nonfiction sermons and retreat addresses. With thanks to instructor Dreux Carpenter, who inspired us to gather, my first group met weekly for years, presenting draft after draft of short stories and novels-in-progress.

Thank you, Jeanette, Henri, Larry, Doug, Nancy, Fauna and Molly.

Thanks, also, to my present writing group, still ongoing, who invited me in, and kept up their feedback when I was lagging, until the final push through. They are: Molly, Nona, Fran and Notty.

I wish to acknowledge the tremendous volunteer effort that has yearly produced The Mendocino County Writer's Conference, attracting authors from all over the country, especially at this time, in the midst of the pandemic.

I would never have persevered without friends, far and wide, published authors themselves: Sarah Rossiter, Jeanette Boyer, Marilyn Hagar, Larry Smith, Julia Slayton, Harriet Gleason, my neighbor Suzanne Lewis, and countless others who have asked, "How's Rose?"

Thank you, Shari McCullough, for being one of the first to read the whole book and encouraging me to keep going. Also, Martin Smith, whose English perspective I appreciated, and my friend Lisa McElaney's unique point-of-view.

Acknowledgements

If it had not been for Don McCullough, another first reader, who nagged me for weeks, I would never have submitted a book proposal to Wipf and Stock publishers. I am so grateful he did, and for the consistent courtesy and efficiency shown me by W&S through the entire production process.

Finally, I am so grateful for the love and support of my family. You are each so dear to me.

England, April 1947

— 1 —

ROSE GRAY SITS IN her flannel nightgown on the back doorstep, enjoying the light and shadows of an early spring morning. Her cat, a tabby hunter with battered ears, keeps watch beside her, alert to sounds Rose fails to hear and movements she thinks are the wind chasing dead leaves. Across the farmyard a ruckus comes from the piggery: the clang of buckets, a man cursing, machinery starting up, stopping. The cat growls and swishes his tail. Rose runs her hand down his spine.

"I love you, Moggy-cat." She buries her face in his fur, smelling the sweet straw where he sleeps high under the barn roof. A deep rumble rises in his throat.

Steamy water gushes from an outdoor spout, splashing into the drain below. Rose listens to her mother's familiar smoker's cough. She should be helping with the washing up, but the heavy cat pushes his way onto her lap and kneads her bony knees.

"Ouch, that hurts!" She lifts Moggy's front paws so they work the air. Still she dawdles, relieved to be outdoors after winter's burst pipes, snow drifts higher than the window sills, and chilblains, cracked and itchy from sitting too close to the fire, even as her back froze in the draughty, poorly insulated house.

A lanky girl with plaits, tall for her age, Rose started her period six weeks ago. Her mother warned it might happen soon and showed how to wrap sanitary towels in newspaper and burn them on the small coal fire in the living room; but only when her father is out working on the farm. Besides her mother, only Rose's best friend knows. It was Annie who informed Rose she now could have a baby. Like Rose, Annie recently had her thirteenth birthday. They made a bet that the first to get her period would buy the other a tube of gumdrops. The minute she heard the news, Annie marched Rose to the sweet shop and made her bring her ration book. Annie ate the entire roll in front of Rose, refusing even to share the green ones. The ritual left them both with an indelible connection between gumdrops and menstruation.

Rose gazes across the farmyard. The housefront overlooks the town of Woolston spread out in the valley below. But from where she sits, the land lies flat under a changing sky. No longer visible is an airstrip where warplanes once flew up, like birds of prey, skimming the horizon. The freshly ploughed fields smell of last year's decaying roots, the soil dark, almost black from weeks of melting snow. Ugly steel pylons giant-step across the land, bearing electricity to scattered houses on the government-owned settlement where she lives. In the distance, a water tower looms.

The Jacksons live next door—too close for comfort, Rose's mum says. Fred Jackson recently married a pale and anxious woman named Vera. It was a second marriage for them both. She came with her eight-year-old son Keith, a pasty-faced boy with a constantly runny nose. The Jacksons grow tomatoes in two glass houses, and raise chickens, purchased as baby chicks from the central packing station. Not long ago, Rose took Keith to see the conveyor belt of yellow cheeping birds upended to sort male from female by laughing, joking women, scarves wound around their heads like turbans. Rose showed him the back of the shed door with pictures of pinup girls and rude seaside postcards, but they were chased away and the boy ran home sniveling.

The elder Jacksons and Grays choose not to socialize, each believing they are a class above the other, forced to live in their present conditions because of the war. The thin partitioning walls between the two houses sabotage any attempt at real privacy, information coming through as broken and staccato as an enemy radio.

From her perch, Rose becomes aware of Keith spying from the communal bomb shelter roof and pulls her nightgown around her legs. Not that Keith would be looking at her legs. He'd be far more interested in playing war games if she gave him the slightest encouragement. She pretends not to see him.

Her real hope is that now the weather has improved, Annie will ride her bicycle up from town. Annie lives with her mother and older brother George in a row of identical houses near the school. Her mum, Mrs. Carter, works all day in a cake shop. Mr. Carter died in the war when enemy aircraft destroyed his ship. A telegram came in the night. Annie said her mother knew what it would say: she'd dreamed only days before that he had perished. When she's at Annie's house, Rose sees the framed photograph of Mr. Carter on the piano in the tiny front parlor, a kind-looking man with dark hair neatly parted to one side.

Until Annie's appearance in her life, school for Rose was a matter of endurance. She rode the public country bus with its mix of yelling, boisterous children and long-suffering adults, eager only to return to the steamy comfort of her mother's kitchen.

Both Rose and Annie passed the eleven-plus entrance exam for girls' grammar school, but were placed in different forms. A year went by before they met for the first time one bright November day. Orange and red leaves from great oak trees piled against the playground fence, and Annie was racing around in a game of catch. Rose remembers observing the scene, hands thrust deep in her pockets as she might on a railway platform, never expecting to be spoken to. The girls gathered and separated in endless, chattering interaction. Rose couldn't help longing for a familiar and welcoming face.

Annie was easy to spot, bright-cheeked, seemingly oblivious to the passionate attachments or spiteful exclusions of those around her.

"Hello," she said, "I'm Annie." She quizzed Rose about her name and where she lived as girls came up, lost interest, and drifted away. Annie liked the idea of a farm, probably imagining something more romantic than the muddy fields around Rose's house.

The following Saturday, she arrived at the back door, out of breath from toiling up the hill on her bicycle. Rose's dad responded to Annie's knocking, "What do you want?"

She stepped back. "I've come to see Rose."

Rose, in bedroom slippers, squeezed past her father to stand on the step. Annie firmly announced, "I said I'd come, and I've come."

Rose smiles, remembering. From that day on, she saw things through her new friend's eyes: rundown farm buildings, the stench of pigs, a precarious greenhouse with cracked windows, the shabby, cheaply built housing, and even mud and patches of stinging nettles, all sources of fascination to Annie. When Rose tells the names of plants and trees and animals, Annie listens. She hasn't told her friend everything that happens on the farm.

Rose shifts from one buttock to the other, recalling Mum's warning: a cold step is bad for the kidneys. She stays, face lifted to the pale sun. Moggy draped over her lap, yellow eyes half closed, lazily follows the flight of nesting swallows flitting in and out of the barn. A shadow appears around the piggery wall. Claws dig into Rose's flesh. With a powerful kick, the cat springs down and flees under a nearby forsythia bush. The crunch of her father's boots makes Rose spring to her feet.

"Wait, girl!" He puts down two feed buckets. A heavily built man in brown overalls and cloth cap, he pushes her aside to open the kitchen door.

"Where's your mother?" His hulk blocks any chance of wiggling past.

"I'm here, Stanley." Alice's voice comes from inside.

"Why's the girl not dressed and in the daylight like that? It's not decent. Has she done her chores like she's supposed to do?"

"I thought I'd let her sit outdoors in the sunshine for a while. It's been so long since we could do that." Rose can't see her mother's expression, but she recognizes the tight voice she uses when Dad's worked up.

"I'll do them now." Rose speaks into the back of overalls smelling of meal dust and pigs. He refuses to let her pass.

"What's the matter, Stanley? What's upset you?"

"My best farrowing sow is sick; the whole litter's going to die and she'll be useless."

"You don't know that yet."

"It's you who don't know. I start to get ahead, then some fresh disaster. We might as well pack it in."

"You work hard. I know you do . . ."

Rose joins in. "It'll be all right, Daddy." She pats his back. He shrugs her away, launching into a list she knows by heart of disasters that have befallen him. Rose pictures a farm truck tipping out its load on their sunny kitchen floor.

"And another thing, Alice: the bloody government's going to shut this whole place down one of these days. You'll see. They won't be able to make a go of it. Then we're done for. Or if not that, there's swine fever up north, and there's no stopping it. Then the whole herd's done for. Might as well start digging a hole for the lot of them."

Rose feels the bleakness her father pulls around him like his old army coat. His large frame prevents her running to her mother's side. Her mum, as she always does, tries to reason, point out things might not be as bad as they seem. "They have new medicines. It isn't like the old days."

If only, Rose thinks longingly, Dad would talk of good times—days long before she was born, a life of money and servants and trips abroad. Mum's soothing words seem to rile Dad even more. He shouts, spraying flecks of spit. Rose claps her hands over her ears as Stanley steps further into the small kitchen. She pushes forward in time to see his flung cloth cap skidding across the linoleum.

"I'll go down the road and telephone the vet." Mum talks rapidly now, untying her apron.

"Mr. Vale will help us," Rose echoes, her voice quavering.

"That bloody vet—he's useless." Her father picks up a plate from the counter, weighs it in his hands.

"Stanley, you're wrong. I'm going to phone right now." Mum reaches in a jar for coins. "Put that plate down; you're making me nervous."

"Can't I make you bloody understand? We're done for." He hurls the plate into the sink.

Rose, unable to stand being kept back a moment longer, pushes forward to see shattered pieces of blue and white crockery. "That was Mum's favorite dish."

"Who the devil asked you?" Stanley roars.

"But, Dad, it belonged to her when she was a little girl."

Alice grasps Rose's shoulders, steering her toward the sitting room and stairs beyond. "Go now and get dressed." Rose resists, too afraid to move. From the corner of her eye she's seen her father's raised hand. He shoulders Mum aside. The slap lands hard on the side of Rose's face. Instinctively, arms shielding her head, Rose waits for another blow that comes as a violent shove in the back. From somewhere far away, she watches herself grasp at furniture, staggering to keep her balance. She thinks, it doesn't hurt—I won't let it hurt.

Her mother's voice carries. "Stanley, don't take it out on her."

"That's right, gang up on me, like you always do." The back door slams hard, rattling the kitchen shelves. Rose flees upstairs and falls onto the bed. Horrified, she realizes she's peed on her nightgown.

FOR A LONG TIME, Rose lies curled, knees to her chest, waiting for her mother to come, as surely she will. Over an hour has passed. She sits up, listening: no sounds from below. She imagines her mother downstairs, hands shaking, lighting a cigarette.

"To calm my nerves," she always says.

Rose calls loudly, "Mum!"

She thinks, I've only myself to blame.

"Keep out of his way when he's like that, then you won't get hurt," Mum tells her. Rose knows her father's anger. She's seen him swing steel buckets at the pigs when they crowd him. He kicks the tractor when it won't start. Once, sitting on the stairs, listening, she heard him threaten, "I'm warning you, Alice." Rose thinks, *Warning about what?* Next day, Mum said Dad was riled up, best not to provoke him. She'd added, "And don't go talking to anyone about this. Your Dad works hard and doesn't drink like some do around here, so keep your mouth shut. The walls are thin enough."

Rose bundles her pee-soaked nightgown into a ball and stuffs it under the bed. Looking about the untidy bedroom shared with her mother, she retrieves clothes from a chair and quickly dresses: knickers, vest, an old jersey and pants, shoes and socks. The dusty dressing table mirror reflects her blotched face, a red mark flares across her cheek. Salt tears sting her eyes and she searches a drawer for a hanky, sniffing the faint scent of face powder and Mum's favorite Red Poppy perfume, aching to be comforted. A hairbrush lies on the table. Mum would tell her to stop the fuss. Rose brushes her tangled hair and ties it back with an elastic band.

Downstairs, she walks slowly through the house to the back. There's no one. A half-peeled potato rests on the kitchen counter next to a paring knife. Stubbed-out cigarettes heap in an ashtray nearby. Back in the sitting room, Rose surveys the scene: a folded table where they eat; two armchairs with faded cushions, drawn close to the unlit fireplace; her mother's sewing basket; an Oxford dictionary, pen and crossword puzzle on a closed wooden desk; her father's pipe and tobacco pouch near his chair. The mantle clock says it's nearly time to start the midday meal. Furniture polish and a cloth on the dining table jolt her memory—on Saturdays it's her job to sweep and dust.

Calling loudly now, she hurries back toward the kitchen. The door to the lavatory is closed. She knocks first, and then turns the knob, imagining her mother ill. The wooden seat is up, and toilet paper flutters in the breeze from the propped-open window. She runs upstairs to the other bedroom, where her father sleeps. Mum won't be there, but she feels sick as she opens the door, praying, "Don't let Mummy be dead." The room is dark, curtains drawn; masculine smells, mothballs, hair cream and perspiration permeate the air. An eiderdown and grey wool blanket have slipped halfway to the floor from the unmade bed. A slight movement makes her jump, but it's only her reflection in the mirror on the open wardrobe door.

Downstairs once more, emptiness permeates the house. She goes to the back door and stands on the step, drawing in cool air. The scene that earlier gave pleasure seems stark, with shadowy farm buildings and a vast expanse of metal-colored sky. With unrelenting images of her mother hurt or dead, Rose follows the path to the greenhouse. A blast of warm, acrid air greets her as she opens the door. Among neat rows of newly planted tomato plants are her mother's gloves, fingers curled, next to a ball of twine. The only sounds are the sighing steam pipes and a creaking of the glass and wooden structure.

Outside, her cat leaps from a patch of thick grass. Rose scoops him up, but he struggles free, and stalks off toward the barn. A distant noise: in a far field her father, sledgehammer high above his head, drives a post into the ground. Rose turns back toward the house, prepared to do the only thing she can think to do, which is to start her chores.

She fetches dustpan and brush from the cupboard under the stairs: a space filled with old coats, boots, and a tennis racquet in its press. As soon as Rose unlatches and opens the door, she's hit by musty, familiar smells. It was here she and Mum hid during air raids. Preferable, Alice said, to spending a night with the Jacksons in the bomb shelter. Her father was out with the Home Guard in a coarse, khaki uniform, checking blackout material in everyone's windows. Mum made a game of bombing raids, telling Rose that the loud noises were Old King Cole stomping around in the heavens.

Rose is older and taller now. On an impulse, she steps into the slanting cupboard. The low shelf where they sat is still there. She crouches in the dim light, remembering the red, circling patterns Mum made with her cigarette. A memory rises of Dad coming home one night shaking and sobbing. She'd refused to stay by herself in the dark cupboard and the three of them huddled in the sitting room, windows rattling, plaster falling from the ceiling while Mum rubbed Dad's hands and feet to stop the trembling. From then on, she never believed it was a game.

Rose suddenly needs air, banging her head as she comes out, calling in vain for her mother. She sets about dusting, though memories still snag and drag at her sleeve. Mum said Dad got up next morning and fed the animals as usual, but from then on he was never really himself. Rose, as she works, wonders what Dad would be like, really himself.

Another hour passes. The chores of sweeping and polishing help distract, but once done, dread weighs on her chest. Her mouth and throat are dry. Mum has never been gone like this without saying something first. There's no other choice; she must approach her father.

From the back door, Rose spots him still in the far field uncoiling a roll of barbed wire. She shouts, but her voice is snatched by an east wind, bearing banks of dark cloud. If her mother is gone, she has to be brave and tell him. That's what Annie would say to dare. She stumbles over matted grass and climbs a metal gate across the farm track. Far from the shelter of the house, wind gusts over the fields, making her eyes water.

"Dad," she shouts. He turns, putting down the heavy sledge hammer, red-faced, sweat pouring from his forehead, dripping from nose and chin. He takes a rag from his pocket and wipes his brow. She catches the scent of him.

"What you doing out here with no coat?"

Rose hops from one foot to the other, arms wrapped around her chest: "Mummy's gone."

Stanley looks at her with pale blue eyes and glances at the house. "Nonsense, girl." He picks up the hammer, steadies the fencepost, and braces himself to swing. "Where would she go?" He jerks his head. "Mind out of the way." The force of the hammer drives the post inches into the ground.

"Dad." She must make him listen. "I need to talk to you."

He grunts, tests the post, and readies himself to swing again.

"I've looked everywhere for her—I think she's run away."

He looks up, "She's coming down the road; use your eyes." Again, he musters strength. Metal crashes against solid wood.

Rose turns to see her mother in the distance, head down against the wind, bicycling toward the house.

—3—

"Mum, I thought you were dead." Rose has run all the way to meet her at the front gate.

Alice's eyes sparkle, her cheeks glow, as she cycles round to the back. "Good gracious, don't be silly—I had to telephone the vet. You heard. Dad's best sow has milk fever and he's afraid she'll die and the baby pigs will never thrive." She leans her bike against the shed.

Rose pictures the red kiosk, only a half a mile down the road. "But you were gone for hours."

"Was I?" Alice says vaguely. " I'm here now. We must hurry and get dinner on the table."

Rose trails after her. Her mother wears faded blue slacks and a knitted cardigan, a flowered scarf tied loosely at her neck, her thick, curly brown hair blown by the wind; not at all like her friends' mothers with their tight, permanent waves. There's a spring to Alice's step as she approaches the back door and stoops to pick a purple pansy.

"You look so pretty," Rose says.

"Nonsense," she says, dreamily pushing back a curl. The house has the lemony smell of furniture polish. "Good, you did the dusting." Light and chatter fill Rose's world as she sets the table with a yellow check cloth and monogrammed silverware left over from Dad's better days. Alice finds music on the radio and hums as she cooks, weaving back and forth around Rose in a tight choreographed dance.

The small space that serves as kitchen has many functions. Pots bubble on the chipped enamel stove as Alice scrapes vegetables in the sink, water running from greenish brass taps. The windowsill above holds splayed tooth brushes, a flattened tube of toothpaste, Drene shampoo, a blue eyewash cup, a yellow bottle of Dettol, and Stanley's ivory shaving brush. In the midst of the clutter, Alice has placed the single pansy in a potted meat jar. The family bathtub, against the wall, supports a wooden board, providing extra counter space. It holds baskets of onions and turnips dug from Alice's vegetable patch. Off the kitchen, there's a small, cool larder where perishables are kept in a meat safe with a mesh door, and milk, in earthenware cooler, covered with wet cloth weighted down with colored beads. Sticky flypaper hangs from a light fixture, moths and flies feebly struggling to get free.

On the way from sink to stove, Mum grasps Rose by both shoulders and turns her face to the light. She gently touches the bruised cheek. "What were you doing in the field talking to your father?"

Rose dearly wants to tell of her ordeal and to ask Mum why she was away for so long, but words lock inside. Knowing her mother is safe is all she prayed for. Rose looks at her feet and sighs.

"What a strange child you are," Alice murmurs. She looks at the clock, "Hurry, fetch some milk and mash the potatoes. The brussels sprouts are ready. I'll slice the cold chicken. Get a move on. Daddy's going to be hungry, and the vet's due any minute."

The radio switches tunes. Alice hums 'I'll Be Loving You.'

After a flurry of serving, Alice removes her apron and settles by the window. Stanley came in around midday, washed his hands and arms with yellow soap at the kitchen sink, and dried them on the roller towel at the back door. The pieces of broken plate have been banished to the dustbin. He eats steadily and silently, his bleak expression the only sign of the earlier outburst. Rose wills him to say he likes the meal her mother has prepared. He says nothing.

"This is delicious, Mum."

Outside the open window, a few sparrows and two goldfinches fight over a bread crust on the feeder. Somewhere below her cat yowls. Stanley frowns, as if remembering something. He takes a watch from his pocket.

"When did that vet say he was coming?"

"As soon as he can," Alice says. "His receptionist said there are a lot of sick animals. When he comes in, she'll give him the message."

She rises to clear away the plates, and Rose helps. There are stewed apples and yellow Bird's Eye custard for pudding, served in blue and white china bowls. Stanley sprinkles on brown sugar and Rose does the same while her mother disappears into the kitchen and closes the door.

She says she doesn't like sweets, but Rose knows Mum has gone to smoke and later will eat from serving dishes, standing at the counter. Alone with her father, Rose wedges her knees against the table to stop them shaking.

"Do you like pudding, Daddy?"

He looks up from his food, "I suppose so."

They eat in silence. She mixes custard and apples and brown sugar, making patterns with her spoon. In the next room, they hear coughing. Stanley glances at the door. He shakes his head and grimaces. Rose scrunches her face too and for a fleeting moment she and her father connect. Then both look away. The mantle clock ticks, unwinding its mechanical spring. If only Mum would come back, or Dad would finish eating. Rose plays with a piece of bread, shaping it into a ball, like putty.

The knocking on the back door is firm and loud. "The vet's here!" Rose says. "Shall I answer it, Dad?" She jumps up, ahead of him. Her mother, already on the way, tidies her hair, stubbing her cigarette as she goes. Rose hears her say, "Oh Annie, dear, I thought you were the vet."

Behind her, Stanley grumbles his way back to his chair.

"Please, Mrs. Gray, can Rose come out to play?" Annie beams at Rose peeking out from behind her mother. "Hello, Rose."

"Hello, Annie." Rose grabs her coat and wool hat from the peg.

Alice steps aside, laughing. "All right, off you go, but mind you two stay out of trouble. She calls after them, "Rose, don't forget your Wellington boots—they're in the bike shed."

— 4 —

THE GIRLS SET OFF across the ploughed field. "Where are we going?" Rose breaks into a run.

Annie points to the water tower on the far edge of the field. "Over there, I'll race you." She leads the way, leaping over ruts, her rubber boots collecting mud from the rich soil. Above them a large crow, tattered wings stretched out, rides with the currents. Rose lags behind, arms wrapped around her small breasts.

Annie looks back. "Why are you running like that?" Her voice reaches Rose above the wind and piercing sweet sound of low-flying birds.

Rose shouts back, "It hurts, if I don't."

Annie stops with hands on her hips and looks Rose up and down. "You need a bra! Not me, though. Ma says I'm as flat as a board." She whoops, and takes off again zigzagging, seemingly pleased with her own wit. Her face hot, Rose follows, feet pounding the dirt, even as she worries that she may be trampling newly planted seedlings.

She finds Annie lying spread-eagled on the concrete slab squinting up at the water tower's iron ladder. Rose joins her, watching small clouds race far above the structure silhouetted black against the blue sky. "It's like being on a ship."

Annie rolls onto one side, props on an elbow and studies Rose's face. "Where did you get that bruise?'

"What bruise?" Rose feels herself blushing.

"The one here . . ." Annie pokes her cheek.

"That hurts."

"It's all different colors! What happened to you this time, clumsy?"

Rose squirms under her friend's scrutiny. "I must've banged into a door." She puts an arm across her face, not wanting Annie to see the lie and all that's behind it.

"You better not fall when you're up there." Annie sits and points to the ladder. Before Rose can speak, she has them both on their feet. "We're going to climb it."

"Climb what? We're not allowed. My dad will kill us if he finds out."

"We have to."

"Why?"

"Because otherwise we can't belong to the club, that's why." Annie's brown eyes are fierce. She confronts her friend, hands on hips. "You took the oath, didn't you? Don't turn lily-livered on me, Rose Gray."

"I'm not lily-livered!"

"Prove it or I'm going home."

Behind her Rose reads red letters: "DANGER: KEEP OFF." Annie starts to walk away. "Wait!" Rose can't bear her to leave. It's true that they have talked for months about starting a club. They'd cleared a space above some pigsties, reachable only by climbing a frayed rope once used to haul straw bales. Rose recalls the stink of dung and how the animals stopped to watch as the girls clambered into the dusty loft. Perched on wooden boxes, they discussed a password and that membership would be limited.

"Definitely no boys," Annie had pronounced. "Definitely not," agreed Rose, secretly intrigued by the thought. They argued over what to call themselves and finally decided on "Daring Demons." Then a ritual that Annie insisted all secret societies do: pricking fingers with a darning needle, and mingling blood and spit.

"The water tower will be our initiation rite," Annie declares. She's shorter than Rose and sturdy, her brown hair sticking out from under her hat. She appraises the tank about twenty feet above.

"I thought we already had an initiation rite."

"You mean the blood and spit? If we are going to be Daring Demons, we have to do things that take real nerve."

Rose hates it when her friend makes up rules as she goes along.

"You go first, Rose, and I'll steady the ladder. Here's a piece of chalk. We'll have to make a mark at the top to prove we did it." She thrusts the chalk into Rose's pocket.

"Who says I have to go first?"

"I do, because I'm the chief. If you do this, you can be chief next time."

Rose looks up—the ladder seems to stretch forever. She grasps a bottom rung; rust flakes. More than anything she wants Annie to think her brave. Taking a deep breath she climbs, hand over hand.

"Don't look down." Instructions float up from below.

Rose tightens her grip. The tank looms; racing clouds above make her dizzy. She can barely hold on. Closing her eyes, she feels suspended in time. The cold metal bites into her palms as the wind bangs against the tower. Rooks sail past, throaty caws jubilant as their dark shapes circle around.

"What's wrong, Rose?"

She dare not move her head. "I feel giddy." The landscape reels. "I'm going to fall." She imagines her body's thud on the concrete, bones breaking, her stomach split open like the dog she once saw run over in the road, its warm insides steaming, spilled out. The ladder shakes. "Annie, what are you doing? She feels a firm grip on her ankle.

"Only eight more rungs and you'll reach the top."

"I can't!"

"Pretend you're climbing the ropes at the gym in school."

"I'm hopeless at gym. I want to come down."

"Come on now, one step at a time."

Shakily, Rose climbs another rung. "I don't think this ladder will bear us both."

"Then we'll die together."

"Don't make jokes. I don't like this one bit." Gritting her teeth, Rose climbs until her eyes level with the tank. Grey-green lichen covers the corrugated surface. The wind blows in fierce gusts and drums in her ears. Annie stays quiet. Rose sees only the top of her head.

"Annie?"

"What?"

"Do you remember me telling you about that boy, Patrick Murray?"

"Who? I can't hear you."

"Patrick Murray?"

Rose flinches as her voices echoes. It feels irreverent to be shouting a dead person's name. Far off, the cry of a bird sounds like a person calling.

Annie climbs higher; her arms reach around Rose's waist as she grasps the ladder. Rose feels a warm cheek pressed against her back.

"Wasn't he electrocuted?" Annie says.

The heat of her friend's body acts as a shield—both a comfort and a distraction.

"He was climbing a pylon and touched a live wire."

Rose knew the sickly looking boy from Sunday school. From the start, she'd had a feeling he'd die young. Such uncanny thoughts alarm her, especially when they come true.

"Why'd you have to remind me?" Annie mumbles. The ladder shakes as she climbs down. Without Annie's protection from the wind, Rose doesn't dare attempt the last few rungs or to reach in her pocket for the chalk.

At the bottom, the girls collapse. Rose's world spins and the concrete slab seems to move beneath her. She rolls over to see Annie wiping her eyes with her sleeve. Rose reaches out to touch her.

Annie says, "I can't help thinking about when my dad died, and how sad Ma was."

Rose can't imagine having a father like the one Annie treasures in her memory. She wonders if her friend was afraid on the tower too, thinking they might fall, and about death. Rose offers a hand, "Let's go home."

Annie holds back. "We'll do it again one day soon, won't we? We'll climb all the way to the top?"

"Of course we will," Rose, strong again, pulls her friend to her feet.

They take the long way back along the lane, arm in arm, bumping hips. The ditches run with clear, fast water; small birds fly in and out of the hedgerows and the girls pick bunches of pale primroses, violets, and polished yellow celandine. They hold on to each other as a man passes them high up on a tractor. Over the rumble of machinery, they call to him: "We're the Daring Demons!" He cannot hear them, but he touches his cap.

— 5 —

THE GIRLS CLIMB THE gate to the farm. "Rain is coming." Rose lifts her face. "I smell it in the air."

"All I can smell is manure." Annie, balanced on the gate, points to the greenhouse. "Look, the lights are on."

"Mum must be in there working. She'll love the flowers we picked."

"Any chance of strawberries for tea?"

"They won't be ripe for ages. Might be oatcakes, though."

Outside the greenhouse, they wipe their muddy boots. Rose holds a coarse grass blade between her thumbs and blows.

"You sound like a dying duck." Annie tries but soon gives up, sputtering with laughter.

They spy through the windows: Alice is bent over, stringing delicate tomato plants.

"Promise me, Annie, you won't tell about the tower."

Annie winks, pushes her shoulder against the door and barges into the steamy interior. Not sure her friend's to be trusted, Rose follows. The first patters of rain hit the roof.

Mum winces, straightening her back. She fishes in her pockets for cigarettes and matches. "What have you two been up to?"

"Nothing, we went for a walk." Rose hangs back. She loves the acrid smell of sun-warmed plants and often joins her mother, helping where she can. Having her friend here is different. Annie knows nothing about the awful row in the morning or that Mum was gone for hours. The tower, too, must be kept secret. Rose wonders if her hands still bear the imprint of the metal rungs, and if her sharp-eyed mother will see them. She holds tight to the bunch of wildflowers.

Annie settles on a low heating pipe, stretches her legs, and pulls off her hat. She acts at home, flattened hair sticking out in all directions, eyes bright and inquisitive, prattling about their walk across the field and back along the lane. Inwardly, Rose smiles, remembering a water rat in the ditch, hidden except for its wet, black tail.

Moods shift like the afternoon sky—if only she could find her cat and curl up with him in the straw barn, alone with her thoughts. She sees Mum's fondness for her friend and how easily they get along. Annie grins, beckoning her to hand over the flowers. Rose reluctantly relinquishes them.

"How lovely," Mum buries her nose in the yellow petals. "Thank you, girls, they smell of the woods."

The rain, heavy now, sluices down the windows and slaps violently against the glass roof.

Annie, raising her voice, keeps up the chatter: "We saw a lapwing along a furrow in the ploughed field. It acted as if its wing was broken."

Alice takes a deep drag, tips back her head, and makes two smoky circles that float lazily to the ceiling. Annie applauds. Alice joins her on the warm pipe, "Did you notice its strange cry?" she asks.

"Yes. Like someone calling." Annie imitates the bird's two-toned mournful sound. Rose remembers hearing it too, from the ladder. Annie has no idea how much trouble there'll be if they are found out.

This time it's Alice who claps her hands, "That's why the bird's other name is pee-wee."

"Should we rescue it?"

"Goodness, no! It's how the female protects her young—she acts as a decoy by pretending to be injured. She's guarding her nest from a hawk, perhaps, or an owl."

Annie looks thoughtful. "Supposing the hawk swoops down and flies off with the mother? What would happen to the babies?"

"Yes," Rose finally speaks. "What would happen?"

Alice laughs at their serious faces: "I expect she's much too clever a mother to be caught!" She takes a last puff and grinds her cigarette end into the soft soil with her heel.

Hands pushed into the small of her back, she says, "Now, girls, I need to finish this last row. Rose, I want you to find your father and tell him tea will be ready in fifteen minutes, but don't hang about bothering him."

She steps close to Rose, touching her hair, retying loose ribbons. "Why are you so quiet? Look at me when I am speaking to you."

"I'm okay."

"Then cheer up." And louder, so Annie can hear, "In ten minutes, I want you to put the kettle on, and set the table for tea."

Annie says, "Any chance of oatcakes?"

Alice hands Annie her hat and mittens warmed from the pipes. "As soon as the weather clears you should go. It'll be dark soon, and your mother will be looking for you. I'll give you a cake to take home."

Outside, they slosh through puddles; a steady drizzle, mixed with dirt, creates a sea of muck. A mud-splashed green Hillman drives up behind them and comes to a stop at the straw barn. Annie grabs Rose's arm and points. A man in a tweed jacket, brown corduroy trousers, and high boots climbs out and waves. He carries a bulging leather bag and hurries toward the pigsties, his collar turned up against the rain.

"It's the vet," Rose says excitedly.

Annie runs after him and Rose follows, calling out, "We mustn't be in the way." Then she mutters, "It's hopeless!" The rain hits her face. She's glad the vet has come, and that Annie, who is her best friend, likes this muddy place where she lives.

They arrive at the piggery door and Rose pushes back the heavy bolt. Pigs on either side are in uproar, anticipating feed time. The girls hold their noses. Rose signals Annie to look behind and she jumps back. A huge white boar leans on hind legs against the edge of the stall, its fangs flecked with white foam. Its little, pink-rimmed eyes fix on Annie, and Rose yanks her away. Her father has warned the animal could kill. One time she saw Dad enter the stall and the boar charged. With surprising agility, he kicked at the great pig and was outside and bolting the door before it could turn on him again.

Rose leads the way along the corridor to the furthest sty. They hear men's voices, a pig's soft grunting, and occasional squeals of baby pigs. Instead of the odor of dung, there's the smell of clean, fresh straw. The dividing wall looms high and the girls hoist each other up, leaning on their stomachs. A sow lies on her side, piglets clambering all over her. Rose quickly estimates at least ten: a good-sized litter. The vet kneels in the straw, gently pushing the babies aside as he runs his hands over the sow's flanks. The animal lets out a series of dusty sighs. Stanley, on one knee beside him, points to the inflamed and swollen teats. At first the two men don't notice the girls hanging over, watching.

Rose admires the vet's strong features and gentle expression as he talks to the mother pig. She likes that he is young, and has a thatch of brown hair, unlike her father's balding head, which gleams in the light. He speaks to Stanley respectfully and in businesslike tones. "I'm going to give her a shot now, and another tomorrow. We'll have to separate her from the youngsters, at least for a night or two. I'll give you some formula."

He glances up: "Well, look whom we have here. Hello, Rose."

Rose blushes, thrilled that he remembers her name. Her father frowns but she knows he'll say nothing with the vet there.

The man takes out a syringe, readying the shot. He has removed his jacket, rolled up his shirtsleeves. Rose can't help staring at his muscular arms, one with a long, white scar. He strokes the pig's snout: "This will only take a minute, love." She flaps a leathery ear and sighs again. The pig squeals loudly as the needle penetrates her thick hide, and she struggles to her feet, spilling piglets.

The girls watch, fascinated, as the two men create a barrier with a board, and skillfully herd the babies away from the mother. Annie sees something and shouts, pointing to a corner of the stall: "Look, there's a tiny pig over there by itself, buried in the straw."

"That's the runt," Stanley tells her curtly, "It won't survive."

"Oh please, Mr. Gray, couldn't we have it?" She ignores the tugging on her sleeve. Rose knows little can be done to save the runt from being trampled or eaten by the mother.

The vet looks up. "Who's your friend, Rose?"

"I'm Annie." She leans so far that Rose grabs her coat to stop a head-first fall into the sty.

"And I'm David Vale. I'd shake hands, but I have to pay attention to the old girl here, and all her babies. She's feeling quite poorly. Rose's dad is right: there isn't much we can do for the poor little nipper over there, so we concentrate on keeping the other ones healthy." He grabs one of the wriggling, protesting piglets and puts it in the makeshift pen with the others. The runt, half the size of the others, pale as candle wax, lies still.

The sow flops down heavily again, making a cloud of dust, her big head stretched out in the straw, one frightened eye open as her babies are taken away.

"Let's move the poor old girl into the next stall, Stanley, so she can have some peace and quiet."

Annie persists, "Please, please Mr. Gray, let me and Rose take care of the runt."

Stanley's neck jerks. He talks past Annie to Rose, "I want you girls to run along now."

David Vale speaks over the commotion: "By the time we're through, Rose, we're going to need a cup of tea."

Stanley nods, "Tell your mother the vet's here and he's going to need his tea, and hurry up about it."

"Oh help," says Annie. "We forgot about the kettle!"

— 6 —

ON THE WAY TO the house Annie asks, "What will happen to the runt?" Rose put that question to Dad once, and he said if the sow didn't kill it first, he'd probably knock it on the head. She doesn't want to tell Annie this, or how she found a little body tossed on the manure heap. Mum had reminded her that they live on a farm as if that settled the matter.

"It's like the time we found the baby bird, and kept it in a shoe box, and fed it worms. It died anyway."

"But at least we tried," Annie says. "I don't know why your dad doesn't let us feed the poor thing with milk from a bottle." She trudges along, hands thrust deep in her pockets. "He can't let it die all by itself—I bet that nice vet would let us do it. I think your dad's cruel."

"Oh Annie," Rose says helplessly, "He's not. He's been ever so upset about the sow being sick."

"My dad wouldn't let a baby die, because it's the littlest. Our mum says he was the kindest man she ever knew. He wouldn't hurt a fly."

Rose wants to defend her father, to somehow explain him, but no words come, and they walk in silence. For the first time she notices the rain has turned to a fine mist and it's almost dusk. As they reach the house, they see a young man waiting in the driveway.

"It's George." Annie runs to greet her brother. Rose has met the tall gangling youth before, but he seems not to notice her. His neck is long and skinny with a pronounced Adam's apple. Large ears stick out from beneath his cap. He wears a gray, plastic raincoat and baggy trousers secured at the ankle with bicycle clips. Annie says that when their father died in the war, George had to be the man of the house though he was only a young boy.

He ignores Rose. "Ma sent me to fetch you, Annie. You're to come home straight away or you're in trouble."

Annie collects her bike and turns on the small light on the handle bar. "Goodbye, Annie," Rose says miserably.

"Cheerio." She pedals off quickly behind her brother without looking back. Rose watches until their lights are hidden by the trees, wanting to run after them, to tell her friend to wait, that somehow she'll beg Dad to let them take care of the little pig. She'd do almost anything not to have to endure the emptiness she feels now, the worry that Annie will stop being her friend. Being a Daring Demon, she decides, is about being brave, facing things that frighten you, like rats and poisonous adders, thunderstorms, and great heights, war, explosions, and being trapped by falling rubble. As she makes her list, in her heart of hearts, she knows there are other things, inexpressible things, of which she is even more afraid.

Looking out over the valley, the damp air feels fresh. A smattering of lights appears in the town below. Bats swoop by so fast she sees them only from the corner of her eye, but her keen ears detect their high-frequency squeaks. She knows she's supposed to make the tea, but doesn't want to go in yet. Her head is full of ways she could prove to Annie she's not lily-livered, imagining saving her friend from drowning in a raging river, or pulling her from a building on fire. "Hold tight, Annie," she calls into the gathering darkness. "I'm coming to get you."

Rose thinks at first that the cracking of twigs in the bushes is her cat, but the noises become louder and she swings around in time to see a shape ducked down among the wet branches. "Who's there?" she calls sharply.

"Who you talking to, Rose Gray?"

She recognizes the squeaky voice of the boy from next door. "What are you doing spying on me?"

"I ain't spying on you, Rose."

"Yes you are, you horrid boy. I saw you hiding in the bushes."

"I saw you up the water tower, you and that girl, and you're not allowed. My dad said."

"What water tower? You don't know what you're talking about, and it's none of your bloody business anyway." Rose walks over to him, clenching her fists.

"I did see you, Rose Gray, so there!" In the dark his face is a white blob. Rose dances around him, ready to punch his stupid runny nose. That's how she thinks of him—stupid—but she's afraid too. He steps back, as though ready to run home. Rose sniffs, like her cat with a mouse. The boy smells of wet vegetation and pee. Defiantly, he says, "You climbed first, then you got scared and she came up the ladder next, then you both chickened out." He starts to make clucking noises, and Rose goes to slap him, but misses.

"I'm going to wring your nasty skinny little neck." She is so angry she's worried she'll cry. Neither she nor Annie saw anyone when they were up the tower. He must've been spying from one of the deep ditches near the field, along with the water rat.

She grabs his arm, "Have you told anyone?"

"Ouch, you're hurting!"

When she momentarily slackens her grip he says, slyly, "Maybe I did. Maybe I didn't. What's it to you?"

Inwardly, Rose shakes. As her mother would say, there'll be hell to pay. Rose dreads the scene, especially if her father hears about it from Mr. Jackson. Dad can't bear his neighbor, and picks fights with him all the time. She peers through the gloom at the boy's shifty eyes darting in all directions. He hops from one foot to another, whimpering and trying to escape. It surprises her how wiry he is, taking all her strength to keep a grip on his skinny arm. Slowly, it dawns on Rose that he's afraid of her; she has power over him. It's an unfamiliar feeling, and makes her draw back. She tells herself he's only a little boy.

"Don't I play with you, Keith?" Her tone is kinder, but she's not quite ready to let him go.

"Yes, sometimes."

"Don't I play war games with you when I don't even like war games?"

"Yes."

"Would you like to climb the tower with me one day?"

"When Rose? Yes please."

"Soon, we'll do it soon, but it has to be a secret. You mustn't tell anyone. Have you told anyone?"

"No, honest, I ain't said nothing."

Rose believes he's telling the truth, or hopes he is. She takes both arms, but gently this time, pulling him close, so she can feel the beating of his heart.

"Good boy. I'm sorry I said you were horrid. Now do you swear, cross your heart and hope to die, you won't tell?"

In the dark, he makes his promise, and Rose hugs him quickly before he disappears into the gloom. She turns toward her own house and sees all the lights are on, and her heart sinks; she'll be blamed for forgetting the tea. Then she remembers: Mr. Vale will be there, and she starts to run, knowing nothing will be said, and perhaps there'll be oatcakes after all.

—7—

ROSE HAS GONE TO bed willingly enough, tired after the long day, but now she's wide awake. Unlike the years of blackout, when there was only darkness, moonlight patterns the room. She hears her parents downstairs. Her father soaks in the bath, while Mum finishes tidying the kitchen: a Saturday night ritual from which Rose is banished. She cringes. Recently, she accidentally walked in on Dad in the tub. It was only a glimpse of his rounded, white belly and, below, the dark hair and outline of his penis floating, marine-like, beneath sudsy water, before he roared for her to "shut the damn door." The harder she tries not to think of her father's naked body, the more the image comes back, and his reaction to her intrusion that makes her shrink with shame.

If only she could fall asleep. Her limbs are heavy, the old mattress full of lumps, however much she wriggles to find a comfortable spot. Suspended between wakefulness and oblivion, she has the sensation of falling—dozing fitfully, then jerking awake. Her brain refuses to switch off.

After Annie and George left, and after the tussle with Keith, she'd gone in to find Mum busy in the kitchen. Alice had changed into a blouse she'd sewn herself out of yellow parachute silk. She'd put on pink lipstick and a dab of rouge on both cheeks. "Where on earth have you been, Rose?" Mum scolded, but, without waiting for an answer, gave her the best teacups to carry to the table.

David Vale and her father were there. Mum poured their tea. Lying in bed now, Rose remembers staring at the vet, his jacket hung on the back of his chair. She pictures his hands holding the cup, the same hands that had caressed the flanks of the sick sow. Shirt sleeves rolled down, the snaking scar was invisible, except for a small white mark on the inside of his wrist. She reconjures the smell of clean cotton and wonders who washes and irons his shirts.

Her father had been quite talkative, complaining to Mr. Vale about what it was like to work for the government, and his distrust of the farm manager. Dad boasted of the hundred acres of prize arable land in Sussex his then-wealthy father had plans to buy, and for him, the oldest son, to farm. "Then the stock market collapsed, banks failed, and everything went to hell."

Rose doesn't like it when her father talks of hell.

Mr. Vale listened and drank his tea. "It's been a hard time for a lot of people, Stanley." Rose worried that he was bored. She'd seen the vet sneaking a look at his watch. The shabbiness of the house, with its cheap furniture and worn slipcovers, was an embarrassment. Not that Mr. Vale was stuck up—he sat right down and made himself at home like it was his own living room. It was her mother who seemed nervous, talking too much, and plying him with oatcakes. She offered to bring out a bottle of port, but he said he had to go. "There's a sick horse I must attend to."

When he was gone, the house became very quiet. Mum put on a housecoat over her blouse to do the washing up. Her father stayed, smoking his pipe and staring into the fire. Rose put away the tea things and fed her cat.

Rose likes to think of Mr. Vale as David, which is what Mum calls him. She practices saying "David," and then says it again, softly: "David."

She turns over her pillow to find a cool spot for burning cheeks, and feels the bruise on her jaw; and then the memory of wetting herself, mocking the very notion of David Vale liking her. In horror, she recalls the damp nightgown stuffed under the bed. But when she turns on the light for a second, and hangs down to look, it isn't there. Mum must've found it.

In the dark again, Rose worries about the runt and wishes she and Annie hadn't quarreled. The tiny pig, alone in the straw, could be dead by now, its body stiff and cold. The stark image spirals her thoughts downward and she breaks into a sweat.

Like a swimmer bursting the surface, Rose sits bolt upright. The reality of death constantly pulls her into the depths. There's no escape: the dread of Mum dying is always there; there's no explaining it. She fights the inevitable that she too will die, and so will everyone she knows. Rose moans, struggling with terrors that come in the night. She tries to think of "forever" in time, pushing the thought until her mind reaches a precipice beyond which there is no time. Space, too, has no end to it, yet its limitlessness is past anything she can imagine. Her mind scurries for exits, like a small wild animal in a cage. Shadows made by the ash tree outside the window dance on the wall. She wants to cry out, but once when Rose spoke aloud of her fears, Mum said she had no answers, and tiredly told her to go back to sleep.

Rose kicks back the covers and pads barefoot to the window. The rain clouds have blown through, and a half moon, ghostly and beautiful, hangs in the night sky. Her grandmother, far away on the south coast of England, says that it is everybody's moon. "Even Hitler's moon?" Rose once asked.

"Yes," Granny said. "It's the same moon that Hitler sees, but Hitler must grieve God terribly."

"Mr. Baxter, my Sunday school teacher, says Hitler's going straight to hell, and that's where we children are all going too if we are not good and don't believe in Jesus."

"Don't listen to that silly man," her granny had told her. "Look up at the evening star and never forget: God loves you and so do I."

Rose sees a gleam of gold on the darkened sill. She picks up the small cross, a gift from Granny, and wraps the chain around her hand, holding it tight. Like a nagging toothache, Rose misses her grandmother. Until she was five, they all lived in the same village: she and her parents and Granny and Grandpa. Her aunt and uncle and two boy cousins lived only a few miles away. Then one day the moving van came. Men walked up and down the path of their stone cottage, carrying boxes and furniture. Rose remembers standing to one side clutching her favorite doll, its half-glued wig tipped over one china blue eye, revealing the mechanical workings in its head. Even if she'd been able to look into her parents' heads and known their thinking, nothing prepared her for the move north that would take her away from everything familiar. The year was 1939. How could anyone have foreseen that the whole world was about to change?

Rose presses her forehead against the cold windowpane. The moon rides high, in and out of the clouds. Tomorrow, she thinks, Mum will make me go to Sunday school and I can't stand it. A prefab hut is not proper church, unlike Granny's, with its embroidered hassocks, stained-glass windows, and stone tower. Just because Mr. Baxter was a missionary in China, it doesn't make him a real vicar. She tried complaining in a letter, but her granny wrote back and said God might prefer prefabs to cathedrals, but she did agree Mr. Baxter had odd ideas. Perhaps her parents would take her to the lovely church downtown.

Rose closes her eyes and prays. Her first prayer is always the same: *Please God, don't let there be another war.* She tells God she's sorry she upset Daddy, and asks that the sick sow will be better soon, and for the babies to thrive, especially the little runt. She doesn't pray everything in her heart, but Granny says God knows anyway. After a while, shivering with cold, she crawls back into bed. Downstairs, the bathwater gurgles down the drain, doors open and close, and someone turns on the radio.

Sleep must have come after all. Rose wakes to rustles and sparks and wafts of Red Poppy, as Alice sheds her blouse and climbs into bed, disturbing the warmth with her cool body. Rose snuggles against her.

"Mummy," Rose whispers, "Where did you go on your bicycle this morning?"

"What are you doing awake? I told you, I went to ring the vet."

"For more than two hours?"

"Now, why are you going on about that?"

"Were you talking to David?"

"It's none of your business. For God's sake, go to sleep."

Rose lies quietly listening to steady breathing as Mum's body gradually slackens. Pins and needles prickle her arm. Slowly, she extracts herself from her mother's embrace and moves to the bed's furthest edge. The sheets are cold, and she curls into a ball for warmth. Her father's snores rumble through the walls and, next door, the rhythmic squeak of Jacksons' bedsprings. Rose lifts her head to catch Moggy's guttural meowing, off on his moonlit prowl. She imagines small furry creatures listening too, hiding in the long grass.

— 8 —

THE BANTAM COCKEREL WAKES her first, strutting up and down his pen, lifting his feet high and stretching his neck, this way and that, to crow to the new day. Rose tries to sink back into sleep, but someone has let the cat in, and he jumps on her bed, treading all over her with sharp feet.

"You win." She sits up as the cat slides into the warm place she's left, and settles in the hollow. "What have you been doing all night?" The cat merely washes himself with his rough, pink tongue.

In a fog, Rose pulls on her old dressing gown, two sizes too small, and gropes for her slippers. Bright sunlight decorates the wall, rests on shoddy furniture and here and there; sparks shoot out from glass and metal objects around the room, catching the gold cross and chain. She slips it over her head. Memories, like dust motes, float up from the night. Rose remembers its Sunday and she has a plan.

Familiar smells greet her as she stumbles downstairs. At the stove, her mother cooks Dad's breakfast: bacon, eggs, fried bread, and bottled tomatoes. Alice squints through smoke from a dangling cigarette. Rose brushes her teeth at the sink, barefoot. Her mother pours hot water into a basin for Rose to wash, but after their first greeting remains oddly quiet.

"What's the matter, Mum?"

Alice slides food from the frying pan to a plate and pushes it under the grill to keep warm. At first she says nothing, but then turns to Rose, wiping her hands on her apron. "Mr. Jackson came to the back door. He says some animal got into his baby chicks last night. He thinks it's a weasel. He's gone to talk to Dad about it."

Rose's heart sinks. She sees her mother's troubled expression, and thinks it's because Dad dislikes Mr. Jackson, and there will be another shouting match.

"How's the sow and her babies?" she asks.

"Don't know yet. I'm waiting for him to come in for breakfast."
Mum casts a critical eye, "You need to get dressed. Then come back with
a hair brush."

The only dress Rose owns is green velvet, bought in a jumble sale,
and which, up to now, she's rejected as too *dressy*. She tries it on in front
of the mirror, tying the sash in a bow at the back. It's the best she can do
for real church. Her school shoes are all she has.

"Mum."

Alice looks up from her crossword.

"I want to go to St. Bede's today instead of Sunday school. Granny
would approve. I can ride my bicycle into town. I hate Sunday school. It's
boring, and Mr. Baxter keeps saying we children are all going to hell if
we're not good, and he has bad breath."

Her mother puts down the paper, and wields the brush, pulling on
knots and tangles in Rose's long hair. "I don't want you going all that way
by yourself. It would be different if the bus ran on Sundays."

"It's not far if I take the cart track, and everyone else rides their bikes
into town. Annie's allowed."

"I said no, and don't wheedle."

Rose persists: "Last week the hall smelled of beer and cigarettes from
last night's social and Mr. Baxter made us pray for sinners who drink and
smoke." She ducks away from the fierce tugs. "Ouch, Mum, that hurts."

" You're giving me a headache. It's very good of Mr. Baxter to volunteer his time." She pauses brushing, "Did he really say that?"

"Granny says Jesus and his friends drank wine—it's in the Bible."

"You're driving me mad, Rose, and so is Granny. I don't have time to
take you to church. Besides, what does Granny know about my life here?"

"She does know, Mum. She says at least you have me."

"When will I get to see her again? I'm overwhelmed with work and
she's too old to travel across London by herself. I can't believe she made
the trip here when there were doodlebugs, stubborn woman."

"I miss her too. Next time, please take me with you. I don't like it
when you leave me here with Dad."

"You can't miss school."

"Suppose Granny dies suddenly like Grandpa?"

"Why so morbid? Maybe Mr. Baxter's bad for you, after all. He'd
smoke too if he had my nerves. Sanctimonious little squirt!"

Rose giggles, "I told you, Mum!"

Alice silently plaits, yanks and tightens. Footsteps approach the back door. Rose takes a quick bite of toast and Marmite.

Her mother's voice softens. "I see you found that nice frock to wear." They listen as Stanley scrapes his boots outside.

"If I let you, you'll be careful on your bike, won't you? The cart track could still have icy patches."

Her father bursts through the door, his face purple. In a panic, Rose thinks Keith must've told Mr. Jackson about the water tower. Mum gives her a sharp push. "Go, quickly, or you'll be late for church—leave by the front, check your bicycle tires; the pump's in the shed."

At the door, Rose hears, "Whatever's wrong, Stanley?" She doesn't wait for the answer.

She takes the shortcut, riding her bicycle down the steep rutted track between fields whitening with daisies. The old plough horse, Violet, looks up from grazing in the lush grass. Rose pretends she's clinging to the mane of a palomino pony, riding bareback, pigtails flying.

Holding tight to juddering handlebars, she's almost thrown off when the front wheel hits a rock. The adrenalin tingles on the backs of her hands; she recovers, straightens her bike, and pedals faster. Past the mill-pond, she goes, where she and Annie fish for tadpoles, past the hedges white with hawthorn, slowing a little to cross a wooden bridge. She sees a flash of glorious blue as a kingfisher skims the chattering stream below.

Cart track changes to smooth tarmac. Rose coasts through quiet streets. She passes the old stagecoach inn, The King's Arms, and further on, the public library, and the Odeon Cinema, where she and Annie sometimes go on Saturday afternoons. Elated by new freedom, she follows her reflection in shop windows—a young girl on a bicycle, her skirt riding above bare knees, ribbons coming untied from the wind. For the first time in her life, she wonders if she's pretty.

Bells peal wildly across the rooftops. Turning up a back street, the massive medieval church appears with its tall steeple. Rose props her bike against the yard wall. Suddenly shy, she joins others in their Sunday best, walking up the worn steps. Stone gargoyles lean grotesquely with lolling tongues.

A smiling man, handing out leaflets, ushers her to a high-backed ancient pew. Rose kneels to pray as her grandmother taught her. Eyes closed, she envisions Dad's darkening face. Thoughts switch to being halfway up the water tower with Annie, in full view of the farm. Did Keith tell on them? Someone in a waft of perfume bumps the pew from behind. Rose sits up, embarrassed she's knelt too long. People are assembling; there's a low buzz of whispered greetings. She takes in the scene: women in fine dresses, little veiled hats, and elbow-length gloves; and the men, if not in military uniform, dressed alike in dark suits, white shirts, and striped ties. A girl in front, about Rose's age, sits between her parents in pink frills, ribbons to match. Her head leans against her father's shoulder. Music pours from the tall organ pipes as a red-robed boy, with white ruffled collar, lights candles at the high altar. Rose recognizes him as part of a boys' school group that hangs around the bus stop. From afar she's admired his reddish blond hair, and shiny bicycle with dropped handlebars. When he wears cricket-team whites, she thinks him quite handsome. They've never spoken.

The people stand for the first hymn and a procession slowly moves past led by a solemn-faced man carrying an ornate brass cross. The choir follows with its powerful range of male and female voices, and then a young man swinging incense, the fragrant clouds wafting over the congregation. Close to the aisle, Rose could reach out and touch the heavy, brocade robes of the three clergy, so different from Granny's village church and its vicar. Very last, a small man sweeps by in an embroidered white cape and tall hat, carrying a shepherd's crook. Rose sings, head up, freed from any teacher's judgment, giving herself to music that soars to the rafters, where curls of smoke still linger.

In the leaflet, she reads that it's Eastertide: the man, with the shepherd's crook, a visiting bishop. He climbs the stairs to the high pulpit. Rose expects to be bored. Instead, he begins with a story about himself as a young boy whose brainy, atheist parents were mystified that he wanted to go to church. Looking back, he speculates on what on earth got into him, walking several miles every Sunday to attend services. In these postwar times, he says, we're desperate to start over, but many of us have lost our way, undecided what to do next. With a sweep of his arm, he says, "Friends, the Spirit may be leading you. Watch where your feet go."

Rose feels him looking down at her, his expression grave. He says the words again. "Watch where your feet go." She touches her face and wonders if he sees her bruises.

The bishop continues. "The war is over but there's still staggering human suffering, especially the children. Millions are refugees. Although we have celebrated Easter, the whole world is still in deep mourning. We need to start the hard work of forgiving one another, including those we've thought of as our enemy."

Rose's mind drifts, remembering German prisoners in grey uniforms, with armed guards, working on the farms. She was warned not to "fraternize with the enemy," not understanding what that meant. One day a prisoner called to her, saying she looked like his own little girl in Germany, and how he didn't know if the child or her mother were alive. He gave Rose a doll he'd fashioned out of straw. How could she think of him as her enemy?

She wakes from her reverie. The service for Holy Communion has begun at the High Altar. The congregation goes up, including the girl in pink taffeta with her parents. Not yet confirmed, the ritual is a mystery to Rose. She remains in the pew. A direct sunlit path through stained glass bathes Rose in iridescent purples, reds, and gold. She breathes in the smell of candles and incense, and the heady scent of Easter lilies, convinced this is where she's supposed to be. Worshippers file by shaded by the tall pillars, their faces thoughtful, some sad. Rose fingers the gold cross at her neck. Granny would approve of her being here.

Organ music reverberates against the ancient walls as they rise for the last hymn. She joins in, her heart filled to the brim. As he processes by, the bishop bows slightly in Rose's direction, perhaps seeing the glow in her face. The service over, some stay in their pews to listen to the music; others gather in the aisles greeting one another. Not quite brave enough to talk to anyone, Rose slips out by a side door.

— 9 —

ON THE WAY HOME, the cart track is mostly uphill. Halfway, Rose dismounts, not because she's tired, but to listen to the chorus of birds singing, echoing the hymns still playing in her head. White blackthorn is in glorious bloom; she stands still, her eyes absorbing the beauty. Violet, the old horse, is there keeping her nose in the grass and swishing flies away with her tail. The blades of the water mill turn in a light wind, rippling the green surface of the pond.

A movement turns her attention to the field's far side. Gradually, a couple comes into focus: they are lying on a blanket. The woman's clothed body stretches on top of the man, moving in rhythm with his hands that ceaselessly stroke the length of her back. Rose watches; curious but timid, she realizes they are kissing. Her own body responds with fluttery sensations. She moves on, stops, and looks back, astonished that they are out in the open, not caring if anyone sees. She and Annie have agreed upon, and giggled about, the unlikely facts of sex. Much as Rose strains her eyes, she can't decide what, exactly, the lovers are doing.

Continuing on, she thinks of the altar boy in church and envisions a future: they'll ride fast down the cart track together, he on his shiny new bicycle with the drop handle bars. She has to pause here, changing him, like one of her paper dolls, from red robe, to cricket whites, to tee shirt and shorts. Her bike is not as good as his. Perhaps she'll fall and he'll carry her home on the crossbar. No serious injuries, but he'll come again, making sure she's okay. Or maybe, he'll be the one to fall. The story is so absorbing Rose scarcely notices she's reached her own driveway. She opens the back door to the smell of Sunday roast. Her stomach tells her she's very hungry. Mum's back is turned, removing a small joint of beef from the oven.

"Hello, Mum." Rose offers an affectionate kiss and immediately senses something is wrong. Through the door, she sees her father in the living room reading the paper, his face hidden. Rose explains why she's late: the service was long, and the bishop was there. Alice cuts her off, telling her to help with dinner, handing over a bowl of steaming potatoes.

"What's the matter?" Rose takes the dish but puts it down on the counter, waiting.

"Why do you always ask me that question?" Mum says. "Why don't you ask your father for a change?"

"Did the sow die?"

Her father has come into the kitchen, glasses on the end of his nose, holding the newspaper in one hand. She thinks, *Oh God, Keith did rat on me . . . ?*

Alice says, "You tell her, Stanley."

Caught between her parents, Rose looks from one to the other. Finally, her father says, "Your cat has been killing Mr. Jackson's baby chicks."

Rose stares, "No, Daddy, that's not true. It was a weasel. Mum said."

"There's no mistake about it. It was the cat. There were feathers everywhere in the barn."

Her father looks at her with an expression she's never seen before: wary and defensive. "There was no other choice."

Rose feels her mother's arms tighten around her waist, but struggles free.

"What are you saying? Where's Moggy?" Her father retreats back to his chair in the living room. Rose pursues him.

"Is Moggy dead?" Her voice comes out as a squeak. "Did you knock him over the head, like the little runt?"

Mum tries again to hold her back, but Rose fights her off. "Did you know about this?"

"You can't keep a cat on a farm once it starts killing chickens." Rose refuses to understand. All she wants is for her mother to tell her it's not true, or to share at least in the horror that her beautiful cat is dead. Instead, Mum says, "I thought if the cat had to be put down, Mr. Vale would have done it as a favor."

"Mr. Vale wouldn't kill Moggy," Rose cries. "I know he wouldn't. You couldn't make him." Convinced, she pictures the vet soothing the sick sow, gently handling the babies.

"Dad did it, didn't he?" She addresses the question to her mother, but Rose, in the pit of her stomach, knows the answer.

"Tell her, Stanley," Alice says for the second time, but her husband pushes his way past them, reaches for his coat and cap. "Wait," she calls, "You haven't had your dinner."

"I'm not hungry," he says in a voice that Rose finds nothing to hold on to, leaving her fearful, calling after him, "Dad, come back."

They watch from the window as he strides, shoulders hunched, across the yard. With a sob, Rose crumples to the floor and her mother kneels, stroking her hair. Half to herself, she says, "Your father shot him . . . used his old rifle from the Home Guard. I had no idea he'd kept it." This time Rose leans into her mother's embrace, head on her shoulder, and together they weep.

— 1 0 —

Monday morning and Rose has barely slept. Her mother calls up the stairs, telling her to come down . . . immediately. Rose finds no comfort in the bed without her cat to greet her—but still she lies there like a sheep fallen on its back, wool so heavy she can't move. Her parents have stopped speaking to one another. It was after dark when her father came in. He ate his warmed-up dinner and went upstairs.

Some time in the night, Alice crawled into bed; her body so tense Rose thought she was crying. She'd pressed her cheek against her mother's back, "It's all right, don't cry. Moggy had a good life."

"You don't get it. This is not only about you and your cat." Mum had pulled away, tugging the blankets, leaving Rose exposed to a thin strip of cold air.

The morning call comes more sharply this time. "Get up this instant, or you'll be late for school."

Rose thinks if only she hadn't insisted on going to St Bede's, Moggy might still be alive. She'd have pleaded with Dad not to shoot him. Maybe it's God's punishment for spying on the couple in the field. Mr. Baxter would say so. The lovely feeling and goose bumps during the service seem far away—probably imagined. She sits up, gets out of bed, and drags herself downstairs.

She doesn't want to go to school. Her mother insists, ironing her uniform, plaiting her hair, and packing up her books in her satchel. Rose listlessly complies. She puts on her coat only when Mum holds it in front of her, forcing her arms into the sleeves. Alice lectures as she fastens the buttons. "The only way you'll ever get away from here is to have an education." Rose makes no reply. Her mother jams her school hat on her head and pushes her out the door.

A small crowd huddles at the bus stop, coat collars turned up against a biting east wind, waiting for the green county bus to grind its way up the hill. The neighbor, Mrs. Jackson, is there in an old coat and felt hat pulled low, a large handbag over one arm. Keith shelters behind his mother in short grey trousers and wool socks, his bare knees blue and exposed. They avoid looking at her; a sure sign, Rose decides, they know about her cat.

A woman prods her in the back, "Get in the queue, dear. Here comes the bus." The conductor jumps from the platform and hurries them on board. Rose sits in the front, as far away as she can from the Jacksons. The bus follows a circular route through the farm estates and village, picking up school children, workers, and housewives. By the time it lurches back down the hill, every seat is taken. Rose gives up hers to a young woman with a crying baby. Country turns into town. The bus stops, letting off workers at the jam factory with its warm, fruity smells. They pass the high walls of the asylum—always a mystery to Rose. Through an iron gate, she glimpses deserted grounds and imagines souls trapped in locked wards. Annie says her aunt went there with a nervous breakdown, was given electric shock treatment, and lost her memory. Rose gets off at the stop nearest school and plods along, past the playing fields, thinking she wouldn't mind having her brain shocked so she could forget Moggy's awful death.

School starts with morning prayers in the assembly hall attended by all four hundred girls, except for a few Catholics and Jewish girls, who are exempt. All are dressed in identical navy blue uniforms, with Saxe blue blouses. The wood-paneled hall has a balcony where the sixth formers sit. Miss Gordon, the dour Scots headmistress, leads the service. Annie is in the choir, near the stage. She sends a cheerful wave. Rose is relieved her friend is not still cross. The prayers, recited by rote, offer little comfort. There's none of the joy she felt singing in the big church. Even then her cat was doomed.

At noon, Annie, fresh from gym class, meets Rose in the quadrangle. She's eager to know what happened to the sow and her babies, especially the littlest pig. "They're fine," Rose says, though she doesn't know for sure. She suspects the runt is dead.

Annie suggests they share her lunch under a big oak tree, where they won't be seen. Next time they are at the shop, they'll buy sweets with Rose's lunch money and a coupon from Annie's ration book. So far, no grown-up has found out their scheme, but the time the two girls spend together has made Rose unpopular with her own class. They tell her she should always eat with them in the cafeteria, not only when the weather is bad. One girl in particular, Pamela Rawlings, threatens trouble if she continues her friendship with Annie. Rose tries to ignore her, but other girls are siding with Pam.

With their backs to a large oak tree, Annie shares half a soggy egg and cress sandwich. She next meticulously bisects a Mars bar with a penknife, allowing Rose to choose the piece she wants. Annie eats fast. She loves chocolate, but one bar is a month's ration. Rose usually takes small bites to make it last. Today her stomach hurts and she puts her piece in her pocket. She blurts out, "Moggy's dead." Rose hears herself say the words and is almost as incredulous as Annie, who immediately makes her repeat them. This time her voice is louder. "My cat's dead."

Annie's face flushes. "He can't be. I saw him yesterday. He ran up to me. He was rubbing himself against my legs and purring. Was he run over? Did some animal kill him?"

"It simply happened," Rose says vaguely.

"He was such a healthy cat. Somebody must have poisoned him."

"Oh Annie, who on earth would poison him?"

"There's something you haven't told me." Annie's eyes bore in, as if she sees right into Rose's soul. Rose shifts on the uneven ground, fighting the urge to bang her head against the tree trunk. She dare not even hint at how Moggy really died. Mrs. Carter would surely never let Annie near the farm again.

Desperate to change the subject, Rose announces, "My period's two days late." She knows this. Like her mother, she marks it on the calendar in the kitchen. The topic is usually of endless interest to Annie, but she won't be distracted.

"He did it, didn't he?" Annie's face is inches away. She has cress stuck in her teeth.

"I don't know what you're talking about."

"Your father did Moggy in, didn't he?"

Rose wavers. "Of course not! My dad would never . . ." She struggles for words, "He liked Moggy!" Then out of nowhere comes a memory of her father adding bacon rind from his own plate to the cat dish.

Rose mumbles into clasped knees, "Mum and I found Moggy in a ditch when he was a tiny kitten. He was all skinny and wet. Someone must've tried to drown him."

The school bell clangs across the lawns and they scramble to gather up lunch wrappers.

"I have an idea," Annie says. "We'll make a grave for Moggy and put flowers on it, and find a rock as a marker. We'll have a funeral. I'll come to your house next Saturday."

Rose nods. She has no idea where the body is and thinks dismally of the manure heap. It's a relief when the bell rings again.

Joining the crowd, they each head off to their classrooms. A big-bosomed girl, her gym tunic cinched at the waist, bumps against Rose. "Traitor," she hisses.

Rose turns in fury: "Bugger off, Pam Rawlings, and leave me alone." She breaks into a run, but the girl, with an evil look, overtakes her and barges ahead through swing doors into the hall.

"Rose Gray swore at me," she screams.

A circle of girls surrounds Rose with jabbing, accusing fingers. Others crowd around to watch until a teacher enters the room, forcing them to sit down, be quiet, and take out their books.

ON THE BUS HOME, Rose tries to insulate herself from yelling, shoving, unruly school children. A boy behind tugs on her plaits and tips her hat over her eyes; she turns round and shouts, "Shut up!"

"I didn't say anything," he says. He and his friend laugh idiotically, until the bus conductor threatens to throw them off. Rose hunches in a corner, face toward the window, registering nothing of the passing buildings and scenery. The bus stops and starts again. Housewives with heavy shopping bags climb on board, complaining of tired feet. The conductor forces two boys to give up their seats. Engine fumes hang in the air. Rose grits her teeth.

The scene in her head plays, unrelenting. Her father lifts the gun, takes aim. The last time she saw Moggy he was settling down in her bed. Stanley pulls back the covers, the sleepy cat instantly alert, arches his back, smelling danger. Then what? Did he seize Moggy by the neck and drag him down downstairs? Or, worse, did he use sweet talk and promises of food to lure the animal to his death?

The bus jolts forward; Rose's hollowed eyes, reflected in the window, stare back. Dad used to clean the gun when he was in the Home Guard, spreading pieces on newspaper on the table. She remembers the smell of oil squirted from a small bottle. He kept a box of shells in a kitchen drawer, along with nails, saved bits of string, paper clips, and wrapped cough lozenges. She saw him practice outdoors, hoisting the rifle, shooting at life-size targets painted on plywood. Thoughts come of Mum alone with him and his unpredictable moods. Rose presses clenched fists against her heart to quell its violent beating. Still, fear sweeps through, like the searchlights that raked the night in the darkest times of the war.

The bus reaches Rose's stop; she pushes through to the front and down the steps. As the bus drives off, in a cloud of noxious fumes, she stops by the roadside, fighting nausea.

"Are you feeling poorly, Rose?"

She hadn't heard the green Hillman approach until the driver called from the rolled down window. Without looking around, Rose recognizes the voice.

"Why don't I give you a lift," David Vale says, "I'm on my way to your house."

Rose hangs back, fighting nausea.

"Were you a bit bus sick? Get in and I'll drive slowly. We'll keep the windows open so you have some fresh air." He speaks in the same unperturbed tone he used with the sick pig.

She goes around to the passenger side while he shifts a pile of *Farmers Weekly*, with their yellow covers, to the back seat. Rose rarely rides in a car and sits leaning forward, her satchel of books still on her back. When she doesn't speak, he says, "The old sow seems to be doing well on her medicine, and the little ones are thriving. They're a bit skinny, but with the formula they should fatten up in no time."

Rose stays silent, concentrating on keeping her head still as the queasiness subsides. She feels him glancing.

"I'm afraid the wee runt didn't make it. I know you and your friend fretted about that, but sometimes it's how nature takes care of things." Rose hears the wheels on the gravelly road and magazine pages fluttering. Her panic slowly subsides, but she's afraid to speak, and stares miserably ahead. She senses him waiting. Finally, in a small voice, she asks, "Did you hear about my cat?"

He slows the car, pulling over to the roadside, and a flock of starlings flies up from the hedgerow. The black shapes wheel out and disappear into the grey sky.

"I did hear he got into your neighbor's chickens, and I know your dad was ever so put out, and you must be too."

Rose holds her body rigid, listening to the quiet rumble of his voice.

"I've been thinking. There's a lady up the road who says she needs a cat to scare off mice. She'd treat your Moggy right well, and let you visit whenever you want. I was going to talk to your parents."

He prepares to drive on, when her face crumbles. Rose tells him nothing, but she feels his hand lightly on her shoulder. "What is it, love?" he asks. "You don't have to tell me, if you don't want to." He turns off the engine and sits quietly as she covers her face. The warmth of his presence releases grief she has tried hard to keep hidden. Sobs shake her body.

When he tells her again that the woman who wants her cat loves animals, Rose shakes her head.

Finally, very gently, "Rose, I may be wrong, but if you're that upset, I'm guessing . . . is it your cat? Is he dead?"

Rose nods, letting out a wail.

He mutters, "Damn!" under his breath. "I'm sorry," he says. "I didn't know." She senses he wants to say more, but instead restarts the car and drives on until they're parked in front of the straw barn.

With a sigh, he reaches across to open her door, "Come on, Rosie, let's go to the house and look for your Mum."

Rose doesn't move, struggling to regain composure, not wanting to walk with him to the house and have Mum see her crying.

The vet reaches in his jacket pocket and produces a folded handkerchief. When she takes it and dabs at her face, he says, "No, that won't do any good . . . Blow your nose; give it a good blow and clear the old airways!"

Rose giggles.

Out of the car, David Vale takes his time, pointing out a clump of daffodils in full bloom, their heads bobbing in the wind. "Those always cheer me up," he says. "However down in the dumps I've been in winter, they come back." He looks up, "Look, here comes your mother."

How pretty she looks, Rose thinks, as Mum approaches, her face alight with a welcoming smile. "Well," she says, "here are two of my favorite people." Rose looks sharply at David Vale. Her keen eyes notice a flush rising rapidly from his neck.

Alice draps an arm around Rose's shoulders. "Can you believe how tall she's grown?" When David is noncommittal, she confides, "I don't know when it happened, but she often mothers me more than I mother her."

"She's a grand girl!" agrees David, while Rose squirms free. She dislikes Mum's high-pitched voice when she's talking to David.

"I gather something happened to her cat." He speaks in a forthright manner.

Alice says, "Rose, go in the house and put the kettle on."

The vet shakes his head, "No, let her stay. I thought she and I could check on the baby pigs."

Only Rose catches her mother's fleeting frown.

"Where's Stanley, by the way?"

"At a tenant's meeting, with the new manager." Rose has heard about this man, new to the estate, and the sleek Jaguar he drives. She inwardly winces when Mum goes on, "Let's hope Stanley doesn't pick a fight with him. That's how he lost his last two jobs, arguing with his boss."

If the vet's interested in this information, he makes no comment. He opens the boot of the car for his bag. "Your idea of a cuppa sounds marvelous, Alice. We'll be back in a jiffy."

With a slight toss of her curly hair, Mum turns back to the house.

Rose follows him along the dimly lit corridor. She likes the vet's medium height and his broad back under a wool jacket; the way he stoops to unbolt the sty door and lets her through.

"Now Rose," he says, "do you think you can give me a hand?" One by one he examines the small pigs and then gently hands them back to her to place in their stall. She loves the feel of the wriggling bodies. She grows in confidence, holding their hard little bodies close when they squeal.

"Let's look at the sow now," the vet says. "She's was a good mother to her last litter, but she's too poorly to suckle this lot until the infection clears up." Rose kneels in the straw while David does his careful examination. She runs her hand over the pig's warm sides and feels the wild beating of its heart.

Later, they stand together in the open doorway, listening to the sow's peaceful grunts, and the occasional cries of her babies next door. "I don't like to separate them," David says, "but this is the best we can do right now." He packs his bag and they walk slowly back to the house, "When I was in the army," he tells, "I trained dogs to sniff out and rescue people who were trapped under rubble. One dog I especially loved, a Welsh Collie called Bess. Smart enough and little, she could get into small spaces, and she always stayed with me, unlike the other, bigger dogs we kept in the kennels. Then one day she triggered a land mine, and it could've been me. I was injured, but Bess was killed outright."

A slight lowering of his voice makes her glance quickly at his profile.

David turns to face her. His expression is one of gentleness and concern. "I'll never forget her, Rose, and you'll never forget your Moggy. No one can take the memories away, whether it's an animal or . . . a person that's been special to us."

"I know he was only a cat," Rose exclaims, "and I shouldn't go on about it. Mum says it's because we live on a farm. Animals die. In the war, people died all the time."

"When Bess was killed, I told myself the same thing—she was only a dog and people were being killed every day. But you can't measure feelings like that." David muses, "Perhaps all the losses and sadness collect. When an animal we love dies, we grieve. I went back to base that night and I cried my eyes out."

Rose, made shy by his emotion, asks, "Do you have a dog now?"

"I'm not sure I'm ready to take that on, right now. Bess is not easy to replace."

This time, Rose is the one to point out purple violets hidden in the grass along the piggery wall.

They arrive at the back door. "You make a good assistant, Rose. You have a way with animals. The sow calmed down because you were there."

— 1 2 —

INDOORS, HER MOTHER HAS piled a plate with toasted cheese, and another with homemade oatcakes. The table is set in the living room with the best cups and saucers, and a large pot of tea. A newly lit fire burns in the grate.

Rose stands next to the vet as he washes his hands, ready to pass him a clean towel. She again notices the deep scar on his inner left arm that travels all the way to the wrist. She wonders if it hurts, and would like to brush her fingers lightly along the white zigzag line. He sees her looking and smiles, "I was lucky—I might've lost my arm. Many did, and far worse."

They join Alice in the next room, where she pours the tea. Rose wonders where she should sit, unsure in the presence of their guest. David pats the chair next to him. "Come over here by me."

Her mother looks up. "Before you do that, go and change out of your school uniform. Look how dirty it is. I'll have to clean it before school tomorrow." Upstairs, in the bedroom, Rose catches scraps of conversation. Exact words are hard to make out, and yet the chatter flows up the stairs like music. So different, she feels, from the strained voices of her parents, or, harder to bear, their awful silence.

David welcomes her when she returns and tells her she looks pretty in her civvies, as he calls them. She looks at the floor, blushing, and notices he has taken off his boots, and there's a hole in one of his socks. Her mother, in the middle of telling David a story, motions Rose to sit at the table. She continues.

"I'll never forget the excitement here on VE Day. All of England gripped in the midst of a heat wave—so unlike the usual weather in June. Everything seemed unreal, and very quiet—except for the radio announcers, mad with joy that the war finally was ending." Rose drops

48

a sugar lump into her tea, watching it dissolve into the swirling, brown liquid. Next to her, David casually rests his arm on the back of her chair, gravely listening. Rose hopes her mother will go on talking forever.

"Not a plane to be heard," Alice says. "After years of throbbing and droning in the skies, and wondering how soon the sirens would start. For the first time we could leave the curtains open and let in the night air. We could see the smoke of bonfires all across the valley, and I knew people were celebrating. I wanted so much to be there and dance in the streets."

Rose watches, astonished by the shine in her mother's eyes, the high color in her cheeks. David leans forward as though he too sees what Mum is remembering. Sitting quietly, Rose thinks of his closeness as they tended the baby pigs. A piece of straw has caught on his shirt collar. She wishes she dared reach over and pluck it off. Her eyes dart toward the door, worrying Dad will walk in, bringing with him the heaviness he often carries, like a sack of pig meal.

Mum reaches in her pocket for her cigarettes and then changes her mind. "No chance of taking the train to London, where the hullabaloo was going on, but I did at least take Rose down to the village. Stanley wouldn't come, said he hated crowds. He was strangely downhearted."

Listening, Rose experiences again the intense heat of an enormous bonfire, people cheering as they burned an effigy of Hitler, its face distorted and melting. Everyone held hands wildly dancing as they circled the fire, but Rose broke away, crying, imagining the horror of burning human flesh. Annoyed, her mother took her home, telling her she'd spoiled the fun.

David turns: "What do you remember, Rose?"

The way he asks feels real, not like the kind of questions grown-ups ask when they don't really want an answer. Rose believes if she told him about the bonfire, he'd listen, and perhaps understand, but she holds back from casting a shadow on her mother's mood.

"I remember Mum waking me in the morning, and hugging me and saying the war was over. She hung a big Union Jack from the window, but there was no breeze to make it flap . . ."

"What about you, David?" Alice asks.

"Well, I was in Germany and there was unspeakable suffering—as it turned out, far worse than any of us knew."

His voice drops. "And soon after, of course, there was Japan . . ."

Rose stares. David's brown eyes are different from her father's. Dad's are blue and guarded, reminding Rose, sometimes, of an animal that's been injured, wary of anyone coming too close. When David looks at her, she sees affection and warmth and wonders whether he'd like to have children of his own.

She becomes conscious of the vet studying her, almost as if he can read her thoughts. Abruptly, he changes the subject. "Tell us more about the good times, Alice!" He clears a space on the table for his elbows. "How about that bottle of port wine you offered me the other day?"

After a while, Rose moves to an armchair near the fire. She takes out books for her homework, hoping the two adults will notice her absence. Her heavy sighs do nothing to divert them from their animated talk over the opened bottle. She quietly looks into the glowing embers, lulled by David's voice with its slight North Country accent, her mother's lilting laughter, the clink of glasses and creak of their chairs.

"I worked side by side with the Land Girls," Alice says. "You must've seen the posters: 'Lend a hand on the land.' It probably sounds strange, but we had marvelous times in spite of the war. The girls on the farms were younger, but they loved to tell me about their boyfriend troubles. The GIs were here, hanging around, with more money than we'd ever seen and lots of sex appeal. Of course the real boyfriends were away fighting, poor devils."

David gives an odd laugh. "I know about those Yankees. My ex-fiancée is living with one in Texas." Rose raises her head slightly. It takes a moment to realize what he's said, and that although he laughed, it's something sad.

Her mother keeps on with her stories. He offers to pour more wine. "How's the homework, Rose?" he calls. She stays quiet, pretending to be asleep. Through closed eyes, the fire burns red and she hears the quiet settling of coals turning to ash.

Memories come of riding on the back of trucks to different farms, sitting on her mother's lap, or passed around to be held by one of the younger women with their makeup and cigarette breath. They laughed and screamed over the engine, sitting on the hard benches, bumping along farm roads. Sometimes Rose was allowed to ride on the tractor, clinging to the driver's back, while the women followed, picking up potatoes in a cloud of dirt. In strawberry season she helped pick, eating the luscious red fruit until her tummy hurt, and Mum made her lie down on a pile of itchy hay. Her mother had worn a red, white, and blue halter top, her bare shoulders brown from working outside. She tied her hair back with a ribbon, or a bright scarf. The American soldiers in uniform, who were everywhere, gave Rose sticks of gum and candy. Rose squirms a little now, remembering the way they'd ask if she had an older sister and laughed when she looked puzzled.

She must have dozed. Rose wakes to the sound of Mum and David talking quietly, almost whispering. The fire has died down; her open book slipped to the floor.

Alice's voice: "Yes, yes, she's asleep—tired girl, she barely slept last night. I had to force her to go to school. She'd had that cat since he was a kitten. Did she tell you what happened?"

"The poor wee lass. I wish Stanley had spoken to me first. I could've found the animal a good home."

"It was the way he did it that frightened me. He flies into rages whenever anything goes wrong. I wish he hadn't kept that Home Guard rifle . . ."

"Alice, I shouldn't say this—maybe it's the wine. I've known you and Stanley for a while now. To be honest, I wonder . . . well, how the two of you ever got together—you're that different."

Rose holds her breath. It's as though everything has happened before. She almost knows what Mum's about to say, because she's heard it somewhere else, at another time. Without turning around, she pictures the two of them, their heads close together.

"You mean, why did we ever marry? Funny you should ask—someone else asked me that question the other day on the phone."

"Look, Alice, we Northerners can be too blunt. It's none of my business. I should leave before Stanley comes home." A chair creaks.

"Please stay. Stanley won't be home until the pubs close. I can't exactly hang over the garden fence and chat with the neighbors about my life. You've been a good friend to us both."

"I'd be a hypocrite if I didn't say it's your friendship I care about."

Familiar sounds fill the room—the strike of a match, her mother inhaling deeply on her cigarette and slowly breathing out.

Mum speaks softly: "I was only eighteen when Stanley and I met. He was ten years older, handsome, with prospects of his own estate. My head was turned by his attention. I know it sounds shallow. Stanley had had a rather wild life up until then. He was ready to settle down. But the market crashed, and banks collapsed. His family fortune was gone. I didn't care about that, partly because I was young and naïve. My father was editor of the local paper. We never had much money. Mother called it genteel poverty—she'd always scraped to get by. But it hit Stanley hard. He was bitter, as a lot of people were, and angry. Then the news came that his father died suddenly in a hotel in Berlin."

David makes a small noise, like a groan. "I remember headlines in the papers when the market went out of control. My parents weathered it, somehow. I wasn't much more than a lad when all that was going on."

Rose never knew her father's father, nor heard Dad speak much about him. Yet it's a story she's heard before.

David asks, "What happened then?"

"Stanley was devastated. He idolized his father. We were engaged. I didn't feel I could walk away, although I knew by then, for all kinds of reasons, it was a mistake. My parents . . . it was all so complicated. In the end, I'm afraid I may have betrayed myself and, sadly, Stanley too."

"Alice, I . . ."

"It's all right, David. It's a comfort simply to have you listen. It's been a long time since I told anyone that story. I should never have had that third glass of port. Let's change the subject—talk about the woman you nearly married. Was she pretty?"

In Rose's half-waking state, the sense of déjà vu is still there. Like a disappearing ghost, she wants to catch the memory by its heel, but it escapes into a haze of steam and smoke.

Pictures emerge: She's much younger, a little girl. Fleetingly, she sees a tall man, a stranger, in a railway station. She stands between him and her mother, looking up. They are oblivious, lost in each other's eyes. There are sounds of trains shunting, and the smell of coal. Travelers, many in uniform, stream by.

Behind her, David and her mother are chatting softly. The memories almost slip away, but there they are again at the station: the three of them at a small table in a café. The man, wearing glasses, writes on a piece of paper with a black, gold-nib pen. Words are indistinct. A scene so vivid Rose takes a sharp breath. Mum and the man are embracing. Her mother weeps. The little girl cries too, tugging on her mother's skirts. Then, in a rush, she remembers being lifted up, the man kissing her, first one cheek, then the other, before he is gone.

Rose has no idea how much time has passed. The room has become very still. She stretches, and stirs the dying fire with a poker, resisting looking back.

Caught between past and present, Rose trusts neither. She closes her eyes, searching her heart, believing she will somehow find the truth.

"Who were you?" she whispers, and worries that Mum and David will overhear.

There's only the sound of crackling fire. She imagines their heads close together, perhaps holding hands, lips almost touching. Slowly, Rose turns. Shadows dance on the wall, but the chairs are empty. Stumbling across the room, she puts her ear to the closed kitchen door. She hears a man's voice: not her father's. She thinks of Dad, coming home any moment, into their circle of warmth.

Rose paces. Minutes pass. The convergence of memories and the reality of Mum and David in the next room make her head spin. She resolves to ignore them, to do her homework. A single shout of male laughter, then a low amused response from her mother, have Rose running back to the door. This time she turns the knob.

—1 3—

OH, THERE YOU ARE, sleepy head." David reaches to tousle her hair, but Rose pulls back. She surveys them in the tiny room: her mother's hands plunged in soapy water at the sink, and him next to her, drying a plate with a checked tea towel.

"Doesn't look like she did much studying." Alice reaches to dry her hands on David's towel and lifts her cigarette from the ashtray.

In rolled-up shirtsleeves, David's scarred left arm is visible; his elbow appears misshapen. Rose wants to be cross with him, but can't remember why.

"You must have needed that snooze, Rose. It's been a hard week." He waves away the smoke from Alice's cigarette.

"I wasn't asleep."

The two adults glance at each other.

"Nonsense," her mother says firmly. "We practically heard you snoring. Now say goodbye to Mr. Vale, and go finish your homework. It's almost bedtime and you have school in the morning."

Rose mutters goodnight and sharply closes the door behind her. Ear pressed against the wood panel, she hears David say, "It's been a hard day, Alice. She's a grand girl. Let her be."

Back in the sitting room, she strips off her wool cardigan. "Stupid," she mutters to herself. Stupid to imagine they were up to something, when all they were doing was the washing up. Mr. Vale must think her a complete idiot. She gathers her books. Her cat crouches in a corner, slit-eyed, watching. She reaches to stroke him. It's only a shadow. Rose stifles sound with her fist, forcing herself to sit at the table. Breadcrumbs swept away, she opens her Latin primer. David's chair, pushed aside, is as casual as his presence. She drains the last few drops of port, finds it bitter. There's a test in the morning—she must make a list of verbs.

Even as she works, thoughts race off in all directions, like walks with Moggy in the fields when he'd fly up a tree or chase after leaves. Rose copies words into an exercise book and her fountain pen runs dry. She retrieves black ink from the bookshelf and carefully fills the pen, and again she hears deafening blasts from steam engines, garbled words over loud speakers, and, through it all, the man's voice and her mother's, talking urgently. He takes out a notebook and writes words in black ink for the little girl to read.

Rose looks down at her books, at her hand holding the pen, and the bottle of ink. Once, Dad spanked her hard over his knee for spilling ink on the tablecloth. She carefully replaces the cap, pushing the memory away. She wonders where her father is.

"*Ex-pug-nare.*" She sounds it out. And the meaning: "Take by storm." She shivers. David could rescue Mum and her. Take them by storm, far away from here. At last, Mum would be happy. The thought persists—the three of them. She'd help him with the animals, like today with the baby pigs. The thrilling idea fades as soon as it appeared. Dad would be left lonely, with no one to cook his meals. She, Rose, must stay, so Mum can be free. Dismayed by a future of self-sacrifice, she hasn't heard someone open the door.

David Vale stands behind her chair. "Cheerio, Rose. I'm off home now. Thanks for a grand evening."

Rose covers the words with an arm, as if they'd reveal what she'd been thinking. He leans over her shoulder, "I had that same textbook. Thought it was a useless dead language, until I studied to be a vet."

Rose smells port on his breath. She keeps her head down—her upper lip trembles, however hard she wills it to stop.

"Well, goodnight. Good luck with school tomorrow."

She makes herself say, "Good night, Mr. Vale." Surely he has seen the pulse jumping on her lip. There is much more she wants to say.

He seems to understand. "Thanks for your help today."

Her mother waits in the doorway, swaying slightly, holding his coat. "Don't forget this, David. It's cold tonight."

The Hillman bumps down the driveway. Rose runs to the window in time to see red taillights swing out onto the road. She wishes she'd asked him how many years of Latin it takes to become a vet.

"*Belligerare*—to wage war."

"*Tradere*—to betray." Two Latin words that Caesar used a lot.

"*Amare*—to love." Everyone knows that one. She recites: "*amo, amas, amat.*"

"Stupid Latin." Rose mutters.

The kitchen door stays tightly closed. She hears water running.

Minutes pass. Coals have turned to ash. The room cools. Her mother is calling.

She lifts her head, "What, Mum?"

"Come here a moment, please."

Rose puts down her paper, opens the door a crack. Wafts of damp warm air and the scent of lavender. "Mummy, what are you doing?" She almost falls over a basket of vegetables, barely able to see because of the steam.

"What does it look like I'm doing?" Alice stretches out in the bath, her head resting on a folded towel, damp ringlets stuck to her forehead. "Come here, you're in time to wash my back." She waves a beckoning hand. "I thought I'd take advantage of the lovely hot water from the fire we've had going. I'm afraid we've used up a week's worth of coal."

Rose has seen her mother naked before. But with new eyes she stares at the full breasts and dark nipples, the rounded belly, and triangle of hair between her mother's legs. Not long ago, she would've climbed in with her, tangling legs and knees. Now Rose wants only to bathe alone. At the same time, she misses the sharing, talking and playing in the warm-scented water.

Mum reaches with her toes to adjust the taps. Taking a deep breath, she slides down, submerging her head. Rose sits on the edge giggling as her mother's hair floats out like seaweed. She comes up in a rush, water spilling over the side. Rose cries, "Mummy, you look like a mermaid."

Mum passes a yellow sponge, and Rose soaps her long spine, slowly tracing where the sun has browned her neck and shoulders.

"Isn't David Vale a nice man?" Alice says.

Rose squeezes the sponge; droplets run down her mother's back. "I liked helping him with the baby pigs."

"I always thought he was married, but I found out he's never had a wife. Poor man was jilted."

Rose trails a hand in the perfumed water. "When's Dad coming home? Won't he want his supper?"

It takes a moment for Mum to hear the question. Finally, she says, "They must have all gone to the pub."

"Dad never goes to the pub!"

"I know, dear, but I told him that if the new manager asked him, he really should go." She raises one leg out of the water and points her toe like a ballerina. "Besides, it will do him good to get out for a change."

Rose's hesitates, and then says, "Do you remember that time we went to stay with Granny during the war? We were on the train and they made us put on gas masks and we had to wait for hours on the tracks, and it was freezing cold, and everyone was frightened?"

Her mother sits up, pours gold liquid from a bottle into her hand to shampoo her hair. "Why don't you talk about how I used to make lovely picnics and we'd go down to the river?"

"I know, you always say that—it's just that I think that was the time a man met us at Victoria station. He was tall and wore glasses, and we sat in a café at the station, and you and he were talking." She pauses, filling the sponge and squeezing, filling it again, watching droplets break the water's surface. "Who was he, Mum?"

Alice methodically massages shampoo into her scalp, as though she's not heard a word. Once more she slides under the water. Rose holds her own breath until it feels her chest will burst. In a sudden movement, Alice rises, gasping. Water streams from her face, the earlier dreaminess has changed to a look of fierce questioning. Rose bends to push a strand of wet hair from her mother's eyes and Mum grasps her hand.

"How is it you remember? Why bring this up now?

"I knew I couldn't have dreamt it. He had a black pen with a gold nib, and he wrote something down. I think it was for me. At least tell me his name."

Her mother unplugs the bath with her foot. The water eddies and gurgles. She keeps a tight hold on Rose's hand, searching her eyes.

Rose persists. "It won't hurt to say his name. Say it, Mum!"

"It's Graham . . . Graham Faire . . . Does that satisfy you?"

"Graham . . . that's it. I remember you and he were kissing, and you were crying. It made me sad."

In one swift move, Mum pulls herself out of the bath. She stands shivering in the harsh light, confronting Rose, "You may not speak of him . . . Do you understand? Especially in front of your father."

"Wait." Rose runs to the airing cupboard and comes back with two warm towels.

Mum snatches them. "I want you to swear never to mention his name again—tell me you won't."

"I swear." A promise Rose wonders if she can keep. "Come and sit where it's warmer—I'll make you a hot drink. You'll feel better."

In the kitchen, Rose heats milk. She quietly says his name, "Graham Faire."

She spoons Ovaltine into a cup, adds hot milk, and then sugar. It's what they do for people in shock.

"Go to bed." Mum kneels close to the fading fire wrapped in towels.

"Here, sip this. I'll hold the cup . . . Your hand's shaking."

"I'll be all right. Leave me alone." Alice turns her head away.

"Are you ill?"

"I had too much wine—I'm not used to it. Don't tell Dad."

At the foot of the stairs, Rose calls, "I love you, Mum."

There's no reply.

She undresses in the dark, climbs into bed, and tries to pray; God feels very far away. She's still awake when car lights slide across the ceiling. A door slams. Her father calls goodnight. His loud voice sounds jovial. She hears him greet Mum and pictures her close to the hearth. She hopes they won't fight. Rose pulls a pillow over her head and escapes into jumbled dreams.

— 1 4 —

THE LUMINOUS BEDSIDE CLOCK says 3:00 a.m. The house is very still. Mum has not come to bed. Rose turns on the small light. Her mother's nightgown hangs over a chair. Rose tiptoes out onto the landing. About to call out, she notices the faint outline of two white towels on the floor outside her father's bedroom. She slowly slides to a sitting position and leans against the wall, hugging her knees. Moonlight leaks in from a high window.

No noise comes from the closed door, not even their breathing. Rose waits, not daring to knock. Her head drops to her chest and she sleeps a little. Then the distinct sound of voices: an insistent, low rumble. It goes on and on.

It's been a long time since she remembers her parents sleeping together. Mum began coming into her bed when the sirens sounded, holding her close until they were forced to dash for shelter. They'd wait, listening to planes flying overhead, worrying about Dad off on his nightly rounds. Then it became a habit: mother and daughter snuggled together in sleep, their room an untidy mix of clothes and belongings.

The whispering has stopped. The towels maintain their ghostly shape on the carpet. Mum must be naked. Rose's mind flashes to the couple in the field. Then to Dad's anger when she saw him in the bathtub. She thinks about how her mother holds on to her sometimes, like a person drowning. Bereft, Rose creeps back to bed, missing the furry comfort of her cat.

It's almost daylight when she hears her mother opening and closing drawers in the semi-darkness, pulling on clothes. Rose stays still, listening to the brisk movements that betray nothing. She raises herself on one elbow. "Why were you in Daddy's room last night?"

"Good morning to you too, Rose."

"I thought you didn't like his snoring."

"I don't; he sounds like a helicopter. Now since you're awake so early, you can help tidy up. It's worse than a pigsty in here."

Rose rubs her eyes. "Keith says his parents always do."

This gets Mum's attention: "Keith who? Always do what? You're not talking about the Jacksons, I hope. Sit up when I'm speaking to you."

Rose takes her time swinging her legs over the bed, sensing she's on shaky ground—too late to backtrack. She says, casually, "Keith-next-door and I were on top of the bomb shelter. You can see right into their bedroom. I asked him if his parents sleep in the same bed. He says they do and he has his own room."

In fact, Keith had been disinterested in the conversation—busy throwing handfuls of pebbles onto the house roof and watching them rattle down into the gutters. He'd only answered when she kept after him.

Rose attempts to duck away but Mum has her by the arm. "Ouch."

"Where people sleep is nobody else's business. Especially the neighbors—what other personal things have you two been discussing? Anyone else you've been spying on lately?"

"Nothing . . . nobody. It's just that . . ." Rose flounders in a hopeless muddle. "I missed you last night."

Alice abruptly lets go, moves to the window and stands surveying the farmyard. Without turning, she says, "Come and look at your father struggling out there in the mud. See how hard he works?"

"I know he does."

"When he came in last night he was in a good mood for once. Maybe it was the beer. Or the fact the new manager treats him with respect, unlike the last horrible ex-officer type. Anyway, I was cold from my bath. Your father suggested I come into his bed to warm up. Neither of us could sleep. We talked in the dark. I don't know what we're going to do—but we can't go on like this. Last winter nearly did us in."

The morning sky is streaked with red. Rose stands behind, both arms wrapped around Mum's waist, chin resting on her shoulder. Together they watch Stanley trudge across a field followed by half a dozen black and white pigs.

Rose says, "If only we could win a million on the football pools . . . Daddy would be rich again, and happy."

Her mother laughs. "There's no guarantee money and happiness go together, but it certainly wouldn't hurt." She turns from the window and kisses Rose on the forehead. "Right this minute, I'd give a fortune for a pack of cigarettes but I'm broke. You, my nosey-parker daughter, must get a move on for school."

— 1 5 —

THE SCHOOL CLOAKROOM FILLS with girls pulling off hats and coats, elbowing each other for space around the mirror, over the washbasins. No makeup is permitted, but some of the older girls sneak a smear of lipstick or dab of rouge for the benefit of boys who gawk over the hockey field fence. Rose practices invisibility, moving in a dream-like state on the edge, close to the walls. The room exudes a mix of smells: soap, grass, leather, sweaty feet, and unwashed gym clothes. Someone pulls on her plaits. She spins round to see Annie's beaming face, cheeks red from bicycling to school. Annie shouts over the din of slamming wooden lockers, girls calling like magpies.

"I've something to tell you."

"What happened?"

"I'll tell you later." She winks. "Meet me by the blasted oak at midnight . . . I mean, lunchtime."

A sudden hush descends. Annie nudges Rose in the ribs, eyes rolling toward the door. Whispers ripple from girl to girl.

"Gordy's on the warpath again," a girl mutters. "Hold on to your hats!"

"Silence!" The reedy Scottish voice freezes everyone like a game of statues. Miss Gordon ploughs her way through the room, kicking aside objects in her path, working herself into a lather of recrimination for their slovenliness. Flecks of spit form around her mouth. Her tantrums are notorious in the school, but, like any violent change in the weather, hard to predict.

A teacher appears in the doorway, meekly enquiring what the girls have done. Rose steps back as the headmistress sweeps by. A book she has nervously dropped skids across the dirty floor. Miss Gordon, small, bosomy, and white-faced, kicks it before her, along with a gathering pile of other objects: hockey sticks, shoes, odd socks, hairclips, and sweet wrappers. She whirls back, passing by for a second time, snorting disgust. For a split second, Rose registers fear in the woman's eyes. The connection leaves Rose shaken, distrustful of what she's seen.

In a trance, Rose follows orders to retrieve her property and proceed to the assembly hall for prayer. There are so many school rules she despairs of obeying them, especially ones that make no sense. If she complains, Mum insists one must bow to authority, no matter what. Dad, poking his head around the newspaper, agrees; says that's what won us the war. Annie claims Gordy lost a university job when the men were demobbed, and Rose should feel sorry for her. Annie has a way of saying things that leave no room for argument, especially if the source is her own mother.

Word comes for the girls to stand. The headmistress, no hairpin out of place, leads morning prayer. Miss Conroy, the music teacher, plays the piano as the girls sing "All Things Bright and Beautiful." She waves an arm for them to sing louder. Someone in the choir trills descant. The hymn promises "all things well." Rose mouths the words, not trusting her own voice to stay in tune.

In the classroom, everyone talks about Gordy's latest outburst. Someone keeps watch at the door. Suspicion mounts that no one will escape today without an order mark, or extra homework, or both.

"She's completely bats," someone says.

"My dad's a solicitor—he says she should be reported."

"At least we're not caned, like my brother's boarding school."

"I'd rather that, and get it over with," one girl mutters.

"It's a reign of terror."

Rose ventures, "Did you see her eyes? She's frightened."

Backs turn and the conversation continues in whispers.

It's no surprise. Reprisals for swearing at Pam Rawlings were inevitable. The old saying, "sending people to Coventry," meaning deliberately ostracizing them, is Pam's favorite pastime. At her desk Rose withdraws into herself, pretending not to mind.

The first lesson is Latin. Miss Harrington distributes test papers facedown. She wears round steel glasses, her hairstyle short and bobbed, and beige clothing. Some girls complain she's too strict, but Rose likes her no-nonsense way of controlling the class.

"A passage from *The Gallic Wars*," she announces. "If you girls did your homework last night, it should be easy."

Rose turns over the paper and joins in the moans.

"You have twenty minutes to complete this," the teacher says, "so get started."

For the first few minutes Rose stares blankly at the page, but, gradually, here and there, a word, then a phrase, falls into place. She remembers David Vale: the warmth of his breath as he leaned over her shoulder, his North Country accent, and the way he spoke of his fondness for Latin. Concentrating now, she retrieves words, makes sense of them, and puts them in order.

Miss Harrington strolls between the aisles amid the scratching of pens.

Fifteen minutes into the test, the classroom door opens. An older girl with a prefect's badge announces, "Miss Gordon wants everyone in the hall immediately."

There's a hasty scraping of chairs and hubbub of voices. Miss Harrington stands at the front of the class, viewing the girls over her glasses, tugging on her cardigan hem. She seems to have no clue what this is about. Calling for quiet, she tells them they must leave, single file.

A girl behind Rose whispers, "Do you think there's been a disaster?"

Other voices join in. "I didn't hear a siren."

"Please, God, don't let it be the Russians."

"Perhaps someone has died?"

"It's probably Gordy . . . Did you see her in the cloakroom today?"

"Silence, girls." Miss Harrington appears irritated by the disruption, a fact that Rose finds comforting.

In the assembly hall, Rose spies Annie and signals her with a half-wave. Her friend, who looks solemn, shrugs her shoulders, eyes to heaven. Apparently she too is in the dark about this turn of events.

The teachers assemble on the platform where a row of chairs has been set up. The games teacher, Miss Cowper, remains below, organizing the lines of uniformed girls, blowing her whistle in short blasts. Rose shrinks in her seat. She knows what it's like to be subject to Cowper's biting sarcasm on the hockey field.

Miss Gordon, already on the platform, paces. She wears her academic robe, a relic from her former life. Rose thinks of a bat she rescued from the rain barrel, its wings spread out like Gordy's gown. Even the woman's small, pale face and beady eyes remind her of the half-drowned creature.

Many of the teachers have been at the school for years. The story is that they're unmarried because so many men died in the First World War. Rose studies the way they dress alike: drab colors, Lyle stockings, and sensible shoes. She wonders if the reason young teachers don't stay long is because Gordy rattles their nerves, stalking the corridors, peering through classroom windows. Observing them now, Rose is sure of it, as they cross and uncross their legs and examine their bitten fingernails.

Mrs. Case, the English teacher, strolls up the steps and takes a seat. Her white sweater, turquoise beads, and flowered skirt create a welcome contrast. She glances at the school clock as if impatient to get back to teaching. Once, after school, Rose saw Mrs. Case climb on the back of her husband's motorcycle, and roar away in a cloud of exhaust smoke, her skirt billowing.

Responding to a signal from Gordy, Miss Cowper gives a last shrill blast and moves to one side, arms crossed; apparently ready to block the path of any attempted escapee.

Miss Gordon steps up to the podium. The girls become quiet as her eyes sweep the rows. "Someone . . ." she begins, with a quiver in her voice. "Someone in this school is a thief." She points and swings her arm in an arc over the upturned faces. "One of you here," she repeats, "is a thief."

Rose has a sudden urge to pee, but she daren't move a muscle. Two girls whisper behind her, shuffling their feet.

"Quiet!" the headmistress shouts.

Gordy's glare strafes the rows. Each girl, on either side of Rose, sits absolutely still. Sunlight filters from the tall windows, resting on the headmistress's face. Her eyes reflect a yellowish tinge.

"Money is being taken from the cloakroom, and some very evil girl here knows who's doing it." Miss Gordon turns to the teachers. "I want every classroom and if necessary, every girl, searched until we find the thief in our midst. None of you will leave your seat until the culprit comes forward, or is found; and I promise you, she will be, even if we have to sit here all day."

The teachers leave the stage. Rose's heart jumps like an insect in a jar. She remembers money hidden in her desk from when Annie shares her lunch from home and Rose's lunch money is saved to buy sweets. Rose is pretty certain it's against the rules. Girls around her shift uneasily in their chairs. Rose imagines contraband lipstick, mascara, gum, chocolate, and scribbled notes they'd die if anyone read.

Sounds echo of desks being opened and closed. No one dares speak. Guilt has been laid on every girl. Rose feels it in the air. Only the most resilient can resist it. A wild thought of confessing is quickly suppressed. Rose draws a deep, shuddering breath and exhales. The girl on her right gently nudges her arm as if quietly defying Rose's exile to Coventry, offering a secret truce.

The school clock on the wall strikes eleven. Miss Gordon remains seated in her big chair on the stage, watching proceedings. Rose reads gold-lettered names on the wood paneling, listed for academic excellence over the past fifty years. Only one or two have gone ahead each year to university. Many marry soon after leaving school. They already have their hope chests, collecting linens and bits of silverware. The alternative is secretarial, teaching, or nurse training. All of which feel as distant to Rose as the moon. She smiles. Granny says she wants a ticket on the first voyage to the moon, convinced it will happen, though unlikely in her lifetime. If it does, Rose vows to go with her.

Miss Cowper approaches the headmistress and whispers. The girls crane their necks. Rose turns in time to see a girl on her feet, climbing over chairs, pushing toward an exit. She almost makes it to the door when Cowper leaps from the stage and sprints after her. Rose's hands fly to her mouth.

Gordy shouts, "Stop that girl."

$-16-$

IT IS NOON. THE school clock bongs in synchrony with Big Ben, miles south in the heart of London. The girls are spilled out onto the freshly mown lawns. For once, they've been left to their own devices while the staff has an emergency meeting. Rose and Annie find each other under the oak tree's great branches. The mean grey days of early spring have given way to warmth and a rush of new growth. Above, leaves in brilliant shades of green shake out like umbrellas after rain. Rose inhales the fresh sweet air.

Break time has been indefinitely extended while the teachers meet with Miss Gordon. Small groups of girls hang together, nervously glancing over their shoulders. All are aware of the girl left standing on the stage, accused of theft. Now and then, Annie and Rose hear peals of laughter across the lawn—the giddy sound of relief and guilt.

"Phew!" Annie flops to the ground.

"Bloody hell!" says Rose.

"That's swearing."

"I don't care. I feel sorry for that poor girl. I don't even know her name." Rose squats beside her friend, idly digging in the moss for last year's acorns.

"It's Doreen Driscoll." Annie has the tone of someone in the know. "She's in fourth form, new this year. She was at my old school. Her family moved away for a time, something to do with her parents' divorce. Her dad ran off with his secretary." She leans back against the wide tree trunk. "Good thing they caught her—that's what you get for stealing."

Rose stops her digging. She'd felt for the girl, hunted like an animal hidden in the last unmown patch of wheat at harvest time. "You're heartless." She tosses a lump of moss at Annie, harder than she intended. "Besides, you're breaking a rule yourself."

"Am not. And don't throw dirt at me."

"You're sitting on the grass."

"It's not damp."

"Prove that to Gordy."

Annie explodes, "Bother Gordy. I hate rules . . . Did you see how Miss Cowper tackled Doreen?"

"I bet Cowper played rugby in the army."

Annie laughs. "Probably . . . either that or she was in the S.S." She extracts a paper bag from her satchel. "Did you bring lunch?"

Rose says she hasn't, that she keeps asking, but Mum says she should have a hot meal at noon. That's when she and Dad have their dinner at home.

Annie inspects the bag's contents. "I heard your ma is not the only one who wants you in the cafeteria."

"Who told you that?"

"It's all over school. Pam Rawlings wants her lackeys around. No exceptions." Annie smirks. "Did you really push her down and swear at her?"

Rose describes the scene, boasting a little, not at all sure that it was worth the repercussions.

"Golly, I wish I'd been there to see it," Annie says admiringly. "At least you've only been sent to Coventry, and don't have to ride through the streets naked on horseback like Lady Godiva—though, come to think of it, your hair's long enough. Now if it was me, my hair would scarcely cover my ears." Annie chortles.

Rose can't help smiling, though she doubts her friend has any idea how spiteful Pam Rawlings can be.

"In my class," Annie persists, "no one gives a hoot where I eat or, for that matter, if I eat. In fact, I could do it standing on my head. Shall I try?"

"Don't bother." Rose scrambles to her feet, stretches and looks across the lawn at a small cluster of girls. Most have responded to a bell calling them inside for lunch. It all looks so peaceful. A breeze ripples through the sunlit branches, lifting the leaves' silvery undersides. On the far side, someone's mowing the tennis courts.

"Watch me." In a burst of energy, Rose plants her hands and kicks up her legs into a wobbly headstand. Her skirt slides over her face, exposing her regulation, navy blue knickers. Her plaits fall in the dirt. She doesn't care.

"Look out, you're going to land in my lunch." Annie gives her a push. Both girls fall in a heap, and for a while they wrestle. It's an even match.

Rose pins Annie to the soft ground and lies on top of her, their faces close. Annie smells faintly of carbolic soap and her mother's cold cream.

"*Pax*," Annie pleads. She pretends to cry. Rose giggles and lets her go. The girls brush each other off and survey the food.

"I'm starving!" Annie says. "I thought they'd never let us out of there." Her mother has packed two sticky buns from the shop, as well as a thick sandwich and two apples. "Help yourself." Annie bites into a bun. "Looks like Mum put in extras for you. She says you need fattening up. George agrees."

"George? Your brother said that?"

"Our George is like that. He notices things. Mum says that's why he wants to be a photographer. Anyway, have half a potted meat sandwich."

Rose takes a bite. She studies her friend, silently envying the way Annie's whole attention fixes on the bun, turning and licking the sugary glaze on the top. She's too embarrassed to ask what else George said about her. Suddenly self-conscious, Rose compares her long, scrawny limbs with Annie's sturdy body. As for Pam and her friends, they already have shapely curves, bound to attract older boys like Annie's brother.

Envy turns to irritation. "How can you eat like that, after what Gordy has put us through?" Rose hadn't meant to sound peevish. She softens the question with a teasing smile.

Undeterred, Annie pops the last piece in her mouth. "That was good, but I'm still hungry. Where's the other half of that sandwich?"

Rose won't be put off. "How did you feel when they said we had to go to the hall? Someone in my class was scared World War Three was starting."

"I was glad to get out of Geography." Annie munches on an apple. "Want a bite?"

Rose waves the apple away. "What's going to happen to that poor girl? How long do you think she's going to have to stand there? It's worse than the stocks."

"She'll probably be expelled. Do you want that other bun or not?"

Rose stretches out on the mossy ground and looks up into the tree. She should know by now: if Annie's mind's on food, that's where it stays until the last bite. A red squirrel hovers, tensed for a leap to a branch surely too insubstantial to hold its weight. The animal flies into space and lands clinging and chattering in a mass of swaying leaves. In contrast, Rose feels her body in full contact with the solid earth. Annie flops, face up, beside her. Rose gently traces her friend's profile with her forefinger: the upturned nose, round cheeks, and strong chin.

"That tickles."

"Annie . . ."

"What?"

"Nothing . . ." They lie, arms touching, watching the squirrel's aerobatics. Rose eventually murmurs, "What was it you were going to tell me this morning?"

"Guess."

"They gave you a part in the school play?"

"You mean as Romeo? Not blooming likely. Sadie Willets is Juliet and I'm six inches shorter than her. My job is stage props. Guess again."

Voices come near, setting off the squirrel's chatter. Rose sits up. "Oh no, we're about to be invaded."

Two girls, Margaret and Fiona, from Rose's class, join them. They've heard the police have been called. The punished girl's plight creates a brief alliance, but when Rose and Annie have nothing to add, they wander away. Moments later, Pam Rawlings arrives with a small retinue. They smell of overcooked vegetables and something fried. Pam fixes Rose with an evil look.

"Can we help you?" says Annie.

The big girl addresses Rose. "For your information, those two weren't supposed to be talking to you."

"Is that all?" Annie leans back against the tree. "Then please move on. You're blocking the sun." The girls wheel away, snorting like a group of ponies.

"Good riddance," Annie says. "Where were we?"

Rose could kick herself. She should have known right away. "Don't say you've started your period."

"All right, then I won't say."

Rose jumps up and does a little dance. "Why didn't you tell me before?"

"I don't know . . . I suppose I wanted you to guess."

"Annie, I'm sorry. I wasn't thinking. When did it happen?"

Annie forgives her. She says she woke this morning and found blood on the sheets and at first she was scared. She called her mother, who, of course, knew exactly what was going on. "I knew too," Annie says, "but it was still a shock."

George, who pretended not to notice a bloodstained sheet soaking in the bathtub, said he'd get his breakfast at work. He has a girl friend, Annie says. The two of them sit in the front parlor and neck. She knows this because she spied from the bushes under the window. The girl's name is Dora and she smells of strawberries from her job at the jam factory. She wears gobs of makeup and lately has a peroxide streak in her mousy hair. Annie says she peeked in Dora's handbag once and saw a box of tampons but hasn't dared ask how they work.

Lying now on her back, Rose sees bright patches of blue through light green foliage. Annie wraps the remains of her lunch, still talking. Her mother produced sanitary towels and a belt, and showed where they'd been hidden at the back of the airing cupboard. That's where she'd kept her own supplies until her periods stopped, brought on by the shock of being a widow and only a tiny pension to support two small children.

Annie looks thoughtful. "No wonder Ma calls it the curse."

"I should buy you gumdrops," Rose says.

"You don't have to . . . You won the bet by being first." She grins: "But you can if you like. I've a coupon saved."

Rose looks longingly in the direction of the school gate and the road beyond. "The sweet shop's so close," she says.

"You could be there and back in fifteen minutes." Annie's eyes sparkle. "Go on, I dare you. You'll get extra Daring Demon points if you do."

"I can't—the money's in my desk, unless it was confiscated this morning."

Annie reaches in her pocket. "Here's a shilling you can borrow."

Rose looks over at the small knots of girls. The school grounds have become oddly subdued as though no one quite knows what to do next. She turns to Annie, "I daren't."

"I know," Annie says.

Minutes later the clanging sound of the school bell reaches them. A prefect runs up and tells them to return to their classrooms.

They walk toward the school buildings. "Cheerio," Annie says. "I'll see you later. Think I'll buy lunch next week and sit with fat Pamela in the cafeteria." She runs ahead.

Rose is not sure if that last remark was meant to be a joke. Not taking the dare leaves her with a queasy feeling she's let Annie down. She joins the throng entering the building. School secretary Miss Keene stops her in the doorway.

"Rose Gray, Miss Gordon wants to see you in her office."

GIRLS SPILL INTO THE darkened interior, bringing with them the restiveness of more than two hours of freedom; ribbons and sashes untied, hair uncombed, shoes scuffed. A smell of the outdoors stirs the musty air. They crisscross the assembly hall to their different classrooms, stopping to stare at the stage. The accused girl is not there. The school buzzes with speculation. Miss Cowper blows her whistle incessantly and tells everyone to keep moving. Rose makes her way through, weak with anxiety. They must have discovered the money in her desk and think she stole it.

She reaches the front office, but no sign of the secretary. Unsure of what to do, she perches on a chair outside Miss Gordon's closed door. She hears the headmistress's voice and wonders who could be in there with her. An uncovered typewriter sits on Miss Keene's desk, and beside it, neatly stacked papers. Rose fixes on a single brown folder. Even from a distance, she can read the label: "GRAY, ROSE."

She stands. Blood roars in her ears, the edges of her vision blur. She taps on Miss Gordon's door; the voice pauses and then continues. Could Gordy be on the phone, talking to the police? Rose considers sneaking back to her class. Then she remembers Cowper prowling the hall.

When all seems quiet, she timidly knocks again. The door flies open. Rose steps back, startled that she and Gordy are almost at eye level. The woman's face has a grayish pallor, and her forehead glistens with tiny beads of perspiration. Strands of hair escape the tight bun, and a steel hairpin dangles loose. Rose almost reaches out to catch it, but stops. Miss Gordon's cold stare warns against even the smallest gesture.

"Who are you? What do you want? Can't you see I'm busy?"

"I'm Rose Gray. Miss Keene said you wanted to see me."

"Why are you so grubby looking? You're a disgrace. Have you been stealing too?"

"No, Miss Gordon."

"You're lying, aren't you?"

"No, Miss Gordon." Rose pictures the two shillings in her desk. Should she confess? She steps back and bumps hard into the doorjamb.

"Stay there and don't move."

The headmistress pushes past into the secretary's office. "Where's Miss Keene? How can she leave me with this mess?"

Rose isn't sure if the questions are addressed to her. "I don't know," she says. Miss Gordon picks up her file. There appears to be a note clipped to the inside. Rose waits while Gordy reads. Through the window she sees a group of girls run by, brandishing hockey sticks. Miss Cowper jogs in their wake.

The headmistress looks up. "Behavior like this is against school etiquette. Come with me into my office."

Miss Gordon pushes Rose ahead, points to a chair on one side of her enormous desk. She sits opposite, leans forward and hides her face in her hands. Rose swallows. The headmistress's scalp shows pink through her thin, grey hair. Her ringless fingers clutch like claws.

Abruptly, the headmistress sits up and skewers the escaping hairpin into her bun. She glares, "Do you call yourself a Christian, Rose?"

"Yes, Miss Gordon."

"How can you do this to me?"

"I don't know what I did." Rose sits straight in her chair, digging fingernails into her palms.

"Do you have any idea why Miss Cowper sent you here, even though she knew the kind of day I've had?"

"Not really." Rose can't bring herself to mention the lunch money.

She dreads her parent's anger and disappointment. "Haven't we enough problems, Rose?" her mother will say. She fears her father's reaction, like a bomb.

"Well let me read this to you." Miss Gordon adjusts her half-moon glasses, unclips the note from Rose's file, and reads aloud:

Dear Headmistress,

Rose Gray was seen cavorting under the big oak tree with a girl from another form. They wrestled on the ground, and Rose lay on top of the other girl in a most unbecoming way. Before that, Rose did headstands showing her underwear to the entertainment of town boys passing in the street. The pupil with her was not named but I have my suspicions. The one reporting is a reliable witness: she's observed, as I have, that Rose is a poor team player. She told me that Rose spends more time with this other girl than her own classmates. I thought you should be informed of this behavior before it gets out of hand.

Yours faithfully,
Gwen Cowper

Listening, Rose fixes her attention on a framed black and white photo of a small white dog. She suspects the dog is dead, like her cat.

Rose cannot help it. Tears come. Her friendship with Annie is starting to feel too much. She wants to go home, to climb up in the straw barn and hide. There's no escape from Gordy's piercing look. "I only did one headstand and I am wearing gym knickers. I didn't see any boys."

"Why were you lying on top of this other girl?"

"We were only playing."

"Playing? How old are you?"

"Thirteen."

Miss Gordon rises, walks to Rose's side of the desk. "Do you think it proper to play games like that at your age?"

"No, Miss Gordon." *I hate you*, Rose thinks. A hand clamps on her shoulder.

"Who is this girl you are so fond of, Rose?"

"She . . . she's from another class."

"I see you're not going to tell me Annie Carter's name." The hand moves to the nape of Rose's neck. She fights the fusty smell of Gordy's gown brushing her face.

"You think I haven't noticed the times you spend with your special friend."

Miss Gordon returns to her chair and flips through Rose's file. Her tone changes. "I see your parents live on the government settlement. Do they have extra rations since they work on the land?"

"I think my father does." She pictures the bacon Mum fries for Dad's breakfast and the extra butter.

"Did you know your lunches here are subsidized?"

"I suppose so." Rose has no clue why Gordy is asking these questions.

The gimlet eyes don't let up for a second. "You look unhealthy. You are to eat in the cafeteria from now on. As for your friend, Annie, stay away from her."

"Why? She's my friend. I'm sorry we were wrestling. It was my fault. We won't do it again, I promise."

The headmistress points to the door. "You may go back to your class now."

Rose pleads, "I don't see what we did wrong."

"That's precisely the point. It's my job to protect you from moral danger. It's for your own good. One of these days you'll thank me. I'm having a dreadful day. Please leave."

Rose has reached the secretary's office when Gordy calls her back. "I see your marks not as bad as I thought. Your teachers think you have potential. You'll require extra Latin if you ever apply to university. In the morning, I want you to see Miss Keene to set up tutorials with me once a week."

Rose stops midway across the deserted assembly hall in a state of indecision. All the classroom doors are closed. Accustomed to bells and schedules telling her where to go next, she tries to think what class she should be in. Her mind, filled with echoes of Gordy's words, refuses to register the time. Transfixed, she stares at the clock. The pendulum, indifferent to her mood, keeps its steady rhythm. Almost imperceptibly the minute hand moves forward.

Rose tells herself to concentrate: the last period of the day has already begun. Half the day's lessons missed, she is uncertain what subject, and who will be teaching it. Most classes are in homeroom, but others, like chemistry or home economics, move around. She considers going door to door, peeking through the windows. The thought of being seen, or walking into the middle of a lesson, is too dreadful.

Barely aware of where her feet are taking her, she heads to the cloakroom. There will be no bus for another hour but she reasons she could walk home. The thought lifts her spirits, imagining shortcuts through town into the quiet countryside.

In the cloakroom her plans dissolve. Softly, she recites, "Any girl leaving the school premises without permission will be strongly disciplined."

She sits on a low bench and leans back into the hanging coats. There's no sound except the gurgle of a water pipe. Whatever she does now, she fears, will result in worse trouble. Gordy has released her, but with a verdict as hard to bear as being accused of stealing. Rose pulls a coat around her head to muffle cries of protest.

"I hate her, I hate her . . . I won't let her stop me seeing Annie."

How was it possible the time under the oak tree with her best friend was bad? Worse, the hurtful insinuation it was unchristian. Tucking her feet up on the bench, Rose retreats further into her hiding place; she rocks from side to side. She thinks, *Gordy's worse than Mr. Baxter. He loves to quote the Bible: "If your right hand offends, you pluck it off."* Rose grits her teeth. Gordy wants to lop off Annie. Her favorite pastime is plucking bits off other people, leaving empty spaces where their limbs are supposed to be, like soldiers back from the war.

It's for your own good, Rose thinks bitterly. That's what Gordy told her. Grown-ups always say that. "It's for your own good," Mum will say when I tell her about the extra Latin.

Gradually, her spinning thoughts slow to an awareness of where she is. The coats emit a smell of wool and vague body aromas, mixed with her own stale breath. Soon, the school bell will echo soon through the halls, and everyone will crowd into the cloakroom. She's sure to be discovered. One more excuse Pam Rawlings and her consorts will find for ridicule. Rose despairs; the more she tries to avoid attention, the more she seems to attract it. Even the fact that she's been ostracized means everyone notices. Rose *wills* herself to disappear; to tighten her body into an ever-smaller space, but all that happens is she's left gasping for breath.

"Oh Rose, is that you under there?" The voice is matter of fact. Rose parts coats enough to catch a glimpse of brightly patterned fabric. A warm hand reaches in and grasps her arm, firmly pulling her toward the light.

Mrs. Cave, her English teacher, smiles. "I was hoping those were your shoes I saw peeking out. I almost walked right past them." Rose looks up, mortified; the teacher she most wants to impress has flushed her out of hiding.

"Goodness, your face is all red. It must have been stuffy in there. Come over to the mirror and tidy up." Mrs. Cave beckons Rose to follow. A foot taller, the teacher makes a show of smoothing her own short dark hair and arranging the row of turquoise beads she wears over a white sweater.

Rose stands, disheveled, beside the tall, graceful teacher. She attempts to brush dirt from her uniform, a reminder of the time outdoors with Annie.

"May I?" Mrs. Cave picks a leaf from Rose's sleeve. She looks at her watch. "We better hurry. I left everyone reading *Hamlet*, and we are at the part where Ophelia tries to defend herself and Hamlet behaves as though he's completely insane."

She starts toward the door, stopping to let Rose go ahead, but talking all the time. "I thought you liked Shakespeare. You do, don't you? You don't look bored like some do. There are days when I think we teach him at too young an age. Do you think that's the problem?"

Rose, hurrying to keep up, wants to say she loves Mrs. Cave's Shakespeare class, and she didn't realize that it was English she was missing. But the teacher, striding along in her flowered skirt, gives her no chance to speak.

"When I thought about it, I decided Shakespeare writes for all ages. He helps us to think about what it's like to be human, to love and hate and betray, to fight and kill each other, and to go mad."

They arrive outside the classroom door. "I thought you might know what I was trying to say. Then I realized you were missing."

Rose, for the first time, understands what other girls mean when they say they have a pash on a teacher. She wants to be like Mrs. Cave, to dress like she does, to talk about serious things, to be able to climb on the back of a motor cycle and ride away.

Rose asks shyly, "How did you know where to find me?"

"I didn't know. I remembered seeing you earlier in the day when I was up on the stage in assembly hall. I went first to enquire at the school office but no one was there. Then I went to see if your coat was gone."

Mrs. Cave sighs. "What a strange day it has been."

Through the glass, Rose meets the curious stares of her classmates and hastily steps out of view. Mrs. Cave blocks her way. "I have no idea what you were hiding from, but I don't want you missing lessons again. There is nothing in there you can't face."

She reaches for the door handle. "Chin up," she whispers.

— 1 8 —

ROSE IS GREETED BY an ominous murmur, like worker bees when approached too close to their hive.

"Be quiet, all of you." Mrs. Cave writes the homework assignment on the blackboard. The buzzing stops and notebooks are opened.

Rose retrieves *Hamlet* from her desk. Her breathing slows; her heart settles to its normal beat. Fifteen minutes later, it's as though she's never been away, drawn into her teacher's passion for Shakespeare. Mrs. Cave reminds them this ought to be their second reading of the play; midterm exams are coming up. This is the time to be steeped in every scene's drama as the story unfolds.

Rose's chair and her desk create an island of safety. Sounds are muted: the scratch of chalk on the board and the occasional light rap for emphasis, the soft shush of the teacher's skirt against her nylon stockings, and clink of silver bracelets sliding on her wrist. The afternoon sun captures motes of chalk dust. Outside the windows, sparrows congregate in the branches of a tree. Rose envisions Mrs. Cave's husband coming soon to whisk her away, out onto the open road, taking her wherever she wants to go.

Mrs. Cave handwriting flows with loops and curls. She reads aloud what she has written, lingering over the words as she imagines Ophelia might have spoken them:

"O, woe is me, to have seen what I have seen, see what I see!"

They are to write a brief composition on two questions:

1. What has Ophelia seen, and sees now, that is leading to her madness?

2. What is about to happen that she does not yet fully know?

Copying the words, Rose aspires to change her plain, schoolgirl writing to loops like her teacher's. The last bell resounds through the school. Books slam shut and the minute Mrs. Cave leaves the room there is uproar. Some of the girls start clutching their foreheads in mock distress: "Woe is me!" Soon nearly everyone joins in, outdoing each other.

Rose concentrates on collecting her books. She must find Annie to warn her about Gordy's ban. Fiona Foster, the prettiest girl in the class, sidles up. Others gather around. Fiona perches sideways on Rose's desk. "We're all dying to know why you were sent to Gordy's office."

Rose admits, "Extra Latin."

"Extra Latin," Fiona reports back to the others. They seem satisfied with the answer, even impressed. "Miss Gordon tutored my sister in extra Latin," someone says. "So she could apply for university. She was accepted at Cambridge, went for a year—then left to marry her history prof. Woe is she! He's a frightful bore."

"I told you Rose was a rotten swot." Pam Rawlings barges by. "Too bad she doesn't know one end of a hockey stick from another."

"Oh shut up, Pam," Fiona hisses. Rose wishes she'd said it louder. The girls' friendliness tempts her to stay but she needs to find Annie. On the other hand, following too closely in Pam's wake could be trouble. Rose senses Pam is out to pick a fight. She decides to stay and join in the talk.

Everyone is curious about the accused girl. Word is out that she spent hours standing on the platform in disgrace. Fiona asks, "Do you know anything about her?"

Rose says she's heard Doreen's parents are divorced, omitting to say the information came from Annie. She stops short of adding the bit about the father's secretary. Either way she scores points, drawn into a cozy circle of gossip.

Fiona confides she's heard something juicy—Rose must swear she'll keep it secret. She whispers, "Doreen's dad ran off with a floozy." Rose rubs the ear that tickles from Fiona's breath. She doesn't know anyone who's divorced, and she's not sure she'd recognize a floozy if she saw one. There is more. Fiona continues, "A senior told us Doreen was expelled from her last school for something *very bad*. Now she's forced to live with her father and the floozy."

She shouldn't have stayed so long talking. When she reaches the cloakroom, Annie's coat and hat are gone. If Rose moves fast, she might still find her at the bike rack. Grabbing her things, she heads for the door.

"Where do you think you're going, Rose Gray?" Pam's arms stretch across the doorway, her palms flat against the frame.

"Let me through," Rose demands. "I have to catch a bus."

"You want to be with your darling Annie."

"I can be a friend with whoever I want."

A girl shouts from behind. "Come on, Pam, let us in. We need our coats."

"Pick on someone your own size," someone yells, which causes laughter from the growing crowd.

"I'm not moving until she admits Annie Carter is a little twerp."

"Leave me alone, you idiot." In a fury Rose hurls herself forward, encountering solid resistance. Pam shoves back and kicks her in the shin. Rose yelps. The crowd shoves from behind, catching Pam off balance. She stumbles and falls, almost landing on top of Rose.

In the confusion, Rose looks for an escape. A howl goes up, "I'm bleeding." Pam sprawls on the floor, clutching her forehead. Horrified, Rose offers a hand, but Pam ignores it, scrambling to her feet.

Pam spits, "You pushed me, Rose Gray."

"I never pushed you. It was the girls behind you."

"You liar—you and your precious friend, always shoving people around."

"That's ridiculous. Annie hasn't done a thing to you." Rose fights tears of frustration. She looks around wildly for an ally.

Pam sneers, "I'm reporting you to Miss Gordon."

"You did that already," Rose says. The blood unnerves her: a small but steady trickle drips to the floor. Pam must have cut her head on the bench.

"Did she really report you?" a girl asks. "Was that why you had to see Gordy?" She looks incredulous. "That's like turning someone over to the Gestapo."

Rose says, "She told lies about me and Annie."

"Don't believe anything she says," Pam screams. "Look at me, I'm bleeding—Rose did it. She's a liar."

"Me thinks the lady doth protest too much," the same girl mutters. But even she retreats to the back of the crowd.

Pam makes the most of her injury, dabbing at the cut with a hand-kerchief. Huge tears start to well, her bottom lip quivers. Immediately, girls surround her. With a sinking heart, Rose realizes she'll never catch up with Annie. The doorway finally clear, people rush by to grab coats and hats, running to catch their buses. Pam's closest chums stay, circling around Rose, amusing themselves with taunts.

Rose says, "It wasn't my fault."

The girls point and giggle, mimicking her. "It wasn't my fault."

Much as she struggles to get by, with every move, someone bars her way. "Leave me alone," she cries. "Can't you see Pam's faking? She's a big baby."

Like throwing a rock into a lion's cage, Pam's fury is let loose. The others jeer and jab fingers. They accuse Rose of being an outsider who will never fit in. She's queer looking, her clothes don't fit, and her father is a pig man and dirt poor. They imitate the way she holds a hockey stick, knock kneed, always missing the ball. They say Annie is stuck-up and a drip too. Rose yells back, "Sticks and stones may break my bones; words will never hurt me." She cringes at how pathetic she must sound: her words as effective as dud fireworks.

"What on earth is going on here?" A prefect appears in the doorway. She has to raise her voice to get their attention.

"Pam Rawlings hurt her head," someone announces. "Rose Gray did it."

The senior girl walks over to Pam, who is suddenly subdued. She inspects the cut that's no longer bleeding. "How did you do that?"

Rose holds her breath, waiting to be blamed.

"Rose pushed me," Pam stammers.

Dressed in the neat skirt, blue blouse, and school tie worn by sixth formers, the prefect looks skeptical. "You are almost twice her size. Don't you play defense on the hockey team?"

Pam nods, shifting from one foot to the other.

"Well, looks like you'll live. You've had worse on the sports field."

She looks at her watch. "None of you have any business being here at this hour. I want you to clear out, before I report you all. I don't know what else has been going on, and I don't want to know."

Everyone quickly departs. Rose rushes to the bike rack. As she suspects, Annie is gone and she's missed her bus.

— 19 —

ROSE WALKS, HALF LIMPING, past rows of small houses with the same lace-curtained windows and meticulously kept gardens. Satchel straps cut into her shoulders, the heavy books bumping against her spine each time she jumps a curb. In rhythm with her steps she recites, "Sticks and stones may break my bones." Her feet nimbly miss the cracks in the concrete, jogging fifty steps, and then fifty paces walking, "Words will never hurt me." Her shoes kick up pink petals, remnants from blossoming cherry trees, mixed with dirt and sand and cigarette ends.

Even via the cart track, rather than the bus route, the walk home is almost four miles. Sweat trickles down her face and into her collar. She stops to unbutton her coat and, breaking a school rule, removes her hat and stuffs it in the satchel. An old man, digging in his garden, stops to watch, leaning on the front gate.

"Ever so warm for this time of year, wouldn't you say?"

Rose nods a reply and sets off again mumbling the incantation that she cannot get out of her head: "Sticks and stones may break my bones."

She comes to a public footpath that runs along a high wall. Annie once showed her this shortcut through town, but Rose enters hesitantly, afraid she'll lose her way. In the sudden stillness, away from the busy street, her pace slows; the childish song recedes, as if silently absorbed by the centuries-old stones. She trudges along, wishing she were home. She shouldn't have dallied.

According to Annie, the ancient footpath follows Woolston's old city wall, although prewar housing has sprawled beyond it. Rose comes upon the place where lovers, long ago, scratched their names. She and Annie had lingered there until her friend confessed she'd be in trouble if her ma knew they were on the footpath. There'd been a murder there of a young woman, during the war. The victim's killer was never found. In the end, they'd made a pact, promising next time to follow the path's full length, to the park beyond. After all, they were Daring Demons.

Too tired to turn back, and, above all, wanting to impress Annie with her bravery, Rose sets off again, hobbling from her throbbing shin where Pam kicked her. The path emits smells of trampled leaves, wet, cold rock, and an odor Rose suspects is human urine. Sounds are low, rhythmic: pigeons cooing and, not far away, the distant drone of traffic. She comes upon empty bottles and soiled bedding, with the feeling someone has quite recently slept there. On the left, opposite to the wall, are narrow back gardens with high wrought-iron fences and locked gates. Beyond, grand houses, some with boarded-up windows, the bomb-shattered glass not yet replaced.

Rose keeps going, seeing no one, but with an uneasy sense of being followed. She looks back: nothing but deep shadows. Perhaps all she heard a moment ago was a squirrel foraging for acorns. Onward she goes, beneath the high wall but it is no protection from the attacks replaying in Rose's head.

Another sound, closer this time, makes her sharply turn her head. In a rush, a man in ragged clothing pushes past, brushing her shoulder, while muttering an apology in a thick, guttural accent. Rose steps aside in the wake of his stench. He charges forward, sack slung over one shoulder, containing, she guesses, all he owns, besides the tattered blankets where he sleeps. The shock of the stranger's sudden appearance leaves Rose's heart beating fast. Only a distant patch of sunlight, beyond the green tunnel of interlacing branches, gives her the courage to push on.

The footpath merges into a main intersection. Traffic streams from a gateway in the city wall heading north out of town. A motorist slows, allowing Rose to cross the busy street. She cuts through a park, past two tennis courts, and the public swimming baths with a sign that reads: "CLOSED." Families are out enjoying the warm, late afternoon. Husbands and wives walk arm in arm, their children racing ahead. A small headache, forming behind Rose's eyes, grows steadily worse.

She reaches the entry to the cart track as the late afternoon sun touches the treetops. At the mossy bridge, Rose pauses, relieved at last to be in familiar surroundings. She takes deep breaths, hoping to see the kingfisher she saw earlier. Below, a mother duck bobs her way in the fast stream, followed by six tiny ducklings. Rose watches their progress but the headache is affecting her eyes, as though seeing through shivered glass. Leaning over the dizzying, swirling water, she abruptly throws up

the remains of Annie's sticky bun. Bits of sick catch on dark green ten-
drils, spinning out of sight. Rose stands, clutching the railing, bewildered
by how she became ill so suddenly. She must pull herself together. No
choice but to keep going. That's what Mum would say.

If there is any depression in the grass where she saw the courting
couple, it's too far away to see. Better not to think of that Sunday. Memories of her cat only add to her misery. The track, at last, turns into smooth
paved road. A few old houses and a pub are all that remain of the original
village. From there, rows of small brick houses, allotments with glass-
houses and outbuildings, stretch in a straight line from the central farm.
The road continues with its elm trees and untidy rookeries, ditches and
bristling hedges; the sun sits low in the west, the sky spilled across with
reds and orange, casting a golden light on the ploughed fields.

Walking in the fresh air calms her, as though the grasses, wildflowers, and trees are more than they appear. Warblers are busy in the hedgerows. A rabbit hops across the road ahead, pausing before it disappears.
She imagines the trees' swaying branches gently accepting, not accusing
or judging. Thoughts drift to Ophelia adorning herself with flowers and
herbs: rosemary for remembrance, rue, columbine, and daisy. Surely,
even in her madness, Ophelia believed the plants offered healing against
the unraveling of her world. Rose decides Mrs. Cave will be happy she
has understood.

"Where were you?" Mum is sure to ask. "Did you miss the bus?"

Rose walks fast, head down, determined not to look up until she
reaches the red telephone box ahead. At the edge of her vision, dande-
lions flash golden, nestled among jagged-leaved nettles that, were she to
fall into them, would raise itchy red welts. She comes abreast with the
kiosk. Several neighbors use this phone, including Mum. The silent box
reveals no secrets. Its glass sides reflect only the surrounding greenery.
Rose braces as thoughts break down the wall between home and school.
Like storm clouds, the two parts of her life threaten to collide. The sun
disappears as she walks up the driveway.

— 20 —

SHE'S THROWN HER SATCHEL on the kitchen floor and snapped on all the lights. Tea things are out on the counter: the barely warm teapot, sugar and milk, and a plate with two pieces of bread and butter. Three cups and saucers are stacked in the sink.

Rose runs cold water, rinses a cup, and fills it, drinking thirstily. When she calls no one answers. She thinks, *Mum's probably in the greenhouse, or maybe went to look for me at the bus stop and is dawdling on the way back, admiring the sunset.* Hoping food might settle her stomach, Rose sprinkles sugar on a piece of bread and folds it into a sandwich. Standing, eating at the kitchen sink, she sees the dark shape of the greenhouse. The only lights come from the piggeries. The soft bread catches in her throat. This time she won't panic. Mum will be back soon. If only her head didn't hurt so much. She walks out into the yard for fresh air.

"What are you eating, Rose Gray?"

She should've known he'd be there, sprawled on the bomb shelter roof spying on her.

"None of your business," she shouts.

Keith jumps down and runs to her side. "Can I 'ave a bite?" He still has on his school uniform with short grey trousers, grey jumper, and falling-down socks, boney knees exposed. In the light from the kitchen window, his big ears are rimmed in red. Rose notices a dark patch on the front of his trousers and a smell like cat pee.

"Here," she gives him the sandwich, no longer hungry.

She watches him stuff the whole thing in his mouth, chewing, cheeks bulging. She traces a pattern with her toe in the dirt. "Have you seen my mum anywhere?"

"Maybe . . ." The boy picks up a stick from the ground and parries with it, an imaginary sword fight.

"What do you mean, maybe?" She tries to grab him but he dances away.

"Maybe I did, maybe I didn't. Do you 'ave any sweeties to give us?"

Rose lunges and grabs the stick. She takes a swipe at his bare legs, "I'll give you sweeties, you idiot boy!"

"Ouch." Keith hops around, rubbing his leg. "They went off in the green car." He whimpers. "You hit me, Rose. I'm going home."

"I didn't hit you that hard. Don't be a baby. I'll go and get you a sweetie." Rose gives him back his stick, guiltily aware of her own sore shin.

She goes into the kitchen, dizzy with worry. It must have been David Vale's car. Have they run away? She scans the room, spots a lollipop she'd saved resting on the edge of her mother's ashtray.

Outside, she tells him, "Here, it's strawberry flavor."

"But you already licked it."

"Was it the vet's car?" She deliberately takes a lick. The lollipop tastes of ashes. She waves it in front of him until he snatches it, crunching greedily. Rose waits, trying to breathe normally.

The boy looks back with his squinty eyes. "Your mum got in the car with 'im and they drove away."

"Did you hear what they said?"

They both hear Mrs. Jackson calling for Keith to come in for his supper. In two seconds he'll be gone, running home as he always does when there's the chance of food. She has to know where David Vale and her mother went, what they said to each other, and what the boy overheard.

Rose has him by both arms, her face inches from his. His breath reeks of strawberries and unwashed teeth. "Tell me what you know." Holding him down, like an animal about to bolt, she sees his cunning. He knows he has power over her.

"Take me up the water tower. You promised, Rose."

"I'll take you up the tower." *And throw you off it.* "I'm not letting go of you until you tell me." Her head feels ready to explode.

"They went to look for you." He wrenches away. "They thought you didn't come home on purpose because you found out about your cat." He darts out of reach and runs to the bomb shelter, scrambling onto the low roof.

"What about my cat?" she screams. Bats swoop by his silhouette against the evening sky.

Rose strains to hear his squeaky voice. "Didn't anyone tell you, Rose Gray?"

"Wait, Keith!" She hovers below, afraid if she climbs after him, he'll jump off the other side. "For God's sake, what were they were saying about Moggy?"

She reaches for him but he evades her. "We can climb the tower together this weekend if you like," she wheedles.

"My mum says not to tell you but I will, 'cause you crossed your heart."

He dances free. "It wasn't your Moggy that killed the chicks. My dad found out it was a fox, and he borrowed your dad's gun and waited up all night. When the fox came, he shot it dead." Keith closes one eye, aims his arm, points a finger and pulls an imaginary trigger: "Bang! Bang! Bang!"

Rose hears his feet hit the ground and the sharp slam of a door. It's the fox that first forms a picture in her mind. She's seen one slinking along the edge of the field. She pictures its full bushy tale and reddish coat, tongue lolling, ears pointed in pursuit of some invisible prey. Impressions come quickly now of her slain cat and bullets ripping into the fox's flesh, fur and bones and sinew mingling, as though the two animals in her mind will never be apart.

Back she goes, into the house, and the silent kitchen. Her head pounds and there's a ringing in her ears. Rose clings to the banister, climbs the stairs. Too exhausted to even unlace her shoes, she lies on the bed and waits for someone to come.

—21—

"I FOUND HER—SHE'S UP here in bed." Rose stirs. It's her mother's voice, but who is it she's shouting to? She opens her eyes a slit and quickly closes them. Everything hurts. If only she could escape back to her dream. But it won't keep still, evading her reach, moving further and further away.

"She's fully dressed, lying here in the dark."

All this noise pains her ears. Why so loud? "Let me sleep," Rose murmurs.

She is in a boat, water seeping in, slowly rising over feet and ankles. Must keep rowing to get to shore.

"Rose, dear, you're dreaming. Wake up." The boat rocks. Someone shakes her arm.

Time and place return with a jolt. "Mummy, you came back!"

"Of course I did, dear. Don't I always? Silly girl, you were the one who was missing."

"I thought you and Mr. Vale had run away."

Her mother responds in a fierce whisper, "What absolute nonsense. Be quiet; he'll hear you." Loudly, she says, "Mr. Vale kindly drove me into town to look for you."

"I missed the bus."

"You've never missed the bus."

"I walked home by the cart track."

Her mother's body relaxes. "All that way?" She touches Rose's forehead and strokes her face. "No wonder we didn't find you on the road."

A man's voice calls from below. "Is she all right?"

Rose stiffens. She hears footsteps on the stairs different from her father's heavy tread.

"She feels awfully hot. I think she must be feverish." Mum's voice, high pitched, sounds odd, like she's in a play.

Rose struggles to sit up. Walls and ceiling abruptly tilt and she collapses back on the pillows. "Is that Mr. Vale?"

"Yes, it's me," he calls.

The hall light casts a ghostly glow into the room, outlining her mother's shape. His shadow moves in the doorway.

"Do you want me to take a look at her?"

"Yes, please do. I'm afraid she's not at all well."

"No, Mum!" Rose fiercely whispers. She doesn't want him to see her, her clothes dirty and wrinkled and the bedroom a mess.

He enters and turns on the overhead light. "Hello Rose. I told your mother we'd find you home. It happens all the time. Someone rings me in the middle of the night and says their horses got out, or their dog ran away, and we drive all over the countryside looking for them and there they are back in their own yard."

Alice clears off a chair. He comes closer. The reality of him fills the room. He sits, pulling forward so his knees touch the bed with a slight jolt. She clutches at the sheets to right the spinning room.

"Rose, you're really poorly. You can tell I'm not a people doctor. I come barging in without even asking if you mind."

"I'm sure she's very grateful," Alice says.

"Shall I take a look, or do you want me to leave you in peace?" David addresses only Rose.

"Stay," she says in a small voice.

"Your own doctor will give you a proper exam, but let's take a look and see what's going on here." He takes her wrist and feels for her pulse.

"The stripes on your tie won't keep still," she says.

He laughs. "Sounds like vertigo. Does it feel like you're on a ride at the carnival?"

"Yes. Though I've never been on one."

"Try keeping your eyes open and concentrate on a spot above my shoulder. Things should settle down."

He takes a watch from his pocket, timing her pulse rate. His fingers on her wrist are cool. He smells of some kind of shaving lotion, and a mix of animals and antiseptic.

After a minute, he asks her to open her mouth wide. "Say ah." It hurts to open her jaw. He probes her neck, asking if it's stiff. She tells him her arms and legs feel funny, and she has a headache. He says he sees no sign of a rash, but to let him know if her skin is itchy. The vertigo subsides a bit. His features are clear now: the weather-beaten cheeks and light stubble on his chin, thick eyebrows and strong mouth. David's face is so close she wants to touch it. He examines her eyes with a bright light that stays patterned against her eyelids. In the background her mother tidies the room.

"I want to try one thing," David takes a pin from the lapel of his tweed jacket. He hesitates. "Alice, I'd like to examine her feet."

He and her mother pull back the covers, and remove her shoes and socks.

"I'm going to prick your feet," he says. "Tell me when you feel it."

"Yes," she says. "I felt that." She's not sure. Sometimes she thinks he's tricking her and not really using the needle. Then she looks at his face, intent and serious.

"I think we should take her temperature, Alice," he says.

"The thermometer's downstairs. I'll get it."

Alone with him, Rose is overcome with shyness. He studies her with a thoughtful expression. "How long have you been feeling ill?"

"I don't know." She's embarrassed to tell him about being sick in the stream. Then she remembers. "I had a headache and Mum wasn't home, and Keith next door told me she'd gone somewhere in your car, and it was a fox, not Moggy, that killed the baby chickens . . . and my head got worse."

He looks at her gravely, and with his fingertips gently pushes a strand of hair away from her eyes. "I know, Rose," he says, "I heard about the fox today. It wasn't your dad's fault. He did what he thought was best at the time."

She turns toward the wall. Waves of nausea take hold. David Vale reaches under the bed. He holds a green chamber pot. Vaguely, Rose is aware of her mother stroking her back.

It is soon over. David tells her to lie still. Alice leaves the room again to empty the pot. Mortified by what has happened, Rose avoids looking at him. He seems not to notice, absentmindedly stroking her wrist. Mum returns with a warm cloth and towel. David wipes her face, places a thermometer under her tongue. Quietness comes over the room.

"Where's Daddy?" Words come out as a mumble.

"Keep it in a couple more minutes," David tells her.

Her mother sits on the end of the bed. He stays in the chair, looking around at the piles of books, her mother's cosmetics, and a jumble of their clothing.

David holds the thermometer up to the light. "104.5. I'm not surprised the poor wee girl doesn't feel well." He shakes the mercury back down. "Alice, I think you should run a tepid bath to bring the fever down. Do you have aspirin? If not, I have some in the car." He winks at Rose. "Don't worry, they're not horse pills. You'll need to stay in bed for a day or two. Then you should be as right as rain."

— 22 —

A DEEP, GRUFF VOICE comes from the landing. "What's going on in here?"

The world tips as Rose twists to see her father's bulk filling the doorway. How long, she wonders, has he been there outside the bedroom door? She imagines him stealthily climbing the stairs so no one heard him. Too dizzy to sit up, Rose sinks into the pillow. Her whole body tenses, dreading a scene when Dad sees Mr. Vale in her and Mum's bedroom. Mum should never have let him up.

"Rose is sick," her mother quickly explains. "Mr. Vale has been taking a look at her. She has a high temperature."

A floorboard creaks as Stanley walks into the room. "Last time I heard, he was a vet, not a G.P."

The vet hastily stands. "I was about to come down and have a word with you, Stan. You're right; I treat animals, but I trained in emergency care in the army. Your Rose is quite poorly. I think someone should ring your doctor if her temp isn't down by morning." He lowers his voice, but Rose can hear. "It's probably nothing serious, but you never know these days . . . Early diagnosis makes all the difference."

The light sears Rose's half-closed eyes. A smell of vomit lingers in the small, crowded room.

David yields the chair to her father. Stanley refuses and leans over the bed as the vet retreats.

"All right, Rose?" her father asks.

"Yes, thanks, Daddy."

He places his large hand on her shoulder.

"She's not all right, Stanley," Alice insists. "David thinks we should run a tepid bath to bring her temperature down."

Stanley snorts. "Did they teach that in the army too? When I was a boy they'd heap on the blankets and we'd sweat it out. The girl needs some rest. Right, Rose?"

"Yes, Dad."

The men go downstairs. Without them, the room grows quiet. Alice helps Rose put on a clean nightgown. She appears preoccupied.

"What are you thinking about, Mum?"

"I'm thinking you're not well." Her mother moves around the room, picking up and folding clothes.

She stops. "I should run downstairs and borrow David's aspirin if he hasn't already left. I don't know why your father had to be so rude to him."

Rose pleads, "Stay here. We've a whole bottle of aspirin in the kitchen drawer—Dad uses it for his lumbago." Her mother leaves anyway, telling Rose she needs to lie quietly and rest.

There's no part of her body Rose can arrange comfortably; even her eyelids hurt when she closes them. Bed clothing has become a tangle of sheets and blankets. It's not clear how much time has passed; maybe she slept a little after all. Night has fallen; the window a black rectangle that reflects the dimly lighted interior of the room. Keeping her head as still as possible, Rose slides to the floor and gropes for the chamber pot. Mum must not have brought it back, nor did she come with the aspirin. Below, music plays on the radio, a male voice crooning. She pictures the brown box, light shining through the cloth grill, and Dad twiddling the dials. Rose wonders if Mr. Vale left. No car sounds or voices outside, only the wind against the house. She calls out—they don't respond. Shouting brings on coughing, which aggravates her need to pee. Dizzy or not, she'll have to go down to the lav. She makes her way on weak legs to the landing. Sitting and clutching the rail, she slowly bumps down, a stair at a time. Voices rise and fall through the slightly open living room door. They're talking above the music, which is loud now, like a dance band. Like being in the darkened wings of a stage, Rose leans forward, straining her ears.

Her mother: "I'm saying you didn't need to be so rude, Stanley."

"He had no business in that bedroom."

On the bottom stair, Rose hugs her legs. Her bladder feels ready to burst but she waits, listening, in the draughty hallway.

Mum speaks over clanking fire tools. "What on earth are you getting at? David gave her a medical exam. I was there the whole time. Rose is ill. Can't you see that?"

"You spoil her. You should make her help more outside—that would toughen her up."

On the dark stair, Rose thinks indignantly, *I help Mum all the time in the greenhouse.*

A cold wind whistles through the letterbox. She shivers.

Alice is speaking more quietly. "What did the vet say that has you so riled up?"

"We were talking about pigs. That's what he's hired for."

"Don't drive him away—he's about the only friend we have. Look, he gave us the aspirin that he had in his car. He probably needs it for his shoulder. He's concerned about Rose because there's infantile paralysis around—except he calls it polio, and says it's not only infants. We probably shouldn't be letting her ride the bus."

Rose stands shaky and barefoot in the doorway. They look at her like a ghost.

"Why aren't you in bed?" Alice cries.

Her father looks over his glasses. "Where are the child's slippers?"

"I have to go to the lav."

She goes on through to the toilet, shuts the door, and perches on the cold lavatory seat. Her urine won't come at first and when it does she scrunches in pain. She stands, pulls the chain, watching toilet paper swirl down the drain. But again there's something wrong with her eyes. The water, toilet and tank, walls; everything blurs grey. She calls out, "Mum, I can't see."

It is not her mother but Dad who comes into focus. He is gently laying her on the bed, breathing heavily. She feels the rough scrape of his jersey as he settles her into the pillows. Rose asks, frightened, "What happened?"

"You fainted, dear." Mum's hand touches her forehead. "She's burning up, Stan. We should run her that bath."

"Let the child alone."

Rose listens to their voices, confused. "I was downstairs—my eyes went funny. How did I get here?"

Her parents, dark shapes against the light, lean over her.

"Daddy carried you upstairs."

"Like a sack of pig nuts," her father says, "but not as heavy—there's no meat on your bones." He tweaks Rose's toe through the blanket. "Tell your mother to give you something to eat—bread and hot milk with brown sugar and butter. That's what the nanny used to feed my brother and me when we were ill. And forget about aspirin—bad for the stomach."

"She's soaked with sweat," Mum says.

"I'll take care of that. Go on down and make some supper. Rose is not the only one who hasn't eaten lately."

Mum whispers in Rose's ear, "I'll be back."

Dad pulls up the blankets, and tucks Rose in. Something he hasn't done in a long time. She lies quietly watching his slow and deliberate movements, fetching the eiderdown from his own room and heaping it on. Moments later he appears again with a paraffin stove. She listens to his grunts as he bends to turn up the wick and strikes a match. The flame leaps up with a small whoosh, and he adjusts it to a quiet flicker.

From her cocoon of bedding, light patterns dance on the ceiling and the stove emits warm, oily smells. He doesn't say a word, perhaps thinking she's asleep. She hears him going downstairs. In her feverish state, Rose draws on her father's silent, physical strength.

—23—

THE SOUND OF SOMEONE coughing drags her through layers of fitful sleep. The noise persists like a dog barking. Why doesn't someone tell it to be quiet? She sits up in bed gasping. The coughing is hers, rattling and bubbling up from her chest. Her mother, instantly at her side, pounds her back until the spasm subsides. She stacks pillows and coaxes Rose to take small sips of water.

Rose moans, "I dreamt the house was on fire—flames everywhere. I thought I was in hell, like Mr. Baxter said we'll go if we're not good." Rose coughs again, long and hard. She drinks more water. "There was a singeing smell, burning—some animal trapped under the bed. I kept calling for you, Mum, but you didn't come."

"I'm right here. I've barely left your side. You've been tossing around, talking in your sleep. Doctor Harris says I should give you medicine every four hours." Her mother walks over to the window and cranks it open, letting in fresh air. "That's better," she says.

A slip of wind makes the flames on the paraffin stove flutter.

"When did you speak to the doctor?"

"You don't remember? He was here this morning."

Rose stares at the clock and rubs her eyes. "You mean in the middle of the night?"

"No, it was after breakfast—he was starting his rounds. He's coming back later this afternoon . . . insists you stay in quarantine."

"Mum, I'm mixed up. I thought this was nighttime."

"No, it's afternoon, dreary because of the rain, not more than a drizzle now. When I went to the phone early this morning it was pouring. Must be the medicine making you so sleepy."

Vaguely now, she remembers a shadowy figure, a male voice talking in low tones to Mum—she'd thought it was a dream.

"Why quarantine? Will we have to burn everything like they did for that girl who had scarlet fever?"

"Oh, I don't expect so. It's a precaution in case . . ." Her mother pauses. "Well, just in case."

"In case I have polio?"

"Now, where did you get that idea?"

Rose thinks, but doesn't say, *You know what gave me the idea—I heard you talking to Daddy.*

"Will they put me in an iron lung?" Horrified, she remembers hearing of a boy, paralyzed from the neck down, his head sticking out of a machine.

"What nonsense you talk." Mum brings water, making Rose drink a full glass. "Doctor Harris says you must have lots of fluids." Together they struggle to take off her sweat-soaked nightgown and put on a clean one that smells warm from the airing cupboard.

Rose lies back, exhausted and closes her eyes, imagining herself so ill she could die, like Beth in *Little Women.* Tears prick her eyelids. She thinks, *Annie must wonder why I'm not at school.*

Dr. Harris returns as promised. He is of medium height with short arms and delicate hands, dressed in a rumpled suit that smells faintly of the rain. He removes a stethoscope from a black bag, pulls up Rose's nightgown and listens to her chest; he does the same for her back, telling her to take deep breaths, which makes her cough. Rose endures the exam, embarrassed for him to see her nakedness. He extracts other instruments from his bag, checking her temperature and blood pressure. When he probes with a light into her eyes and ears, his face is so close Rose can see the pores on his nose and bristles of his moustache. Her mother chats nervously in the background. He's a quiet man, asking only terse questions. What childhood diseases has she had?

"Only chicken pox," Alice says.

He does the same test as David Vale with a needle. Rose reports when she feels the pricks on her feet and legs, and when she doesn't. She winces as he flexes her joints, bending both arms at the elbow, and then knees, and rotating her ankles. The exam over, he makes notes using her mother's dressing table as a desk, sitting sideways on the small stool, elbow in danger of knocking off an array of bottles. Rose watches his reflection in the tilted mirror, the way his glasses slip to the end of his nose as he writes. His stooping shoulders give him an air of weariness.

He looks around, jots down another note, and then swivels to face her. His expression is stern. "Rose, I am going to ask you some questions, and I want you to answer them as accurately as you can. When did you start to feel ill?"

Rose tries to remember but it all seems a terrible muddle. Her mother volunteers, "Rose missed the bus from school yesterday and walked home. I went to look for her and when I got back she was lying here in bed obviously unwell and quite feverish."

Dr. Harris asks Rose, "What were your symptoms?" She describes her headache and feeling dizzy, and that she threw up and Mr. Vale helped her.

"Who is Mr. Vale?" the doctor asks in a tired voice.

"He's the veterinarian," Alice explains. "He was helping us, and took Rose's temperature, which was very high. He recommended we should call you."

"Ah yes, David Vale, the vet." Dr. Harris writes something in his notebook. In the mirror Rose sees his moustache twitch in what could be a faint smile. He asks, "Have you been around anyone recently who is obviously sick?"

An image comes to mind of Pam Rawlings, blood trickling from her forehead. "No," Rose says. She feels Dr. Harris scrutinizing her, like a specimen in the school chemistry lab.

"What about physical contact with other children in the last few days? Have you shared food and drink with any of them?"

Rose pictures Annie eating lunch under the tree, wrestling with her afterwards. She flinches, remembering Gordy's hand on the back of her neck. Dr. Harris waits for an answer. "No," she lies. She has a sudden thought. "I shared a sandwich and a lollipop with Keith yesterday."

"Who's Keith?" the doctor asks.

"He's the neighbor's boy next door," Alice tells him. "Rose, you shouldn't have anything to do with him. Everything about him is grubby."

Dr. Harris makes a note. "The parents should be informed and he must be watched for symptoms." He asks to speak privately with Alice. Rose gives up straining to hear what they are saying through the closed door.

Dr. Harris returns to collect his bag. "Goodbye, Rose," he says. "I'm prescribing you different medicine and a tonic. We'll have to see how you are in the next day or two. Otherwise, we may have to put you in hospital. For now, no visitors."

They leave. She listens in vain for the rumble of her father's voice. She hasn't seen him since he lit the stove. A breeze comes through the partially open window. The curtains billow. She's heard of children with polio in isolation wards, not even allowed to see their parents. Some of them have to be in wheelchairs or wear iron braces on their legs.

It takes all Rose's energy to make her way to the window. She sniffs the moist air. A broody hen clucks loudly and indignantly. Over the farm buildings the immense sky is a monochrome grey. She prays on her knees, *Please God, don't let me be paralyzed.*

"Rose, what are you doing?" Her mother sets down a tray, grasps her under the arms and half drags her back bed.

Rose cries, "Dr. Harris thinks I have polio, doesn't he?"

"It's not going to do you the slightest good to make a fuss. He says he's not sure. You've obviously contracted something, and you have to rest. He's going to discuss your case with a specialist."

"You're bothered too—I can tell."

Mum brings over the tray. "I'm bothered you're not eating. Look, I've boiled you an egg the way you like it."

Mum feeds Rose with a spoon, insisting she swallow, though her throat is raw. Finally, too tired to take another bite, Rose sinks back. She imagines strength leaking from her body, out through her heels, like air from a slowly deflating balloon. She's never felt like this before. She grasps Mum's sleeve. "Do you think God's punishing me and that's why I'm sick?"

"What questions you ask!"

"I'm serious, Mum."

"You get ideas like that from that awful man in Sunday school. Your granny was right. I should never have sent you there."

Rose persists. "Answer me. Is this all happening because I'm bad? Is that why Moggy got shot when he hadn't even done anything? Is that why Gordy won't let me see Annie any more?"

"If you really want to know, I believe if God punished us for our sins, I'd be dead by now. And if your being ill is God's way of getting at me, I want nothing to do with him." Her mother's eyes flash. She pulls away and goes to the dressing table. Perched on the stool, she examines her face in the mirror and picks up a lipstick.

"Now I've upset you," Rose croaks.

Alice applies the lipstick and blots it with tissue. "I was merely thinking what a fright I look. Dr. Harris was such a nice man. I hope I didn't scare him."

Dishes clink on the tray as her mother descends to the kitchen. Rose rolls over onto her side. Across the room she sees the tall black stove and wonders when it went out and whether her father will come and put things right.

— 2 4 —

HER WORLD HAS BEEN reduced to a sickroom—nothing like the school nurse's office, with its one neat shelf of medical supplies, gleaming sink, and smell of disinfectant. Bottles of linctus accumulate on the bedside table, leaving sticky brown rings. The stale air reeks of menthol ointment and body secretions. Alice's dressing table serves as a repository for basin, water jug, and towels. Days merge into nights when Rose's temperature runs high. She's never imagined illness like this. The worst was chicken pox with itchy, blister-like spots that turned into scabs. She remembers her cat welcoming the warmth of her mild fever, keeping her company with his throaty purrs. This sickness assaults her body, reminding her of enemy planes that flew over the house one night, wave after wave, on a mission to destroy a city in the North. As soon as she starts to doze, thoughts fragment like shattered glass, and she wakes in terror.

Her father comes in the evening to put paraffin in the stove and light it. He stands at the end of the bed, rocking back and forth. "All right, Rose?" he asks. "Feeling better?"

"Not yet, Daddy," she tells him.

He says the same thing each time: "Well, that's good." She wants him to stay, to somehow halt the onslaught, a battle Rose is afraid she and Mum are losing.

He squeezes her toes through the bed covers. "Feel that?" he asks.

"Yes, Daddy."

"Think I'll go downstairs and listen to the radio. Nothing worth turning on . . . always more bad news. I don't know what the world's coming to."

"Thanks for coming up."

He pads back down the stairs.

Then one day, as dawn is breaking, Rose wakes with loss of feeling in her feet. Her mother, exhausted from restless nights, has taken to sleeping on the floor, on a thin pallet. Rose fights the temptation to wake her. Instead she lies, alert, watching the light appear, grey and chilly. Numbness is creeping up her legs.

She will focus on something else—Annie's cheerful face, for example. There's been no word from her since they were together under the oak tree. If it's polio, how will Annie find out? "Did you hear the news?" Pam Rawlings is sure to gloat. "Rose Gray is in an iron lung." Maybe word will spread to the boys' school. Perhaps the altar boy from church will hear and visit her in hospital. Imagination transports him along corridors, clutching a bunch of roses, like her name, stolen from his parents' garden. His vivid face grows solemn as he comes to her side in the hospital room. He steps back aghast when he sees the contraption that encases her body. A rhythmic sound fills the room: the ugly sighing of the machine pumping her paralyzed lungs.

Rose sits bolt upright, a pain shooting down her spine. "Mum," she cries out, "I can't feel my legs!"

Two hours have gone by and much activity. Rose lies marooned in bed. Mum sweeps and cleans around her. She behaves calmly, the way she always does when there's a real crisis. Like the time two Spitfires were in a dogfight with a German plane directly over the field close to the house. No time to get to shelter. Mum pulled her under the dining room table. They crouched, listening to the rapid fire of anti-aircraft artillery.

The noise went on and on until Mum seized her hand and together they ran outside in time to see smoke and flames streaming from the enemy plane and two parachuted men slowly drifting into a field of corn. "Look," Mum shouted, pointing to the sky. "They shot down those poor devils."

Rose scans her mother's face, alert for confirmation of her worst fears. She sees only distraction as Mum clears a path for the two doctors, due in half an hour. Dad is out on the farm. It's her mother who has half-lifted Rose onto the chamber pot and later fetched warm water to bathe her, vigorously toweling legs and feet, which Rose says she can barely feel.

Before it was fully daylight, after Rose had woken her, Mum rode her bicycle to the red box and rang Dr. Harris. She came back, her hair wet from a drizzle of rain, and said the doctor was on his way, this time bringing a specialist in infectious diseases.

She's in a state now about the shabbiness of the house and the hopelessness of making the place presentable. Even in the midst of illness Rose feels it too, embarrassed by the cheap furniture and sheets so threadbare that they've been patched, end to middle. Alice changes into slacks and her good silk blouse. She stands at the window.

"The rain is making a sea of mud," she says, "and they are going to track it all in."

They arrive with an air of gravity. Alice ushers them in, her voice strained.

"We've been so worried about her," she says.

The specialist, a tall man with a booming voice, dressed in a pinstripe suit, has to bend his head as he comes through the doorframe. Dr. Harris, shorter and round-shouldered, follows. They peer at Rose, her brushed hair spread out on the pillow. Rose closes her eyes, to block them out.

"Wake up," the tall man instructs her, "I need to examine you." He stretches and pulls her limbs, and flexes her neck until she cries out in pain. The two doctors converse over Rose's head. They make her sit up, then stand and walk across the room. Her legs threaten to buckle.

"I can't feel my feet." She almost collapses. The doctors each take an arm and force her to keep going. Pain shoots through her legs and she cries out. Rose sees the doctors glance at each other.

The specialist tells Dr. Harris that growing cases of infantile paralysis spreading among children may not be a virus. "Could be caused by poison in the wells, or the soil, maybe lead or arsenic, or some other toxin."

"Poison," Alice exclaims from across the room. "How could that be?"

The tall man continues to address remarks to Dr. Harris, the two doctors still on each side of Rose, holding her up. Sweat runs between her shoulder blades.

"There's no treatment; that's the problem. We have to figure out what's causing it. God knows what was in those bombs."

"Or what was used on the military bases, like the one up the road," Dr. Harris says. "Good thing we got to Hitler when we did. Could have been germ warfare we're dealing with."

He gives Rose a worried look. "You're not going to faint on us, are you?"

"Sit on the bed," the specialist orders. He positions himself on a chair opposite and holds her foot, telling her to push back. Rose feebly pushes.

"Harder," he orders.

With gritted teeth, she pushes so hard her bare foot slips from his hand and lands on his soft, ample belly.

"Well done," he says. "Now let's try the other one."

The examination continues while the tall man keeps up a commentary with his colleague. He manipulates Rose's back, and makes her get on her feet again and touch her toes. Listening to her chest, he pauses to discuss the new mobile X-ray units, testing for tuberculosis. Rose's mother listens quietly, at a distance.

"Of course, there's poverty everywhere," the specialist says. "Look around you. A third of the kids I see show signs of rickets and malnourishment."

He orders Rose not to resist as he picks up each arm and lets it drop. Abruptly, the exam is over. With an absentminded nod, he picks up his bag and heads for the door. Dr. Harris follows. On the way out, still talking, the specialist says, "These are fascinating cases . . . especially the girls . . . hard to diagnose."

Her mother hurries after them. "May I offer anyone a cup of tea?" she calls.

Rose lies in bed waiting. Her body feels beaten. Her joints ache. Outside, there is a commotion: an engine revving, men shouting, and a deafening squealing of pigs. Her mother walks into the room carrying a tray.

"I made you porridge with brown sugar and creamy milk from the top," she says. "I didn't like that specialist one bit. I'm sick and tired of people implying I don't feed you."

"What did he say, Mum?"

"He walked right past your father downstairs and barely nodded at him. Dr. Harris was on his heels. I don't think those doctors have a clue what's wrong. Meanwhile, the pig lorry is here and I have to change and go outside to help. I haven't worked in the greenhouse in a week, and there's a batch of eggs that need grading and cleaning before tonight."

Her mother takes off her good clothes, folds them away, pulls on a pair of overalls—everyday movements that make Rose realize her own weakness.

"Mum?"

Alice is sitting in front of the mirror tying her hair up in a scarf. "What, dear?"

"Do you remember the Spitfires over the house, and the German plane crashing and those two men floating down on parachutes?"

Mum pauses, a grimace on her face. "We hid under the table. But then we went outside and the sky was so blue and our little Spitfires were wheeling around like lovely silver gulls, and that huge, evil-looking Dormer, twisting and turning, trying to escape them. And then there was all that black smoke, and the flames."

"Were you frightened that day, Mum?"

"Of course, but I was angry too, so glad we were fighting back. That's what you have to do Rose. You must fight back."

Rose punches her pillow, the feathers inside flattened long ago into hard lumps. She thinks of her father in his old work clothes, stubble on his chin, and the two doctors marching by without saying a word. The tall man didn't listen when she said couldn't feel her feet—forcing her to walk anyway, pushing her around like a mechanical doll.

Doors slam, men call, and the pig lorry with its cargo jolts its way past the house, en route to a destination Rose would rather not think about. The sound of grinding gears gradually dies away. It takes longer for her mind to erase the animals' cries, for quietness to return.

Mum's words "fight back" buzz in Rose's head. *All right for her to say,* Rose thinks, *but she can climb stairs and go out and work in the rain. She doesn't understand about the weight that's pinning me down, like in* Gulliver's Travels. As a little girl, she'd been fascinated by an illustration of Gulliver tethered to the ground by a hundred tiny ropes. She used to imagine taking sewing scissors and snipping away, a thread at a time; but then terrifying herself at the thought of setting the giant man free.

Her thoughts drift, fatigue muddling one image with another, like the rain mixing with dirt, collecting into muddy pools. When drowsiness comes at last, it is as an unexpected guest tiptoeing around, wrapping her in soft covers, slowly, irresistibly, lulling her into blissful sleep. Only occasionally she surfaces, floating like a swimmer on her back, before sinking again into oblivion.

—25—

THE WHOLE ROOM IS suffused with a soft pink light. Her mother's face, leaning over, reflects the same glow. Her brown eyes sparkle.

"Wake up, Rose. Guess who's here to see you."

"Not that horrible specialist, I hope." Rose rubs her eyes. "How long have I been asleep?"

"It's almost teatime . . . You've slept all day. It's not the doctor. Guess again. Who's here to see you?"

Rose yawns and stretches. Half way through another yawn she exclaims, "Is it Annie?"

Her mother sits at the mirror, tugging at her scarf, loosening a mass of dark curls. She picks up a hairbrush, "No, not Annie. Guess again."

"I wish it were Annie; I miss her." Rose feigns sleep, reluctant to relinquish her dream.

"Rose, open your eyes and look at me."

Carefully, Rose bends a knee and straightens it. Something has changed while she was sleeping. She tentatively stretches the other leg. There's tingling in both feet. Rose wants to be quiet, to be sure. Her mother shakes her shoulder. Rose bursts out, "I don't know anyone who'd come looking for me, except Annie."

"It's David Vale." Her mother makes it sound as though Rose had won the football pool.

"But Mum," Rose says in alarm, "Remember how Dad was last time?"

"I know. That's why you must get dressed and come downstairs."

"What about my legs?"

"You can walk. I saw you with the doctors. Get up; I'll help you."

"Daddy doesn't like Mr. Vale."

"Of course he likes him. They're in the piggery right now talking about whether the sow can be bred again. They'll be in soon."

"What if I have polio?"

"For heaven's sake. Anyone would think you *want* to be ill." Her mother hovers: a silhouette rimmed in gold against the window, reminding Rose of an avenging angel ready to confront any disaster, plague, or feeble excuse that bars her way.

"Rose Gray, listen to me . . . Get out of bed! We are going downstairs."

"Is David really here for me?" All at once, Rose wants to see him, trusting him more than any doctor to make her well.

"How many times do I have to say it? Yes, he wants to see you." Alice raises her by the underarms to a sitting position and then to her feet.

Her father and David Vale are deep in conversation, slowly making their way across the farmyard. Rose shades her eyes. Mum has dragged faded deck chairs from the shed and positioned her, wrapped in a blanket, by the back door. The temperature has risen since the morning rain, the air pleasantly warm and muggy. A slight steam rises from the piggery roof.

The two men pause outside the greenhouse. If it hadn't been for Mum's insistence, Rose would never have believed she'd have the strength to come downstairs. Now she waits eagerly for David Vale. Surely, he will be surprised when he sees her outside in the garden. She frets he hasn't spotted her sitting in the low chair, partially hidden by a clump of purple irises.

Her mother sets up a small wooden table and spreads a brightly colored cloth. She has taken off her jacket, exposing bare, suntanned arms. Humming, she disappears back into the kitchen.

Rose wonders if the vet has any idea how ill she's been. It was David who first worried she might have polio. Squinting into the sun, she sees David with her father. Even at a distance, she loves the way he looks and believes he will listen to her in his quiet, unhurried way.

Alice brings four plates and cups and a plate of homemade biscuits. Stanley and the vet have not made much progress. The rays of the late afternoon sun illuminate the men's heads and shoulders as they stand face to face. They are of equal height, but Rose's father is a heavier man, his complexion ruddier from working outdoors, his forehead deeply furrowed beneath his cap. The vet, younger and slighter, appears to be listening, nodding sympathetically. He stands with legs slightly apart, feet in mud-caked boots, solidly on the ground. Bareheaded, his brown hair glints red in the sunlight.

Alice gingerly lowers herself into a torn deckchair. She takes out a half-smoked cigarette from her pocket, straightens it, lights a match, and cups her hand. She inhales and slowly breathes out the smoke in a long, drawn-out sigh.

"My last damn cigarette," she remarks.

"What's wrong, Mum?"

"I wish your father would stop talking. The tea's getting cold."

"What do you think Dad's saying?"

"Probably about how this place is going to wrack and ruin. As if David doesn't have enough troubles of his own."

"How do you know he has troubles? When did you talk to him?"

Her mother's face becomes a mask. She smokes, staring in the direction of the two men through half-lidded eyes. It's as if she has gone somewhere else, quietly closing the door behind her.

Rose says irritably, "Talk to me."

Alice stirs, flicks ash from her cigarette. "Hush. They're coming."

The men approach. Her father goes directly inside to wash his hands. David Vale stays poised in front of them. Rose has to tilt her head to see his face. He greets her, broadly smiling.

"Well, this is a pleasant surprise to see you out of bed. I heard you've been quite poorly." As he speaks, David Vale bends and gently tugs at a lock of hair that hangs loose around her shoulders. She does not anticipate her response: like sea-surf across warm sand.

"She's really been a worry," her mother interrupts. "Neither of us has had a wink of sleep."

"But I slept today, almost the whole day . . ." Rose stops.

Tongue-tied, distracted by his closeness, she feels energy emanating from him. He remains standing, a little awkward, as though he too feels shy.

"Sleep is good for you," he says. "I've observed that with animals all the time. They seem to know it instinctively."

"I thought I was dying . . ." Rose begins. She wants him to understand. He looks at her kindly, listening.

Her mother interrupts. "Rose is always so morbid." She indicates a chair. "David, do sit down and make yourself comfortable."

"I must be on my way. Thank you anyway." He looks at his watch.

"Not for a quick cup of tea? I made biscuits with the last of the month's butter ration."

"No really, I must go."

"All right then, off you go." Alice savagely stubs out what's left of her cigarette.

Rose witnesses David slowly turn his attention toward her mother, leaning to murmur in her ear. Mum's face relaxes. For a brief moment, his cheek touches hers. Rose pulls the blanket around, averting her eyes. She concentrates on a single purple iris, drawn to its center where delicate yellow sepals lie sheltered, like speckled eggs in a nest. David and Alice talk quietly: casual snippets of conversation about the rain's sudden clearing, the approach of summer. It's the tone that stirs Rose, their voices warm and intimate, as though they speak in a language known only to them. Stuck in her chair, Rose feels there's no place for her. He'll be gone soon. Sounds come from the partly open window: water running, the rattle of the soap dish. She pictures her father's slow, careful movements as he washes his hands, working the lather up to his wrists and brawny forearms.

Listening, Rose suspects Dad's too far into his misery to see what she sees. If only he looked about him, he might wake up and really notice. He wouldn't ignore Mum's birthday, as he did last month, even though Rose reminded him twice. He'd smile at her sometimes, thank her for the meals she cooks, the work she does outside, and tell her she's pretty, that he loves her. Instead, he mostly stays in his own brooding thoughts. Rose dreads his outbursts, as deadly as the unexploded shells that still lie buried beneath the ground. When he flies into one of his rages, she and Mum walk around the house wary and jangled for days.

She shudders. Supposing Dad looks out and sees Mum and David, their heads close together, whispering? Would he attack him, like he did her cat? She mustn't think such terrible thoughts. *David.* Even without looking, Rose feels his power. Futile to remember the way he touched her hair. Yet not to think of something is to think it. Her body has its own sensations, inwardly tying her in knots. She senses David knows on some level and cares; although it is Mum who claims him for her own.

Soapy water gushes into the outdoor drain. Rose lifts her head to the sound of the roller towel as her father dries his hands. She calls out in a clear voice, "Mr. Vale, do you think I have polio?" Startled, David straightens and draws back from her mother's chair.

"Of course she doesn't have polio." Stanley has appeared on the doorstep. "If she did, that bloody doctor would have her in hospital in isolation. He couldn't be bothered to tell us. Isn't that right, *Doctor*?"

"I'm a veterinarian, not a doctor, though in America they'd use that title." David turns toward Rose, "I'm inclined to agree with your dad.

Illness is a mystery for people, and animals. We never quite know what causes the symptoms. Strangely enough, they are sometimes the body's way of healing itself."

"Here's your tea, Stanley." Alice hands him his cup. "I made biscuits. Unfortunately, David can't stay."

David takes car keys from his pocket. "There was a small fire on a farm down the road. They had it out in no time but all the commotion scared the animals half to death." Rose studies him. His cheeks are flushed; otherwise he delivers this speech with his usual easy manner.

The three of them watch him walk across the yard toward his car. He looks back once and waves. "Cheerio, Rose, good to see you up and about." Rose raises her hand.

Her father salutes with his mug of tea.

"What did David say about the sow, Stanley?" Alice asks.

"He says the infection is likely to recur. He doubts if we can breed her again." Stanley drains his tea, tossing the dregs into the grass. "We're done for, Alice."

"I heard several other tenants are making a go of it."

"Well, I'm not one of them, am I?" He bangs the mug on the table, walks away, shoulders bowed, as if he has already picked up the wooden yoke with its buckets of feed.

Alice clears the table. "Well, so much for my tea party!"

"David didn't come to see me, did he?" Rose cannot keep the trembling from her voice. "You put me out here like . . . like a trap."

Her mother looks at her, incredulous, "A trap?"

"Yes, a lure to get him to stay for tea."

"Really—do you think so? You mean like a honey pot at a picnic?" Her mother snorts. "It didn't work did it? At least we got you out of bed into the sunshine."

"It's not funny," Rose frowns, thinking of David off visiting the people who had the fire, taking care of their animals, probably stopping to chat with them.

"I'm not making fun of you. Cheer up; we have to have a good laugh now and then—better than crying." Alice aims a kiss in her direction. Not quite ready to forgive, Rose turns her face away. Her mother carries things inside, whistling. Whatever David said to her, it apparently improved her mood.

Left in her chair, Rose surveys the farm and its dilapidated buildings. Black and white pigs, held in by a barely visible electric wire, root in the rough grass. The fence is not always turned on. She and Annie experimented and touched it; the shock was like a hit on the elbow by a hammer. The animals learn quickly, as she and Annie did, never to test it again.

Mum appears, "It's getting chilly. I think what you need is a proper bath. I've been heating the water."

— 2 6 —

Rose lies soaking while Alice chops vegetables. The board over the tub has been removed, cleared of its baskets, including a hamper of dirty clothing ready for the wash. The bath taps are closest to the kitchen sink. Rose leans at the other end, watching her mother work. Unlike Annie, who jokes about bumps on her own chest, "like gnat bites," she's draped a flannel over her rounded breasts. The scented water soothes her limbs, but emotions teeter on the edge of speech. Mum scrapes carrots like there's no secret, only a meal to make for her family. In the background the radio plays a familiar tune, and she turns to Rose, waving her knife to the beat. Together, they sing, "We're happy in Blue Heaven."

A bubble of laughter arises as Rose remembers. "Did you see the way my foot slipped and I kicked that stuck-up doctor in the belly?"

Her mother pauses, knife midair, "I wish you'd kicked him lower down." They both laugh now. Each time their mirth subsides, one of them starts again. The music switches to "The Way You Look Tonight." Alice turns up the volume, dreamily swaying from the hips as she works. Mum's been misty-eyed over that song a lot longer than she's known David Vale.

"I've been thinking," Alice says. "Now you're feeling better, we could visit Granny. She sent me a little money for my birthday. I ought to spend it on bills. But imagine: we'd be there in a day, and you could convalesce. It'll be a little holiday."

Already, Rose is transported to her grandmother's house with views of the Sussex hills. She can hear the click of the garden gate, their footsteps on the gravel path, past flowering beds of white hydrangeas and honeysuckle, welcomed at the door into open arms. Her whole body stretches, luxuriating in the bath's warmth.

"Will Miss Gordon let us?" she asks.

"You're forgetting—half term is coming up. She won't expect you back until after that. Besides, she'll want to be sure you're out of quarantine."

Rose had hoped to hear, "Who cares what the old bat thinks?" But it doesn't matter. Clearly, Mum is as excited about the plan as she is. Another concern surfaces: "What about Dad?"

"I'll talk to him—we'll only be gone a few days."

"Granny's prayers work, don't they, Mum. See what I can do?" Rose raises her leg out of the water. "It's a miracle."

"Maybe." Alice picks up a peeled onion and begins vigorously chopping it.

Deflated, Rose lowers her leg. "I couldn't do that before."

Her mother stops to wipe her eyes with the corner of her apron. "I wasn't going to tell you this, but I had a long talk with David about your illness."

"Why? What did David say?"

"He ran into Dr. Harris right after the specialist saw you. You may not remember, but you'd told him Mr. Vale examined you when you were first ill."

"I didn't know they knew each other."

"Neither did I, but apparently they went to school together, years ago, up north. Dr. Harris asked David about your early symptoms. He said the specialist found no physical cause for numbness in your legs, but Dr. Harris is not sure he agrees."

Rose pulls herself out of the bath. "I didn't make it up—you were there, you saw. I couldn't feel my legs."

Alice passes a towel. "There's no need to snap my head off. Both doctors should come back and talk to us. David agrees. He says he saw a few cases like yours in the army for people in shock. They call it hysterical paralysis. It's why I got you out of bed to see for myself if you could walk."

Rose bursts out, "Is everyone saying it was all in my head?"

"For God's sake, be happy you're feeling better. What David is talking about hardly applies to you. As I told him, we lead a perfectly ordinary life."

Rose can't help herself. She doesn't trust anyone to tell the truth. What else have Mum and David been discussing? She poises on a slope of words, heart beating fast, prepared to pour out her accusations. But accuse them of what?

"You and David were laughing at me, weren't you? Does Dad know?" She sees her mother's startled look; it takes a moment for Alice to regain composure.

Mum approaches with open arms. "Of course no one's laughing at you."

Rose pushes her away. "You smell of onions." She tightens the towel around herself and steps toward the doorway.

"And you're being tiresome. As for your father, there was so much upset about the pig, I doubt he and David had a minute for anything else. Don't forget yours isn't the only crisis around here. Where are you going?"

To stay would only make their bickering go from bad to worse, but Rose can't resist a parting shot: "I'm going to take my imaginary body upstairs to my imaginary bedroom." She departs on unsteady legs, leaving a trail of damp footprints.

In spite of efforts to create order, the aftermath of recent days is still there: the unlit paraffin stove with its smoky residual smells, Mum's rolled-up pallet, and the dressing table with its mix of pill bottles and cough medicines. Rose looks around with a curious sense of detachment, as though the sickness had belonged to someone else. She tests her bare feet on the floor.

In a fit of rebellion, she drags the pallet to the opposite wall. From now on, she decides, this will be her bed. She pulls, pushes, and shoves a bookcase into the middle of the room, creating a divider. The strenuous exercise leaves her gasping, open-mouthed; she waits to regain her breath. The draped towel from her bath drops to the floor. She keeps going, puts her full weight against Mum's dressing table, but either she's weak or it's too heavy to shift. The mirror swings crazily, reflecting her naked, lanky body, hair wild and loose, face screwed up with determination. She flops down in her new, makeshift space, walled off by the back of the bookcase. Disturbed spiders cling precariously to their webs. The room's new configuration feels chaotic, nothing like what she'd imagined; but it's her creation, and whatever Mum says, Rose likes the way it is.

She rests, even dozes, until woken by a loud noise. A sheet clutched to her chest, she peers out into the fading light. Squeals and banging come from the piggeries. It must be feeding time.

Staying below window level, Rose moves a lamp to her new space, plugs it in, and appraises what she has accomplished. She borrows a pillow and, with Dad's eiderdown wrapped around, sits cross-legged on the palette, determined to have a good think.

While she was sick, time merged into itself. Now, it's not only the furniture that has shifted—it's as if she'd been reading an absorbing book, put it down, and lost her place. Rose uncrosses her legs and stretches, pleased with the island she's created. She doubts they'll let her keep it, but for now it's hers. The eiderdown's masculine smells compete oddly with Mum's Red Poppy. Rose ponders, *What would it be like to have different parents?* Her Aunt Betty and Uncle Archie, for example, living now in the South near Granny. They always seem so jolly together and never cross for long with her cousins, though those two boys were always getting into scrapes, bringing home stray friends and dogs and cats, and once a snake to Granny's tea table.

Her mind jumps to David and sets off again like a hare across a field. She frets that he didn't stay to talk to her. Maybe she's like poor Hamlet and thinks too much: "Sicklied o'er the pale cast of thought." Is that what's wrong with her? The thought of doctors joking behind her back raises prickles on her bare skin. Chilly and embarrassed, she searches for clothes. Nothing is where it was before.

A smell of onions cooking wafts up into her hiding place; Rose realizes her stomach is growling. She dresses. Mum greets her in the hallway. "Oh there you are," she says. "I was coming to get you. What on earth have you been up to? Never mind. I've been waiting for your dad to come in for supper. The buildings are dark, and he doesn't answer when I call from the back door. I'm going out to look for him."

Rose follows to the kitchen, where the scent of lavender from her bath mingles with savory smells bubbling on the stove. "I'll come too," she says, suddenly anxious, as Mum reaches for her coat.

"You stay here, set the table and stir the soup." Alice takes a large torch from a shelf. "I'll be back in a minute."

—27—

ROSE STANDS AT THE open door, watching the light bobbing as her mother heads toward the piggeries. Night has fallen; no moon or stars are visible. She quickly finds bowls, spoons, and cloth napkins, and puts them out with a loaf of bread on a wooden board. She goes back to the door. Somewhere in the darkness, her mother calls Stanley's name. No lights go on in the buildings. Rose shouts, "Mum," but no response. A large moth brushes her face and she beats it away. *I'll count to fifty*, Rose says to herself. *If Mum doesn't return, I'm going out there*. The count begins slowly: one, two, three water glasses filled from a tap; four, five, six stirs of the soup.

She speeds up and runs to the open door, where there's a flurry on the step. Distressed, Rose kneels and inspects the moth, with dusty outspread wings. "I'm sorry," she cries, "I didn't mean to hurt you." She carefully lifts it, feeling the scratch of tiny feet. The moth revives and flutters away. Rose grabs her coat and sets off into the dark.

At first the black night envelops her and she walks on unsteady feet, hands outstretched. She stares and stares into the darkness in the vain belief that if her eyes are wide enough open, she'll be able to see where she is going. All around there are small rustlings in the undergrowth and the occasional whoosh of wings. Her nose detects the distinct musky smell of fox somewhere in the shadows. Or is she dreaming? Gradually, her vision adjusts. The greenhouse looms large to her right. Ahead, a glimmer appears from inside a building and disappears. Rose shouts for her mother, stumbling over clumps of rough grass, tracking where she saw the light. She shouts again, more loudly. Disoriented, she searches the dark piggery for the door, repeatedly calling into the night. A blinding light shines into her face. "Stop making so much noise. The neighbors will hear you."

"Mum," she cries, "why didn't you answer me?"

"I told you to stay indoors," Mum says. "I can't find your father—his bicycle is by the shed, and his cap. He wouldn't have gone very far without telling me."

"Why are the lights all out?"

"Stanley must've thrown the main switch. It's at the other end where his office is. I was about to go down there. Either that, or a fuse has blown."

Rose pleads, "I want to come with you."

"Okay, but stay close, and don't make a racket. We don't want to get the pigs going." Alice takes her hand, and with the torch leads Rose into the building. She calls, "Stanley, are you there? Stan, answer me."

They make their way down a corridor that stinks of fresh manure. Alice shines a light into each stall. Enormous pink pigs lie on their sides, white-lashed eyes tightly closed. Rose peers into dark corners. "Daddy, where are you?"

Mum squeezes Rose's hand. "It's my fault. I should have found out what's upset him. He gets so down when things goes wrong. I hope he hasn't done anything foolish."

"Daddy, answer us," Rose calls. "Tell us where you are."

"Shush, Rose." They've come to a half door into the next building. Alice leans over to unbolt it.

Empty stalls seem cavernous in the darkness. Threads from webs that festoon the ceiling catch in Rose's hair. She holds tight to her mother's coat.

"Look," she whispers, "this is where the baby pigs are." Rose hoists herself up for a better view of the piglets in a circle of light, sleeping on top of one another in a pile of straw. Her mother moves on to the next stall. Rose wonders if her father could be close by—surely not in the dark. Again, she climbs and leans over to see the mother pig, separated from her babies.

Mum shines the torch; the beam sweeps over the sow's pale flanks and rests momentarily on her teats, which appear dark and inflamed. "Oh my God." Alice puts out a hand to shield her daughter, but Rose has already seen the pig's face, its jaw half shot away, a gaping hole in place of the eye, and the straw dark with blood. "Mum," she cries. "Is she dead?"

Alice says sternly, "I want you to stay here, and not move until I find Dad."

"No. Don't leave me." Rose clings to her mother. "I'm frightened." Without warning, dim lights go on throughout the building.

Mum pushes Rose behind her. "I don't know what's wrong with you, Stanley," she calls loudly, "but you're frightening us to death."

"I'm here." His voice comes from the end of the corridor.

"Dad," Rose yells, but her mother puts her finger to her lips, moving slowly, keeping Rose behind her.

"It's time for supper, Stanley," Alice calls, her voice calm. "I made barley soup, the kind you like."

There's no reply. Alice keeps talking, edging forward; she tells him the table is set, he must be hungry, that everyone has had a long day.

They come across him in the lit mill room, seated in a wooden chair near a makeshift desk piled with ledgers and farming manuals. Everything is covered in fine dust from the mill.

"I'll come in a minute," he says.

Rose hangs back, clutching her mother's coat. Her father's hair sticks up from the ridge made by his cap, and his bloodshot eyes have a wild look. A wave of pity gives way to the horror of the animal's ruined face in blood-soaked straw. Rose tugs to pull her mother back as Mum goes to him, putting a hand on his forearm. "Stanley, you've sat long enough in the dark. Come along now. You're done in, and you need food."

"I had to put the sow down."

"Yes, of course you did. Let's go up to the house. We'll talk about it there."

"Rose, is that you?" her father says.

Rose hangs back. "Yes, Daddy, it's me."

"Feeling better, are you? Come over here so I can get a look at you in the light."

"The gun, Stanley," her mother says. "Where is it?"

"Christ, Alice, I'm not going to shoot her; nor you right now, for that matter."

Rose emerges from the shadows. She points to the wall, "There's the gun," she says, "on the rack over Dad's desk."

"Her father says again. "Come here, I've something to show you."

Her mother gives her a little push. "It's all right," she says.

Rose stands in front of her father. He takes a small silver box from a shelf and rubs dust away with his sleeve. "I've been keeping nails and screws in this," he says, "but I'd like you to have it. My father gave it to me for cigarettes, for my twenty-first birthday. See, he had my name engraved: "Stanley F. Gray." We could add your name to it if you like."

He puts the box in Rose's hand. "It's quite heavy, isn't it—that's because it's solid silver. You could use it for jewelry."

Rose holds the tarnished box, not knowing what to say. She doesn't own any real jewelry, unlike Annie, who has a charm bracelet.

"That's lovely, Stanley," her mother says. "Rose, say thank you to Daddy."

"Thank you, Dad." Rose feels more is required. Or that there's something she's left undone. She stands, trembling, her mind in a muddle. Then, with startling clarity, she remembers, "I forgot to turn off the soup," she says, and bursts into tears.

The three of them walk down the corridors, her father at the rear. Rose puts a hand over her nose and mouth. The dust and manure smell like blood. Alice leads the way toward the house, lighting the path ahead. Rose follows in her footsteps, her father close behind, carrying his own torch. The air feels moist and heavy as though it might rain again.

Inside, they are greeted by the warm fragrance of soup. Rose rushes to the stove; the pan has not burned. "We'll add water," her mother says.

They sit in their customary places. Stanley eats hunched over. The only sound is the slurping of soup. The faint smell of sage rising from her plate reminds Rose of dried herbs hanging in Granny's kitchen. She wonders, miserably, if the planned trip will be cancelled. Rose composes sentences to say about the meal; words that in the end stay unsaid—too trivial before the indelible, haunting image of the slain pig.

The silence continues: the clink of cutlery, the clock ticking on the mantle. Her mother puts her spoon down and folds her napkin. "How are you going to get that pig out of there, Stanley?"

He pushes his plate away and shrugs his shoulders.

"I don't understand why, if the sow was no good for breeding, you didn't send her to market. At least we could have made good money for her meat."

Rose sits straight in her chair. Her father works his jaw, fists opening and closing.

"Mum, don't."

"Don't what?" her mother snaps.

Rose collects plates. "May I be excused?" She escapes to the kitchen. They're still at the table, not speaking, when she returns. She pecks them both goodnight on the cheek; she might as well have kissed two blocks of wood.

Her legs have barely made it up the stairs. When Rose snaps on the light, the bedroom's disarray is a shock, as if the carnage of the pig could have somehow changed what went before. She scarcely remembers the energy she'd had to make the room different. Too tired to do anything about it now, she undresses and settles on her makeshift bed. Downstairs, her parents quarrel. Rose gets up, turns off the overhead light, closes the door, and clambers back over the furniture. She pulls the eiderdown over her head, but still she hears muffled voices, and the weird intermittent shriek of an owl, like someone in distress.

She's awoken by a crash. "What the hell is this?" The light goes on. Her mother's face glowers over the bookcase.

Rose rubs her eyes. "I want my own room."

"And I want a lot of things I can't have, too. I don't think my nerves can take any more." Her mother slams a drawer shut. "Has everyone in this house completely lost their mind?"

Rose curls up on the pallet, listening to her mother banging around. "At least you have the bed to yourself now," Rose says.

"I'm too damn tired to care." Lights go off. Bedsprings creak.

Rose asks into the dark, "Why did Dad shoot the sow?"

"I haven't the foggiest idea. I do know I'll never again let him frighten us like he did tonight."

Rose, missing Mum's comforting body, resists going to her, staying where she is, reliving her own fears.

"There's something I've been meaning to say, though," her mother says. "And then you must sleep."

Rose raises her head "What, Mum?"

"Whatever you and your imagination, or anyone else for that matter, may think—David Vale's an honorable man."

— 2 8 —

IT IS MIDMORNING WHEN Rose stumbles down for breakfast and finds the letter propped against a cereal box. Unmistakably, the large, untidy handwriting is Annie's. On the back she has scrawled, "SWALK." Rose giggles at the meaning: "sealed with a loving kiss." She slits open the envelope with a table knife.

Dear Rose,

Do you really have the plague? I don't believe it. Neither does my mum, who says she bets it was a bug you picked up on the bus. Either that or the potted meat sandwich had gone off. Of course, there's no telling what sort of meat's in it these days [says Mum]. Last week I was sick myself twice on the way home from school, once in the gutter, and once leaning over someone's garden fence, right on a rose bush! Ma made me stay home the next day—I'd been hoping you'd be back in school so we could compare notes. Then, when I dragged up the hill on my bike and your dad said you were ill and not receiving visitors, I was afraid we'd poisoned you. I hope you got my message!

Speaking of poison, Pam Rawlings is spreading nasty rumors that you have infantile paralysis and everyone is going to get it. She thinks we should wear our gas masks. I still have my regulation Mickey Mouse one somewhere—remember having to wear those things??? I think I'll use mine to fumigate the air when Miss Big Chest Pamela waltzes by.

Anyway, thank goodness Gordy announced in assembly today NO ONE has been diagnosed with polio in the school, but there are some cases in town, so they won't be opening the swimming pool. Gloom!

Yippee! Half-term hols start soon. I had a smashing idea—remember the old ruined house we found in the woods? Let's

121

explore the cellar. Extra points for the Daring Demons! I bet there are rats, and there could be ghosts of former inhabitants. EEEEEK!

Seriously, I hope you feel better soon. Send me a letter or a smoke signal, or something to let me know when I can come and see you. I MISS YOU!

Lots of love from your friend,
Annie.

P.S. Sniff this notepaper. Can you smell the violets? George gave me a box of stationery as a bribe to stay away when he and Dora are necking. Can you imagine wanting to kiss my brother? Yuk.

P.P.S. How are the old sow and her piglets? Did the nice vet come back?

Rose presses the letter to her face. The paper smells of talcum powder, not like the woodsy scent of violets she and Annie pick along the lane. She pours cornflakes into a bowl. Under the milk jug there's a note from her mother: "I'm in the greenhouse if you need me." Rose rereads Annie's letter while she's eating—there is no earthly way she can tell her friend what happened to the sow, or about Dad sitting in the dark, not answering when they kept calling him. The silver box in its tarnished state still rests on the mantle like a reproach. Rose takes it into the kitchen. From the window she sees Dad at the far end of the vegetable garden. She idly watches him dig, piling earth behind him. She frowns—what possible reason did he have for not mentioning Annie's visit? Retrieving silver polish from under the sink, she rubs away layers of dirt, turning the rag green. The rotten egg smell of the cleaner reminds her of experiments in the chem lab. The box, Dad said, could be for jewelry. Annie has one that is the most beautiful thing Rose has ever seen. It is black lacquered, and when opened a ballerina twirls on a mirror to the music of *Swan Lake*. Rose will show Annie the silver box and the name etched on the top: "Stanley F. Gray." Annie will remind her that her own father is dead.

Rose washes her hands. Stanley is still out there, bent over, shoveling dirt. It is her mother who usually works the vegetable garden, but in the spring Dad helps by forking over the heavy soil. Turning off the tap, Rose resolves to go out and show her father the gleaming silver; it surely will please him. Trembling slightly, she reaches for her coat. Halfway through putting her arm in a sleeve, it dawns on her: Dad's not gardening but, instead, digging a grave for the dead pig. With morbid curiosity, she returns to the window, watching him work, almost waist deep, dirt piled all around. After several minutes, convinced she's right, Rose turns away, puts the box back on the mantle, and goes in search of writing paper, a pen, and stamps, so she can write to Annie.

"Don't rummage around in my things," Mum's voice hums in Rose's brain as she eyes the oak desk against the living room wall. She reasons: pages ripped out of an exercise book won't do, not compared with Annie's scented notepaper. Mum has a whole box of stationery, the quality of fine white linen, a birthday gift from Aunt Betty. Rose runs her hands over the desk's wooden surface, exploring the nicks and scratches. It once stood in her grandfather's office, where he was editor of the local newspaper. She tests the lid. It's locked, but Rose is a close observer of her mother's habits. She feels along the top of Grandpa's framed portrait above the desk, and under his slightly narrowed gaze locates the small brass key.

There are no neat pigeonholes like some desks—instead a jumble of papers, bills, receipts, and letters with postmarked stamps showing the solemn profile of the king. Rose has poked around under her mother's watchful eye, begging to be shown snapshots of herself as a baby. She's seen photographs of her dad's childhood home: he and his brother in sailor suits, on a pony cart, and a younger sister, with thick braided hair. A groom holds the pony's reins. Their parents pose, unsmiling, in front of a large house. Rose never knew them. She pauses over a photo of Dad as a young man, his blond hair slicked down, dressed in whites, holding a tennis racquet. He has the look, she thinks, of someone who already owns several silver boxes and a lot more, besides. One day she asked to see photos of her mother as a little girl and Mum said they were mostly in albums at Granny's house. "What about pictures of you and Dad getting married?" Her mother said there were none—not a brass farthing for a photographer—and for Rose to leave her in peace to write her letters.

Rose puts the photos back and continues her search. The letters she finds are mostly in Granny's tiny handwriting. No sign of the blue aerogrammes the postman occasionally pushes through the box. She carefully lifts a brown manila envelope marked "POETRY" in blue ink. At one time Alice wrote poems and occasionally read them aloud. Writing always seemed to cheer her up, especially the time a magazine published a poem entitled *Thaw*. Now Mum says her present cabbage existence has deadened inspiration, and she's given up crying for the moon. Rose replaces the package; it hurts when Mum makes remarks like that, as though happiness is always in the past.

It doesn't take long to uncover the box of stationery. She extracts an envelope and a sheet of fine white paper, looks guiltily around, and steals another piece. Annie will be impressed. Rose glances at the clock. It wouldn't hurt to look a little longer. Papers scatter as she digs to the bottom of the pile. Her probing hands encounter a large stiff envelope— more photos, she assumes. Scarcely worth the effort, or the mess; but she tugs at it anyway. It smells of sealing wax. The label, "Mrs. Alice Gray," and their present address are typewritten—Rose guesses more poems and rejection letters from editors. She shakes the envelope; two glossy black and white photos fall out, ones she's never seen before.

Rose blinks, her eyes widening to take in what she's seeing. In the first, her mother poses in a sunlit, wooded clearing. She's barefoot; arms over her head, dancing, her dress swirls around her. The second photo has the same dappled light. Her radiant mother holds hands with a smiling, dark-haired man. Rose's mind opens to memories, like a bud slowly bursting into flower: the crowded railway station, and two of them embracing; the way he bent to kiss her, a little girl, with such tenderness. And she remembers his name: Graham Faire.

Rose hurries to push the photos in their envelope down deep, closes and locks the desk, and replaces the key. Only then does she see on the floor a torn page from a notebook with strange handwriting. It must've fallen out with the photos. She quickly stuffs it in her cardigan pocket.

$-29-$

ROSE SITS AT THE table, her pen poised over her mother's finely textured paper. She has written, "Dear Annie, thank you for your letter . . ."

Ten minutes have passed. She stares into the fireplace with its cold ashes. She pictures Annie's face, eager and curious to read what she has to say. Every subject that comes to mind has its censure. She cannot stop thinking about the photos: when and where they were taken and who took them. Even if Annie were right in front of her, how could she tell her friend what she fears?: that there's a man in Mum's life who's not her husband. She groans as a blob of ink falls onto the page, and spreads like tentacles. Blotting paper makes matters worse, creating a shape resembling a flattened insect. She tears the whole thing up, takes the second sheet, and starts again: "Dear Annie, thank you . . ."

The dress Mum was wearing in both photos is the color of the sky on a cloudless day. Rose knows this because one day she pulled that same dress from the back of her mother's wardrobe, and asked why she never wore it. Mum said something about wearing it in better days, and dismissed the subject.

> Dear Annie, thank you for your letter. I was so happy to receive it. My dad must have forgotten to tell me the day you came. I was sort of ill . . .

Should she tell Annie about the paralysis? Heat rises in her cheeks, ashamed the doctors didn't believe her. She throws down the pen and on shaky legs goes upstairs to the bedroom. Sure enough, the dress is where she thought it would be. She buries her face in the full skirt. Her heart overflows with images of Mum in the woods free and dancing, and him watching. The actuality of the material against her skin, the slight camphor smell mixed with Red Poppy, makes it all real. The old wardrobe creaks as she hangs the dress in the farthest corner and pulls both doors shut.

> Yes, let's explore the old house soon and its cellar—what fun and how creepy! I think Mum is taking me to visit my granny over half term. Can't wait to see you after that! Lots of love, Rose

She stamps and addresses the envelope. Annie has mentioned nothing about Gordy's ban on their friendship; maybe she doesn't know. Rose rubs her forehead where an ache is gathering. She grabs her coat and slips out by the front door to mail her letter.

Like the first plunge into a cold pool, she steps into a biting wind. In spite of an overcast sky that broods across the countryside, there's a glare that hurts the eyes. She walks cautiously, dismayed by pins and needles in both legs and feet. Ahead, the tall, red postbox stands like a distant sentinel. Enormous trees heavy with new growth crack and groan. Every few steps, birdsong erupts from deep in the foliage, and, invisibly, a thrush sings its own distinct song. She'd run and skip as she and Annie do when they set off to play, but her feet are heavy. Haunted still by the photo of Mum dancing, Rose lifts her arms, bowing and swaying with the wind, and for a moment she is set free.

The noise of the trees muffles the sound of a farm truck until it draws alongside; the driver rolls the window down and gives a long, low wolf whistle. "Want to dance with me, sweetheart?" the young man says, before he roars off.

Rose shouts, "I'm not dancing." She stomps on numb feet to the postbox and all the way home frets that what she wrote was not good enough for Annie.

Her mother is waiting for her by the front gate. "Why are you limping?"

"I'm not."

"I watched you coming down the road. You were dragging your feet and scowling like you were in pain. We should talk to Dr. Harris."

"I won't see him."

"Why does everything have to be an argument?" Alice sighs. "Come in the house. It's far too cold for you to be out in this wind. Where did you go?"

"I went to post a letter to Annie."

They face each other in the tiny front hallway. "I guessed that was Annie's handwriting, and in such a pretty envelope."

"Where's Dad?"

" He's changing his overalls in the kitchen. I have to do the wash."

Rose fiddles with the zipper on her jacket. Even her fingers are numb from the cold.

"Here, let me do that." Alice pulls her close. Rose wishes she were small again and could rest her head on her mother's shoulder, smelling the mix of cigarettes, tomato plants, and her warm, scented skin.

"Did Dad have blood on his clothes from burying the pig?"

"Do it yourself."

"Do what myself?"

"Get your own coat off."

Rose follows her into the living room. "Now what have I done?"

Her mother attacks the dying fire with a poker, sending sparks up the chimney. "You can't leave well alone, can you?"

"What's going on?" Her father appears from the kitchen dressed in a wool shirt, corduroy trousers, and his old plaid slippers. Unusual for him: he has not shaved and he walks stiff-backed, as though in pain.

"Nothing." Rose dodges past, and heads for the kitchen, "I'll set the table."

She loiters in the small, dark pantry, looking at shelves with no idea what she's supposed to be doing. She takes a loaf from the bin but dreads returning to the kitchen for board and serrated knife. Her father's clothes soak in the bathtub, the water stained a dark, rusty red. Rose throws the bread back and runs through to the back door, out into the cold wind.

Huddled against the house wall, she immediately senses being watched. That boy must spend his life on the bomb shelter roof.

"Go away, Keith," she says.

"It's not just your roof, Rose Gray. Is it true you have polio?"

"No, and none of your business, anyway."

"My Mum says I can't come on your side because it's catching."

"Good riddance. Leave me alone."

"I ain't doing nothing."

"That's a double negative—what do they teach you at school?"

She thrusts her hands into her pockets and discovers the scrap of notepaper. With her back to Keith, she takes it out. Writing, in black ink, covers the page; except at the top, penciled in childish lettering— "ROSE GRAY."

The words jump from line to line, like a game. It was a game. She remembers his black, gold-nib pen, the table at the station café, the smell of coffee that made her tummy hurt. He'd shown her how to play with words. She'd forgotten; but there they are in his writing: "Faire Rose; Gray ham; Rose, roes, sore, EROS."

"What are you looking at, Rose Gray?"

"Be quiet," she says, distracted. The word "EROS": the name for the god of love. How could she have known that then? Was he using her to flirt with her mother?

She turns over the page and reads, in black ink: "Alice, Celia." Rose draws in her breath. Celia is Granny's name. Did she know about Graham Faire, and if so, what was their connection?

The wind comes in gusts, blowing grit, almost ripping the paper from her hand

The boy hops around on the bomb shelter like an underfed bird. "Get indoors, Keith," she says, "before you catch your death."

"Why did your dad dig that big hole?"

"To bury nasty little boys in—now go away, and leave me alone."

She escapes back to the house, where she finds Mum on her knees, leaning over the bathtub as she attacks bloodstained clothes with a wood and metal plunger.

"Sorry I snapped at you," Mum says. "My nerves are so strung out you could play 'God Save the King' on them." She sighs. "I need help hanging these on the line. First, take Dad a glass of water and two aspirin—his lumbago's acting up, and you and I are going to have to do the feeding tonight. He's asking what you've done with the silver box."

It takes two more rinses, watching pink water sluice down the drain, before Mum's ready for Rose to crank the mangle. Outdoors, wet clothes flop in their faces as they peg them. Together they push up the line with a wooden prop and, like a sail, the wind catches Dad's shirt. His heavy overalls remain inert, reminding Rose, when she looks back, of a news picture she once saw of a postwar hanging.

Mum says, "Now maybe we can return to normal."

They go in to find Stanley in the living room, resting his aching back. Rose, at her mother's prompting, shows him the polished silver box. He nods approval.

In the evening, Alice hauls the buckets, Rose's legs still not strong enough to help. Together they watch the growing baby pigs feed on their formula, laughing at the way their noses are flecked with milk. Neither of them mentions the empty stall next door.

"You work hard, Mum," Rose says.

"It's not the work I mind. But I never imagined life quite like this."

"What did you imagine?" Rose puts her hand in her pocket, feeling for the folded paper. She's had no time alone to return it to the desk.

"Silly thoughts, mostly." Alice inspects the back of her hands. "Can you believe I used to paint my nails?

"Are you happy, Mum?"

"Oh Rose, what a question. Are *you* happy?"

"I was today in the wind—there were white petals flying everywhere and my feet wanted to dance."

"Funny girl. Where did you come from?"

"You always say that. Was I adopted?"

The cries of the young pigs have changed to quiet grunts as they settle down to sleep. Alice takes Rose's arm, pulling her toward the door. "No, you were not. I should know—I was there when you were born."

"Sometimes," Rose says, "I feel more like a foundling—remember you used to say you found me under a gooseberry bush?"

"It was a joke."

"I know." For now, Rose staves off the thought that whatever Mum says never quite adds up. She asks, "Why don't we have any of my baby pictures?"

"Oh, we must have somewhere . . . Granny probably has them."

It's tempting to keep prodding—best not. Rose kisses her on the cheek. "I love you, Mum."

They walk slowly, arm in arm across the yard, stopping to admire the sunset. "It looks like the sky is on fire," Rose says. She risks, "Mum, when did you last wear your blue dress?"

Alice stops. "Have you been nosing into my things again?"

Rose reddens, like the sky, "It's there in the wardrobe. I was thinking: you must have looked pretty in it."

"I should put it in a jumble sale . . ." Mum pulls her arm away.

Rose starts to say, "Save it so I might wear it one day." But she stops. Her feet feel numb and heavy as they walk toward the door.

— 3 0 —

Next day, Alice is out in the vegetable garden, thinning and weeding a row of carrots. She leans on her hoe. "That's all there is to it. We can't go. I'm as disappointed as you are."

"It's because of Daddy, isn't it?" Rose, who has come out to find her, kicks at a clump of dirt. "What's Granny going to think?"

"Don't blame me—your father's barely moved since he hurt his back. I've been working non-stop—you've seen me. How can we leave?"

"But Mum, I was so looking forward to going."

Alice hacks at a patch of weeds. "Don't grizzle at me. We can't go, and that's that."

"It's because he hurt himself burying the dead pig," There, she's said what everybody knows anyway. From Mum's look it would have been better to keep quiet.

"I don't remember asking for your opinion . . . Go to the house and do your homework, and mind your father, like I told you."

"I came to ask what I should pack . . . Dad's all right; he's sitting in his chair." *As silent as the grave*, she's tempted to add.

Like freshly dug earth in a cemetery, the mound is quite visible. Rose can't wait for weeds to grow over. "I still don't understand why he shot her in the first place."

Mum, on her knees now, separating a row of radishes, tells Rose to drop the subject, return to her books, and say nothing about their cancelled trip.

Indoors again, Rose slams her history book on the table, emitting vague inky smells of school. The afternoon stretches endlessly, like a moldy gym mat; a thought that brings up unpleasant reminders of Miss Cowper's whistle blowing at close quarters. Rose anticipates the games mistress will have no mercy for weak legs. She extracts more books from her satchel. Her father stirs.

"Feeling better, Dad?"

No reply. His eyes are closed. She has no idea if he's awake and ignoring her, or asleep. Flickering sounds come from the fire. Rose picks up a pencil and quickly sketches him, following the lines of his profile: prominent, almost Roman nose, hair sprouting from the nostrils, downturned mouth, square chin, and pendulous ear lobe. She pencils in a fringe of blondish hair with streaks of grey. It's not a fair likeness—she crumples the paper and throws it in the fire.

Her attention wanders the room, resting on objects so familiar Rose has ceased to see them. Mum's desk is there but Dad unknowingly guards it, like a sleeping lion. For two days she has planned to replace the note, restoring it to the envelope with photos of Mum and *him*. She's reluctant to say the name, even to herself. For a brief time, she'd thought of *him* as "faire," like a medieval knight, come to rescue her mother and herself from their enclosed existence. Now, the more she thinks about it, Rose resents the way he played with her name and its anagram.

She reaches in her pocket for the note, only to realize she's wearing a different sweater from the day before. Panicky, she tiptoes out of the room and up the stairs. The bedroom furniture sits back against the wall. Her mother had insisted, relenting only about the pallet on the floor. Rose's cardigan hangs on the door, and she quickly checks and rechecks both pockets but the paper is not there. She lifts books, and shakes out clothes and bedding. Mum's old woolen jacket pockets yield only an empty cigarette packet and a grocery list. Graham's note has gone—either lost or taken away.

If Stanley hears Rose sneaking back into the room, he merely shifts his position. Her heart beats uneasily as she wonders if Mum might've found the note and returned it to the desk. As silent as a mouse, she approaches Grandpa's portrait and runs her fingers along the picture frame. It isn't there.

"Stir up the fire, Rose." Her father's voice makes her jump, knocking the picture askew.

"Did you know him, Dad?"

"Who are you talking about?"

"Mum's father?"

"Oh yes, I knew him all right."

Rose crouches over the fire. There is only a faint glow in the coals. "Did you like him?"

"He was alright. Lent us some money. I don't think he thought much of me." Her father leans forward. "You're putting the fire out, poking at it like that. Add some coke."

Rose scoops coke from the scuttle. Billows of dense smoke rise, but no flame. She blows on the embers. Ashes fly in her face, making her cough.

Her father grumbles, "Here, move out the way. I'll do it."

"No, let me." Rose kneels, takes a double sheet of newspaper and stretches it across the small fireplace, creating a vacuum. The paper sucks in toward the chimney. Rose holds tight. Suddenly the fire roars, the paper scorches and bursts into flames in her hands.

Her father shouts, "Get a grip, girl."

Rose thrusts the burning paper into the grate and bits fly up the chimney. "I did it!" she exclaims.

"Good thing you didn't burn the house down. Where did you learn that trick?"

"Watching you," Rose says proudly.

"Well you better go outside and make sure you didn't set the chimney on fire. That's all we need." In a fright, she runs outside in her slippers to see a column of black smoke rising from the chimney, bits of ash drifting lazily. Her mother appears around the corner, wheeling her bicycle.

"Mum," Rose cries, "Dad thinks I've set the chimney on fire."

Her mother glances up. "Better luck next time."

"Mum!"

"Just joking; the chimney's fine. Be glad we don't have a thatched roof."

"Where did you go?" Rose asks.

"I went to phone David Vale." Alice leans her bike against the shed.

Rose envisages another crisis. "Why? Is another pig sick?"

"I invited him to drop by after his evening rounds." Alice stoops to pull bindweed from the flowerbed. She straightens, meets Rose's gaze. "You can close your mouth now. He said he'd be delighted. It will make up for not staying for tea the other day. Now come with me and help tidy things up. It looks like you already got the fire going."

Rose, who dare not ask about the missing paper, trails after her mother, sighing heavily.

❦

David arrives as it is getting dark. Rose is the one to jump up and greet him at the door. Under the light, it looks as though he's combed his hair and changed clothing. He's wearing a clean white shirt that smells of ironing. She ushers him into the living room, where her mother welcomes their guest with a smile. The vet shakes Dad's hand and settles in a chair on the opposite side of the fire.

"How are you Stanley?" he asks.

"Fair to middling."

"Is it your lumbago?"

Alice interposes, "I've been doing the feedings. I can barely drag those feed sacks—I don't know how Stanley manages to hoist them on his back."

"It's probably muscle spasms," David says. "Have you tried heat?"

"I've been giving him hot water bottles, haven't I, Stan?"

Stanley grudgingly admits his back has immobilized him and that the sacks, far too heavy for his wife, weigh a half a ton.

Rose observes the interaction. Dad doesn't appear to mind David talking like a people doctor; in fact it's perked him up. No one mentions the sow, though Mum confided to Rose she'd filled David in on the phone. She said he'd become so quiet she thought he'd hung up. Rose suspects it's why he agreed to come over. So far, he doesn't think any of the other tenants know and if anyone asks about the hole to say it's a drainage ditch. Rose thinks, guiltily, of her conversation with Keith.

Mum brings up the subject of the cancelled trip south. David says he knows a strong lad who could do the feedings. When Stanley objects to the cost of hiring someone, David says the boy owes him a favor, and he's sure he'd do it for nothing.

Rose asks boldly, "What favor?"

"I operated on his dog's hip when the lad couldn't afford to pay me—it was a golden retriever. You should see the way she runs now." He beams.

All is settled over a glass each of port, her father joining in, though he rarely drinks. Rose is given ginger ale. Observing her parents come to life, she's reminded of a mechanical village scene she and Annie like to visit at the town library. When you press a button the toy figures all go into action. David Vale seems to have that effect on her family.

Alice suggests Stanley go with them, but he quickly says no—he hates crowds. "You used to enjoy travel," she says.

"You two go," Dad says gruffly.

After an awkward silence, David says he's glad Rose will have a chance to convalesce before school, and he offers to drive them to the station.

There is much in preparation: meals for Dad while they are gone, clothes to pack. Mum bewails she has nothing decent to wear and that Rose has grown out of almost everything.

Dad insists on going out to the piggeries, doing what he can with Alice's help. The lad will come the day they leave. It's obvious from the way he walks that his back hurts, but he refuses to see a doctor. Rose, given chores to do, feels the lingering effects of her illness, and is often tired. Mum is the one who has taken on "a new lease on life," as she puts it. She says it is because she's happy she'll soon see her mother.

At last Mr. Vale comes and they are on their way. Rose is so excited she can scarcely believe it. The image of her father on the step waving them off stays imprinted on her mind—she'd kissed him on the cheek, with a mixture of guilt and elation. She sits in the back the car with a grey-muzzled black lab resting its head on her lap. David tells them the dog's owner was forced to give up his farm because of ill health. "Winston really likes you, Rose," he says to her reflection in the mirror. She basks in the compliment.

"I feel guilty about leaving Stanley," Alice says.

"I'll look in on him from time to time—that's a strong young lad he'll have helping him." David changes gears as they head down the steep hill. "It'll do you both good to get away."

Rose listens, stroking Winston's silky ears until he drools. In front, David and Mum chat, the easy conversation of two friends.

"We're only going for a few days," Alice says. "Even the Jacksons next door have their holidays in Blackpool, not that I'd want to go to there." *What a snob she is*, Rose thinks, but David acts oblivious, no doubt bedazzled by Mum's smart red hat and lipstick to match. He'd been nice enough to admire Rose's green hand-me-down coat, but he'd have noticed the too-short sleeves exposing her boney wrists, and her ugly, lace-up shoes.

The scenery speeds by, familiar because of the bus to school, but everything is different as though someone has turned on spotlights, like in a play. The fragrance of her mother's perfume wafts toward the back seat. David asks about the South of England, where Mum was brought up. He speaks nostalgically of his own childhood in the North, and the Lake District, where he dreams of moving back one day.

"I hope you don't plan on doing that any time soon," Mum says lightly.

They arrive in the station parking area. Winston has to be disturbed. David Vale carries the bags to the vestibule, and waits while Alice buys tickets to London, booking through Southern Railways to their destination. He offers to purchase a platform ticket and help with the luggage. Alice says she knows he's busy, and they say goodbye. He touches Rose's shoulder. "Have a lovely time," he says. She watches him walk away, and wishes he'd hugged her.

—31—

THE CROWD AT LONDON's King's Cross Station flows likes a river. Rose stays close, afraid of losing her mother. "Isn't that where we take the Underground?" Rose points to a line of travelers disappearing down a moving staircase.

"How are your legs?"

"Fine, I think," Rose says as someone bumps into her from behind.

Her mother puts out a steadying hand. "Come on," she says, "Let's take a taxi."

"But we can't afford it."

Her mother pulls her along. "Remember the sixpences I've been saving in a jar? Well, thank the Lord I didn't spend them on cigarettes. It will be fun."

Rose marvels that her mother knows what to do, leading them beyond a long queue at the taxi stand. They cross the street at a busy intersection where red double-decker buses, commercial vehicles, and private cars rev their engines, waiting for lights to change. Alice steps into the road, thrusts out her hand, and hails a taxi. A black hansom cab pulls over to the curb.

"Hop in," Alice says to Rose.

While the driver stows the luggage in front, they collapse back in the shiny leather seats. The driver, a muscular Cockney with prematurely grey hair, moves off into the stream of traffic.

"Where to?"

"Victoria Station, please."

"Bob's your uncle."

Mum squeezes Rose's hand so tight it hurts. "Can you believe it? Look around you; we're in London."

She leans forward. "Driver, could we go by some of the sights for my daughter to see?"

"Right you are." the driver does a U-turn, ignoring the horns and shaking fists of other drivers.

He and Mum chat while Rose absorbs the sights and sounds. The driver's accent reminds her of the song, "Oranges and lemons . . ." She hums it to herself, abashed when he picks up the tune and bursts into in a gusty baritone, "I owe you three farv'ings, say the bells of St. Martins." Her mother joins in, "When will you pay me? Say the bells at Old Bailey." Mum nudges Rose, and the three of them sing, "When I grow rich, say the bells at Shoreditch."

Rose puts the window down to fully hear and smell London. In a department store window, a young woman wrestles to dress a blank-faced mannequin. Men walk by in pinstriped suits and bowler hats, with rolled-up umbrellas and newspapers tucked under their arms: caricatures of themselves, like Punch cartoons at the library. She laughs out loud.

"You'd never know there'd been a war on," Alice says.

"You don't have to look far." The driver turns up a side street and stops in front of a block of buildings, some blown open exposing wallpaper and wires that hang down, remains of furniture strewn about on each floor. Rose gapes, trying to imagine the people who lived there. Did they escape? Or was death sudden: ordinary people sitting down for supper, tired of responding every time they heard they heard sirens? She only half-listens to the taxi driver's tale of rebuilding efforts, stalled by last winter's brutal cold, followed by the river flooding. Fuel and building materials are in short supply, he says, and many are still in temporary housing.

They drive on. He points out the dome of St. Paul's Cathedral still standing. He'd been with the fire brigade the night of the Blitz, fighting the firebombs. "A bleeding miracle," he says. "Everything else was on fire." He proceeds along the Thames with its barges and bridges. Seagulls drift with the wind, their underfeathers catching the light against a cloudless blue sky. History lessons fall into place. The driver relates gory details of the Tower of London and sings, "Here comes a chopper to chop off your head. Chip chop chip chop the last man's head." Rose shudders, envisioning her own neck exposed to the cold steel of the executioner's axe, and morbidly speculating if the head knows, even for a second, it has been severed.

The sweep of the Houses of Parliament and Westminster Abbey comes into view with more stories of heroic efforts to save historic buildings. Crews are at work clearing away piles of rubble. Big Ben, the great clock, begins to strike twelve. "It's like we hear on the wireless," Rose says. She pictures the brown box with its white knobs at home, and how they'd listen to broadcasts from Downing Street, Mr. Churchill addressing the English people. The resonating bonging of the clock—the real sound—stirs her deeply as she thinks what it must be like to be a Londoner. She glances at Mum, who seems lost in her own thoughts too; a sad, wistful look. For the whole ride, she's never let go of Rose's hand.

"What time's your train?" The driver seems to sense their mood.

"One o'clock," Alice says. "I've already bought our tickets."

He turns down the flag on the meter. "We have time for young miss to see the changing of the guards."

A crowd has gathered outside Buckingham Palace; the guards in their smart red uniforms and tall bearskin hats are doing their drill. "Get out and have a butcher's," the driver says.

He stands behind Rose, whispering, "See the royal flag? It means they're home. The king and queen never left, even in the worst part of the bombing. Princess Lillibet has recently turned twenty-one, and she's got a beau, Phillip from Greece. My missus says there'll be an engagement soon, and there's nothing like a royal wedding to cheer Londoners up, even if clothes rationing is still on."

Rose thinks, *If only Princess Elizabeth and her handsome Phillip would appear on the balcony, like at the end of* Snow White.

He drops them off outside Victoria's imposing entrance. Alice tries to tip him extra but he refuses. "Cheerio," he says. Handing Rose her case, he winks, "I feel sorry for your dad. He's going to need a big stick to scare off the boys."

Mum looks up at the clock. "Our train leaves in twenty minutes. We'll have to hurry."

"I need to spend a penny."

"Can't you wait 'til we're on the train?"

"I'm dying to go."

"Follow me."

The vast station with its war-damaged steel and glass roof reminds Rose of an aviary: the medley of voices and screech of trains, like a thousand chattering birds. She tries to keep track of Mum's red hat darting ahead. Her legs slow her. The sight of a café with a faded striped awning makes stop and stare. Formica-topped tables spill out into the station. It all looks smaller, more crowded, travelers with luggage piled around them, drinking tea from thick white cups. Not the rendezvous she'd imagined: no white tablecloths or silver coffee pots, or men in uniform saying goodbye to their sweethearts. Had she only seen that in a movie?

"What on earth are you doing?" Her mother has come to find her. She fishes in her handbag for a penny. "Our train leaves on platform one. I'm going to buy a newspaper. Meet you at the gate, but hurry."

The white-tiled room echoes with slamming doors, and the sound of copper dropping in brass slots. Rose, shy among strangers, sits on the toilet, peeing in slow dribbles. She washes her hands, surrounded by women powdering their noses and applying lipstick in front of the mirrors.

There's no sign of Mum at the gate. Alice is not at the newspaper kiosk. People rush by, holding out their tickets. She checks the platform number—no, this is right. Like tickertape, one imagined scene follows another of Mum ill, or leaving the building, or accosted by a stranger. Rose makes herself take deep breaths. Seconds later, she sees a patch of red across the station, momentarily obscured by a streams of people. She runs in that direction, in time to see her mother in her red hat hanging up the phone and pushing open the kiosk's glass door.

"Mum, we're late. Who were you calling?"

"No one—they weren't home. Here, take your bag."

"I don't understand—who wasn't home?"

Her mother says over her shoulder, "Are you coming or not?"

"Hurry up Missus." The man inspects their tickets. They run the length of the train: past porters stowing the last of the luggage, men and women in smart clothes settling into first-class compartments, and the dining car with waiters in white aprons ready to serve lunch. Level with third class, Alice keeps going, Rose close on her heels, until a guard shouts, "All aboard." They clamber on. He slams the door behind them, blows his whistle, and waves his green flag.

In a series of shudders, the train pulls out of the station. Rose, overheated in her wool coat, follows her mother along the swaying corridor. "There are seats here," she calls, as they pass half-filled compartments. Her mother seems not to hear, negotiating the passage between linked cars, oblivious to Rose's fantasy of slipping through to their death on the tracks. At last she slides open the door to a compartment thick with cigarette smoke. A male passenger in a shiny brown suit jumps up to help hoist their luggage onto the rack. He makes room for Alice to sit next to him. Rose, opposite, takes the only remaining seat, wedged between two large and corseted ladies. She closes her eyes to regain her breath.

The sounds of the train begin slowly and then faster and faster as the signals turn green. Rose silently chants, "Off to see Granny," until she can no longer keep pace with the rhythm. Passengers around her light up their cigarettes and pull food from carrier bags. The man next to Mum asks her help with a crossword clue. The two ladies begin chatting about black-market nylons, speaking across Rose as though she's part of the upholstery. They pause only long enough to allow her to extricate herself. As soon as she's upright, the space she occupied fills with their overflowing thighs.

Her mother looks up. "Sorry I dragged you this far, dear. I needed a smoke."

"It's all right," Rose mutters.

The man in the brown suit puts down his newspaper. "Need some fresh air, does she?" The whole carriage becomes quiet, listening.

None of his business, Rose thinks. She pulls open the sliding door, creating a draught, and murmurs of complaint. She hauls it shut, sealing her fellow travelers in a blue haze. Someone has opened a window in the corridor—Rose lifts her hot face to refreshing cold air.

— 3 2 —

THE TRAIN CHARGES THROUGH city outskirts, rows of low brick houses flash by. *What must it be like*, Rose wonders, *to live so close to a railway that walls shake and people look right into your living room?* Small children lean on fences at the end of gardens and allotments, wildly waving. Rose waves back. She imagines people in first class languidly raising an arm, like the king and queen in their royal carriage. The train stops at a station; a crowd of schoolboys pushes by. One boy lingers in the corridor, standing close, jostling Rose with his rucksack. She hangs on, determined not to give up her space by the window. It doesn't matter that her legs ache—she's not going back into the stuffy compartment. The boy sticks his hand out into the breeze, his shirtsleeve flapping. Rose catches a strong whiff of underarm.

A guard comes through. "Don't go sticking yer head out," he warns, "or you'll get yer block knocked off." With a swoosh the train enters a tunnel.

Only a faint electric light illuminates the corridor. Rose stays facing out, smelling the damp, dark smells of the tunnel. Instead of scenery she sees the dim reflection of herself and the boy, side by side.

"I say, shall we close it?" he asks, "We'll be covered in soot." The tall youth pushes the window up. His hand, back on the railing, rests lightly over Rose's, a warm, rough hand. She wonders if it's an accident, not sure what to do. The tunnel, surely, will come to an end soon. She thinks of her mother in the darkness, crossword put aside. Casually, she pulls her hand away; her heart thumps. The boy says nothing, the swaying motion occasionally bumping his shoulder against hers. The train slows, braking, metal screeching on metal, and comes to a complete stop. In the dim light with nothing to look at but the walls of the tunnel, everything seems eerily quiet.

"What's happening?" Rose asks.

"Maybe something's on the line." The boy reaches in his trouser pocket and takes out a packet of cigarettes. "Care for one?"

"No thanks." She thinks him too young to smoke. But when he strikes a match she detects the slight shadow of a moustache.

She asks. "You mean like a body?"

"Rather, don't you think? Probably some old tramp crawled in the tunnel to get out of the cold. It'll be hours before we get out of here."

"How ghastly—the poor man." Rose feels sick. "Can't they put up fences to stop people wandering into the tunnel?"

"People are stupid. Now we're going to have to wait for the scraper."

"The scraper?" For the first time Rose turns and looks at him. In the half-light she thinks him the handsomest boy she's ever seen.

"Yes, it's a special machine for scraping up bodies . . . There's one with its driver in every tunnel."

" I'm not stupid!" Rose says indignantly stepping away. "I don't believe you."

"I say . . . I don't believe me either. We've stopped for a signal—it happens every time." He grins, steering Rose by the arms so both face their reflection. "Don't we make a handsome pair? What shall we do while we're waiting in the dark?"

She's never seen herself like this, next to a boy, as if they are a couple. His height makes her look small beside him, not the way she usually feels—too tall and gangling. Flustered, she says, "You're so conceited."

He laughs. "I know."

He's daring me, Rose thinks, waiting for me to bolt so he can have the whole window to himself. She grips the railing. The boy casually smokes his cigarette, flicking ash onto the floor.

The train starts to move; within minutes they are in brilliant sunshine. One of the women from the compartment appears and heads toward the toilet. The boy grins at Rose as he flattens against the window to let the lady squeeze by. The look he gives is conspiratorial as though she and he own the corridor. Bolder in the daylight, Rose inspects the way he wears his school tie loosely knotted to one side, his cap pushed back on blond, crinkly hair.

"Don't look so cross," he says, his blue eyes teasing. He puts out his hand, "I'm Duncan Algernon Fisher. Who are you?"

"Rose Gray." She doesn't even have a middle name.

"I didn't hear you."

She speaks louder. "Rose Gray."

"I say, what a nice name . . . but you're still cross, aren't you?"

"No."

"Yes, you are. Promise me you won't be cross." He leans toward her.

Rose says, "It's awfully hot—please, let's have some fresh air."

With an easy motion he pulls the window down, the breeze rushing in. "Have you noticed," he says, "that the further south we go, the warmer the air feels?"

"I have. Everything seems greener too, and the hills so much prettier than where I live." She keeps her gaze on the passing fields and woods, sensing him studying her. His hand moves closer to hers; she moves away. He's right: she is cross. But he makes her laugh, imitating the whistle blasts, lurching from side to side as though on a ship, riding the waves.

Duncan tells her he's on break from boarding school and he and his friends are on their way home for half-term. "Are you ever homesick?" Rose asks.

"I was at first—I cried my eyes out."

Rose steals a look at him. She can't imagine him crying. "How old were you?"

"I was five; my father and mother were in Singapore."

"How awful—you were so young. Are your parents back in England now?"

"Mater is and my stepfather—that's where I'm going."

"What happened to your dad?"

"Didn't make it out of there—ended up in a Japanese prison camp."

Accounts of survival in prison camps have always fascinated Rose; but the ghastly details of conditions give her nightmares. "I am so sorry," she says.

His stiff manner puts her off asking any more questions. A silence falls between them. The train hurtles on through small hamlets. *He'll be getting off soon*, Rose tells herself, *and we will go our separate ways.*

He says, "Are all the girls at your school as pretty as you?"

She looks at him suspiciously. "Why do you want to know about the girls at my school?"

"I'd rather know about you." He pulls on one of her plaits. "How old are you—these pigtails make you look about twelve."

"I'm older than that." She glares. "Much older." Then, before she can stop herself she asks, "Should I cut them off?"

He laughs. "Why do girls always ask questions like that?"

Rose presses her forehead against the window to hide her burning face. A soft, golden light illuminates the gentle rise of the chalk downs. Already, her grandmother must be putting on her hat, getting ready to meet them at the station.

"That was an idiotic question about my hair," she says.

Duncan leans on the railing, looking at her sideways. "I like that you asked me."

She's given up trying to tell if he's serious. The train slows. He picks up his bag. "This is my station. I say it's been jolly meeting you. I think you should definitely resist cutting your hair, and never have a perm. Wear it long and loose."

His friends burst into the corridor. "We saw you two kissing in the tunnel," one boy shouts.

"No you didn't," Rose shouts back.

This sets off a chorus. "Got a new girlfriend, mate?"

"Nice, isn't she, Duncan? Does she know she has soot on her face?"

"Don't mind them—they're jealous." Duncan stretches his arms across the corridor, blocking their way, his face toward hers. He kisses her softly on the cheek. The guard calls out the name of the station. They all crowd past, jostling and laughing.

"That's three in a row. Duncan gets the hat trick," someone says.

He waves from the platform. Rose stays by the window, wiping at the soot, smearing where he kissed her. He pantomimes placing a hand on his broken heart. The train pulls away. At the last minute, she blows him a kiss.

"Good gracious, Rose, who was that?" She hasn't seen her mother emerge from the compartment.

"No one—it was no one."

"For someone who says she doesn't like boys, you certainly seemed to be attracting a lot of attention from that mob."

"I wasn't!" Rose frowns. "Anyway, what about you and that man in his shiny suit and his crossword puzzle?"

"Oh, you're being silly." Alice takes a handkerchief from her pocket. "Your face is all sooty. "Here spit on this, so I can wipe it off."

"Don't baby me."

"There's no need to be grumpy. I came to see how your legs are—don't you want to sit down?"

"I'm okay. I'd rather be out here." She'd forgotten all about her legs.

"All right—we'll be there soon. I'm going to the loo to tidy up. You should too."

For the rest of the journey, Rose dreams about Duncan: the touch of his hand, blue teasing eyes, his crinkly hair, and the things they talked about. What must it have been like to be a small boy in boarding school, his father in a concentration camp? She touches her cheek, imagining kissing him back. She doubts his kiss counts as a first. Annie might know. The conductor calls the next station; people emerge into the corridor with their luggage. Rose puts daydreams aside, in a pocket of her mind, to be pulled out next time she's alone.

—33—

"THERE SHE IS." ROSE spots her grandmother at the end of the platform, tall and erect, amidst a small crowd.

"I see her too. Run ahead. I'll catch up with the bags."

The train belches steam and images wobble, but there she is again, waving her walking stick.

Granny greets her with open arms. "You've grown so tall. Are you limping?"

"Only a little bit."

At one time, Rose would have flung herself into her grandmother's embrace. The lapse in time since their last visit has made her hesitant. It is Alice who rushes up, drops the luggage, and allows herself to be enfolded. "Mother," she says, "I can't believe it—I never thought we'd get here."

"Well, you're here. I think I must be dreaming. Come here, Rose, and pinch me."

"Rose laughs, and she too is scooped into the embrace. The three of them do a small dance on the platform, and Rose inhales the mix of Pear's soap and Red Poppy perfume.

"Mum says my face is all sooty," Rose says.

"Well, how can one not be sooty traveling on a train," her granny laughs. "Come on, let's go home and you can wash there. I've made a batch of scones to go with your favorite blackberry jam." She leads the way, elegant in a lilac linen suit, the skirt long, almost to her ankles, old-fashioned buttoned shoes, and a brimmed hat tipped to one side.

"Need some help, Mrs. Whitham?" a porter asks.

"No, thank you, Robert," she says. "How's your wife? Better, I hope, after that wretched influenza?"

"Yes, ma'am, she's back on her feet, thank the Lord."

Alice murmurs, "Is there a person in town who doesn't know you, Mother?'

"Oh, that's your father's fault. Everyone knew him because of the paper." She looks around. "Captain Oaks is supposed to be waiting for us with the car—stay here." She strides off, stick in hand, in search of him.

They wait in front of the station. Rose perches on a suitcase. A breeze blows through bearing a hint of the sea.

"It breaks my heart to see how she's aging," Alice says.

Rose protests, "Look, here they come. That man's having trouble keeping up with Granny."

"Yes, I know, but . . ." Alice sighs.

Captain Oaks owns the country hotel in the village and runs a small taxi service. Rose, sitting behind, tries to imagine him in charge of a ship. There's dandruff, like snow, on his dark collar and a strong smell of what she guesses is whiskey. Her mother sits with her in the backseat and Granny in the front. The grown-ups talk: bits of information about what's been happening in the village, comments on the weather, flooding along the river paths.

Soon they turn off the main road and into the valley. High hedges and ancient trees form a cool green avenue with deep ditches on either side. Everyone stops talking as Captain Oaks navigates past an oncoming lorry with a tall load of hay. A dog runs out from a gate, barking furiously. Rose looks back to see the mongrel following, loping along, until finally it stops for a good scratch. She thinks of Winston in David Vale's car—impossible to believe it was only this morning. Like Winston might've done, she puts her nose to the window crack and sniffs the smell of cattle, green vegetation and the sweet aroma of burning bracken from someone's bonfire.

The road curves downhill. Between the trees, Rose catches a glimpse of the village at the heart of the valley. "I see your house, Granny," she shouts.

"We're almost there." Her grandmother reaches back for Rose's hand and squeezes it. "You've been so quiet I thought you were asleep."

"I'm awake. There's the field where the farmer keeps his Shetland pony. Perhaps he'll let me ride it again."

Church bells ring out. "They must be practicing," Granny says.

Captain Oaks pulls into the graveled driveway and parks in front of an ivy-covered brick house with lattice windows. Two fair-haired boys appear, one of them walking on wooden stilts. "Charles and Mark," Rose exclaims. "Look, Granny, those are the stilts Grandpa made us."

"You didn't tell me they were here, Mother." Alice jumps out of the car. "Where's Betty?"

"She wanted to surprise you."

A woman in a flowery cotton dress appears at the front door. She is larger and heavier than her sister and almost knocks Alice over as she runs to hug her. Rose, positioned directly behind, rescues the red hat from falling to the ground. "Hello, Aunt Betty," she says shyly.

Her cousins are instructed to help Captain Oaks with the suitcases, which they do with dispatch, once it's established that Charles may not attempt the task on stilts.

"We're on half-term," they tell Rose. " Here only for the afternoon—come on, we were having a game of cricket on the back lawn but gave up. We need someone to field for us."

"Rose, your legs . . ."

"I'm fine, Mum."

"Tea is in half an hour," Granny says. "Everyone must come in when I call."

The older boy gives a mock salute behind his grandmother's back. Rose hopes Granny didn't see, in spite of her claim to have eyes in the back of her head.

The cousins, a few years older than Rose, have always bossed her around. When she was little they simply picked her up and moved her about to serve as wicket keeper or fielder. They made jokes about her being "silly mid off," depositing her in front of a flowering bush only to have to retrieve her when she wandered away. Rose tells them, "I won't play with you unless you let me bat."

She's never actually thought of them as boys. She tries not to stare at their lean, muscled bodies, and hairy legs clad in loose khaki shorts. They too apparently see her differently, especially Mark—when she stumbles and falls, he runs to help. "Are you all right?" he asks. Even Charles says, "Good try," when she misses the ball, rather than, "Clumsy clot."

In the bathroom, before tea, she stands at the washbasin, letting warm water run over her hands. She washes her face, dries it on a soft towel. Her eyes look bright in the mirror, and cheeks pink from running. Hoots of laughter come from the living room. Rose finds them at the table, where her grandmother presides over the teapot. The cousins are already wolfing down scones. "I told you boys to wait," Aunt Betty says.

She's only pretending to be cross. Rose can tell by the way her aunt laughs, even when she's scolding them.

Alice says, "I wish Rose had an appetite like that."

Mark pats the chair next to him and plops a scone on her plate. "Not with your fingers, Mark," Granny says.

"Your grandmother received second prize at the Women's Institute for her scones," Aunt Betty announces proudly.

Charles wants to know why not first, speaking as a boy accustomed to prizes.

"They loved the taste but didn't like the shape."

"Ridiculous," Granny says. "Who cares about the shape when you bite into it?"

"They're delicious," Rose says truthfully.

In the evening, when the cousins and Betty have left and the supper dishes are done, they listen to music on the wireless. Granny knits. Alice lies on the settee, almost disappearing into cushions. Rose sits with a fluffy ginger cat on her lap, stroking its fur. She basks in the afterglow of her cousins' attention. After tea, they had dug out an old croquet set from the back of the garage and set up hoops on the rough lawn—the raucous game came to an end when Aunt Betty came to say it was time for the boys to get in the car. Mark rolled down the window and promised Rose he would write.

"I wish Betty didn't have to run off so soon," Alice says.

"It's an hour's drive home, and they're all leaving for the seaside to-morrow. I'm glad you didn't miss one another," Granny says.

A deep sigh comes from the depth of the settee. "Archie takes them on such nice holidays."

Rose pictures her Uncle Archie loading suitcases into the car, Auntie Betty in front and her cousins in the back. "I wish we could go the seaside."

"Betty's life always was fabulous." Alice says. "Remember how she was invited to parties at manor houses and had lovely clothes to wear? When I came of age those days were gone—the gentry were broke and so were we."

"That's an exaggeration, dear." Granny says. "Besides, you were much more of a tomboy than Betty and more interested in jodhpurs than hand-sewn gowns."

"I'd have loved to go to parties, Mother, if I'd had the chance. Stanley was full of promises about all the places we'd go once we were married. I know it wasn't his fault the money vanished, but we still could go to a social at the village hall. He refuses—says his dancing days are over."

Granny, counting stitches, says nothing. Rose prays silently, *Be happy, Mum.*

Her mother rearranges cushions, and kicks off her shoes. "I'm sorry to grizzle. Isn't this bliss, Rose—being here with Granny?"

Mozart's Piano Concerto fills the room. Rose lets her thoughts float with the sound, remembering the train ride and Duncan's stolen kiss. She inwardly smirks: *Sweeter for the theft.*

"Betty says she's put on a stone, but she doesn't know where she's put it," Alice says. She pauses. "I do . . ."

"That's not very charitable." Granny catches Rose's eye and smiles. "Maybe it's a good thing you don't have a sister."

"I wish I did, or a brother."

"I wonder . . ." Alice murmurs.

For no good reason the ginger cat takes offense and jumps off Rose's lap. Alice stretches and yawns. "What are the plans for tomorrow?"

"I need to take barley soup up to the shepherd's cottage—it's a lovely walk; the weather forecast is good. I thought you and Rose might like to go with me."

Rose remembers the old shepherd and his dog. "I'd love to see the lambs."

"As a matter of fact," Alice says, "I thought I'd go to London tomorrow. I can catch the early bus to the station."

The knitting needles stop clicking.

"But we only just got here," Rose protests. "We drove all over London this morning."

"That was the touristy bits. I want to go to Knightsbridge and look around the shops, or maybe take in a matinee. You don't mind, do you, Mother? It will give you a chance to spend time alone with Rose."

Granny stuffs away her knitting. "Time we all went to bed," she says. "Regardless of my opinion, you've obviously made up your mind." She moves around the room, winding the clock, raking embers, replacing the fireguard, and switching off all the lights, leaving Rose and Mum no choice but to leave or sit in the dark. In the hallway Granny says, "I put a hot water bottle in your bed, Rose. Sleep well." Alice has already drifted off in the direction of the bathroom.

The small bedroom used to be Aunt Betty's. Rose guesses it was her aunt who chose the wallpaper with pink roses and trailing vines. The bedspread is white candlewick and simple whicker furniture decorates the room, including a small bookcase. Rose sits on the bed, scanning familiar titles: *Wind in the Willows, Grimm's Fairy Tales, Alice through the Looking Glass*. In the end, she selects *Little Women*, which smells slightly mildewed. She discovers her nightgown wrapped around the hot water bottle and quickly undresses. On the way to the bathroom, she hears voices coming from the lighted kitchen. Rose pauses to eavesdrop. According to Annie, she has the ears of a bat.

"I am simply saying that we see each other so little—why do you have to leave the moment you get here? Your visit is far too short as it is."

"You know I can't be away for very long . . . There's so much work to do on the farm. Rose has to go back to school."

"And you know perfectly well that's not what I'm saying."

"I never get away by myself—don't begrudge me some time alone for a change."

"When are you coming back?"

"Late tomorrow evening, unless I stay the night. I'll ring and let you know."

Granny's sigh is audible. "There's no point in arguing . . . We should go to bed."

Afraid she'll be caught, Rose flits down the hall to brush her teeth, mulling over what she's heard. She spits in the sink. Whatever Mum's up to, she's not going to let it ruin her holiday with Granny.

− 3 4 −

ROSE WAKES TO THE sound of the front door opening and closing, then footsteps on the gravel. She scrambles out of bed in time to see her mother hurrying down the driveway, hatless, her dark hair bouncing as she walks. Rose undoes the latch and opens the window, only to hear the country bus rumble by. She leans out: the morning air smells of lilacs.

There's a gentle knock. "I thought I heard you up." Granny is wearing a gingham apron over a blouse with rolled-up sleeves. She has the air of someone who's been awake a long time, and accomplished half a day's work. "I brought you a cup of tea."

Rose hops on one foot back into bed and takes the cup. She moves her feet to make room for Granny to sit. "You spoil me."

"You look as though you could do with a little spoiling. How are your legs today? Your mother thinks the walk up to the shepherd's cottage might be too much."

"My calf muscles ache a bit."

"I'm not surprised after all that running about with your cousins. I heard you fell at least once. Those boys are too rough."

"But it was fun. They let me bat." For the first time, Rose suspects they'd been told about her recent illness. They kept encouraging her to rest.

"Did you hurt yourself when you fell?"

"I banged my knee . . . not much, though." She doesn't want to admit it's sore.

Granny takes her cup. "Show me."

Rose gingerly pulls the blanket to one side, exposing the bruised knee. Her grandmother lightly runs her hand over it. "I am going to prepare you a bath," she says, "and add Epsom salts. You can borrow your Grandpa's old dressing gown, even though it'll be far too big. I wear it sometimes—couldn't bear to throw it away."

In the bathroom, Granny adds more than salts to the steaming water. Rose has heard stories of villagers seeking her out to cure their various ailments.

"Your mother and Aunt Betty accuse me of being a witch," Granny says, sprinkling what looks like dried nettles. "But guess who calls on me when they're the least bit sick? It's the same with prayer. They say they don't believe in it, but then expect me to do the praying as soon as someone's in trouble—as though they can't talk directly to God themselves."

Rose, newly modest in her grandmother's presence, stays enveloped in the heavy robe. In spite of framed photos all over the house, she has only a hazy memory of her grandpa. She pictures a kind old man often in front of a typewriter, with a shock of white hair. He died of a heart attack shortly after the war began. When the telegram came, Rose begged to go with Mum to the funeral. Mum said she could only come if she promised not to make a fuss, especially in the church, where there'd be a lot of people. No one in the family cried, not even when Grandpa's coffin was lowered into the ground. Rose had let out a sob and Aunt Betty led her away. "Stiff upper lip, dear," her aunt whispered, handing Rose a hanky, making her wait by the church gate until the service was over. Next time Mum travelled to see Granny, she left Rose at home with her father.

As though reading her thoughts, Granny says, "Grandpa loved you. He'd be happy you're wearing his dressing gown." She turns off the taps. "There, it's all ready for you to have a good soak." She picks up the basket of herbs. "I'll make porridge for your breakfast."

Rose lowers herself into the scented water, luxuriating in the warmth. She soaps her whole body, slowly washing her small breasts, running her hands over her belly, and between her legs, exploring the first growth of hair. Fronds of ivy scrape and rustle against the window, giving the light a greenish tint. A tap drips. Mum must be on the train to London by now. Anxious feelings gnaw like a mouse at the edge of her consciousness. Who was it that Mum tried to call at the station? Nothing quite falls into place. Rose yanks on the bathplug chain and stands up, streaming bathwater. Bits of swirling nettle have stuck to her skin. She rubs at them vigorously with a towel. Granny says to talk directly to God: *Please bring Mum safely back.*

"There you are," Granny says as Rose appears with her hair tied back in a ponytail, ready for breakfast. "That was quick." She eyes Rose sharply as she dishes out a plate of porridge. "I wish your mother had stayed too, but we mustn't be selfish. She deserves a day to herself."

It's a mild reproach. Rose lowers her spoon into a dish of golden honey, lifts it high, and lets it fall, slowly twisting onto the hot oatmeal. She says, "This smells wonderful, Granny."

The propped-open kitchen door lets in pale ribbons of sunlight, views of the garden, and beyond, the distant rolling hills. After a while, they go out to the vegetable patch and pick a first crop of peas from tall vines. Granny brings a folding chair and a colander for Rose to shell peas while she picks flowers for the church. "We'll go and arrange them on the altar."

Content, Rose snaps open green pods, tasting the tiny sweet fruit as she works. Sounds of sheep drift down from the hills, and the low buzz of bees from nearby hives. "My knee feels so much better, Granny," she says. "I'd like to go with you to the shepherd's cottage."

Granny doesn't answer—she is staring over Rose's shoulder. "May I help you?"

Rose turns around—a tall, bearded man, wearing wire-rimmed glasses, has appeared at the back-garden gate. He carries a wooden staff and a haversack slung on one shoulder. Rose immediately thinks he must be one of the tramps that wander the countryside. She looks anxiously at her grandmother.

The man opens the gate and comes closer, taking off his hat. "Mrs. Whitham, Celia—don't you recognize me?" His eyes are dark, deep set in a long face with sunken cheeks, his skin pale and translucent in the morning sunlight.

"Yes, now I know who you are," Celia says coolly. "You've changed since we last met, Graham Faire."

Rose jumps up, gawking at the stranger. Granny has said the name, but she struggles to connect it with the person she remembers, or the photographs of a much younger man.

"I'm looking for Alice."

"My daughter hasn't lived here for years."

Bewildered by the coldness in Granny's voice, Rose says, "She went to London."

"But that's where I came from. I took the milk train and walked here from the station." He sounds distressed.

"She must've passed you on the bus," Rose says.

"That's enough." Granny's tone is sharp.

The man paces. "I didn't see the bus. I walked here along the river path." He looks around, distracted. "I must go back and find her." His eyes focus on Rose. "Did you say your name is Rose? It can't be—you were such a little girl when I last saw you."

"I'm thirteen," Rose says. His black hair and beard have streaks of grey, his looks not handsome, not at all as she imagined. The clothes he wears are splattered with mud and foreign looking, with baggy trousers, black jacket, and collarless shirt fastened with a stud. It's the intense way he looks at her that feels familiar. She sums up her courage. "I remember you. You're Graham Faire."

"*Oui. C'est moi, Mademoiselle.*" He reaches for Rose's hand, as though to kiss it, but Celia pulls her away.

"My daughter is a married woman."

"Yes, I heard she was married."

"Don't be disingenuous with me, young man. As far as I remember, you were quite interested in stopping the marriage."

"You also may recall that I solved everyone's problem by going abroad."

"How do you know my granddaughter?" Celia asks, her voice still cold.

Rose pipes up, "We met . . ." She stops as Granny tightens her grip. Rose wonders what "disingenuous" means.

Graham says, "Alice and I met at Victoria Station when I was on leave as a war correspondent. Rose was with her."

"When was this?"

"It was before the war officially began. Hitler was unstoppable. I was living and working in France. I worried about Alice's safety traveling through London with a child."

"She never told me this."

"She wanted to tell you, but it wasn't a good time. She was on her way to her father's funeral. I am sorry, Celia. I meant to write. I respected your husband; he was good to me. You both were."

Mouth open, Rose cannot stop staring. Graham leans heavily on his staff. He appears worn out from his walk.

"John appreciated the articles you wrote about him. He had a high regard for you, as you must know." Rose detects a slight catch in Granny's voice.

Graham straightens his back, "But not my falling in love with his daughter . . ."

"This is not a suitable conversation in front of a child."

"You haven't changed much, Celia—as moral as ever." Graham Faire picks up his bag. "I was hoping the war softened you. Do you at least have it in your heart to tell me how to contact Alice?"

Rose slips from under her grandmother's grasp. She wants to say, *I've seen their pictures. I know more about them than you do, Granny.*

"I have no information to give you." Granny stoops to gather the flowers she's let fall in the grass. " I'm going to walk down the garden a little way. By the time I come back, I want you to be gone." She begins to turn aside. "Alice has enough troubles as it is, without you in her life again."

"For God's sake, Celia—I know how unhappy she is."

"Whether my daughter is happy or unhappy is none of your business. I'm sorry you've come all this way when you're obviously in poor health. Alice is not here."

Granny walks away, motioning for Rose to follow her.

Rose hangs back, speaking rapidly, "Mum said she might go to Knightsbridge to look at the shops, and then maybe a matinee."

Graham pulls the battered hat out of his pocket and puts it on. "I should go. Thanks for the tip, Rose. I can't quite see your mother lingering in Harrods. I'll have to see what plays are on in London. Perhaps she's even looking for me."

He attempts to brush some of the mud from his clothes. "The river path has flooded in parts—I think I'll walk back by the road. I heard there are no buses this time of day. Let's hope I can hitch a lift. I'm afraid I look like a tramp."

Rose giggles, "I thought you were one, at first."

"Did I frighten you?"

"Not once I realized who you were."

Graham glances in her grandmother's direction. "And who am I?"

"You're the man at Victoria Station."

"All those years ago, you remember?"

Rose colors. Unconsciously, she puts her hand to her cheek. The kiss from the boy on the train had left her with a sensation she'd never had before. She feels older, wiser. The photos of Graham and her mother were a shock when she first found them. She remembers now how happy they looked.

"Tell your mother I was looking for her," Graham says.

"It may have been you she tried to ring in London yesterday—we nearly missed our train." Out of the corner of her eye, Rose sees Granny coming toward them.

Graham steps closer, speaking rapidly, "I wasn't there when she called. Tell her I have to see her. It's urgent."

Celia calls, "I thought you were leaving, Mr. Faire."

Graham persists. "Rose, please tell your mother I am going back to France in a few days."

"I won't do that," Rose protests, not knowing why. The sun is so bright—she can't think straight. Her legs ache. If only Mum hadn't gone to London.

"You look like your mother," Graham says softly. He steps toward her. Abruptly, Rose sits down on the grass.

Graham leans over, a concerned look on his face. "Are you all right?"

"I should never have left her alone with you," Granny pushes her way between them.

"Dear God, Celia, you know I would never do anything to harm her."

"She was ill recently. Help me get her in the house."

Rose hears their voices as though from a distance.

They pull her to her feet. She can walk. On either side, they each take an arm until they sit her at the kitchen table. Graham takes a handkerchief from his pocket and mops his face.

Granny pours everyone a glass of water. "I feel fine," Rose says weakly. She doesn't really know what happened. "My legs gave way."

Graham hovers by the door. "I should go."

Granny stands, arms crossed, appraising him from head to toe. "You look worse than Rose. Sit down before you faint on me as well. When did you last eat? Such a pity, you used to be such a nice-looking young man. You'd better wait here for the afternoon bus. I'll heat up the barley soup I was going to take to the shepherd. He'll have to do without."

Graham collapses in a chair. Granny busies herself. For a while they sit in silence. Graham leans toward Rose and whispers, "I think we've been given orders." He takes out a notebook and a pen from his pocket and starts to doodle.

"I remember you doing that at Victoria Station," Rose feels better. At least he will stay for a while. "You made words out of my name," she says.

He scribbles, and looks up. "It's a habit; I'm a writer—I hope I didn't offend you." He scribbles again, and slips her the notebook. "Dear Rose, please don't be SORE."

"You're impossible," she writes back, "It's not FAIRE."

Celia sets out plates, and dishes out the soup. Graham eats hungrily. She brings bread and cheese and apples. She and Rose sit across from him, watching him eat.

Celia says, "You look as though you've gone through a lot since we last saw each other—how many years?"

"It's been ten since I was last in this village—I worked that out on my walk here. Longer than that since you and I last spoke."

"You were in France all that time?"

"Yes, except for the rare times I could get home on leave."

"So you were there during the Occupation?"

"At considerable cost to people I cared about."

"God help you. Were you involved with the Resistance?"

"I'm sorry, Celia, I can't talk about it. I lost too many friends. It's all too recent."

"I can't imagine what you saw. I know the unspeakable horror my son went through in the First War. May I at least ask about your health?"

"I've been in England for medical treatment, mostly for the afteref-fects of dysentery and malnutrition. Yesterday I was released from hospi-tal. I go back to France in a few days. I have to see Alice."

Rose sits quietly, listening. Granny's questions make her aware that the person sitting opposite her has suffered. She examines the lines etched in his gaunt face, sensing her grandmother's pity, and at the same time her resistance to his reappearance in their lives.

"I can feed you, but I can't help you with Alice." Celia collects the soup bowls and stacks them in front of her. She stays at the table.

"You mean you won't."

"That's correct. I'm sorry."

A bumblebee hums loudly around the room. The smell of mint and thyme drifts through the open door.

"We seem to be at an impasse," Graham says.

"Couldn't there be a truce?" Rose asks timidly. "It's such a lovely day—we could walk with Graham to the church, Granny, and take the flowers for the altar."

"Marvelous idea." Graham perks up. "First, how about a glass of your homemade blackberry wine, Celia?"

"It's hidden under the floorboards. If the Germans invaded England— and it looked like they would—I didn't want them drinking my wine."

"If you'd seen what those Nazi bastards plundered in France," Gra-ham hits the table with his fist, "you can be sure you did the right thing."

He turns to Rose with a glint in his eye. "Go out to the tool shed, and hunt for a crowbar."

Her grandmother gives him a steely look. "I'd prefer you moderate your language." She pauses, apparently thinking it over. "As for the wine, why not? I've been wondering if it's still drinkable after all these years."

—3 5—

ROSE HAS NO LUCK finding a crowbar, and is suspicious Graham has sent her on a wild goose chase. She looks around at the neat shelves with labeled boxes of screws and nails. The shed feels warm from the sun, a peaceful, pleasant work area as well as a place to store garden tools. She remembers stories of her grandfather liking to hide out here when all three grandchildren were visiting at once. He made up for his absence by crafting simple toys like the stilts her cousins were using yesterday.

Rose finds a chisel, and weighs it in her hand. Granny's behavior has been strange—quite unlike her usual welcome to visitors. A fly buzzes around Rose's head, breaking her train of thought. Absentmindedly, she swats it away. At least Granny has gone along with Graham's plan to retrieve the blackberry wine. Rose scours her memory: if Graham was around before her family moved north, she has no memory of him. Yet, in a strange way, he feels familiar. Rose shakes her head to clear her thinking. She's fairly certain of one thing: at one time Graham and Granny knew each other very well, and perhaps liked each other.

Taking a last look around the shed, she notices a piece of paper, the edges curled, pinned to a corkboard—on it is a rough sketch and written measurements; probably one of her grandfather's projects. She speaks into the silence, "You knew him too, didn't you, Grandpa?" She pictures the two of them, in this actual shed, but the vision slips away. The walls, which still hold the smell of wood shavings and paint and turpentine, tell her nothing.

She closes the shed door, follows the flagstone path to the kitchen and through the open back door. At the sound of her footsteps, they stop speaking.

"Did you find a crowbar?" Graham asks.

"I didn't." Rose finds his jovial tone annoying, convinced he'd wanted her out of the way so he could talk to Granny.

He shoots a quick, apologetic look. She holds up the chisel. "I found this."

"We may not need it," Celia says. "Help me move the furniture and roll back the coconut matting."

Celia pushes back the table and chairs, boasting a little about her strength as a woman in her seventy-ninth year. Graham assures her that once he's had a few sips of her extraordinary wine his full vigor will be restored. Wide wooden boards are exposed under the matting. Exclaiming at the dirt, Celia fetches a broom and makes Rose hold the dustpan as she sweeps. "See the lever I had installed," she says to Graham; "pull on the ring and lift."

It works perfectly, revealing a row of dusty bottles. Graham waits for permission. Celia nods, and he carefully pulls out a bottle, holding it to the light so they can admire the dark purple contents. "The Germans would have found this cache in a minute," he says.

"They wouldn't have been looking," Celia says tartly. "I already had a plan to offer them tea as soon as they came in the house. People in the Channel Isles say our so-called 'enemy' was mostly made up of young boys, half starving themselves. It was as I suspected—I even kept a tin of biscuits for such an emergency."

"I think, Granny, you and I were in a different war," Graham says.

Celia addresses him sternly. "I don't remember any of my children giving birth to you. You may address me as Mrs. Whitham, or by my Christian name, if you insist. But I'm not your grandmother."

Rose looks from one to another. Graham hangs his head, reminding her of a small boy who's been scolded. He has the bottle of wine in his hand. Suddenly, he grins, "May we open this, Celia?"

First, the boards, matting, and furniture have to be put back in place, then a long hunt for a corkscrew. Fine crystal glasses appear from a cabinet in the sitting room. Rose is poured a tiny amount. She pretends she loves the bitter taste. Celia sips hers appreciatively, saying the wine has aged well, recalling the lovely summer she picked the blackberries, and how no one believed England would actually go to war. Graham says it is as fine as the wines of the Loire Valley. He downs his fast, chiding Celia that her glasses are no bigger than a thimble. He gets his wish for a refill, the cork then replaced and the bottle put away on a shelf.

Graham sighs, stretching out his long legs. "Hills, lovely beyond the telling," he says, with a gesture that takes in the view of the downs. Rose has never known anyone like him: the way he speaks, his clothes, the fact that he earns his living as a writer and lives in a foreign land.

"You have no idea, Celia," he says, "what it's like to find myself sitting in a kitchen surrounded by ordinary objects like this table and these chairs and those blue and white plates on your dresser, and not to be hiding in someone's cellar, or afraid of my own shadow out on the street, or in a hospital ward surrounded by maimed, dying people."

Granny looks around the peaceful kitchen, as though, Rose thinks, seeing it through Graham's eyes.

"I expect, to you, things look much the same, but in this village alone over two hundred gave up their lives. Others have come home shattered by what they've seen and heard, struggling to return to life as it was, which, of course it isn't."

Graham turns to Rose. "I don't mean to be depressing—you're very quiet. What are you thinking?"

There are so many thoughts—about this man in her grandmother's kitchen and who he is in their lives, and a longing for her mother to come back and explain it all, to put things right.

She explodes, "I detest war—everyone says I'll understand when I'm grown up. But I'm thirteen and a quarter and I still don't know why people have to kill each other. It's stupid and I hate it, and I always will." She rubs her hand across her eyes, afraid if she cries she'll be banished.

"Hate is a strong word in any circumstances," her grandmother says quietly.

"But she's right, Celia: war *is* hateful—absurd what we do to one another, humanity at its most illogical and dangerous."

Celia gathers up glasses, taking Graham's right out of his hand. "That's enough talk," she says. "I must change my clothes before I take the flowers up to the church, and if you intend to come with me, Rose, you should tidy up too."

"What about Rose's idea that we all go together? Would you mind, Celia?" Graham runs his hand over his beard. "I probably should do something about my appearance—Rose thought I was a tramp."

"No, not really . . ." Rose mumbles.

Her grandmother frowns. "We may run into people who know you."

"I haven't committed a crime. I may even have a few friends left here."

"Very well, as long as you don't miss the bus. John's shaving things are in the bottom drawer in the bathroom."

As soon as Celia has left the room, Graham mutters, "Your grandmother drives me mad, but there again maybe I'm insane—what in God's name am I doing here?"

Rose can't decide whether he is talking to himself. He walks, a little unsteadily, to a small mirror hanging over the sink. "What do you think, Rose? Would your mother admire my beard, or should I use your grandpa's razor and shave it off?"

"Dad tried to grow a beard once, and Mum didn't like it." It seems disloyal to be talking about her father. She changes the subject. "A boy told me recently not to cut my hair."

"You're interested in what boys think already?" Graham raises his dark eyebrows in mock horror. She glares, but before she can answer he joins her at the table, reaching for her hands.

"Dear one, whatever any boy says, choose what's best for you. Don't listen to what everyone else thinks you should do. Ask your mother about that. You're a clever girl. Follow your intuition."

"Dear one"—no one has ever called her that. Rose reacts, freeing her hands, and alarmed by his intensity. "I must go and change," she announces. The telephone rings in the front hall and Graham overtakes her at the door, listening. Rose's heart beats fast.

He returns, shrugging his shoulders. "Something to do with the Women Institute.

I thought it might be your mother—I think you did too. Did she tell you she was going to ring?"

"No." This was true. It was only what Rose overheard Mum saying to Granny, but she feels guilty for misleading him.

"When is she coming back? Tell me, should I wait here, or go back to London and try to find her?"

"I don't know—I don't even know if she wants to see you."

"You said she might have tried to ring from the station. What do you remember?"

He hovers, blocking her view of the hills.

"I remember her red hat," Rose says.

"What about her hat?" Without taking his eyes from her, Graham pulls up a chair and sits opposite. He smells of mud from his river walk.

She takes a deep breath. "I'd been to the ladies and we were to meet at the platform gate, but Mum wasn't there, and the train was about to leave. I was worried and kept looking for her, and then I saw her red hat coming out of a phone box."

"It was me she was trying to reach."

"She didn't say it was you," Rose says, doubtful. "She said that whoever it was she'd tried to call wasn't there."

"I was in hospital again—she didn't know that."

"There was no time. We had to run for the train; the guards were blowing their whistles." She looks down, trying to avoid Graham's stare. His hands rest on the scrubbed, wooden table, long-fingered like a musician's—not at all like her father's large hands, calloused from work.

"Why, then, did you think it was me she was calling?"

"I don't know." How could she explain that sometimes she felt she *knew* things?

"What's troubling you?"

"I found photos in Mum's desk of the two of you holding hands. Mum was wearing a blue dress—it's still hanging at the back of her wardrobe."

"Ah yes, the blue dress. Go on."

"A scrap of paper fell out with my name scribbled all over it. It was with the photos and it made me remember you and Mum at Victoria Station."

He smiles. "Such a little girl you were, but you already could read a bit, and write. Did you tell your mother about what you'd unearthed?"

"I'm not supposed to look in Mum's desk—she'd be cross if she knew. I put the photos back right away, but I kept the note, and then I couldn't find it. Though I'm positive I left it in my cardigan pocket it simply disappeared. I'm afraid Mum found it, or my dad."

The confession brings only momentary relief, as Rose shakes her head in a confusion of mixed loyalties.

"How you must have worried." Graham sits back and pats his shirt pocket. "Voila! I have a surprise for you, dear one." He produces a piece of many-times-folded paper. "Is this what you lost?"

Rose pushes back her chair, trying to snatch it. "How did you get this?"

"Actually, a postman put it through my letter box, and a friend delivered it to my hospital bedside. You've no idea how happy it made me. There was also a letter from your mother saying you two were planning to come south. She didn't know exact dates."

Rose holds the paper in disbelief. "Why didn't you show it to me before?"

"I've waited for so long for the chance to see you again. Now I'm certain your mother's looking for me. You'll help us meet, won't you?"

She goes to the door. "You and Mum and your secrets—why should I help you?" Emotions constrict her throat. "You pretend you like me, but not a bit—you're using me to get to my mother." Graham sits slumped in his chair, expressionless. Her voice cracks. "I want you to leave me alone . . . If you don't stop, I'll . . ." She flounders. In the hall, Celia's voice continues on the phone. He closes his eyes, crosses his arms, a half-smile forming.

Rose says in a low, furious voice, "Go to hell. If you don't stop bothering me, I'm going to tell my Granny about you and my Mum."

Graham opens one eye, "Don't bother, dear one . . . I suspect Celia already knows."

$-36-$

THEY SET OFF FOR the church. Celia carries a wicker basket and has changed into a full-sleeved blouse with pearl buttons, dark wool skirt, and a straw hat. She sets the pace, using her ivory-handled walking stick. Graham accompanies her, pointing to houses, asking questions about villagers. His beard hasn't been shaved but he looks more respectable, his longish hair slicked back with a wet comb. Rose walks quietly next to him. She clutches some of the church flowers, a mixture of asters and irises that almost match the pattern of her shirt. He makes no comment on her appearance. Secretly, she'd hoped he would. He has scarcely spoken to her since her outburst.

At first she'd felt exhilarated. She'd never told anyone to go to hell before, especially not a grown-up man. It was an expression her father used, but usually indirectly, about his next-door neighbor. Afterwards, in her room, her hands trembled so much she had trouble buttoning her blouse. If Granny overheard anything, nothing was said—only that everyone should hurry.

Walking beside them, Rose worries they're ignoring her—their version of sending her to Coventry.

A jangling bicycle bell causes her to jump. An old man peddles slowly by. His bike wobbles as he raises his hat. "Afternoon, Mrs. Whitham."

Graham asks, "Who's that? He looks familiar."

"Jack Wright," Celia says. "He's been church sexton for years and still takes care of the building and mows the grass in the cemetery."

"I remember—he's the gravedigger. No wonder he's so bent over."

"I hope he's around to perform that service for me—I'd much prefer Jack digging my grave than some greasy-haired youth with a bulldozer."

"At least you know where you'll be buried." Graham takes the basket from Celia and carries it, his head bent, listening intently. Rose, who has dropped behind, notices how frail he looks, almost as thin as her grandmother.

She comes to a row of thatched cottages so close to the road she can see directly into tiny sitting rooms decorated with chintz-covered furniture. They appear empty, like cordoned-off rooms in a museum. Only the lingering smell of cooking suggests someone might be home. A frowsy tabby cat sits on a window ledge. Rose reaches out and the cat butts its head against her hand, purring. Rose makes believe it's Moggy's ghost. She strokes the strange cat with fierce, hard movements. The animal, distracted by the flowers in Rose's other hand, stiffens. Without warning, it leaps, clawing wildly at her arm, drawing blood.

Celia and Graham are waiting by the church iron gate.

"Granny asks. "Are your legs bothering you again?"

"She's bleeding," Graham says.

"I'm all right—a cat scratched me."

Granny takes the flowers from Rose and hands them to Graham. "Was it that mangy creature on the window sill?"

"It wasn't his fault." She lets her grandmother dab at the deep scratch with a handkerchief.

"Rose and her cats," Celia says. "How's that Moggy-cat of yours? He must be quite a hunter by now." Celia ties the hanky around the injured arm.

"Moggy died," Graham says. They both stare. The flowers make purple shadow patterns on his face.

"You know?" Rose asks.

Granny says curtly, "Know what? How is it you've learned so much about our family?"

"I shouldn't have said anything . . . I thought you would know about it."

"That Rose's cat died?"

"Well, yes, and everything else . . ."

Rose feels Graham looking uneasily in her direction. "Please don't," she says.

"'Don't what?'" her grandmother says sharply.

"It's none of my business," Graham says. "Is it Rose?"

Rose looks down at her arm. Blood seeps through the white handkerchief. She shakes her head.

"For heaven's sake, give me those flowers before they completely wilt." Celia's stick raps sharply along the path, past tombstones so ancient they lean into each other.

Rose pulls on Graham's sleeve. "What else did Mum tell you?"

He puts his finger to his lips. Bells ring out from the Norman tower. They pass through the porch door, leaving the sunlight, and enter the cool interior. The bell ringers, two men with their sleeves rolled back, pull and release, and pull again the thick white ropes. Graham stands close. The clamor of bells drowns out his voice. His mouth forms the words, "I'm sorry."

Rose finds a pew where Granny always sits, next to a plaque for her son, Mum and Betty's older brother, killed in the First World War. Graham delivers Celia's flower basket to the sacristy and chooses a seat near the front. Two women appear to help Celia with arrangements in tall brass vases. Graham is leaning forward, as if praying, head propped in his hands. The bell ringing comes gradually to a stop. In the silence, Rose begs God's forgiveness for telling Graham to go to hell. A fit of shame scores through her. How could she have said such a terrible thing? She peeks through laced fingers. What could he be saying to God? She closes her eyes and prays harder. The pew creaks as Graham takes a seat beside her.

He gently lifts her wrapped arm, "Does it still hurt?"

"Mostly my pride—I thought cats liked me."

"Well, I like you," Graham says. He grins. "Pax?"

Rose looks to see if he's mocking her but his eyes are serious. "Pax," she says.

He leans back, propping his dusty boots on needlepoint linen, arms stretched across the pew back. His sleeve lightly brushes her neck; Rose imagines resting her head on his shoulder, her cheek against his coat.

"Have you been watching those women?" he says in a low voice.

"Yes—they seem awfully busy."

"Busyness is probably what saves them. That's what they did all through the war; knitting socks and balaclavas for the soldiers, sending food parcels, running canteens."

"But the war is over now."

"Yes, but I suspect they each lost someone—a son, husband or sweetheart. They need this to fill what's missing."

A young man in a black suit and circular white collar has entered from a side door. The women gather around—a cluster of hats. Only her Granny stays apart, working with the altar flowers.

"I always admired your grandmother," Graham says, "even though we had our differences. She could lead this church a lot better than that callow young man over there, if they'd let her." He adds, "Even Celia can't live without explanations."

"What explanation?" Rose asks.

"I mean her religion. Like everyone else, she wants reasons—why did her only son and two of her brothers die in the Great War; why another war soon after, and more suffering than any human heart could have imagined? Suppose none of it means anything, Rose? Supposing those women are polishing brass and silver for nothing?"

Rose draws into herself, thinking about what he is saying. She asks hesitantly, "Don't you believe in God?"

"Your grandmother does. I used to. Listen to her, not to me. I'm not thinking right; the doctor gives me tablets. I'm like those women, empty inside, or maybe they're fine, and it's only me. You're so young; I shouldn't be saying these things. It's stirred up a lot being back here, seeing you and your granny. Before I go back to France it's urgent I see your mother. I'm positive Alice wants to see me—will you help me? At least give her a message?"

Rose has edged into the pew corner. She searches the sanctuary and sees her grandmother at the lectern, deep in conversation with the vicar as he turns the pages of an enormous Bible. Graham is waiting for an answer. He knew about Moggy. Rose draws breath, remembering how dreadful Dad looked the night they found the dead sow, Mum acting more afraid in the dark piggery than in any overhead air raid. Did she tell Graham about that in her letter?

Rose says, "What makes you think seeing you would make Mum happy? You're leaving again, aren't you?"

Graham removes his arm and sits straight with his hands on his knees, staring ahead.

The afternoon sun glows through stained glass; iridescent light dances among the somber altar hangings. The air is filled with the scent of newly polished brass. Next to her, Graham's smells are alien. His silence, as much as his words, opens up a cavern of doubt.

A man with white hair appears and sits at the organ. Celia looks in their direction and waves, signaling she'll be a few more minutes. Graham touches Rose lightly on the shoulder and nods toward the door. She follows him past the bell ringers finishing off their mugs of afternoon tea.

—37—

ONCE OUTSIDE, GRAHAM SAYS, "I'd like to see your grandfather's grave—will you show me where it is?"

Rose leads him to a secluded place beneath an ancient yew tree. Patches of bluebell grow wild around the grave and someone has gathered some in a vase by the headstone.

"He showed me a bluebell wood once, a day's hike from here," Graham says. "Your grandfather said it was rare to see them like that, untouched under the beech trees. At first I thought the deep blue was water stretching for miles. It was a grand day. On the way home we stopped for a pint at a pub. Your grandpa loved to talk."

Rose sits on a wooden bench. In the fresh air she feels lighter; curious about the way Graham speaks of Grandpa with such affection, wishing she too had seen the bluebell woods. She makes room for him. "How did you two meet?"

"I'd come down from Oxford, trying to decide what to do with myself. My parents lived not very far from here. They were both in poor health, and in my selfish way, I was bored. I picked up a copy of the local paper my dad had been reading. The writing impressed me, especially the editorial. I went to the local library and found out your grandfather had been a war correspondent in the Great War. I rang John and asked if I could do a story on him."

"And he said yes?"

"Not right away, but I kept pestering him, and finally he said I could come and see him, but only once. You'll laugh at this, Rose—I heard Celia in the background saying, 'Invite the poor man to dinner.'"

A blackbird hops around the grave, watching them with beady eyes; abruptly it flies onto a low branch. "Was Mum there when you went to their house?" Rose asks.

"Yes, but I hardly noticed her. I was so busy interviewing your grandfather. I have vague memories of her in riding jodhpurs—she'd turned sixteen, not that much older than you are now."

"Wasn't that the age she left school?"

"Indeed. I found out later how hard up your grandparents were. They'd sent Betty off to secretarial school, but Alice had to contribute to the family income. She found a job mucking out stables at the local riding school."

Rose remembers. "Mum told me she loved exercising the horses." She omits Mum's envy of Betty's opportunities.

"That's like your mother—she always found a way to enjoy life. I bet you take after her. When I saw you today in Celia's garden, my heart almost stopped—I thought you were Alice."

"Well, I'm me," Rose says irritably. The hard bench cuts into her thighs. She feels vaguely out of sorts. "RIP" it says on the tombstone. If only she could ask Grandpa if you really rest in peace when you're dead. None of the grown-ups she knows, except perhaps Granny, *feel* very peaceful. Graham reminds Rose of her cat: wound up, and ready to react to the slightest noise or movement. She asks suddenly, "Did you know my father?"

"Stanley? He appeared on the scene two years later, bronzed and fit from living on a farm in Denmark. He came to buy land with his father's money, but that caused some controversy around here."

"What do you mean?" She's nervous now about bringing up her father's name.

"It was complicated—a dispute about common land. Anyway, it got into the papers and he and your grandfather were at loggerheads. John and I had become close friends. I think he and Celia thought of me as a son. By then I was assistant editor for the paper."

"What about Dad?"

"He swept your mother off her feet—he was rich, handsome, and he noticed her."

"Which you didn't," Rose reminds him.

"Perhaps, subconsciously, I was waiting for her to grow up. I didn't see it happen. It took me completely by surprise when she and your dad announced they were engaged. It was then I woke up and realized I was in love with her."

"But she didn't love you," Rose insists. "She loved my dad."

"That's what was tragic. She'd always loved me, but thought I didn't care. When I told how I felt, she couldn't believe it. She promised she'd break off the engagement."

"Poor Dad. Was that when he lost all his money?"

"Exactly, and his father died suddenly. Stanley had to leave for several weeks to settle his father's estate, which really meant paying off all the debts. Your dad lost everything."

"But he didn't," Rose says. "He has Mum and me."

"Rose, dear one . . ."

"Don't call me that—I'm Rose, not your dear one." She struggles not to cry.

"I'm sorry. The last thing I intend to do is upset you."

Rose says nothing, sitting with her arms wrapped around her chest. Graham, too, sits quietly, perhaps waiting for her to speak. Her heart hurts. She focuses on the vase of bluebells nodding in the breeze. What would Grandpa say about their conversation? Why did Mum choose Dad over Graham? *There are no words*, Rose thinks, *to say how I feel about him showing up like this.*

She looks back toward the church. "I expect it's time for your bus."

Graham says, "Yes, and look, here comes Celia."

"I thought this is where I'd find you." Granny holds up a finger. "Listen to that blackbird singing its heart out. John would have loved it. Come now. I hadn't intended to be so long—the new vicar's always in a dither about something. Let's hurry. I'm afraid, Graham, there'll be no time to offer you tea before you leave."

They walk quickly through the quiet tree-shaded village. In the distance, there are sounds of cricket practice: the crack of a ball on a willow bat, followed by hoots and cheers. The bus appears, stops, and let's out a family: two small children carrying buckets and spades, both parents red-faced as lobsters, back from an outing to the seaside.

"I forgot there would be no school children today," Granny says. "The bus turns around at the village hall—that gives you less than ten minutes before it comes back."

"I'll run ahead and get my bag . . . I assume the door is open." Half limping, Graham jogs ahead.

By the time Rose and Granny reach the driveway, the front door is wide open. Rose realizes it may be her last chance to see Graham. She runs up the steps. His tall frame blocks the front hallway, the telephone held to his ear. Celia, close behind, pushes past. "Is that call for me?"

Graham turns his back. "Wait for me there, Alice. Please, stay right there. I'm leaving now to catch the next train. Yes, I've been here all day with Rose and your mother."

"Is that my daughter? Give me the phone, immediately. You've no right." He ignores her. She raps him hard on his bony shoulder with her cane.

"Ouch!" Graham clutches the phone. "Celia hit me. I must run for the bus. Promise you'll wait for me." He dodges Granny and relinquishes the receiver to Rose. "Your Mum wants to talk to you."

"Mummy—where are you?" Rose sobs.

Instead of her mother's voice, it's the operator. "You have thirty seconds . . ."

"Rose, dear, what's wrong? Why are you crying? I'm still in London at the station. I can't talk." Her mother weeps too. "Tell Granny, I'll ring back as soon as I can."

"Mummy, please come home."

"Let me talk to her," Granny says.

"It's no good—the phone's gone dead."

Through the open door they hear the sound of the bus roaring past the house.

Rose says, "He didn't say goodbye."

"I thought he'd changed for the better. Clearly I was wrong." Her grandmother closes the door. She takes off her hat, pauses in front of the mirror, and straightens her shoulders. "What we both need," she says, "is a cup of tea—and how about a scone? It's a good thing I managed to save a couple before your cousins ate them all up."

— 38 —

ROSE WAITS WITH A tea towel while Celia does the washing up. Mulling over their tea party for two, she decides it was a disaster: a honeybee dove into the jam dish, the milk tasted off, and Granny complained the cousins had scoffed her entire butter ration. Rose bore the furious bee in a spoon to the open door and shook it free—only to find it later, on the threshold, in the midst of sticky death throes. "We'll have to kill the poor darling," Granny said. Rose had closed her eyes but there was no escaping the small crunch of her grandmother's foot on the stone step.

Granny lowers the wine glasses left over from Graham's visit into sudsy water. Miniature panoramas of the room float by. Rose captures a single, rainbow bubble, balancing it on a fingertip until it bursts. From habit, Granny has removed the wedding rings she still wears, although they no longer slip easily over arthritic fingers. Purple veins cord her hands as she carefully washes each crystal glass. Rose dries. She lifts a glass to her nose—the smell of wine has gone.

The moratorium on Graham's name enlarges his presence throughout the house. Rose hears the sound of his voice in her head, visualizes him as though his image is imprinted in Technicolor on her brain.

"I need to lie down for a while," Granny says, her chores completed. "I feel a little undone." She looks pale, the lines in her face scored deep with fatigue.

"You never rest in the afternoon," Rose protests. She follows her grandmother to the sitting room, where she reclines on the sofa.

"Even Mr. Churchill napped and there was a war going on."

Rose arranges cushions, brings a crocheted blanket. "Should I fetch someone?" she says. "Are you ill?"

"Not ill, merely old. No need to make a fuss—I am going to close my eyes for a few minutes.

"I feel terrible. I told Graham to go to hell."

"I think he believes he's already there."

"I didn't mean it."

Celia closes her eyes. "I'm afraid all three of us may have said things we regret. It's been a trying day. You must rest too on your bed."

Dismissed by her grandmother—put out, Rose thinks, like the cat—she dithers in the hall, unsure what to do next. Old resentments arise from when she was little, of being made to take naps in the daytime, despite protesting she wasn't the least bit sleepy. Meanwhile, her cousins would be outdoors playing. If Mum were here, instead of heaven knows where, they might've gone for a walk, taking the chalky path up into the downs. Alice would insist they toil without stopping to the highest point, where she'd make Rose draw deep gulps of fresh air into her lungs—as though the air at home was somehow less breathable.

When the war was on, rules were strict—none of the children were to wander from the house. There were rumors that silver paper, collected for the war effort, was booby-trapped. Signposts were turned round to confuse the enemy; there was always a danger of getting lost. More alarming were whispers about a half-crazed man who roamed the hills and lured children with sweets that he kept in his trouser pockets. Once, she and her mother saw a stranger, rifle slung over his shoulder, lurking on the edge of some woods. Mum had grabbed Rose's hand and they'd run all the way back to the village. It turned out that he was a harmless gypsy in search of a rabbit for his supper. Mum said she'd been afraid he was a German spy.

Rose drifts toward her room, resigned to climb under the white candlewick and close her eyes, shutting out the daylight. Clothing lies strewn on the bed from before their walk to the church. "Don't talk about that man," Granny says, but it's impossible not to visualize Graham on the train, heading for London, and Mum on the railway platform, waiting to greet him. In a fit of longing to shake off the mood Rose feels herself falling into, she plucks her cardigan from a chair, puts it on, and makes for the front door. On the way, she sees the hall table with Granny's gloves and leather-bound prayer book. The mute black telephone sits mute—if only Mum would call.

Rose is half way out the door when she hears ringing. She runs back to snatch up the receiver. "Mum?"

"Rose? Is that you? It's David Vale. Is your mother there?"

Like peering through the wrong end of a telescope, she tries to bring into focus the person who, only yesterday, drove them to the station. "Mum went to London."

"What about your grandmother?"

"She's asleep." His voice sounds strained. She adds, "Is everything all right?"

"I didn't mean to concern you. It's your father."

Her immediate thought—*We should never have left him.* "Is it his lumbago?"

"Probably that's it—that, and living off his own cooking."

David has switched to his veterinarian voice. Far from being reassured, Rose recalls the way he sweet-talked the sick sow before jabbing it with a needle. "When did Alice say she'd be back?"

"She didn't exactly. Did Dad ask you to call?" Her father never uses a phone if he can possibly avoid it.

"No. I thought I'd chat with your mum. You'll both be coming home soon anyway, won't you?"

"Yes, the day after tomorrow. I have school on Monday." The thought makes her heart sink.

"Winston will be happy—he misses you."

"Winston?"

"I have a surprise for you." He tells her about a litter of kittens that will need homes as soon as they're weaned. "Perhaps you'd like to see them and choose one."

"In place of Moggy?" Rose tugs on the telephone cord to where she can sit on a spindly chair. She wonders where David is. A dog barks in the background.

"Nothing can replace your cat. I thought . . ."

She inspects the red scratches on her arm. There's so much David doesn't know. "Thank you," she says. "When Mum comes back, do you want her to ring you?"

"I'll not bother her. Must go now and see about a fox terrier . . . caught its foot in a trap, poor dog."

Rose hangs up. She frowns into the hall mirror. Now what is she supposed to do? The prayer book sits impassively on the table. The sitting room stays shut. "Bother it all," she says to her reflection. "I'm going for a walk."

$-39-$

SHE SETS OFF IN opposite direction to the church, buttoning her cardigan against the chill. The days are still short. Windows in the stone cottages reflect the late afternoon sun, like ship lights afloat on a grey sea. She stomps her feet to get the circulation going. David's call implied something's wrong with Dad, perhaps worse than lumbago. A chill runs through her, recalling Dad sitting in the dark the night he killed the poor pig. Rose kicks at stones in the road. Swallows on a telephone wire take off in unison, skimming over thatched rooftops.

Ahead a garden gate unlatches. "Alice, is that you?" A woman appears, her round face framed by a blue chiffon scarf stretched over tightly wound hair rollers. She approaches, in carpet slippers with fur trim, her size hampering progress, reminding Rose of someone pushing along a large piece of furniture.

"Blimey, I thought you were Alice," the woman says, clutching her side.

"I'm Rose."

"You looked like her, coming down the street."

"Alice is my mother."

"Yes, love, I'm assuming that, but last time I saw you, weren't you in nappies?"

"I'm thirteen." Rose squirms under the woman's inquisitive gaze. She wants to say, *I don't like being inspected like meat at the butcher's.* She attempts to step around but her way is blocked.

"I could've sworn you were her—at a distance, mind you. You don't have her curly hair, or those brown eyes. She kept us all guessing, that's for sure."

Guessing what? Rose wonders. The woman has an odd chemical smell—must be from her home perm. Rose eases past, brushing against a flowering hedge, causing a cascade of pink petals.

A warm hand grasps Rose's shoulder. "Keep still a minute—you've got some in your hair." Close to, the woman appears younger, her eyes mischievous, bright blue, like cornflowers. "We never knew which one she'd marry," she laughs. "My hubby said that they were taking bets at the pub." She picks a few more petals from Rose's sleeve and gives her a pat. "Tell your mum you saw Gracie Miles, and to come by. She'll remember me—we mucked stables together. Tell her my Bertie died and I got fat."

"All right," Rose mutters, pulling away.

"Cheerio—don't forget to say you saw me."

The sun lies low on the hills—too late in the day to climb them. Turning back might risk another set-to with Gracie Miles. Rose veers down a side road, past a cluster of houses until the lane becomes a grassy track through green fields sloping toward the river. This must be the way Graham walked up to the village. She inspects the soft ground for footprints but there are too many: dogs, horses, cart wheels, and perambulators, as well as people. At a gate, she stops to watch a man unharness a plough horse. The huge animal makes snickering noises, restless to be let loose. The man, middle aged, weather-beaten face, with a battered hat, greets her with a cheerful wave. "Feels like there's a nip in the air. Nice day, though, weren't it?"

"May I stroke him?" Rose asks, shyly.

"Better 'urry—he wants 'is supper."

Rose climbs the gate and jumps down. She runs her hands over the powerful, groomed neck, inhaling the stable smells. "I wish I had a sugar lump."

The man takes a carrot from his pocket, "Try this, but keep yer palm flat."

Rose giggles as velvety lips pluck at her hand. The horse chews, tossing its head, spraying her with orange bits.

The horse feeds, breathing dustily into a metal trough. The ploughman chats to Rose as he smokes a cigarette. He knows her grandmother. "That lady," he says, "walks to town no matter what, either along the river, or if it's flooded, on the road. Won't go on the bus, or let anyone give her a lift." He appraises Rose's lanky looks. "I'd say you take after her."

He tosses the cigarette, unclips the bridle. Ears pricked forward, the horse gives a deep-throated whinny. Rose jumps back, amazed by the creature's sheer size and powerful haunches. It sets off, a slow trot at first, then kicking, galloping, dark tail and mane flowing, circling the field.

"'E's 'appy." The man hoists the harness on his shoulder. He opens the gate and lets Rose go through. "I best be off 'ome." As she turns back toward the river, he cautions, "I wouldn't go too far on your own, Miss . . . the paths are slippery, and you never know who's loitering about down there."

She should turn around before dark. If Granny wakes, she'll worry. Rose tarries by the gate, watching the sun slide out of sight, leaving a crimson and turquoise sky. The horse grazes in the corner of a field turned to gold. At first she thinks it's the wind she hears sighing in the trees. She listens. Even the horse lifts its head, as if it too hears the low, ceaseless music of the river.

Daylight is fading fast. She'll only stay a minute or two, to see how high the tide is running, and to smell the rivery smells that since she was a little girl conjure images of Rat, Mole, and Toad of Toad Hall hiding in the bulrushes. The cart track makes a right-angle turn around the fields. Straight ahead is the opening to a trail through woods, then steep steps that lead down to the water's edge.

"*I dare you*," Annie would say. "*Bring me back something from the river so I'll know you've been there.*" But Annie is miles away. Graham, on the other hand, would have emerged from his river walk at this very place this morning, his clothes spattered in mud. She conjures his dark eyes, quizzical, slightly mocking, one eyebrow raised: "*Dear one, you can do anything you set your mind to.*"

She shouts, scaring a nearby jay on a fence post: "Who cares what you think?"

Beyond the trail entrance, Rose enters into a green vault of overarching trees, bushes, and tangled undergrowth. Within minutes, meadow sounds fade away; a strange, dull silence descends, like entering the hushed, darkened interior of a cathedral. Damp leaves muffle her footsteps. Old beech trees form a tangled roof far above the well-trodden path. Weak, filtered light casts dark blue shadows. She catches her foot on a root and almost falls. The moss-covered trees, like watchtowers, stand as ancient witnesses to passersby. To the sheltering trees she calls, "I took the dare, didn't I? Don't trip me up again." She keeps going through the gloom, barely able to see her way, but always keeping her eyes on the faint glow ahead.

Rose bursts into a clearing bathed in light. The bright disk of a full moon floats above, reflected in the deep, fast-moving river below. Thirty-nine wide steps cut out of the chalk cliff face, known by locals as Jacob's Ladder, and zigzag down to the river. There's no railing to hold on to, and the steps are uneven in height. Rose has never made the descent alone, but she knows the way. Once, Granny and Mum brought her to see two swans building a nest in a thicket of reeds, making the birds hiss and stretch their long white necks. Another time, further up stream, they rented a rowboat, drifting with the current, scattering ducks and moorhens in their path. Dad was not with them—he'd never wanted to come back after *the incident*. Rose stops to rest her trembling legs. Almost halfway down: twenty-one steps to go. Moonlight lights her way.

She would've been almost five years old when *the incident* occurred. It was shortly before they moved to the farm. A hot summer's day, perfect for a family picnic. Her parents were both there—Mum in a sleeveless summer dress. Grandpa wore a straw hat, one of Rose's last memories of him. Granny had packed a hamper of sandwiches and lemonade. Aunt Betty and Uncle Archie brought towels, fishing tackle, and a blanket, the boys slowly following, legs barely long enough for the steep steps. Rose had to be carried, her father hoisting her on his shoulders. "You're nearly strangling me, girl," he'd said, but Rose, on her dizzy perch above the river, had been afraid to loosen her grip. They'd almost reached the bottom when Dad missed the last step, staggered several paces, tried to right himself, then fell headlong. Rose catapulted from his shoulders and rolled down the grassy bank into the water.

Remembering, Rose's ears fill now with the unceasing rush of the river, waves slapping against the shore, so different from the lazy current flowing by on the day of the picnic.

Details of *the incident* have changed over the years. The cousins cheerfully refer to it as the time "Rose fell in the drink." They claim that their father, Archie-the-hero, plucked her "like a drowned rat" out of the river—although not everyone agrees, since several people ended up soaking wet. Family lore had it that if any non-swimmer fell in the river, they'd instantly drown. When water closed over her head, Rose believed, without question, this was her fate. Her eyes must have been open. She remembers a greenish light, no struggle, only a deep sense of peace as her body gently sank. If she hadn't clung to her father, half throttling him, he'd never have fallen and had the wind knocked out of him.

A canopy of stars has appeared, too numerous to count. The river beckons: seen now only in silvery patches through tall weeds and cattails. Mud sucks at her shoes as she slips and slides down the steep bank. A dark cloud scuds across the moon. Rose stands very still. Some animal splashes noisily among the reeds. She hears sounds of small rivulets and dripping water, the muffled collision and release of floating debris, and, always, the river's roar on its journey to the sea. Minutes later, the moon breaks free. Her feet are cold and wet, but the temptation to stay is strong. *What it would be like*, Rose wonders, *to run away? One day*, she vows, *I'll come back with Annie and we'll follow wherever the river is telling us to go.*

Rose gropes through the weeds back to the foot of Jacob's Ladder. She starts the climb. One wrong footing and she'd step into space. Halfway, she rests her trembling legs and peers back into the darkness. Far below, a small flame flares. Then nothing. Perhaps she imagined it. Seconds later, she sees a red, bobbing light moving along the path at the water's edge. Rose shouts, "Is anyone there?" Whoever it is may not have heard over the constant sounds of the river. "Hello," she calls, but more cautiously now, remembering the ploughman's warning about loiterers. At the foot of the chiseled steps, the flame appears again, and goes out. Rose scrambles upward. Barely visible in the gloom, a dark shape follows, rapidly gaining ground. In a fright now, Rose climbs faster, her breath loud in her ears. Cigarette smoke, bitter and foreign-smelling, rises from below. Perhaps the splashing among the reeds wasn't an animal, after all, but a person hiding under the cliff. She forces her legs up the last few steps and into the clearing. A hand touches her shoulder. In a fright, Rose stands still.

"I heard you calling—are you lost?"

She'd not expected a woman's voice. The strong cigarette smell pricks her nose. Rose, too exhausted to take another step, slowly turns around.

She gasps, "Mum! What are you doing here?"

"Good Lord, what are *you* doing here?" Alice comes close.

"I wanted to see the river. Granny's home, tired out from your friend's visit. She had to lie down. We heard him begging you to wait for him in London."

"I don't want to talk about that now. I'm worried about Mother—it's unlike her to lie down in the daytime."

"She says she's done in. She won't talk about Graham Faire either. But she fed him barley soup and blackberry wine from under the kitchen floorboards."

"Blackberry wine? She'd never let any of us touch it. I'm too exhausted to talk. My nylons are torn and I've ruined my shoes in the mud. How could I wait there? Don't you see—I had to come back for you?"

The moon shines bright, but behind her mother, so Rose can't read her expression. Alice says she started the long walk to Granny's house when a local woman offered a lift. "I asked her to drop me off outside the village. I took the river path so I'd have time to think."

The ghostly light draws lines around Mum's eyes andmouth, her lips purple as if she too had drunk blackberry wine.

A large bird flaps by and disappears into the dark trees.

"Pax," Graham had said to her, in the church. She takes her mother's arm. "How are we going to find our way back in the dark?"

It takes what seems forever before they emerge at the other end of the trail. Mum insisted she knew the woods "like the back of her hand," but soon became disoriented. They shouted at one another, finding themselves in the midst of prickly briars, disagreeing about direction. Rose's legs felt close to collapse. She's convinced it was the trees that helped them out of the dense brush and back onto the right path.

"We did it," Mum exclaims. "Fat lot of use this lighter was." She thumbs the little wheel. "I can't even light my cigarette."

"Did you see," Rose says, "the way moonlight came through the trees every time we thought we were lost?"

It takes a while to brush leaves and twigs from each other's clothing before setting off, arm in arm, along the grassy track. They stop by the field gate. Rose clicks with her tongue; the big horse lumbers out from the shadows, whinnying and tossing his head.

"Look out," Rose says, "he'll try to eat your sleeve." They pull handfuls of thick grass. Alice reminisces about when she worked in the stables, which reminds Rose of her encounter with Gracie Miles. "She asked me to tell you her Bertie died, and she's grown fat."

"Dear Gracie, she always was plump—I didn't know about Bertie."

They walk on the road now, past the warm glow of cottage windows. Rose doesn't share Gracie's story about bets at the pub. There's one conversation, however, she must mention.

"Mr. Vale rang."

"David called? Why?"

"He said Dad isn't well—he wanted to chat with you about it."

Her mother's arm tightens. "Is it his back?"

"Mr. Vale didn't exactly say. He said maybe he'd have a word with Dr. Harris."

Mum says with a sigh, "Dear David, he's always so good to us."

Granny's porch light is on.

"Thank God we're nearly there," Alice says. "My feet are killing me."

"I can't even feel mine."

As they reach the gate, Alice stops and asks in a low voice, "What did you think of Graham?"

Their arms still linked, Rose feels the drum of her mother's heart. Many responses run through her mind. She chooses the simple truth: "I sort of liked him."

Granny has seen them coming. She's waiting at the door, first greeting Rose as she hobbles up the porch steps. "Where have you been, you naughty girl? I've telephoned the police constable—he's out looking for you on his bicycle. Who's that with you?"

Alice appears from the shadows. "It's me, Mother. I found Rose on her way up from the river in the dark."

−40−

THERE'S A DIFFERENCE BEING in serious trouble at Granny's house versus at home, with Dad's tinderbox moods and Mum nagging not to upset him. The same is true of school, where breaking a rule will end you up in Gordy's office, or, worse still, in public disgrace. Rose contemplates this in a warm, scented bath, soaking off layers of mud, her dirty clothes in a heap. Mum received her share of the scolding right there on the doormat before they were allowed in, and not before they'd removed their caked-in-mud shoes. They must've looked a bedraggled pair. No sooner were they indoors than the doorbell rang, and a policeman's hat was visible through the frosted glass.

Mum had winked at Rose and pulled her into the kitchen. The over-heard conversation was very brief: "Evening, Ma'am. Your granddaughter was seen by a farm worker—he said she was heading for the river, but . . ."

"We found her—she's home."

"A good thing too—there's undesirables out there in the woods."

"I quite agree with you, constable. I'm afraid we've made you late for your supper. Please give my apologies to your wife."

Celia found them at the kitchen table. It was then she dispatched Rose to have a bath. Mum told Rose not to use up all the hot water. To Granny, she said, "By the way, what's this I hear about blackberry wine?" Celia was not amused, instructing Rose to go along because she needed to have a serious talk with her mother.

After her bath, Rose reaches for Grandpa's wool dressing gown and envelops her damp body in its warmth. Mum, looking subdued, leaves for her turn to bathe. Granny stands at the stove, cooking sausages and onions. Whatever she and Mum were discussing lingers in the kitchen like smoke.

"I'm sorry I worried you."

"Of course I was worried—you didn't even leave a note. Do you know what that's like? And I don't enjoy being reprimanded by the local constabulary."

"I'm sorry. Don't be angry with me."

"Let's sit." At the table Granny pours two glasses of water from a pitcher. The blackberry wine bottle, Rose observes, has not moved from the shelf.

"I couldn't imagine where you'd gone," Granny says.

Rose fidgets with her glass. "I went to the river—I thought I could be there and back before dark." She wishes she could explain how the watery sounds and smells drew her there, but the river's pull is a mystery to herself. Instead, she asks, "Do you remember the picnic we had when Daddy tripped carrying me, and I fell in the river?"

"Is that where you went, down those slippery steps? I'd never have allowed that."

For the third time Rose apologizes. She draws comfort from Granny's reputation with her cousins. "She'll forgive you for almost anything."

"What a fuss there was," Granny says, "plucking you out of the water. Poor Stanley; he was trying so hard to fit in with the family."

Rose has never thought about this. "Did he fit in?"

Granny reaches into a drawer for matches. "Your father's a bright man whose circumstances changed. We wanted him to feel welcome, but after shooting-brake picnics, tennis parties, and who knows what else, adjusting to all of us couldn't have been easy." She takes a candlestick from the sideboard, places it in front of them, and inserts a beeswax candle.

"May I do that?" Rose asks. She strikes a match and holds it to the wick, as an orange, blue-centered flame leaps up, spreading a soft circle of light.

"I often think of your parents toiling on the farm," Granny says.

Rose thinks of her father alone in the house. She sighs. "I sometimes think Dad hates it." She runs a finger through the flame.

"Don't do that. You'll burn yourself."

The ginger cat meows outside and Granny let's him in. Settling back in her chair, she says, "Speaking of the famous picnic, I bet you don't remember what sandwiches I made."

There's so much Rose could say—Granny, of all people, might understand what happened that day when she *knew* she was drowning in the river's green, murky waters. But Granny's thoughts are elsewhere. The moment passes. Rose says, "I give up."

"Corned beef and chutney—I wished I'd made more. They were your grandpa's favorite. That was one of his last picnics. He loved the story of Jacob's Ladder—do you know it, Rose?"

"About the angels ascending and descending?—It always makes me think of playing Snakes and Ladders."

Granny laughs. "Life's a bit like that. Grandpa's other favorite Jacob story was when he wrestles all night with the angel for a blessing and is left at dawn with a limp. John once said your dad reminded him of Jacob, only Stanley seemed always to be wrestling with something, and more often than not, with some part of himself out of joint. John wasn't judging him. He saw a lot of your dad's struggle in himself."

Sounds from the bathroom: gurgling in the pipes, a door opening. Rose's asks quietly, "Do you think Grandpa liked Graham better than Dad?"

"Dear, you shouldn't even be asking that question . . ."

The telephone rings in the hall.

"I'll get it," Alice shouts.

Granny listens and then returns to the stove. She picks up a spatula and dishes food onto their plates. "You and I should eat."

The fire sends out heat into the living room. Only one lamp is lit so Celia can see her knitting. Alice was first to claim the settee with its soft cushions. Rose, in her nightgown, sits upright in an armchair, a crocheted shawl drawn around her shoulders. The ginger cat is draped on her lap. In spite of drooping eyelids, she resists going to bed. At supper, after Mum joined them, the conversation was mostly about Gracie Miles. It turns out Bertie did die of an asthmatic attack.

"You should pay Gracie a visit," Granny said.

"Hmm," Alice responded. All through the meal Rose could tell Mum's mind was miles away.

The cat purrs as she absentmindedly strokes his fur. David Vale's offer of a kitten has taken her by surprise; the events of Moggy's death are still too vivid, the future too unsure. Her insides flutter—in three days she'll see Annie at school. Like snow collecting on the roof last winter, successive anxious thoughts sift into consciousness. For comfort, Rose gathers the sleepy, compliant cat in her arms.

Mum lolls full length, enveloped in a pink flannel robe.

"Is nothing of mine sacred?" Granny mildly protests, as she always does when her daughters borrow her things without asking.

"I didn't think you'd mind," Mum says.

Rose studies her grandmother's profile, bent over her knitting, the way she yanks hard on the wool, needles flying.

Granny looks up. "You're not thinking of running off again, I hope."

"You're not, are you Mum?" Rose echoes.

Mum's head emerges from the pillows, eyes flashing, reminding Rose of an indignant bird disturbed from its nest. "Goodness you two—I had a day in London. That's all right, isn't it?"

"You don't have to sound belligerent," Granny says. "You seem to forget, Rose and I spent the day entertaining your visitor." She puts down her work. "I don't like secretiveness—how long has this been going on with you and Graham?"

Rose inwardly groans. *I thought we weren't going to talk about him.*

"Nothing's going on. Graham and I are friends—we always have been. You and Daddy were the ones to invite him into our home. He's been through hell. You saw that yourself. I'd hoped we'd meet today. I tried to find him at the hospital, but he'd left."

"I gather you've been in touch all these years."

"Hardly at all during the war—he was in France. Messages rarely got through. I thought he was dead. Then he wrote—he'd survived. We hoped to meet this time in London—I should've waited yesterday at Victoria."

"You made the right decision, dear," Granny says quietly. "You're a married woman." She adds, "We ought not to be talking about this in front Rose."

"You started it. Anyway, Rose isn't a child any more. She saw us together a long time ago. Now she's met him and says she likes him a lot. Is it such a crime, Mother? I've never stopped caring about him."

Rose weeps. "I thought you wouldn't come back."

Mum crosses the room, pulls Rose to her feet, spilling the ruffled cat to the floor.

"Don't cry, dear one."

Rose pulls away. "Don't call me that . . . You got that from Graham."

"We're all overtired," Celia says briskly. "Come along, Rose, it's time you were in bed." Actions follow Granny's words: the raked fire, cushions rearranged, light switched off.

Mum holds her ground. "Before you herd us out, Mother, there's something else I want you both to know about today. It's premature but, frankly, it's the main reason I didn't stay in London . . ."

"I don't think I could stand anything more tonight," Granny says. "It's been far too long a day." She picks up the cat and sweeps out of the room.

—41—

THE SOUNDS AND SMELLS of Granny's house awaken her senses. For a while, she chases dream fragments; efforts to pin them into words—father, house, field. All evade the fast-vanishing story played out in her sleep. She kicks away blankets, yawns and stretches. Her knuckles rattle a cup and saucer on the bedside table. She'd almost forgotten: in the night, Granny came, bringing hot cocoa and a biscuit.

"Everything will look better in the morning," she'd said. "Drink up— it'll help you sleep." What a picture Granny was in her long nightgown, white hair loose around her shoulders. She must have heard Rose creep to the bottom of the stairs in the night, listening for her mother's breathing, afraid she might run off again to London.

Rose contemplates the empty cup with chocolate dregs and crumbs. "It won't do you one bit of good to worry," Granny told her.

Rose's last thought before sleep was: *Whatever she says, Granny isn't over the liking she once had for Graham Faire.*

The sound of clinking milk bottles and receding footsteps brings Rose back to the present. Time to get out of bed. She yanks back the curtains and opens the window, greeted by wafts of grass, earth, and something delicious in bloom. Dressing takes no time at all—a cotton shirt and pants.

No signs of anyone in the kitchen except for the lingering smells of toast and soapsuds. The open back door reveals a swath of green downs and cloudless blue sky. Granny is at the bottom of the garden, hanging washing on a clothesline stretched from tree to tree. Rose walks gingerly down the steps.

"Good morning, Granny. It's Saturday. I thought Monday was your wash day."

Granny laughs. "And ironing on Tuesdays, like the song? You have a good memory. Those were the days when life was predictable. Besides, I found muddy clothes on the bathroom floor."

"Sorry. I meant to pick them up."

" It's a lovely excuse to be outdoors. Now you're here, I could use some help—hold the end of this."

Together they twist moisture from a wet towel, sparkling drops falling into the grass. Granny says her wrists aren't as strong as they used to be, and she finds it too much trouble to drag out the heavy mangle. "You came just in time."

Rose retrieves clothes from the wicker basket, shakes them out, and hands them to Granny, who takes pegs from her apron pocket. They work together, and when done, hoist the sagging line with a wooden prop.

"I help at home," Rose says. "Mum soaks everything in the bathtub, especially Dad's work overalls. Then we hang it all outdoors. Last winter, clothes kept freezing on the line, and that's how we brought them in—stiff as corpses." Rose demonstrates with her arms.

They stand on the back step, surveying a limp row of clothing and towels. "Not even a breeze," Granny says. "The weatherman predicts thunderstorms tonight and tomorrow the heat wave will be over, temperatures back in the forties. We should make the most of the fine day."

Rose doesn't have to think very long. She saw the children getting off the bus yesterday with buckets and spades. "Let's go to the seaside."

Granny leads the way into the kitchen. "We could take a picnic. We'll see what your mother says."

Rose asks, "Where is Mum?"

Granny fills the electric kettle. Rose waits. Less than hour ago, she'd promised herself not to ask about her mother.

"She was up early this morning but went back to bed." Granny empties wet tea leaves into a basket in the sink and rinses the teapot. I heard her coughing in the night. It'll do her good to lie in for a while."

Granny allows Rose to skim the creamy top from a fresh milk bottle for her cornflakes, but refuses to let her splash a little in the cat dish. "Let him catch a mouse—lazy animal."

Rose takes her cereal bowl to the sink and rinses it under the tap. Another question she'd intended to stay safely in her head pops out. "Did Mum say what it was she wanted to tell you last night and you were too tired to hear?" She says this all in one breath.

Granny leans the broom against the wall, reaches over Rose's shoulder, and turns off the tap. "No, and I doubt it's any concern of yours."

"Do you think it was Graham who rang before supper?"

"For heaven's sake, what did I just say to you?"

There is an awkward pause and then, as though she regrets her sharp tone, Granny says, "Let's hard-boil some eggs for sandwiches." She hands Rose a sharp knife. "What I'd like you to do is cut a lettuce from the garden."

Rose easily finds the vegetable patch. Whereas at home rows of outdoor seedlings are only just appearing, here bright green growth has really taken hold. It's a relief to be in the sunshine, with a job to do, away from obsessing about Mum. On hands and knees in the dirt, Rose slashes at a lettuce so vigorously she knocks off a large snail. "I'm sorry," she says. She picks it up between finger and thumb. "Are you in there?" A long, grey neck emerges with horned head and antennae stretching this way and that, forever tethered to its house. She gently turns the shell right side up, fancying upset furniture, like the bombed-out houses they saw in London, sliding into place. Repositioning the snail in the leafiest plant she can find, she cautions, "Don't tell Granny."

Her grandmother meets her at the door. "Well done."

Mum is there at the table, in a white, sleeveless nightgown that has slipped to reveal a bare shoulder. She looks tired, Rose thinks, but at least she's here. She kisses her mother warmly on the cheek.

"What was that for?" Alice asks.

"Just to say good morning."

"I haven't told your mother about our plan for the day," Granny says.

Alice rises and wanders barefoot around the kitchen, opening and closing cupboard doors. "What plan?"

"Granny and I thought we could all go to the seaside—she's making us a picnic."

With visible effort, Alice turns her attention toward them. "The seaside? Wouldn't you rather be lazy and stay here?"

"I thought some sea air would do us all good," Granny says. "We can ride bikes. There's an assortment in the garage: if the tires are flat, we'll pump them up."

Alice tugs on a drawer handle. "It's six miles to the sea."

"You never used to think twice when your father was alive."

"You two seem to have it all choreographed," Alice says. "All right, but first I must have some coffee." She holds up a bottle of dark liquid. "Is this horrible stuff all you have?"

Celia says, huffily, "I keep that stuff, as you call it, for Archie. It's been a long time since any of us tasted real coffee beans. When did you acquire a taste for it, anyway?"

Rose relives the dark, bitter smell of Victoria Station coffee: how different to fit Graham's actual person to that memory.

Lost in her own reverie, Alice drifts to the window, her body silhouetted against the light.

Rose says, "I can see right through your nightgown, Mum. Did you buy it in London?" She catches Granny's shocked look, and blushes.

Alice ignores her. "I'm out of cigarettes. I think I'll go to the shop and, while I'm there, see if they have Nescafe."

Rose asks to go with her but is told to stay and help Granny with the picnic.

— 42 —

ALICE LEAVES DRESSED IN blouse and skirt, and a borrowed straw hat. Ten minutes later, Celia realizes she's out of butter. She hands Rose money and ration book and sends her off to catch up with her mother. It's a short walk past where the frowsy cat lives and a few yards beyond the church gate. The shop doorbell jangles. Mum frowns, "I thought I told you to stay home."

Rose explains about the butter while her eyes dart around the store. "Granny said I could buy crisps with the change."

Women with shopping bags jostle behind. Someone grumbles that Rose has jumped the queue. An old man serves at the counter. He takes his time, chatting with every customer, bemoaning the half-empty shelves, but it isn't it a lovely weather for a change after the terrible winter? He writes down each purchase: tins of baked beans, sardines, Spam, packets of jelly and Bird's Eye custard, and rationed items, carefully weighed and wrapped. Rose looks longingly at jars of boiled sweets.

"Coffee, Madam?" the old man says, as though Alice had asked for gold. "Are you on our waiting list?" Alice sighs, buys butter and a packet of Players and, prompted by Rose, a bag of potato crisps.

"Wait for me outside," she says. "I need to buy stamps." She points to a grille on the other side of the shop, where post office business is being conducted. Another queue waits patiently with parcels, envelopes, and filled-out forms.

"You can borrow stamps from Granny," Rose says, impatiently. "Let's leave, so we can go to the seaside."

"Do as I as say . . . It's crowded enough already in here. And don't go wandering off."

Rose settles on a bench in front of the shop. She fishes the twist of blue paper from her crisp bag and sprinkles salt. This simple action, and the first salty crunch, reminds her of all the packets she's shared with Annie, down to the last morsel. Annie, without doubt, would love to bicycle all the way to the sea, however many miles.

The steady clip-clop of hooves resounds on the road. The ploughman, leading his great horse, stops to greet Rose. "I see your grandma found you."

The horse snickers softly when Rose strokes his downy muzzle. He seems to remember her from the night before. She asks, "Where are taking him?"

"To the blacksmith—want to come and watch 'im get a new shoe?"

"I have to wait here for my Mum," Rose says.

The ploughman jerks on the reins and shouts, "Giddyup." In its own good time, the horse lurches forward and lumbers on its way.

A shadow blocks the sun. Rose quickly looks up from the bench. She hadn't noticed Gracie Miles coming along the road, shopping basket over one arm.

"Hello, Where's your Mum?"

"She's in the shop." Rose shades her eyes. Gracie's hair, out of rollers, forms a halo of tight, blonde curls. On her feet she has strappy sandals with a wedge heel.

"I was hoping I'd see her. Having a nice holiday?"

"Yes, thank you."

"Give us a crisp."

Rose reluctantly holds out the packet.

"Just teasing. See you in a minute."

The shop door clangs constantly—each time it's someone else coming or going. To Rose's keen ear, the chorus of "good mornings" are quite different from the flat Midlands accent she's used to, varying from Sussex brogue to the clipped tones her mother calls "The King's English." She stretches her legs, relieved to see Alice and Gracie emerge from the shop at the same time, talking and laughing.

"Blimey, that took a long time," Gracie says. "Move over, so we can have a sit down." Rose shifts to the middle.

Mum rips cellophane from a new pack, reaches across to offer Gracie a cigarette. "Blast," she says, "I meant to buy lighter fluid."

"Got a match?" Gracie asks a youth going into the shop. He lights their cigarettes, glances at Rose, and walks away, pocketing his matches.

Gracie says, "Cheeky lad—had an eye on Rose, didn't he?"

Rose glowers.

"Don't embarrass her." Mum laughs.

Squashed between them, Rose bats away the smoke.

Gracie says, "I'm assuming if it was bad news we wouldn't be sitting here—who's that you fired off a telegram to on a busy Saturday morning?"

"What telegram?" Rose conjures visions of yellow envelopes, almost always bad news. Like the one that came when Grandpa died.

Alice, ignoring their questions, draws on her cigarette. It sets off a fit of coughing. She gasps, "I really should give up these filthy things."

Gracie flicks ash. "Come on, Alice—I bet you were wiring your old flame. I heard he was around yesterday, skinny as a rail, poor man. Such a lovely looking chap he was in the old days."

"Shut up, please, Gracie. Does everyone have to know everyone's business around here?"

"I know; none of my blooming beeswax." Gracie pulls herself to her feet, "What are you two doing today?"

"We're going to ride bikes to the sea," Rose says. "Granny's making a picnic."

"Sounds just like something your grandmother would think up. I'll walk with you as far as her house. All the exercise I want on a hot day."

"Rose, carry her shopping basket," Alice orders.

"Thank you ever so much."

Alice takes Gracie's arm and asks her why she's limping.

"You mean, other than the fact I've put on two stone? War wound—shrapnel in my right leg. At least that's what I like to tell people."

Gracie winks at Rose who stares, curious if metal bits are embedded Gracie's leg.

"A bomb was it?" Alice says.

"No, a chicken."

Gracie stops for a breather. "When Bertie died I volunteered his old delivery van for the war effort, taking food and medical supplies to the hospital . . . often twelve-hour shifts. I enjoyed doing it—took my mind off missing my hubby. One night, I swerved at the last minute to miss a blooming chicken. The van ended up in a ditch. I cried because I thought Bertie would be furious I'd wrecked it. Then I remembered he was dead. And I cried harder."

"What happened to your leg?" Alice asks.

"Broken in two places—me in the hospital when they couldn't spare the bed or a doctor to set it properly. Or, for that matter, a tractor to pull the van out of the ditch. Anyway, end of Gracie as war hero. I suppose I'm embarrassed. The farmer was angry that I'd killed his chicken—said I'd deprived the country of eggs."

"It wasn't your fault," Alice says.

They resume walking. "But, you know," Gracie says, "I've an idea—apart from a few dents, the van's fine and there should be just enough petrol. The lad next door drives it sometimes and puts oil in. I could take us all to the seaside."

Rose says, "What about Granny?"

"She can come too. There's room, with a squeeze, for three in the front. Rose, you can sit in the back. I could do with an outing and a bit of sea air."

They arrive at Celia's gate. Gracie takes back her shopping, says she'll pick them up in half an hour. Alice goes to the house to put the butter away in the larder "before it swoons."

Rose discovers Granny outside the garage, bent over an upturned bicycle, tools scattered about. "Two of the bikes are okay but this one has a flat, and I'm trying to find the leak." Granny mops her brow with her apron.

Rose is dispatched to fill a bucket from the garden hose, and while she's at it, to replenish the birdbath. Within minutes, sparrows flock to the stone bath with a vigorous splashing and shaking of wings, scattering sparkling water drops in the sunlight.

"Annie and I were out on a bike ride one time," Rose chatters. "She rode over a nail and punctured her front tire. We were in the middle of nowhere. I had a repair kit but I'd run out of patches, so guess what we did?"

Granny smiles, "I love the way your face lights up when you mention Annie. Tell me—what did you do?"

"We found a run-over frog in the road, all flattened and leathery, glued it on, and pumped up the tire. Annie rode her bike all the way home."

Granny chuckles, "It's amazing how resourceful one can be in a fix." She holds up the inner tire. "I'm afraid there're more holes in this than a pincushion . . . and I'm clean out of dead frogs."

"Here comes Mum—maybe she'll have some ideas."

Alice makes her way across the lawn, carrying a tray with three glasses of lemonade. She calls, "Did Rose tell you, Mother? We're not going to need bicycles after all."

$-43-$

THEY SIT UNDER AN apple tree on chairs retrieved from a cobwebbed pile in the garage. "I'd no idea Gracie still drives that old van," Granny says. "I heard she wrecked it when she had the accident. Good thing she wasn't killed."

"It'll be quite safe, Mother," Alice says. "Gracie says she'll check the water and oil."

Granny sips her lemonade, her ankles crossed, sunlight dappled on her face. "I'm sure you're right dear, but I think I'll stay here. I haven't kept my promise to bring the shepherd home-cooked food. He works so hard in lambing season."

"What about the picnic?" Rose asks.

"Take it with you—there's a hamper all packed on the kitchen table. You were gone so long I gave up on the idea of butter."

"Should I stay with you, Granny? I'd like to see the lambs."

Granny is resolute: the three of them are to go without her.

"You always were stubborn, Mother," Alice says, taking out her cigarettes.

"That's like the pot calling the kettle black," Celia retorts. "Rose and I both heard you coughing last night, and still you insist on smoking."

"It's funny you should mention my cough." Alice sits up in her chair. "It relates to a woman I met on the train to London. I was about to tell you about her last night."

Rose's mind had been on the beach—what to wear since she'd hadn't packed a bathing suit—but the half-heard conversation puts her on alert.

Granny puts down her glass. "You have our full attention."

Alice holds the unlit cigarette between two fingers and wafts it as she speaks. "She was about my age and friendly. Right away she offered me a magazine to read. It was the slow train. I asked if she'd mind if I lit up, even though it was nonsmoking, as long as the window was open. She said okay, though I could tell she wasn't thrilled. Anyway, we started talking about her work as a respiratory nurse. I had a bit of a coughing fit, and she asked if I'd ever considered quitting cigarettes. I explained I don't inhale. I just have this annoying tickle in the back of my throat."

Granny frowns. "What did she say to that?"

"She wanted to know if I'd heard about the tuberculosis epidemic. There's talk of setting up mobile X-ray units round the country."

Rose vaguely recalls the units mentioned by Dr. Harris and the consultant. Her mind leaps to sanatoriums and heroines with bloodstained handkerchiefs. "Mum, does she think you have TB?"

"I haven't finished. I promised her I'd keep it in mind. Then, to change the subject, I told her about Rose's illness, which she found interesting."

"Any insights?" Granny's tone is slightly disapproving.

"Only that mild cases of polio are hard to diagnose. She'd heard of the specialist who saw Rose and was surprised he didn't put her in hospital. I said I thought it was because of our insufficient insurance. She says the only answer is National Health Service . . ."

"That's an awful lot to discuss with a perfect stranger," Granny says.

"What happened when you got to London?" Rose asks.

Mum's mind has floated off somewhere, maybe having second thoughts about the conversation. She comes to when Rose touches her knee. "Where did you go after the train?"

Alice flicks the lighter wheel and frowns. "We parted at Victoria station and I went to ring Graham. Honestly, Mother, don't make a face. I knew he'd been seriously ill and wanted to reach him. A man answered and told me Graham was back in hospital. I trekked across London on the Underground, only to find out he'd discharged himself."

"He was here," Rose exclaims. She pictures him ragged and gaunt at the garden gate with his staff and battered hat.

"So I heard, but not until I rang you hours later. I couldn't wait to leave that place full of sick people, but on my way out I passed a sign for Radiography."

"Ah, a chance to get a chest X-ray . . ." Granny remarks. "Surely, you'd need an appointment?"

"I thought I'd inquire at the desk. The receptionist was friendly and asked questions. Then she said if there was any possibility of pregnancy, I should not have an X-ray. It got my attention. I didn't know what to do."

"Good God in heaven."

"You don't need to react that way, Mother."

Rose throws up her hands. "Are you saying you're having a baby?"

"Would it be so terrible? Haven't you complained about not having a brother or sister?"

"I don't know, Mum. I still don't understand what you're saying."

"I thought you didn't like being an only child. Don't need to look so panicked. I've only missed one period . . . well, two actually. It's probably from all the stress."

The taste of lemonade and potato crisps rises in Rose's throat.

Granny says, in a calmer voice, "Does the father of this child know about the possible happy event?"

"Mother, I can't believe the mean way you said that. What are you implying?"

"Well," a voice says from behind, "sounds like a fascinating conversation. Is everyone ready for the beach? The van is revved up and raring to go." Gracie Miles, dressed in a red polka-dot sundress, offers a hand to Celia. "I hope you're coming with us, Mrs. Whitham."

Granny coolly shakes Gracie's hand. "Thank you, but I am going to stay here—the shepherd needs his soup."

Alice collects lemonade glasses on the tray. Gracie follows her to the house.

Granny remains in her chair beneath gnarled branches with bright green new growth. Rose wonders what's going through her grandmother's mind. She has shown only politeness to Gracie—no signs of reaction to Mum's revelation. Rose hesitates, unsure whether to stay or go. Granny firmly waves her away. "Bring me back a seashell," she says.

— 44 —

THERE ISN'T ROOM, AFTER all, for all three in front of the van, not without Rose sitting on the gearbox. She clambers in the back with the picnic basket, trying not to breathe in the smell of exhaust fumes and stale beer.

"Off we go." Gracie settles in the driver's seat. The motor chugs nicely. Bottles roll as the van lurches forward. They follow the winding hill out of the village. Rose strives to keep looking straight ahead while her body sways with the van's motion. The concentrated effort wards off thinking about Mum's latest news for more than seconds at a time. On they plunge, through narrow leafy lanes, red sunlight splintering through the trees.

They turn onto the main road.

Gracie calls out, "Okay, Rose?"

Alice glances back. "She's looking a bit green at the gills."

Rose clamps her teeth, waiting for her insides to settle.

"You should have told us, Rosie." Gracie rolls down the window; the damp curls on her broad neck barely stir. She changes gears. "Hold on, we're going to pass that army truck."

The van lurches forward. Rose leans toward the window in search of fresh air. Soldiers in the back of the truck gesture wildly; for a time the two vehicles run parallel. Rose closes her eyes, convinced they'll all die. When she opens them again, a soldier leans out, mouthing words. A bus appears over a rise. Someone screams—was it Mum? Abruptly, the truck slows and let's them pass. The sound of hooting fades.

"Crikey," Mum says, "that was exciting."

"Randy lot, those soldiers." Gracie settles back in her seat. "I miss the Yanks."

"Look," Mum says, "I can see the sea."

Traffic slows as they come into town. Pedestrians wander back and forth across the street.

"Let's park the van and walk to the beach, before you kill someone," Mum says. "Besides, I'd need to stretch my legs."

Gracie pulls to the side of the road and turns off the ignition. The van judders and stops. She stays sitting, hands on the steering wheel. "Mrs. Whitham didn't seem herself this morning. I couldn't help overhearing. Is someone in the family way? Like it was bad news? I know I'm supposed to mind my own beeswax, but . . ."

"Yes do, please, Gracie. I know you mean well."

"It's not Rose, is it?"

"Don't be absurd. She's thirteen . . ." Alice tugs on the door handle. "How do I get out of here?"

"I feel sick," Rose says.

Wrenching the door open on her side, Alice runs to the back. "Quickly, come out this way. Don't throw up in the van."

She makes Rose sit on a patch of grass near the pavement. The nausea passes but not the skittering thoughts. Rose blurts out, "Does Gracie think I'm pregnant?"

"Of course not, dear. Gracie's mixed up—her sister had a baby when she was very young."

A steady stream of trippers passes by; some cluck their tongues at Rose on the ground, her mother's arm around her.

"Too much peppermint stick?" one man asks.

Gracie comes around carrying the food, a string bag with towels, a magazine, and baby oil. She bends, revealing the deep freckled V of her cleavage, "Feeling better, Rose?"

The three of them join a cheerful throng making its way to the sea front. Gracie, in her sundress and wide hat, reminds Rose of a colorful beach ball.

"Can you believe this heat wave?" a woman says, walking with two small boys in tow, all three of them licking iced lollies. "Watch out, we'll pay for it later—back in our woolly undies next week."

"And no coal to put in the grate," another woman replies.

"I'll keep yer warm," a man shouts. Everyone laughs.

Suddenly the sparkling sea is before them stretching to the horizon. Rose had forgotten its vastness. The knot of people spreads out: some drawn to oompah sounds coming from a bandstand while others cross the road to a promenade, where there are steps down to the beach.

Gracie shows the way to an expanse of lawns and gaudy flowerbeds. She says, "I can't walk another step until I've had a cup of tea."

Mum puts down the picnic basket. "Looks like there's a stand over there where they're selling tea. And isn't that the ticket man for deck chairs?"

"When can we go to the beach?" Rose looks longingly toward the sea where gulls scream, stark white against blue, circling and coasting with the wind.

"We'll all go when Gracie's had a chance to rest. Let's eat our picnic first."

The two women settle themselves in striped chairs. Rose sits on the grass and hands out sandwiches—sliced hardboiled egg, lettuce, and salad cream. Gracie reminisces about Mrs. Whitham's picnics when she and Alice were young.

"She was always good to me," Gracie says. "Even when she thought I was a bad influence on your mother, she never gave up on me. Not like my own Mum."

Surf pounds the shore, sea birds keep up their persistent complaint, and from across the park there are sounds of tinny, discordant music.

"Look," Gracie says, "there's a fair over there. I haven't seen one of those since before the war. Here's a bob, Rose. Go and have a ride on the dodgems."

When Rose hesitates, both women urge her to go and have fun. "We'll be here," they promise.

In minutes, Rose finds herself caught up in a world of piercing music, cranking machinery, and screaming fairgoers hurled to the sky and back, around and around—anything to terrify. But it's Rose's mind that's in a whirl. She wanders in a trance, drawn to a merry-go-round, where solemn children circle by astride painted horses and zebras, lions, giraffes, and tigers. Parents stand beside them, waving. There's been no time to digest Mum's news about a baby—was that *really* what she said? Gracie's probably grilling Mum right now, wanting all the details. The shilling warm in her hand, Rose heads for the dodgems. On the way, she wastes sixpence at the Hoopla booth. She'd had her eye on a giant blue teddy bear, with the idea she'd win it for the possible baby. She worries now that losing was a bad omen.

Three times, Rose is outdone by a herd of boys rushing to claim a car. A dark-skinned gypsy man with broken teeth takes her money and the music starts. Sparks fly from the overhead wires. Rose steers carefully around the outside but almost immediately she's rammed from the back by one of the boys. She spins the steering wheel, only to be hit by another from the front. The boys cheer and soon all are in a hopeless jam. Precious seconds tick by. The agile attendant weaves across the rink and shoves them free. Rose evades collision, then bumps a car hard from behind. The driver, a boy with a pimply face, laughs and shakes his fist. The music stops and so do the cars. She climbs out and someone yells, "Stay for another go."

Rose shouts back, "I would, but I'm broke."

She walks toward the far exit, past sideshows and vendors. If only Annie were here. She'd have loved the rides. Everyone is with someone. Couples hold hands. Little children traipse behind their parents, pleading for one more ride. Boys and girls her age dart like schools of fish, from one attraction to another. When one moves, all follow in unison.

"You're such a lucky girl," Mum would say and scold her for not having more fun. Hurrahs ring out from the Show Your Strength booth. Young men, shirtsleeves rolled to show off their muscles, take turns hitting a peg with a hammer while their girl friends hold their coats. No one manages to drive the little puck high enough to hit the bell. She pictures her father, sledgehammer high over his head, fixing fences the day she thought Mum had run away. With his strength, he'd have no trouble hitting the puck clear off its stand. The thought leaves her in a muddle, wondering about Dad's back and what he'll say about Mum being pregnant, and whether he knows about Graham Faire. She sees a narrow gap between two booths and impulsively steps over ropes and cables to a grassless area, where workers have parked decorated, wooden caravans.

The abrupt quiet unnerves her. A skinny horse on a rope snuffles the ground for a few spilled oats. Rose approaches to stroke its nose. The horse jerks its head, lips curled, baring long, yellow teeth. A curtain flutters in one of the caravans. Rose has the distinct feeling she's trespassing. Only a few feet away, on the other side of the caravans, is the park. All she has to do is follow the fairground's outer rim until the sea comes into view. That way she won't get lost. Rose makes a dash for it, past an old man silently watching her from his open door.

"Sorry," she calls, as she hurries by on unsteady legs.

There it is again: the huge expanse of water, greyer than before, with the horizon as straight as if drawn with a ruler. Mum and Gracie are not where she last saw them. Nor are they at any of the tables around the tea stand. Rose scans rows of deck chairs, hoping to spy Gracie's red polka-dot dress. There is only one conclusion: they've left the park without her, crossed the road to the promenade, and gone down to the beach.

—45—

WITH THE EXASPERATED FEELING that once again she's been sent away, so grown-ups can talk alone, Rose pauses at the top of steps leading down to the sea. Rounding her fists, she holds them to her eyes, like field glasses. The sandy shore stretches into the distance. Pale bodies, in various states of undress and reddening skin, sprawl on spread-out towels and blankets. Sandcastles, with towers, moats, and tunnels, built at water's edge, slowly succumb to the incoming tide. Far out, Rose spots a swimmer, head bobbing and disappearing. Otherwise, only small children dash in and out of the surf, watched by dads, trousers rolled to their knees and knotted handkerchiefs to protect bald heads. She lowers her fists. For several seconds she searches the troughs of waves, unable to find the distant swimmer. But there he is again: arms moving in steady rhythm, still heading out to sea.

If Granny were here, she'd insist on walking to a quieter stretch. Mum wouldn't make Gracie do that—not with her limp. They'd be here, at the foot of the steps, where people change bathing suits under towels, not caring who's watching. But she sees no sign of them. Above the horizon, a line of clouds blurs the azure sky, creating a soft pink haze, blocking the sun. Rose takes one last long look, scanning the whole expanse: about a hundred feet away, a group has gathered at the water's edge, some pointing out to sea. Others are stopping too. With an uneasy gnawing in her stomach, Rose quickly descends.

She walks as fast as her legs will allow and reaches the knot of strangers. Mum and Gracie are not among them, but her instincts were right: there's clearly something very wrong. The waves are larger now, rolling in, bringing pebbles and rocks, crashing onto the shore. A woman stands knee-deep in the foam, her dress soaked, wailing. Her cry is terrible. Rose speaks to one of the sunburnt dads she saw from the steps. "What's happening?"

"It's her husband: he's swimming out too far. There are riptides."

"Who can help him?"

The man says, "The only hope is that motorboat over there: they're trying to launch it."

"I saw him," Rose says. "He looks like a strong swimmer."

"The problem is he keeps swimming in the wrong direction. It's all right for him—he's found a way out—but what about his poor wife?"

Before Rose can absorb what's been said, the woman flings herself forward into the waves. Within seconds, two men wade in, dragging her back to shore, though she fights them. Rose cries too; she has never seen such grief.

Next to her, the man who spoke earlier says gently, "You don't need to see this—as my wife says, 'This one will end in tears.'"

Rose takes one last look at the scene: grey water, grey sky, and menacing clouds overhead. She thinks the swimmer disoriented; that surely he would see the shoreline and turn back. Onlookers have backed away from the wife, who kneels, clasped hands held to the heavens, praying in a language Rose doesn't recognize. She prays too. The man says firmly, "Come along, Miss, there is nothing we can do."

The park has thinned out, tea stand closed, chairs upended on tables. The kind dad and his family have gone off to catch their bus. Rose assured them that her mother and Gracie would find her soon. She sits on a bench, swinging her legs, but stops when passersby shoot wary looks. A father follows with a small, crying girl on his shoulders. Others hurry past, pulling out warmer clothing.

"Typical English weather," a woman grumbles. "At least we had a bit of sunshine. Last time we were here they'd strewn barbwire on the beach . . . as if that could've stopped the Jerries."

Thoughts follow one after the other like the celluloid ducks Rose saw at the shooting gallery. Common sense resists scenarios of an accident, or Mum and Gracie off on a jaunt in the van. Perhaps this is what Granny meant about Dad wrestling like Jacob, expecting the worst. Thoughts switch to the swimmer, heading further and further away from dry land. "If you're lost," Mum taught her as a child, "stay there and I will find you." Rose thinks, irritably, *Maybe that was true when I was three. What's the point of staying still when Mum can't be trusted to be where she said she'd be?* To calm herself, Rose makes a plan. It's six miles to Granny's house. If Mum and Gracie don't show up soon, she'll walk, and if she gets lost, she'll stop and ask someone the way.

A cold drizzle has begun. Carnival lights shine in the gloom. Maybe that's where they went and somehow she missed them. Rose sets off, drawn to the hurdy-gurdy music. She keeps going, avoiding hawkers and the watchful eye of a policeman outside the fairgrounds. Only a few steps past the entry, she's swept up into a mob, noisier and more boisterous than the one earlier. Carried with the tide, she realizes there are others pushing back trying to reach the exit. Drizzle has turned to steady rain; sideshow owners are putting up tarpaulins and she overhears someone say rides will close soon for fear of lightning. Rose fights her way to the dodgems. Older boys than last time circle in pursuit of flirtatious, giggling girls. The smell of sparking overhead wires hangs in the air, incendiary, like bombs. But no thought holds fast in the hubbub. She sees no familiar face. Then, from the corner of her eye, a flash of billowing polka dots.

"Rose," a voice shouts.

A Klaxon sounds. The music stops. On the other side of the rink, an attendant helps pull Gracie out of the tiny car. Rose threads a way through the crush to greet her.

"There you are," Gracie says, her cheeks pink. "Isn't this jolly?"

"Where's my mother?"

"She's around, looking for you. I told her we'd find you here. The gypsies didn't snatch you away after all."

Mum appears, her face a mixture of annoyance and relief. "I've been looking for you everywhere."

"I was looking for you too."

"All you had to do was come back to where we were, like I told you."

"I did and you weren't there."

The music begins again. Gracie shouts over the noise, "It's my fault; I made Alice move into the shade—we were nattering and not minding the time. Sorry, Rose. I should've given you more than a shilling to spend— used to be thrupence a ride in the old days."

"I was going to walk back to Granny's house."

Gracie winks at Mum and they laugh. She reaches into her bag. "Look what I won for you: a blue teddy bear." Rose takes it, wishing she could hurl the ugly thing into the sea.

$-46-$

THEY ARRIVE AT THE van soaked to the skin. Rose looks out from the back, through fogged-up windows. Rain explodes on the roof. The whole interior smells of damp clothes and a curious blend of shampoo and chemicals.

"Hope we make it back before dark," Gracie says. "I'd forgotten a headlight's out and the heater's not working."

Alice peers ahead, wiping the glass with her sleeve. "I'd no idea it was this late."

They become quiet as they drive through rain-swept streets. A few pedestrians scurry along with towels over their heads, or wrapped around their shoulders for warmth. Others huddle at a bus stop with backs to the rain like cattle in a field.

They merge onto the main road. Motorists are beginning to turn on lights. In the flickering gloom Mum's profile looks pale. Rose puts a hand on her shoulder. "You're shivering, Mum."

"Can't stop my teeth chattering—I wish we'd brought our coats."

"We'll have you home in no time," Gracie says, "and into a hot bath. We can't have you catching cold in your condition."

Rose draws back. So, they must have talked about the baby. That's what Gracie means by Mum's "condition." It's really happening. She's said nothing about what occurred on the beach: the swimmer's distraught wife, and him far out in the rough, dark waves. She won't, not now. But in her imagination, Rose connects the tiny baby floating in Mum's womb and the man's body adrift in the sea.

Without warning, the van's front wheel hits a pothole, followed by the scream of scraping metal. Sparks fly. Rose bangs her knee hard against the seat in front. Her mother, thrown forward, steadies herself on the dashboard. "What the devil was that?"

"Sounds like the exhaust system. I'm going to have to pull over." Like the captain of a ship in murky seas, Gracie turns the steering wheel hand over hand, across the path of oncoming lights.

Rose sticks her fingers in her ears; but not enough to block out steel screeching across the tarmac and furious honking. Against the traffic, on the wrong side of the road, Gracie deftly swings the van through a gap in a hedge and comes to a stop in front of a building shrouded in darkness. She keeps the motor running. "That was lucky—hope we didn't wreck the hedge. All right, Rose?"

Rose squeaks, "That's the second time today I thought we'd all be killed."

"Gorblimey, Gracie, you're even wilder than I remember. Where on earth are we?" Alice rubs her wrists.

"It's the Black Swan—you remember. We used to call it the Mucky Duck."

"I see that now. Looks different—a bit run down. Stan and I came here years ago on his motorbike."

"I know the owners. I'll go round and have a chat. First, we'd better move this pile of junk off their lawn."

The van makes the same excruciating noises as Gracie eases it onto the graveled driveway and turns off the engine. She opens her door and lowers herself to the ground. "My clothes are so wet they're sticking to the seat," she grumbles. "I'll be back in a minute." They watch as Gracie's large frame squelches its way toward lights at the back of the pub. A dog barks continuously.

Rose shifts her legs to uncramp them and examines her reinjured knee. She speaks to the back of her mother's head, "I hope that dog doesn't bite her."

"Hopefully it's tied up. Besides, she'd probably bite back if it tried anything. I'd almost forgotten how tough she is." Mum laughs.

They sit one behind the other, like two partial strangers on a bus. At least that's how it feels. Not one thing about the last few days has been what Rose expected. This moment, alone with her mother, is the first since their walk from the river. Mum said nothing then about thinking she was pregnant. Yet she seems to trust Gracie.

"Was Gracie your best friend at school?" Rose asks.

"I suppose so, though she left before I did. After that we both worked at the riding stables. We had a great time exercising the horses."

"I don't remember Gracie when we lived in the village."

"She was around, about half the size she is now, and married to her Bertie. We weren't seeing much of each other."

Alice finds a rag. For several minutes she vigorously defogs the windows. A fruitless effort—outside, a fine curtain of rain continues to blur their view of the pub. More lights come on. "If Gracie doesn't appear soon, I'm going in. I'm chilled to the bone."

"I'm coming too." Rose had been quietly thinking of her own friendship with Annie. So much has happened since they last saw each other. Annie knows nothing about Dad and the sow, or Graham, or the baby. Rose leans forward and rests her chin on her mother's shoulder.

"I'm worried about the baby, Mum."

Alice leans her head back so their cheeks touch. "I know you are, dear. Me too."

They stay that way, listening to the patter of rain and occasional yelping barks from the dog.

$-47-$

GRACIE YANKS THE DOOR open. "The owner's name is Mike. His wife is Linda. They're both really busy getting ready for opening time. They say we can wait in the back parlor. Mike has a mate who's a mechanic and he's expecting him any time. I'd go under the van and take a look but I'm afraid it'd take an army to haul me out with my bad leg."

Alice opens the door. "I need to ring Mother."

"We'll ask if you can use the phone. Rose, before you get out, undo your plaits, and here, borrow my lipstick. I told them you're sixteen. I'm hoping they'll offer us a drink from the bar."

Rose stops to greet the dog: a bedraggled mutt on a chain. "Can't we let him in?" The dog whimpers. "He understood what I said!" No one listens. Inside, they are greeted by delicious smells of cooking.

Gracie says, "I'm guessing fish and chips on the menu tonight."

They are ushered into a tiny sitting room by a frazzled-looking woman in a grease-splattered apron and bristly hair rollers. "You can put on a bar on the electric fire, if you like." She closes the door behind her.

"It's almost as cold in here as it was outside," Alice says. She pauses at a mirror on the wall. "Where's that lipstick, Gracie?" She applies it carefully, straightens her damp skirt. "I'll be right back."

Gracie sits gingerly in a small armchair by the fire, stretching out her hands to warm them. "Good thing we weren't stuck out in the middle of nowhere," she says.

Rose wanders the room, examining sepia photographs of unsmiling family groups. Most of them dead by now, she guesses, even the children. It's a solemn thought. Casually, she positions herself in front of the mirror: her loose, damp hair falls around her shoulders, her cheeks reddened by the sun.

"I wonder who you resemble the most," Gracie says. "I can't say you look much like your dad—handsome fellow though, at least when I knew him."

Flustered that Gracie was watching, Rose asks, "Did you know my father well?"

"I was keeping company with my Bertie then—a jealous type. Anyway, I think your dad fancied himself a class above the likes of us."

Rose pictures Dad in his old clothes, hauling buckets of feed. "I never think of Dad as stuck-up."

"I expect he's changed. They say war's a great leveler."

The door opens. A man enters in a hurry like his wife, but with a cheerful smile. Alice appears close behind. "There's a much better fire going in the bar," he says. "I doubt the coppers will be around on a night like this. Besides, I heard this lady's in the family way. Come on in and make yourselves at home. How about a hot toddy to warm you up? Except for you, Missy: I bet you'd fancy ginger beer and crisps?"

"Yes, please." Rose feels a little crushed. He doesn't believe she's sixteen.

As they file out, Gracie whispers to Alice, "What did you say that put him in such a good mood?"

"Oh, I just smiled." More loudly, Alice tells them, "I reached Mother. She insists on sending Captain Oak to pick us up. She says the night's not fit for cats and dogs.

Mike settles them at a table and adds logs to a roaring fire. He busies himself at a long counter, arranging bottles and polishing glasses. Shelves gleam with pewter and brass. Linda has taken off her apron, put on makeup, and teased her hair into a pile of blond curls. Her high heels resound on the stone floor, back and forth, from the kitchen. The two of them talk as they work, occasionally touching as they pass one another with an affectionate pat or squeeze.

"First time in a proper pub, is it Rose?" Gracie asks.

Embarrassed she's been caught staring, Rose admits it is.

"I'm drying out. Can you see the steam rising?" Alice looks around. "I haven't been to a pub in years, but it has the same feel to it: warm and inviting. The only entertainment on the estate is a converted army hut where they have socials and serve tea, beer, and buns. Stanley refuses to go."

"I remember the Yanks crowding this place. That's why the road has potholes like the one we hit today—it's never been repaired. The convoys went right past here." Gracie laughs. "Maybe it's my imagination, but those Americans seemed taller than the English blokes. They had to bend their heads because of the beams. Yanks think they can import pubs like this back home, but they'll never do it."

"Not even with their English wives," Alice agrees.

"David Vale's fiancée married a Yank," Rose says.

Mum gives Rose a quick glance. "Where did you hear that?"

"He said . . ." Too late; Rose recalls she was eavesdropping.

"Who's David Vale?"

"He's the vet," Rose says. "He's nice. And he likes Mum a lot."

"You and your men, Alice . . . I do believe you're blushing."

Rose looks away, avoiding Mum's scrutiny. Through the rain-blotched window, headlights can be seen arriving. It must be almost opening time.

Rose needs to go to the lav. She leaves the fire's warmth and follows signs along a poorly lit corridor. Just as she reaches for the latch, a young man steps out. He holds the door. Rose sidles past, worried she'd entered the gents by mistake. Worse, the man follows her into the small room. "Excuse me, Miss, I nearly forgot my manners—what would my mum say?" He reaches past, puts down the lavatory seat, and with a cheeky grin says, "See you at the bar."

Rose bolts the door. She pees, then washes and dries her hands, wishing she'd thought of something cheeky to say in return. Back at the table, Mum and Gracie are deep in conversation. They scarcely look up.

Linda brings drinks on a tray. She smiles. "Sorry I wasn't more welcoming when you arrived. We're ever so busy. Mike says you're related to Mr. and Mrs. Whitham . . . They were very kind to us years ago." She hurries away.

As soon as Linda's out of earshot, Gracie remarks, "I thought you said it was your smile that earned us these drinks."

Alice shrugs. "I asked Mike to dial Mother's number." She lifts her glass. "Here's to our driver!"

"I hate to admit defeat." Gracie reluctantly lifts her glass. "But I'm afraid the van's about ready for the knackers. I suppose it's my way of hanging on to Bertie." There's a sadness in Gracie Rose hasn't noticed before.

"Surely the van can be fixed," Alice argues. "You said yourself it was the exhaust falling off. All that's needed is some wire . . ."

"And sealing wax and string." Gracie wipes her eyes, smudging mascara.

The room fills: a crowd, mostly men, gather around the bar. Blue smoke curls to the ceiling. Mum and Gracie take out their cigarettes. Their cheeks grow pink. Linda appears with three plates of fish and chips.

"These are on the house," she says.

Gracie and Mum protest they couldn't possibly—not with all the food shortages. Mike, watching from the bar, comes over, and he too insists. He says a couple of the lads will have a look at the van as soon as the rain let's up a bit.

Later, Mum says, "Who knows what good deed my parents did for them—Father was worse than Mother for giving things away. No wonder we were hard up."

"Remember the time," Gracie laughs, "when we stole back a box of your toys from a charity sale?"

"It seems funny now," Mum says, "but even Father was angry, as though we'd robbed the poor orphans in India. My sister Betty hid anything she valued in the attic until the sale was over, but, as usual, she got away with it."

"You have to admire Betty—she was resourceful."

Mum rolls her eyes.

"I bet Rose has done worse than that." Gracie slaps her knee. "Tell us, Rosie, what you get up to when Mum and Dad aren't looking?"

"She snoops."

Gracie roars, "The poor girl's gone all red. You were no saint, Alice Whitham. I remember you and those stable lads."

"Shut up, Gracie."

Mike appears with another round of drinks. "Compliments of those gentlemen over there." Two men with broad smiles and ruddy complexions raise their glasses.

"Oh, lawd," says Gracie.

Mum looks flustered. "Do you know them?"

"Vaguely." Gracie pats her hair. "Just wave and smile. Don't look so stricken, Rosie.

"I shouldn't drink this." Alice takes a sip anyway. "I worked those stables because I had to, so don't go giving Rose the wrong idea."

Rose sticks up for her mother. "Graham Faire says Mum mucked out stables to bring in money for the family, instead of going to secretarial school like Aunt Betty."

Gracie's blue eyes light up. "Did he mention me?"

"He only asked about Mum. He wants to see her . . ." Rose pauses. "Before he goes back to France."

Mum reacts as though stung, raising her voice. "I don't remember you telling me that, Rose." Heads turn in their direction.

Gracie leans across the table, looks briefly around her, and says, "I wish someone would fill me in. How is he, Rose?"

"For heaven's sake, do we have to drag her into all of this?"

"Drag me into what, Mum?"

"Graham had other friends in the village besides you, Alice." Gracie says. "Maybe he came back because he needs friends. There's still talk about the way he left, without so much as a forwarding address."

Gracie's face has changed from pink to bright red and she's breathing hard like someone in a race. She goes on, "As for Rosie, I remember what it was like when I was her age—nobody tells you a blasted thing but you *know* something's going on. It drove me mad, all the whispering about our Meryl . . . She disappeared for a year and not one person told me why."

Mom half rises, knocking the table with her knee. "You're not comparing me to your sister, I hope." Rose, grabbing her ginger ale, wonders if she should stand too.

"For heaven's sake, sit still. Meryl's got more guts than the rest of us put together."

Gracie's tone has an effect: Alice sits back down.

"The irony is Bertie and I couldn't have kids. Meryl gave up her baby and moved on with her life. We'd have adopted that little boy if we knew how to find him. Bertie and I often talked about it."

"I'm sorry," Alice says. "I didn't know."

Cheers burst out across the room. A game of darts is in progress. Rose, glad for the distraction, swivels her chair to watch. The young man she saw earlier stands poised, a feathered dart balanced between fingers and thumb.

"It's a bull's-eye, mate," someone yells. The victor circles the room, fists aloft. He stops: offers his darts to Rose. "Want to have a go?"

Rose hastily turns back to the table, steeling herself to be teased, but Mum and Grace are oblivious, staring into their drinks. Alice is first to look up.

"Let's not quarrel, Gracie. It's taken this long to find each other again. When the war was on, all any of us wanted was for it to be over and everyone safely home. But, you know, not everyone who went away felt welcomed back. You've made me wonder about Graham. Mother didn't exactly receive him with open arms. I lost my nerve and ran away instead of waiting for him at Victoria Station. Rose, tell Gracie what happened when he showed up in Celia's back garden."

Like chess pieces, Gracie moves salt, pepper, and vinegar to one side for a better view. "Start from the beginning."

In the background, the noise has intensified. People are still arriving at the pub, shaking rain from their coats. There's a smell of spilled beer. Rose's mind has been on the dart game, wishing she'd been more daring and at least given it a try. Mum and Gracie lean forward, waiting.

"At first I thought he was a tramp." And so Rose tells her story. It is the realness of what happens that floods back. She describes his height, the scraggy beard and his foreign-looking clothes that smelled of the river, and, yes, he is very thin. She tries to explain Granny's reaction: how at first she was quite cool, but then she fed him and allowed him to retrieve the blackberry wine.

Alice frowns. "I *knew* I ought to have waited for him in London."

"Well, you are a married woman." The jibe, like a hawk over a field, hangs in the air. Gracie turns to Rose, "Word in the village is you and Graham were in the church and you showed him your grandpa's grave."

"He talked about bluebells."

Rose despairs. Nothing he confessed that day can be shouted across the table over the din. Graham Faire, she realizes, has an effect on everyone. For her, it's a strange loyalty. "I don't want to say any more," she says firmly.

Gracie doesn't let up. "Did he upset you?"

"Only at the end," Rose says, reluctantly. "It was running late and he had to catch the bus, so he ran ahead to Granny's house. The telephone was ringing. It was you, Mum, calling from London. Granny was so cross he wouldn't give up the phone, she hit him on the shoulder with her stick, and he rushed off."

"Celia hit him? Did you know about that, Alice?"

"I heard him yelp. Next minute Rose was on the line, crying. I'd run out of change. Try to think, Rose: what did he say about France?"

Words have come out of her mouth. She's heard herself say them, but none of them convey the actuality of Graham, or what it was like to have him drop in and out of her life in a single day. Rose thinks, *I was crying because Mum wasn't there and I didn't think she'd ever come back.*

One at a time, she moves the cruets back to the table center. "I won't talk about it anymore."

$-48-$

THE DARTS SEMI-TOURNAMENT IS over. Someone picks out tunes on the old upright piano and a few people gather around. Lights are low. There's a steady buzz of conversation and the clink of glasses. The log fire sends out crackling heat and a couple sit in a nook close by, where couples have sat for centuries. Gracie is at the bar chatting to Mike's friend about the van, and Mum has gone to the loo. Rose sits at the table marooned. The tall, skinny dart player approaches, carrying a glass of frothing ale.

"Mind if I sit for a minute? I'm Jeff. Who are you?"

"Rose." She frees one hand for a brief shake. The other she keeps under the table, clamped between her knees. Close up, he looks older than first impression. She guesses eighteen or nineteen. His complexion is tanned and his palm calloused, as though he works outdoors. When he takes a takes a swig, froth remains on his upper lip. She giggles.

"You look like you have a white moustache."

He wipes his face. "I told you my mum says I have to improve my manners."

He tells her he's back from a trip on his father's fishing boat, where the catch was good. Now he's celebrating. He talks easily about being in rough waters and spending time hanging over the rail. "At least we weren't worrying about enemy ships, like it used to be when my dad would go out and me and my brothers had to stay home."

Rose begins to relax. "I like rivers better."

"Why's that?"

Rose tells him the sea feels too huge and unpredictable. "Today I was on the beach, and there was a man swimming far out and not turning back."

"He probably knew what he was doing; didn't he?"

"I don't think so. Or maybe he did. His wife . . . she was standing in the waves, crying for him to come back. I keep thinking about him. I'm afraid he drowned."

Jeff looks grave. "You take things to heart, I can tell. I could see you were the serious type, not wanting to play darts and fool around. Sometimes I come here for a bit of fun, but I think a lot and read. The sea scares the heck out of me too, but I'm in love with it. God knows if that man you saw chose the sea or it chose him. There are dangerous riptides. Could be some fishing boat pulled him out."

Rose is surprised by the mention of God. More people have gathered around the piano for a loud sing-along. She has to lean close to hear what he's saying and feels his energy, like he's still on victory parade with the darts.

Jeff says, "I'm Catholic. It's my mum who's religious. I think she believes it's her prayers to Our Lady that keeps the whole fishing fleet afloat. I've thought about being a priest—not so different from going to sea, in a way. Does that sound daft?"

Rose shakes her head. "That woman on the beach—she was praying so hard. Do you think God heard her?"

His eyes are serious. "I suppose God hears, but I've seen too many prayers go unanswered, however much my mum says the rosary. Besides, a lot of German mums on the other side of the channel were probably praying their hearts out too. The man you saw wouldn't be the first to drown out there, and he won't be the last. I have to make up my mind soon—priest or fisherman. I don't know if I have the sea legs for either one. What should I do?"

Rose doesn't hesitate. "Do what you think is best and not what anyone else says you should do. Somebody gave me that advice only yesterday."

"Thanks, I'm glad I came over to speak to you." Jeff looks up. "Here comes your mum and your auntie. They'll be needing their chairs."

This time when he offers his hand, Rose takes it willingly. "I haven't told them about the swimmer. I'm glad you came over." Jeff picks up his empty glass, nods to Mum and Gracie, and returns to his friends.

Mum sits down, her red lipstick renewed. "Who was that?"

"A fisherman."

"Cheeky chap," Gracie says, "but comes from a good family . . . too old for Rose, though."

Mum has spotted Captain Oak having a pint at the bar. He apparently was in no hurry to announce his presence. Gracie says she's going to stay. The two men who bought the drinks want to negotiate about the van, interested in buying it for spare parts. They've assured Gracie of a lift home.

"Are you quite positive?" Alice asks.

She's sure. Rose and Alice won't see her again before they leave. Gracie envelops Rose in a bosomy hug. "Don't be a stranger," she says. "You'll soon be old enough to hop on the train by yourself."

She and Mum tearfully embrace. "Let me know what happens . . . you know, about everything."

"I'll stay in touch," Alice promises.

Halfway across the room, Gracie calls over her shoulder, "You said that last time." The convivial crowd parts as she limps, hips swaying, toward the bar. "Anyone round here going to buy me a drink?"

Rose watches. "Mum, do you think we should leave her?"

"I think Gracie knows how to take care of herself."

They pause at the open kitchen door, where Linda is stooped over the sink, washing glasses. She has kicked off her high heels. While the two women talk, Rose looks around: every counter is stacked with dirty dishes. In front of the stove, a contented black dog sprawls on his back. Rose falls on her knees to stroke his belly.

"Can't stand the smell of wet dog," Linda says, "but I took pity on him, didn't I?"

Captain Oaks opens a large, black umbrella and leads the way. They pass two men in sou'westers inspecting the van's engine by torchlight. Rose realizes the younger of the two is Jeff and she turns back. He smiles, takes her arm, and steers her under the shelter of a jutting roof. "My dad and I are thinking of buying the van," he says.

"I bet Gracie would rather sell it to you than for spare parts. The van belonged to her husband, who died." Rose hesitates. "Good luck with your career decision."

He holds on to her arm. "Will you pray for me?"

"Yes, I promise . . . I won't forget."

He releases her with a quick hug. Captain Oaks has the car door open. She falls into the back seat, her heart beating fast.

Captain Oak's driving is slow and steady through pelting rain and strong winds. Gradually, Rose sinks back into the comfortable leather cushions, lulled into sleepiness by the swish of windscreen wipers and the captain's gravelly voice. At one point, the car stops. Rose looks to see the road partially blocked by fallen branches. A man in a yellow oilskin jacket swings a lantern, directing traffic. Mum apologizes for the umpteenth time for dragging the captain away from his nice warm fire, but Rose has the impression the he's rather enjoying himself.

Granny's porch light is on. Rose goes in first. "Granny, we're back."

Mum follows, calling, "Mother, you wouldn't believe the adventures we've had." Both the living room and kitchen are in darkness. Alice feels for the hall switch and snaps on the lights. "Mother, are you home?"

"Up here." The voice comes from upstairs.

"What's wrong—are you ill?" They find Granny, propped up in her high bed reading.

Before closing her book, she saves the page with a marker, and looks at them over her glasses. "Does there have to be something wrong because I decide to have an early night?"

Rose climbs up on the bed. "Oh, Granny, I missed you so much. We saw the sea, and there was a fair, and you'd have loved the dodgems. I have a seashell in my pocket, but I don't think you want sand in your bed."

Granny feels Rose's hands. "Good gracious, child, you're cold. Let me cover you with the eiderdown." Rose snuggles against Granny's warm body, the way she did as a little girl.

"We were soaked to the skin by the time we got to the pub. They gave us free drinks and fish and chips."

Alice, sitting at the bottom of the bed remarks, "Only because of their undying gratitude to you and Father. What did you do?"

Granny bypasses the question, and asks what happened to Gracie and the van.

"Did you see the lambs, Granny?"

"Yes, there were two, only just born, still wobbly on their legs."

"Any phone messages, Mother?"

"I was out most of the afternoon—the phone may have rung. No unexpected visitors, either. But I should warn you people are gossiping about Graham being seen in the village yesterday. It was a mistake to allowing him to go with us to the church."

Alice reacts sharply. "You mean because that's where all the gossips are? What spiteful things are they saying about him?"

"Graham has both friends and enemies here, I'm afraid. His reappearance has stirred things up from the past."

"What things from the past?" Rose asks.

"Your mother and I need to talk alone," Celia says, pulling back the eiderdown. "You may help yourself to a glass of milk and a biscuit, if you like."

Mum also insists, saying Rose should begin packing. They have a train to catch in the morning. She has pulled up a chair beside the bed. As Rose leaves, she hears Granny say, "How much did Grace hear of our conversation in the garden? Will she be adding to the rumors?"

—49—

It's early morning and Rose is up and ready to go to church. Mum announces she feels rather unwell and instead of fasting as Granny does before Communion, she'll stay back, have some dry toast, and pack for the journey home. Rose says she wants to go and will wait to eat. She and Granny join a few stragglers walking up the hill. The sun is so bright Rose shades her eyes. The temperature has dropped and a bitter wind ripples puddles left by the rain. Granny carries an umbrella against fat drops from overhead branches. Rose doesn't care and skips ahead. Every plant and blade of grass glitters like strewn diamonds.

In the night, a tremendous clap of thunder had awakened her. She lay listening as the sounds growled and reverberated around the hills, slowly fading. She thought about Dad's fear of loud noises since the bomb fell near home. At the first sounds of thunder, he tells her to run through the house, closing all the windows. Counting seconds between flashes and thunder, she'd wondered how he'd manage if the bad weather reached him in the North.

She revisits these thoughts, sitting near Granny in church. She prays, *Dear God, take care of us all.*

There's no music at the early service, no altar boy, and no heat. Rose buttons her coat, thinking the elderly congregation must be chilled to the bone. She observes the young vicar: the nervous way he runs a finger around his clerical collar; his highly polished black shoes peeking out from under long robes; the slightly ruffled hair of someone who may have woken up late; and a shiny gold ring on his left hand, which he waves when preaching. He concludes the sermon with an enthusiastic amen. Rose guiltily realizes she hasn't taken in a word of it.

Alone in the straight-backed pew, Rose watches as Granny goes to the altar rail and joins others receiving Communion. The vicar gives them each a wafer and then wine, tilting a silver cup so each person takes a sip, reminding Rose of how a mother might offer a drink to a young child. He repeats the same prayer as though he really means it. "Drink this in remembrance that Christ's blood is shed for thee."

Granny has seemed solemn ever since they entered the church. Rose wonders what she's thinking. Does the wine she drinks make her think of Christ's blood? Rose shivers. Memories are too recent of the blood-soaked straw around the dead pig, and the bloody way both her cat and the fox were killed. Rose squirms, conscious of her body; aware her period is due soon. Is that blood different from other blood? She tightly shuts her eyes to quash thoughts of Mum's body, her periods stopped because of the baby. How this all could have happened leads to questions Rose doesn't dare or want to ask. She takes up a prayer book and pretends to read it.

Granny returns to her seat and kneels to pray, burying her face in her hands. The vicar clears dishes from the altar. Watching him reminds Rose of her promise to pray for Jeff. Her heart skips. As a fisherman he could have a wife and children, but as priest his church wouldn't allow it. She pictures his lively, cheeky face and wonders what he'll do. "Maybe it's his fate," Jeff had said about the man swimming out to sea. She wishes she could ask Jeff if he believes in fate and, if so, what that means in her own life.

On the walk back, Granny takes Rose's and tells her how pleased she is to have had company going to church.

Celia buys a platform ticket and waits with them for the express to London. She has sent Captain Oaks away to attend to his hotel guests and says she looks forward to walking home. She ignores Alice's warning that the river path, after the rain, could be slippery.

"The river always soothes my soul," Celia says.

Rose thinks, *She must hear the music too.* "I'll miss you, Granny."

"I'll miss you, too. Look, here comes your train."

"Be careful, Mother," Alice says. "Don't turn an ankle."

"You're the one who needs to take care—write to me, dear. Let me know what's happening, or I'll worry."

The train pulls into the station, blocking the morning sunlight, hissing and sighing, spilling passengers. A porter unloads luggage onto a cart. Uniformed boarding school children, their holidays over, receive last-minute instructions from their parents.

"Pay attention, Rose," Mum says. "Hand me your suitcase."

"I love you, Granny." Rose throws both arms around her.

Granny gives a little push. "I love you, too. Now hurry, dear."

Barely settled in their seats, the train starts off again. Rose presses against the window and waves. Granny stands erect on the platform in her sensible coat, walking shoes, and old felt hat. She raises her stick in salute.

"Oh, Mum," Rose cries, "when will we see her again?"

$-50-$

SMALL STATIONS FLASH BY. Green hills give way to fields and hedges. Mum sits opposite in her red hat. She has the *Sunday Times* crossword on her lap, pen in hand, but her eyes are closed. The only other passengers are a silent young couple, sitting close together.

Rose's mind drifts to a memory that seems not just a few days, but weeks ago. Maybe it's the train's rhythm, but there is Duncan beaming, luring her to join him in the corridor, teasing that the tunnel would soon be upon them. Eyes closed, she goes over the scene: if he dared to try anything, would she have the nerve to kiss him back, *properly*, this time? What would it be like to feel his lips on hers? Or, imagine his tongue exploring her mouth, his teeth bumping against hers—like she's overheard from older girls in school. She shudders.

Mum touches her knee. "What are you thinking about?"

"Nothing." Rose moves her leg from her mother's reach.

Rose shuts her eyes tight again. There's no going back. Duncan is gone. She can no more summon him back than sheer willpower could stop the train rushing northward toward Victoria Station.

Rose frowns at her mother's retreating back from the bench, where's she's been left to mind the luggage, while Mum goes to the ladies'. There's a two-hour wait before the train leaves King's Cross. There's not enough money for a taxi this time, so they'll go by Underground. Rose distrusts Mum's promise to be back in two minutes.

A pretty young girl strolls by, dressed in a flared skirt and woolen jumper, ticket in hand, checking platform numbers. Their eyes meet and the girl smiles. Rose thinks, *I can't wait to be her age, traveling alone and not having to sit here, twiddling my thumbs, waiting for my mother.*

The bench groans. An antique woman in a black cloth coat arranges herself and her belongings on the seat, emitting a medley of smells. Rose grudgingly moves over. The woman produces a sandwich wrapped in greaseproof paper.

A few scruffy pigeons appear, pecking at crumbs—one has only one leg and hops around, lopsidedly. The old woman breaks off a crust and offers it to the lame bird, but a two-legged pigeon with a sharp beak snatches the bread away.

The woman scolds, "Get away, you greedy thing."

"How will that poor thing survive?" Rose asks.

"Oh, he's been around a while. He's a Londoner . . . getting by like the rest of us."

"They must come in from the roof." Rose points to the bomb-damaged glass.

"You'd think so, but there's been pigeons living in the station as long as I recall—tough old birds, like me." She chews thoughtfully. "You're too young to remember any of that."

"My mum and I came through London during the war to see my granny."

"Good thing you wasn't both killed."

Rose's memory holds scenes of twisted railway tracks, gas masks, and interminable waiting in darkened trains. She'd somehow kept the danger of those train rides in another part of her brain. The old woman's remark unnerves her. It's a relief to see Alice hurrying toward them.

"Sorry I've been gone so long. I've been enquiring about trains—there're delays on the Underground—we should leave now."

Pigeons scatter. The woman waves her half-eaten sandwich. "Goodbye, young ladies."

Long escalators suck them down into subterranean depths, hot air rising to greet them. When she was little, Rose was timid about stepping onto a moving staircase; now she goes first with her suitcase, riding past advertisements for ladies corsets, hesitating only slightly before striding onto level ground. Eager to show Mum she can find the way, she follows the colored signs through long, urine-smelling tunnels. They emerge onto a crowded underground platform. Mum was right about the delays. She finds a place to sit. Rose stands apart, absorbed in posters for musicals and theatre on the opposite wall. In Rose's imagination, there are darker, newsreel images of Londoners in subways, bedded on concrete, listening to bombs pound the darkened city above. The air feels stale, hard to breathe. More passengers arrive from the tunnels, crowding her close to the platform edge. The third rail lies cold and still, like a deadly snake. A draught of warm wind blows through the tunnel, swirling women's skirts and making men grab for their hats. A deep rumbling sound grows nearer.

Mum grips Rose's arm. "Be ready to push or we'll never get on."

Getting off is an equal struggle, and a relief to spill into the cavernous King's Cross Station. Mum straightens her rumpled skirt.

"After that, I need something to drink."

The station café displays a dismal array of potted-meat sandwiches, curled at the corners, and stale rock cakes. Mum brings tea on a tray and waits for Rose to clear away dirty plates.

Rose plops in a sugar cube and watches it dissolve. "I wonder if Dad's back is better."

Wherever Mum's mind has been, it takes seconds for her to focus: "I don't know how we'll manage if it doesn't heal soon."

"Was it okay to leave him?"

"We both needed a holiday. Look how much better your legs and feet are. He didn't want to come with us, anyway."

Rose asks cautiously, "What will Daddy say when you tell him about the baby?"

"I hope he'll be delighted. Aren't you?"

"Where will we put it?"

"We'll make space. I still have your old Moses basket in the shed. Anyway, a baby is not an *it*."

In the background, there's constant noise. Rose raises her voice. "Will he or she sleep with us?"

"I don't know how things will work out."

"You could go back to sleeping in Dad's room."

Mum takes out a compact and vigorously powders her nose. "I'm in no mood to discuss this now." The compact snaps shut.

A waitress appears with a trolley, collecting cups and saucers. Rose scarcely notices. "You were happy that day at Victoria Station, even though you and Graham were both crying. It's not fuzzy anymore—I can picture your faces."

"What on earth are you talking about?"

"I was only little, but I remember. I've seen the photos—you were holding hands."

The waitress takes her time, wiping the table with a dirty rag.

Rose continues, "Is that why Dad's so miserable all the time?"

"Excuse us," Alice snaps, "we need to get out." Mum gathers their bags and thrusts one at Rose.

Mum shoulders Rose ahead, between tables, and beyond the confines of the café. They stand face to face in the station, suitcases at their feet, and people streaming by. "Do you realize that woman was listening to every word you said?"

Rose hangs her head, "I'm sorry, Mum."

Normally, she would've been thrilled when her mother suggested watching a newsreel and cartoons in the small station theatre.

"Just you go," Mum says. "Come back in half an hour. I need some peace and quiet." When Rose hesitates, she adds, "I'll be right here, I promise."

— 5 0 —

AN USHERETTE WITH A torch directs Rose to a seat. She settles in the darkness to watch a black and white newsreel of ruined German cities. In the film, a woman with a cart picks her way through rubble, foraging for firewood. A male voice comments on the slowness of economic recovery. The scene ends with doleful music. Next is a Tom and Jerry cartoon—Rose flinches each time the cat is mangled, flattened, or blown to smithereens. A man plops down next to her, taking up space, though there are rows of empty seats. Rose leans away. The man laughs loudly at the cartoon, nudges her with his elbow as though to share the joke. She moves two seats over. The man stays where he is, apparently enjoying the cat-and-mouse antics. Rose slowly relaxes and joins in the scattered laughter around the theatre. Next moment, he's beside her again, stinking of tobacco. His shoulder brushes against hers. She shrinks away as he takes over the armrest. Once again, cheers go up when Jerry outwits Tom. The man's elbow slips over to her side. Rose pulls as far away as she can, trying to concentrate on the screen. The man removes his arm and takes out a bag of sweets, offering one. She shakes her head, hating the intrusion, smelling strawberry on the man's breath. She decides to leave as soon as the comic strip is over. The man again lets his elbow fall over to her side, slowly moving downward, then hard into her lap. On her feet now, Rose stumbles in the dark, forcing people to stand to as she rushes out of the theatre.

Scarcely able to see in the bright daylight, Rose searches frantically for her mother. Disorientated at first, she can't find the café but then she sees Mum sitting at an outside table in deep conversation with a man. Alice looks up and waves her over. From the back, the man appears a city type in a dark suit. A fedora hat sits on the table. Rose thinks angrily, *Why is Mum talking to a stranger?* Alice again waves in her direction and the man turns around. Blinking in the glare, Rose walks slowly toward them.

"Rose," Graham Faire says, "whatever's the matter?" He offers his chair. "Why are you trembling?"

She sits in a daze, unable to believe her eyes: Graham has cut his hair and shaved his beard. He's wearing a shirt and tie and a suit that looks too big for him. He asks, "Did something upset you at the theatre?"

"She can't bear seeing films where animals get hurt," Mum says.

"There was a horrible man," Rose mumbles. "I ran away from him."

"Did he touch you?"

Rose stares bewildered at Graham. "Why are you here?"

"Wait . . . I want to know about the man." Graham is crouched down, one hand on her chair, his intense grey eyes level with hers. Café noises and bustle clatter around them. "Try to say what happened."

Rose rocks back and forth, her arms tightly wrapped around her body—memory of the man's prodding elbow in her groin sets off a wave of revulsion.

Her mother says, "Couldn't you move away?"

"I did move," Rose wails. "Twice."

Graham straightens up. "I'm going to find that perverted creep."

"Don't go," Alice says, "there's so little time before we leave for our train."

Rose also begs him to stay, shuddering at the thought of Graham encountering the horrible man. She's astonished that he cares enough to want to protect her.

Graham relents, but insists he goes to order a drink for Rose.

Watching him leave, Mum remarks, "I've never seen Graham so furious. He's as thin as a rail. God knows what could've happened if he and that character got in a fight."

Rose asks, "What's he doing here?" She looks anxiously into the crowd, wanting Graham to come back, afraid the ghastly man will reappear.

"You let slip we were going home today. He took a gamble that we'd be on the morning train."

"I don't remember that. Granny and I heard you on the phone after we came back from the river—you probably told him yourself."

"I said nothing about our travel arrangements."

Reluctant to let it go, Rose asks, "Graham knew you were trying to reach him. Isn't that the whole reason you went to London?"

"Everything has changed. Don't you see?"

There's a table's width between them; it feels like a thousand miles. Then, like the slot at the ladies', the coin drops.

Rose says, "You'd realized you were expecting—that's why you didn't see him."

"I was in shock. Has it really taken you this long to work it out? Graham has suffered enough. In a few hours we'll be home and he'll be on his way back to France. Don't spoil these last few minutes."

There's a question Rose wants ask, even as she recoils from Mum's accusation of spoiling the little time left with Graham. "If he came to meet our train, why didn't we see we him?"

"He hit delays, like we did, on the Tube. By the time he reached Victoria, our train was already in. He didn't know for sure if we were on it, but took a taxi here in case he'd missed us. You should have seen him: in that borrowed suit and hat, and a smile as big as all of Europe."

"I see him coming," Rose says. "How funny his face looks—half white where he shaved off his beard. And he's wearing different glasses. He doesn't look like a tramp anymore."

Graham sets down the lemonade and a straw. "You need to drink this, Rose. You've had a nasty shock."

Alice says, "Our train goes in thirty minutes."

The three of them sit at the café table. Rose sips her drink. Seeing Mum and Graham together brings to mind the time long ago. They are at ease, Rose thinks, as though in a dance—but she's afraid. They're like the fire at home that burns bright a moment before it goes out. Graham sees her watching and smiles.

"I feel guilty—I must have frightened you, appearing unannounced at Celia's."

"I wasn't afraid," Rose says truthfully, "once I realized who you were."

"It amazes me that you remember. I met soldiers in the war who carried photos of loved ones and, at any excuse, brought them out, showed them around. I only had a memory. I'd tell them about this little fair-haired girl and her beautiful mother. I pretended you were mine. In my delusion, there were times I believed you really were, and that you'd both be waiting for me after the war."

Mum smiles, remembering. "You wrote beautifully about how you felt. I thought of sending photos but I couldn't be sure they'd reach you."

The light catches the gleam of her gold ring as their fingers intertwine.

Graham gently removes his hand. "It's hard to justify myself. In the midst of war, rules don't always make sense. Any of us could die in a moment. If there was love at all, one held on to it for dear life. I adore your mother, Rose, but it's wrong of me to make claims on her, or you."

Mum lifts Graham's wrist to look at his watch, then checks her own. "Why are you telling Rose all this?"

"Because I want her to know her mother is loyal in every way. These are the things I love about her. I concede defeat—something I should've done years ago when she chose your father."

Mum shakes her head and says to Rose, "If only you knew—if there's any loyalty left in me, it's for Graham. He's my best friend. But you and I are going home. It isn't Dad's fault. You mustn't think that. Sometimes we don't know whom we love until it's too late. It's not the life your father would have chosen and the farm wears him down. I'll talk to him: maybe we can work out a better way."

The three of them walk slowly toward the platform gate. Graham carries the suitcases. He sets them down. "Time to say goodbye."

Mum hands Rose her ticket, "Find us seats on the train—I need to talk to Graham before we go."

"Don't make me." Rose thinks: *I know Mum. She'll never tear herself away—not after all that talk about love.*

"I'll be there in minutes."

Rose pleads with Graham. "Suppose I see that ghastly man?"

He gently places his hands on her shoulders. "Look, dear one, we need this time. I promise she'll be on the train."

"I'll wait over there, by the luggage cart," Rose says. "I won't bother you. We'll get on the train together, won't we, Mum?"

Beyond the gate, the great steam engine sighs, emitting billowing clouds of vapor. The ticket collector waves people through. Graham instructs Rose, "Stay where you are." He leads Alice a few feet away and turns her face to his.

Rose leans against the luggage cart; afraid if she looks away they'll disappear. Graham has Mum's face cupped in his hands. She is crying. Cripes! They're kissing and everyone's staring.

"Better move yerself, young lady," a porter shouts, "unless you want a spin around the mulberry bush."

"Mum," Rose calls, "hurry up."

—51—

In the end, there is a big rush. Graham pushes them through the gate with their luggage. The ticket collector bars him from following. When Rose looks back, Graham waves her on. "Hurry," he shouts. She follows his tall, thin frame until he's gone from sight. Mum, beside her, says, "Oh Rose, how can I bear it?"

They struggle into the nearest carriage, where passengers grudgingly make room. Alice sways with the train, stuffing their bags into already crammed luggage racks.

"Mind my hat," a woman says.

"I'm not touching your hat."

Rose says, "Where's your red hat, Mum?"

Alice puts her hand to her head, "Damn, I've lost it."

Minutes after they're all settled, Rose needs to go to the toilet. Their late arrival has caused enough fuss and bother. Better to sit still and not cause a disturbance. Every bump and motion makes any thought other than her bladder impossible. Mum frowns as Rose tugs on the carriage door.

In the tiny, cramped lavatory, Rose balances on shaky legs to avoid contact with the seat. She flushes and takes two unsteady steps to the tiny washbasin. Her face wobbles in the distorted mirror."

Someone knocks. Rose hastily dries her hands on a grubby towel. Then she hears Mum's voice. "It's me."

Rose emerges. "It's smelly in there. Someone peed on the floor."

"Wait here. I might need your help."

The train races through miles of rain-drenched London suburbs. Drops of water form and slide down the windows, leaving sooty tracks. Rose clutches the brass rail, at the same time keeping guard. Mum's been in there a long time.

The door opens a crack. "Bring me sanitary towels—they're in my suitcase. Hurry."

In the carriage, Rose reaches for the case. The train lurches and she staggers. All eyes are watching—except for one man who never lifts his eyes from the book he's reading.

"Here we go again," the hat owner says.

Rose is certainly not going to search for Kotex with everyone looking. The case bumps against knees as she hauls it into the corridor. Crouching, she pops open metal fasteners and searches through Mum's clothes and underwear. All the time, a thought hums in the back of her mind.

A boy, in short trousers and school cap, stops to gawk. Rose reacts: "What are you looking at?" He leaps over the case and snags a stocking on his shoe. "Now look what you've done." Rose holds up the torn nylon. He scuttles, scarlet faced, down the corridor, while she stuffs sanitary pads under her jumper and relocks the case.

Mum says she can't come in—there isn't room for them both. Peering through, Rose glimpses water in the toilet, stained red. It dawns: "I didn't think you could get your period when you're pregnant."

"Usually you don't. Stay there." Mum locks the door.

Rose keeps up her vigil. Her mind flits through bits she's gleaned from girls at school: periods, babies, and sex. Mum is bleeding. Annie's aunt had a miscarriage. In a panic, Rose remembers talk about "blood everywhere." She leans against the door, feeling the vibrations against her cheek. She calls, "Mum, should I pull the emergency cord?"

The commotion of their return to the carriage and restowing of suitcase elicits more complaint. Mum has said absolutely not to the emergency cord idea or that Rose should go in search of the guard. Instead, she insists all she needs is to sit down, since her head's a bit woozy. Rose sits opposite and watches her mother's face grow ashen. Annie's story about her aunt returns more vividly. According to Annie, she nearly bled to death.

Twenty minutes pass, Rose as watchful as a hawk. Her mother stirs and pulls her coat collar up to her chin. Rose reaches for her own coat from the rack and wraps it around Mum's knees.

"It's chilly in here," Mum says.

"It's you that's cold. Your hands are freezing." Rose leans forward and swaying with the train, she tries to warm her mother's hands with her own.

"I'm seeping through to the seat. Get me a newspaper or something to sit on."

"Please, can I use that?" Rose plucks a folded newspaper from a dozing woman's lap. Arms around Rose's neck, Alice attempts to stand. Blood trickles down her legs and pools on the floor.

"Good Lord, the woman's hemorrhaging." The sole male passenger throws aside his book. "Everyone, make room for her to lie down."

The hat woman jumps to her feet. "What a mess . . . Who are you to give orders? It's just a heavy period—menopause, I bet."

"I'm a doctor: I've been watching and she's obviously in trouble." He turns to Rose. "Has your mother done something to herself?"

Mystified, Rose says, "She's going to have a baby."

"Stay back, everyone, and give her some space. Someone fetch the guard. We'll have to get her to hospital." He barks at Rose, "I need you to stay here. Look in your suitcases and find soft clothing we can use to staunch this. And hand me down my black bag."

The doctor continues giving orders. He shouts at Mum, asks her name, and when did the bleeding start? "Did you do this to yourself, Mrs. Gray?"

"I'd never do that."

"Rose," the doctor says, "I want you to sit so Mother can put her feet on your lap. That's right, rub them."

Alice says weakly, "I'm so sorry to be a bother."

The guard arrives, takes one look, and gives directions to move passengers and curious onlookers further down the train. He says to the doctor, "The nearest hospital is Woolston. I'll radio ahead for an ambulance."

More orders: blankets, emergency supplies, and a cup of hot sweet tea.

"Who's meeting you?" the doctor asks.

Rose realizes she doesn't know.

Mum mumbles, trying to say something.

"Don't talk." He asks Rose, "Who's at home?"

"My father—we don't have a telephone."

"They'll help you at the station." The doctor looks at his watch. "Your mother will be taken directly to hospital."

"I'll go with her."

"They won't let you—she needs immediate medical attention."

"What will I do?"

"You're a very grown-up young lady. You'll manage."

"Is Mum going to be all right?

"She'll need a transfusion—let's pray the hospital has her blood type."
Mum moans.

"Hang on—we're nearly there, Mrs. Gray."

For the first time the doctor comes into focus: severe blue eyes, thinning blond hair, about Dad's age, but trimmer. His suit jacket lies, one sleeve inside out, flung on the opposite seat, along with his book.

"I'm on my way to a conference in York," he tells Rose. "I won't be getting out at your station, except to make sure they're expecting you. I'll go now to consult with the guard. Whatever happens, don't allow your mother to move."

He packs up his black bag and puts on the jacket. He leans over Mum. "Mrs. Gray, did you hear what I said to your daughter?"

Mum flutters her eyes open, closes them again. "Yes, thank you, Doctor."

He lingers, feeling her pulse. "The train's slowing. I'm going to make sure the ambulance is there and hand your mother over to them. He gives a quick smile.

"We'll be there soon, Mum." Rose kneels beside her. "Don't go to sleep—I can see the church spire. We're almost there."

It amazes Rose the way the doctor trusts her to stay here alone with Mum. She strokes her mother's forehead, praying silently, as though her own strength can somehow be transfused. "You're going to be all right. I know you are." *But*, she thinks, *I don't really know . . . Please God, help me.*

Alice opens her eyes, struggles to sit up, her voice scarcely more than a whisper. "I told him, Rose."

"The doctor says you mustn't move."

"Graham knows I'm pregnant . . . He was angry that I hadn't told him right away. He says he doesn't know about us anymore." She reaches for Rose's hand. "Have we hurt the baby? I really wanted it, Rose; you know I did."

"We talked about finding the Moses basket." Rose pictures Graham forcing them to run for the train. "He didn't seem angry . . . I think he hated saying goodbye. Graham loves you . . . I was there when he said it." Suddenly, with all her heart, Rose wants this to be true.

Mum's hand slackens in hers, her breathing fast and shallow; she doesn't respond when Rose gently shakes her shoulder. Brakes screech as the train slows into the station. The carriage door slides open. Within minutes, two male ambulance attendants have taken charge. They fire questions at Rose: name, address, next of kin? One of them, taking Mum's blood pressure, says, "We have to move her right away—she's fading fast."

$-52-$

ROSE STANDS ON THE platform, luggage in a heap. The siren wails as the ambulance drives away. The stationmaster said a policeman would come to discuss getting word to her father. The guards shout to one another as they unload and reload the train for its journey to York. Mum's eyes were closed, her pallor the color of the grey blanket they'd wrapped her in.

Beyond the station buildings a crimson sunset spreads across the sky. Sounds of the departing train are further and further away. The vibrations along the steel rails gradually cease. The stationmaster has disappeared into his office, grumbling about a delayed schedule and more trains waiting out there on the tracks for signals to change. "The police are very busy," he'd said. "You better wait there and keep a lookout."

Every time she hears a car, Rose runs to the station entrance. No vehicle appears that resembles a black and white police car. Partly relieved, she returns to the luggage. A thought nags, barely formed. The doctor's stern words to Mum: "Did you do this to yourself?" People gather on the platform. Rose frets: *I can't wait much longer.* A plan begins to take shape in her head.

"If you leave them, Miss, you can't retrieve anything until tomorrow." A weary female attendant at "Left Luggage" hands her the stubs, pulls down shutters, and hangs a "Closed" sign. Rose panics—should she have done that? Clutching her mother's handbag, she walks out to the station lobby and stops in front of a map. It takes several minutes to locate the county hospital on the far side of town. In the dim light, street names are barely readable. "Look for the scale," her geography teacher says. Rose measures with her thumb—two miles, at least. She peers more closely and locates St. Bede's—the spire will be her landmark. First, she must turn in the direction of the fading sun.

A voice behind her enquires, "Do you need help with directions?"

She turns to see a smiling face. "Mr. Vale," she cries, "Mum's been taken to hospital."

David Vale enfolds her in his arms as she weeps against his chest. "There, there, don't cry," he says, patting her back. "I'm here now."

The vet had already met an earlier train. "I wasn't going to come back, but something told me I should—I'm around animals so much; it's like I've developed a sixth sense." They are on their way to pick up Dad. Cars ahead move in fits and starts. "There's been a bus accident on the main road," he says. "That's probably why the policeman didn't come."

When she told David what had happened, he went right away to consult the stationmaster, who was in his office having a cup of tea. Rose waited as calls were made. David came out and said they must fetch her father and then go to the hospital. No news about Mum except she's in the casualty ward. "I gave the guard a piece of my mind," David says. "Leaving you alone like that."

It's quite dark beyond the town as they climb the long hill to Rose's house. David talks in his quiet, soothing voice. "I nearly brought Winston but he looked so comfortable in front of the fire I let him be—all worn out, he was, from chasing a rabbit."

Rose barely makes out his profile in the dial-lit car.

"Look, you can see the lights of your house . . ."

Rose tenses. "How's my father?"

"He's been better. His back still troubles him. The lad has been a help doing the heavy work. Stanley's going to be right upset when he hears about Alice."

Tentatively, into the darkness, Rose says, "Did you know about the pig . . . ?"

"You mean the sow he put down."

"He shot it."

They have stopped outside the house. "Don't be too hard on him, love. He feels bad enough as it is . . ." He turns off the engine. "I'll go get him."

She's glad he told her to wait in the car, dreading going into the house with Mum not there. At first everything is pitch-black. Shapes emerge: bats thread in and out of shadowy farm buildings; the glasshouse roof reflects a hazy moon. If Moggy were alive, he'd have darted from under the bushes, ecstatic that she was home. Additional lights go on in the house; shadowy figures of the two men move from room to room.

They're turning off the lights—here they come. Dad will want to be in the front seat. Seeing him lock the back door and walk resolutely toward the car, Rose tries to imagine what he must be feeling, hearing that Mum is ill, taken off the train on a stretcher, and now in hospital. Like a stone, the reality of it all sinks in. Rose scrambles into the rear of David's car.

"Here you are." David hands her a small paper bag. "I brought you a hunk of bread and cheese—heaven knows when you last ate."

"I'm not hungry . . ."

The car bounces as Dad eases himself into the front seat. "Hello, Rose." His voice is subdued. Earthy smells mix with the sharp aroma of mothballs. He's wearing his tweed cap and sports coat. She nibbles stale bread—David insists at least she try to eat. He is quiet too. Sitting behind them both, Rose thinks, *I've never seen Dad drive anything but a tractor, and I never saw him on his motor bike.*

She speaks to the back of their heads: "I hope Mum's all right . . . The doctor said they'll need to match her blood type." She wonders if they have heard. "Dad?"

With a painful grunt, her father twists toward the rear.

"Did you know about this, Rose?"

"You mean Mum expecting? I don't think she knew herself until we were at Granny's house." Rose becomes quiet, withdrawing into confused memories.

Dad shifts again, facing forward. It's obvious his back hurts. He addresses David. "How did you get involved in all of this?"

"As I told you, I went to meet them at the station. When I dropped them off last week, Alice said they'd be back today. She wasn't sure which train."

Rose listens to the hum of the wheels on the tarmac. They reach the center of town, riding through lit streets, past the cinema and library, which makes her think of Annie.

"I hope those doctors know what they're doing," her father says.

"You'd be surprised, Stanley; medicine has changed since before the war."

"They've had enough practice—those poor buggers back from the front."

"Medics saved my life," David says.

Traffic has slowed to a crawl. Rose spots signs for the hospital. Everyone appears to be going in the same direction. David pulls over to let an ambulance go through.

Rose silently grumbles. She'd have been there an hour ago if she'd walked. Mum must wonder why she hasn't come. She leans forward. "Please, let me out. I'll run ahead."

David Vale angles the mirror, speaking to her reflection. "We're almost there. I'll drop you and your dad outside Casualty."

"One of the ambulance men said they had to get Mum there right away, that she was fading fast."

"Nobody told me that," Dad says.

The road clears. David accelerates and the car jerks forward. They pass low hospital buildings, the windows rectangles of dim electric light. Rose imagines rows of beds, people maybe dying.

"Oh Mum," she moans softly.

"Alice's strong—she'll pull through, won't she?" Stanley says.

"They'll be working on her right now," David says. "Here we are. Looks like there are a lot of police around—must be because of the accident." He lets them off.

"Aren't you coming in with us?" Rose asks.

"I have to park. I'll find you."

David was right: the place is crowded with accident victims and relatives. Rose follows her father to the front desk. A woman says a bus went off the road—so far no fatalities but several injuries. A surgeon will examine Mrs. Gray. Stanley's signature may be needed. She refuses to give more information and asks them to step aside.

"You don't understand. I insist on seeing my wife—where have you put her?"

"I told you, she's being attended to—someone will come and speak to you. It's very busy here." The receptionist's expression hardens when Stanley shows no signs of moving. Her eyes dart in the direction of a nearby policeman. Rose tugs on Dad's jacket. He reluctantly follows to the waiting area but remains standing, his eyes fixed on a row of curtained cubicles on the room's far side.

Nearby, a young boy with his mother clutches a wad of bloodstained gauze to his forehead. A strong smell of antiseptic pervades the air; people appear dazed, speaking in muted voices, their movements slow, waiting to be told what to do. A nurse, her shoes squeaking on the polished floor, enters one of the cubicles, revealing a white-coated figure bent over a patient. The nurse quickly closes the curtain.

Rose says, "Do you think she's over there, Dad?"

He sits. "Haven't the foggiest. Talk about what happened on the train."

She pictures the wild dash for the train, the scene in the corridor outside the toilet and her search for sanitary napkins, the shocking sight of blood in the lavatory bowl, and later, pooling on the carriage floor.

"Just tell me what happened, girl. Did she suddenly faint or fall down?"

Rose recoils from his impatience.

"Mum started bleeding on the train and it didn't stop. A doctor saw what was happening and helped us. He arranged for the ambulance."

"Did you know this doctor?"

"No. He was on his way to York. He left me to take care of Mum in the carriage. And I did, until they came."

"Well done."

David joins them. "What did you find out, Stanley?"

"Alice is here, all right, but they don't tell you anything. She might need an operation. Nobody seems interested in anything except the bus accident."

"I just spoke to a policeman outside. More hospital staff has been called in, which seems like overkill. The policeman agrees, but he says but there hasn't been an emergency on this scale since the war."

"Where does that leave Mum?" Rose asks.

"I'm sure she's being taken care of right now," David says.

"But you don't know. Maybe they shunted her off to one side."

Rose's focus returns to the cubicle. No one has emerged. Pretending to tie her laces, she bends enough to peek under the curtain: a man's polished shoes and grey trouser cuffs, and a nurse's white lace-ups—some person must be receiving a lot of attention.

"I have a feeling Mum's over there. Can't we look?"

A woman nearby says, "They won't let you. Strict hospital protocol."

Rose glowers. *Who asked you?* she thinks. The woman's son, dabbing at the cut on his forehead, rolls his eyes.

Rose wants to scream. Her father and David are doing nothing. "Can't either of you make them help us; at least tell us where Mum is, so we can go to her?"

"You have a go, David," her father says. "You're a vet."

"I'll try, Stan. Remember, my job's treating animals. They are much more reasonable."

Rose follows David's progress through crowds to the reception desk. An imposing figure in nursing uniform blocks his way. David engages in what appears to be intense, head-to-head conversation. Red in the face, the usually mild David Vale clenches his fists, but gets nowhere. He meekly walks back. Rose turns to her father and shakes his arm. "Dad," she says, "why are you just sitting there?"

Her father doesn't move. She pushes on his arm again. "We have to find Mum."

The room is filled with mostly elderly men and women, clutching their belongings. They look disheveled and lost. A lady in a pink coat trundles an urn of tea. Rose thinks how helpless the old folks look. Granny would never put up with this. She slings her mother's handbag over her shoulder and walks briskly toward the cubicle. The enormous nurse in blue and white uniform steps forward. "This zone is for medical staff only!"

"I'm looking for my mother." The nurse turns away as someone asks a question. Rose slips past, reaches the cubicle and parts the curtains. She screams at the sight of her mother under a thin sheet, her deathly pale face contorted, body violently twitching. A doctor and nurse lean over, adjusting tubes attached to their patient's rigid arm, the hand, with its thin gold ring, in a tight fist.

The big nurse pushes in front, blocking Rose's view. Glancing up, the doctor says, "Matron, we need your help—right away."

Rose screams, "Mum!" The young doctor, his red tie neatly tied, a biro clipped to his white coat pocket, orders in a steely voice, "If you want me to save your mother, you'll leave now."

Forced outside the curtain, Rose pleads, "Mummy, don't die."

People arrive, telling her she must be quiet, coaxing her away. She refuses. A policeman intervenes, helmet tucked under an arm. "Come along, miss," he says kindly. "The public is not allowed in this area."

David is suddenly there, taking her arm, but she pushes him away. "Rose," he says, "come with me—we found out where your mother is!"

Rose points, "She's in there. I saw her. Her face was all screwed up. I think she's having a fit. I know she's dying."

"Move along," the policeman says, "or I'll have to issue a summons." He takes out his notebook. "Are you this young lady's father?"

"No, I'm a doctor." David says. "Please step out of the way."

"Sorry, sir—she was causing a disruption."

"Come with me, Rose. Your dad's waiting."

She stares at the closed curtain. "Mum's in there. I saw her."

"Some poor person is in there, but I promise you, it's not your mother. Follow me, if you want to see her before they take her to the operating room."

—53—

It's close to midnight before David Vale drives them home. The men chat about everyday concerns. Dad has made no comment on the surgeon's report, other than to say the doctor was in too much of a hurry to answer questions.

Rose listens, thoughts churning, doubting what she'd heard the surgeon say. She can't believe the way the two in front are saying nothing about what they all have been through.

"I don't know how much longer I can keep going," Stanley is saying.

David's old car groans up the steep hill. I'm giving serious consideration to joining my brother . . . He has a small-animal practice up north and could use the help. My shoulder's not going to get any better, especially as arthritis sets in."

In the dark, Rose feels she's about to be sick. It's though nothing has happened in the last several hours; that she's a small child relegated to the backseat, invisible to the men in front. If they're concerned about Mum left alone in hospital, they're not talking about it. Instead, Dad is going on about being a farm student in Denmark, which his father insisted on, in preparation for managing his own acres.

David asks, "Have you ever thought of an advisory job on one of the settlements?"

"I admit it's crossed my mind. The present pig man scarcely knows snout from a tail. They should fire him. Lousy pay, of course, even if a job did come up, and the problem is they can move you around the country. Why—you know something?"

David demurs, says he has no inside leads.

"Good luck at school tomorrow, Rose." David says and drives away.

They enter the house through the back door, turning on lights. Rose is so tired she can hardly stand. She brushes her teeth, spits around dishes piled in the sink, and drags herself upstairs. The room is as they left it, with Mum's nightie and old dressing gown thrown over a chair. With the space to herself, Rose opts for the bed. Soon after, she hears her father coming upstairs. He pauses outside her room.

"Goodnight, Dad," she calls.

"Time you got some shut-eye." Boards creak. His door closes.

Instantly, her thoughts are back at the hospital, replaying the scene outside the curtained cubicle, and feeling David's firm grip, pulling her away. "It's your imagination, Rose," he'd kept saying.

He'd led her to a side room where Mum was hooked up, receiving pints of a stranger's blood. Dad kneeled by her bedside, stroking her free hand.

"Rose, where were you?" Mum whispered.

"I thought you were dying . . ."

In the darkness now, Rose sees, again and again, the woman's contorted face, and her hand, so like Mum's, with its thin gold ring.

They sat in a waiting area outside the operating room doors. David had gone in search of cups of tea when the surgeon emerged, dressed in what looked like green pajamas. Deep marks from the surgical mask he'd worn crisscrossed his face. He'd spoken gravely, explaining they had performed an emergency procedure to stop the bleeding, but further surgery would be necessary.

"She's very weak," he'd added. Then, to no one in particular, "This bus accident was worse than we thought—it's going to be a long night."

Dad asked, "What about the baby?"

The surgeon shrugged. "We found no fetus." After that, he'd hurried away. Rose repeats the words to herself. They make no sense. If only she could have talked to Mum, but they weren't allowed. David came back with tea they didn't drink. Dad said he'd seen the surgeon and it was time to go. When he volunteered no further information, David didn't ask. He just said, "I'll get the car."

Rose reaches for the light. *It's useless*, she thinks. *I'm never going to sleep.* In a few hours there'll be school. Dad has insisted she go. It feels like a hundred years since she was there. Most of the things she'll need for tomorrow are downstairs. She creeps a stair at a time, in rhythm with Dad's rumbling snores. Moving silently, she collects clean underwear and socks from the airing cupboard. *Cripes*, she remembers, *half my stuff's in my suitcase at the station.*

The fire has gone out and the house cold. In the short time they were away, a film of dust has settled on the sideboard, dead flies have collected on windowsills, newspapers lie crumpled around Dad's chair, and the washing up still waits in the sink. Rose heats the kettle. Her mother's apron tied around her waist, she sets about cleaning up. Halfway through, Rose comes across Mum's handbag on a doorknob where she'd hung it when they came in. One by one, she takes out the contents: lipstick, compact, comb, a small notebook and pen, a change purse and a few coins, ticket stubs. Tucked in an inside pocket, she finds, folded several times, a copy of the telegram Mum sent from the village shop, when she said she was buying stamps.

The message is short: "One grief removed. A."

Rose replaces everything, except for the telegram, which she tucks into her satchel pocket. She turns off the lights and sits by the cold fire. It was Gracie who guessed Mum was telegraphing Graham. He'd been seen in the village. Mum had already been to London. Were the words a book title or quotation? What "one grief" did Mum think resolved, and would Graham have understood? He could be on his way to France by now, with no idea what's happened. Rose draws up her knees and pulls a shawl around her bare legs and feet. It's all too much. She must get some sleep.

In the early hours, as it's becoming light, someone is in the room. Rose stirs, rubs a crick in her neck. A broad back comes into focus, bent over the fireplace, stacking kindling on crumpled newspaper.

"Good morning, Dad," she says sleepily.

Stanley adds a few pieces of coal before he asks, "Why are you sleeping down here?"

"I was afraid I wouldn't wake up in time for school."

"You can't be very comfortable."

Rose massages her neck again, gathering her thoughts. "Mum's shawl kept me warm."

"Suit yourself." He lights a match and steps: a blue flame curls along the paper's edge. "I see you did some tidying. Don't know how we'll manage without your mother."

One foot has gone to sleep. It's a relief to feel blood coursing back. Rose waits for the pain to subside before she says, "I didn't understand what the doctor was saying: was Mum not pregnant, after all?"

"That's what I heard."

"Why does she have to have another operation?"

"You were there—you have ears. He didn't say, did he? They never do. Stop asking questions I can't answer. I'll never get the fire going." Groaning as he stoops over, Stanley works a small pair of bellows. The flames catch, leaping upward.

Rose follows her father into the kitchen. "Are you going to visit Mum today?"

"Easier said than done, with this lumbago. They want me to see the lady almoner at noon, like we're in the poor house. We'll be there soon enough, what with my back and Alice in hospital."

"Maybe Mr. Vale would drive you."

"We've used up enough of his petrol as it is." Stanley takes his coat and cap from the peg by the back door. "Besides, I don't want him involved any more in our private affairs."

Not knowing how to respond, Rose volunteers, "If I didn't go to school today I could stay home and cook your breakfast like Mum does."

Freezing air whips into the room as he opens the door. "Don't bother. I've been doing that myself. Get yourself something to eat and off to school." Stanley picks up the ash bucket and winces, ready to head toward the piggeries.

Rose says from the back step, "Is it okay if I leave early and ride my bike—then I can see Mum afterward?"

He looks back at her. Behind him the sky is a wash of pinks and grey. "All right, but don't be late. I've enough on my mind. And don't stand there in your nightclothes. The lad's due any minute to help with the feeding." He fishes in the front pocket of his overalls. "Here's a couple of bob for lunch money."

Deciding that the cart track will be too muddy for her bike, Rose takes the bus route. She coasts down the steep hill, the cold wind stinging her cheeks and making her eyes water; but strength is returning to her legs. She peddles fast, scarcely aware of the scenery, until she comes to the stop where she normally gets off the bus. It's still early. On impulse, she turns up a side street in the direction of Annie's house.

The Carters live in a circle of houses shoulder to shoulder on a quiet street. Rose leans her bike against a low brick wall and unlatches the garden gate. She follows the narrow path around to the back door and knocks.

Annie appears and, with a shriek, pretends to be about to fall in a dead faint. "Rose. Is it you or are you a ghost? I thought you'd died of the plague. Then we heard you'd gone south to warmer climes—to see your granny, I suppose."

Mrs. Carter is at the stove stirring porridge in a saucepan with a wooden spoon. She's a stout woman with grey hair pinned at the back in a tight roll. A blue cotton housecoat stretches over her comfortable middle. "You're a sight for sore eyes," she says. "We've been ever so worried. And what are you doing here so early in the morning? Have you eaten any breakfast?"

"I had a Weetabix."

"Doesn't your Mum give you a hot breakfast?"

Rose's voice breaks. "My Mum's in hospital. She's had an operation and she has to have another one."

"Women trouble, is it?"

"Sort of . . ." Rose's eyes fix on the pattered linoleum floor.

"You don't have to say a word." Mrs. Carter says. "Annie, pour her a cup of tea and add an extra lump of sugar. The poor girl looks done in."

Rose allows herself to be led into the next room and seated at the dining table. A small coal fire burns in the grate. It's a tiny space in which every surface gleams, where Mrs. Carter has scrubbed and polished, as Annie jokes, to an inch of its life.

"Dad let me ride my bike so I can visit Mum when school's over," Rose explains. She looks around for a clock. "I think I got here faster than the bus."

Annie gives her the tea. "We've scads of time—twenty minutes at least. We can ride to school together. I've oodles to tell you. Oh look, goodie, here's Mum with the porridge, and see what we have to go with it." She reaches into a cupboard behind her and proclaims, "A whole tin of Lyon's Golden Syrup."

Annie's brother emerges from the stairs door. "Don't ask where we got it. Ask no questions; tell no lies . . . Hello, Rose, where did you spring from?"

Mrs. Carter interrupts, "Sit down, George, and eat your breakfast, or we'll both be late for work."

"George has bought himself a beat-up old car," Annie says. "He gives Mum a lift to the bakery, and then goes to the studio. That's when he can get it started."

"I'm an apprentice photographer." George points with his thumb to a leather-cased camera, slung on the back of his chair. "I also freelance at weddings, birthday parties, local events—that kind of thing."

"He's ever so good," Mrs. Carter says. She puts a steaming bowl in front of Rose and passes the treacle. "It will give you energy. Your poor father—who's going to cook him his dinner?"

The family chatters on, mostly to each other. George has styled his red hair in a wavy crest like the bantam rooster that wakes Rose every morning. A comb sticks out of his shirt pocket and he reeks of Brylcreem. Annie looks at him adoringly. Seeing the happy faces around her, Rose realizes they know nothing about the baby and Mum nearly dying. Nor does she feel, with George there, she can bring up the subject. "Woman trouble," Annie's mum called it.

Mrs. Carter looks at the clock and says it's time for everyone to get going. She and Annie busy themselves with clearing the table. George doesn't move. "Stay there," he says to Rose. He takes his camera from its case and studies her through the viewfinder. Rose tries to stand but he says, "Keep still." He adjusts the lens. "Smile," he says. "Life can't be that bad, can it?" The camera clicks and clicks again.

$-54-$

ANNIE AND ROSE OVERTAKE the walkers. Rose is dejected to see a long straggle of girls in Saxe blue cotton dresses, white ankle socks, leather sandals, smart navy blazers. She has missed the announcement to change from winter to summer uniform. She's bound to be teased.

Annie, in a new handmade frock, her straw hat stuck on the back of her head, reassures Rose, "Don't worry, no one will notice."

They park their bikes at the rack. The school building, an old, grey stone manor house, has long ago lost its grandeur. What were once handsome stables have been replaced with a scatter of prefab classrooms used by seniors. Across the street, old army barracks serve as a gym with climbing ropes, parallel bars, and leather horses—Rose and Annie call it the torture chamber. Rose sees everything as though for the first time, as jittery as a new girl. She and Annie part company in the cloakroom.

Rose quietly takes her place for morning prayer below the balcony of the great hall. A few girls nudge each other, setting off a babble of voices. A prefect tells them to be quiet. They stand for the opening hymn, stirring the air with smells of disinfectant, chalk, ink, shampoo, and four hundred female bodies. Rose's throat locks; she mouths the words: "Breathe on me, breath of God." Somewhere, in the choir, Annie pipes away: "Fill me with life anew."

Miss Gordon calls them to prayer. Except for a slight quaver, Gordy looks and sounds the same. If anything, her complexion is more sallow, her expression battier. With eyes closed, Rose prays for her mother. She feels sure the doctor in the red tie was afraid. That's why he called to the matron for help. She'd only seen the woman's convulsed face for a split second. Images flit by; nothing stays still. Tricked by her mind, Rose takes long, deep breaths.

In the classroom a crowd gathers around her. "We heard you had the dreaded polio and everyone was scared to death they'd catch it." Girls who normally never speak to Rose talk all at once: "There were rumors you were paralyzed and some parents wanted to close the school."

"Golly, I wish they had closed school," someone says.

"Swimming pool's not going to open. My dad won't let me take the bus any more."

"Gordy had to send out a letter swearing there were no known cases of polio among her students."

"Still," another girl calls out, "they must have sprayed the place during the hols. I can smell the disinfectant."

Rose, emboldened by the attention, says, "I thought that was Gordy's new perfume: 'Eau de Dettol.'" She sits to hide her trembling knees beneath her desk.

Her tired brain barely keeps up with classes. History is especially baffling with its dates of kings and queens of England; she must've missed a hundred years while she was gone. It's like she's jumped on one of the rides at the fair with no time to buckle her seat. Mrs. Cave, dressed in bright pink, suggests they meet soon in the library.

"You'll catch up in a few days," she assures Rose. "Besides, I have authors to suggest whom you'll love reading."

Rose dreads lunchtime. Fiona, who'd befriended her before, suggests they go together to the cafeteria. She wants to warn Rose about a new rule—sixth-formers are no longer free to eat together in their own room. They have to supervise lunches. Four senior girls had been caught skipping to a new Milk Bar at noon. Gordy stripped them of their prefect badges, accusing them of meeting boys, which they denied. Fiona says ever since Gordy suggested the Milk Bar was a den of iniquity, everyone wants to go there. She and Fiona move down the canteen line to receive their slice of pallid Spam and dollop of boiled cabbage. If she had the nerve, Rose thinks, she'd skip out for toasted cheese and milkshake. She accepts Fiona's invitation to sit beside her. Annie is on the other side of the room, but for now, at least, Rose senses a shift. Free to sit quietly amidst the chatter, she no longer feels exiled. Pam, at the table end, may have forgotten all about Coventry; she only has eyes for their allotted, pretty, and athletic senior.

෯

Annie keeps her promise to meet at bike racks after school. "We should go by the shop first so I can let Ma know where we're going."

There are steep steps down into a shop that smells of cinnamon and baked bread. Mrs. Carter offers them each a biscuit. She looks doubtful when Annie tells their destination. "Do you know when visiting hours are?"

Rose shakes her head. "I need to see my Mum—she'll be expecting me."

"Of course you do, dear, but there's no point in going all that way if they don't let you in."

Annie, munching on her biscuit, says, "I promised Rose I'd go with her."

Mrs. Carter locks the cash drawer, takes off her starched white apron, and hangs a sign on the shop door: "Back in ten minutes." "You two wait here—I'm going around back to the bakery to make a phone call."

Through the window only people's legs and feet are visible walking by. Once, the door rattles; otherwise, the place is quiet. Annie goes to a sink behind the counter, brings back water to wash the biscuits down. "I was floored when you showed up at our back door. It's eons since we last talked. I've missed you. I came that time to see you but your dad sent me away. I asked him how Moggy died, and he said it was a fox. I was sad."

"Oh Annie, it's all so complicated." The small shop offers little hope of evading her friend's piercing look. "I can't talk about it," Rose says flatly.

Annie wanders around, inspecting the sparse display of loaves and small cakes in a glass case. If she's offended, she keeps it to herself. A child walks by with a stick, running it along the window, knocking against the glass. A woman tugs at his hand.

"I'm worried about my mother," Rose says at last.

Annie spins round. "And I'm worried about mine too. Look at this place. Unless rationing lifts soon, the shop will close, along with the bakery, and she'll be out of a job. I'm not supposed to say, but when our George gets married, we might have to take in a lodger." She gestures, hands to the ceiling. "I don't want a stranger living with us—especially some lonely brush salesman who fancies Mum."

Annie reacts fiercely to Rose's raised eyebrows. "Don't look so surprised—Ma has had all kinds of gentleman callers. She turns them down, of course." Annie swipes at her eyes with her sleeve. The doorbell jangles. "Shush . . . here she comes."

Rose assesses Mrs. Carter with new eyes.

Mrs. Carter reties her apron and attends to two customers, who followed her down the steps. As soon as they've gone, she says, "I rang a nurse I know at the hospital—they're not supposed to give information, but he did say your mother was operated on today: a hysterectomy." She puts up a hand like a traffic policeman. "Now don't be upset, Rose. One of my sisters had the same thing and skipped menopause. She was ever so glad."

"When can I see her?"

"Not today, dear. She's resting."

"What's a hysterectomy?" Annie asks.

"Never you mind . . . It's your job to take care of your friend. She's had a bit of a shock. You two should ride your bikes over to our house. George will be here soon to pick me up. Rose, didn't you say you have bags at the station? Give me the stubs and we'll pick them up for you."

Annie's Mum stands at the shop door. "Now Rose, don't you go getting yourself all worked up. It will take a while for your mother to be back on her feet. Your dad's going to need you. This is no time for you to fall apart."

THE CARTERS' BACK GARDEN is a long strip of grass with a potting shed. The girls sprawl on a blanket. Annie's changed out of her uniform into shorts and Aertex shirt. Rose takes off her shoes and socks. The late afternoon sun warms their bare legs. "Do you think we should shave them?" Annie says. "Dora does, and when she cuts herself has to borrow an Elastoplast."

"Not likely," Rose rubs her shins. "It would make them all stubbly." Mention of Dora reminds her: "I didn't know George was planning on getting married. I wouldn't think he's old enough."

"He'll be nineteen next month. He and Dora have been going steady for a year. Mum wishes he'd wait, but they've already picked out a ring."

Rose rolls over to face her friend. "What does a lodger do?"

Annie groans. "He'll come and go, depending on his job, and sleep in George's room. Mum says she may cook him breakfast, the occasional dinner. I've always thought I'd inherit George's room when he moved out—it's twice the size."

"At least you have your own bedroom, lucky duck."

"So do you, don't you? Though, come to think of it, I've never seen your room."

"We're almost in the shade," Rose says. "Let's move the blanket into the sun. I'll tell you about this boy I met."

"What's so funny? We could hear you two cackling from the street." George strolls over, camera slung round his neck. Rose hastily covers her knees.

Annie sits up, a huge grin on her face. "You wouldn't believe what Rose has been up to . . . Ouch, don't kick me!"

"It was only my bare foot."

"She met a boy on a train."

"Annie, hush."

"I thought you were the shy type, Rose." George looks into the lens of his camera. "Stand over there with Annie so I can take your picture . . . No, not there; you have your back to the sun."

They pose, arms around each other's waist. Rose can feel Annie's body still shaking with laughter. In spite of herself, she too giggles. Talking about Duncan was a happy memory and she's reluctant to let it go. George sets up the camera on a timer and runs so he too can be in the picture.

Mrs. Carter, appearing from the house, says, "There's one for posterity. I'm glad to see you cheered up, Rose. I'd invite you to supper but you should be off home. George has volunteered to run the suitcases up to your house, and he'll take a sponge cake for your Dad."

Rose zigzags on her bike from one side of the road to the other, standing on the pedals. She is almost at the top of the hill when she sees George's old car coming down. He pulls over and rolls down the window. She wobbles to a stop.

"I found your dad back in his office, a pile of papers in front of him. He looked a bit glum until I gave him the cake. When I told him it was made of dried eggs he gave me half a dozen fresh ones. I'd never seen the speckled kind before. Ma will be chuffed."

Rose looks at George sideways—she's never seen him behind a steering wheel before or noticed the fine red hair on the backs of his hands.

He grins. "Better move on, hadn't I? Sorry your bike wouldn't fit in the boot, or I'd have given you a lift. You must be strong riding up this hill—I'd never persuade Dora to do that. Have to go pick her up. Ta-ta, then."

Rose walks her bike until the road levels. She carries in the suitcases George has left at the back door. Every physical object—every piece of furniture, cushions, curtains, cooking pans, teapot and chinaware—no matter where she looks—all are reminders of her mother's absence. Seated in Mum's chair, Rose contemplates the cold grate. *No one*, she reasons, *knows her as well as I do, nor do they have the foggiest idea what she's been through.* There are things she needs, like her nightie and sponge bag.

Rose looks at the clock. Dad has forgotten to wind it. Judging by the light, it's late. The last bus has gone. She could hitchhike . . . Someone would be sure to stop and she'd explain about Mum in hospital. Rose grips the chair arms, ready for action . . . if only she dared. The walls, with their torn, patterned wallpaper, close in. Rose prays, *Dear God, please show me what I'm supposed to do.*

Silence. An occasional car or lorry rumbles by. Granny believes in prayer, but God must be awfully busy taking care of all the people hurting from the war. Out of nowhere, five words so fleeting she almost dismisses them: *"Watch where your feet go."* No actual voice, but an inner flash like lightning, so distant she could've imagined it, and there'd been no storm. Hadn't Mrs. Carter said it was her job to take over with Mum gone? Rose fetches a broom from the stairs cupboard, with its own jumbled disorder, as though Dad had been searching for something. Once begun, she keeps going: crumbs under the dining room table, and dust beneath the sideboard. Her heart quickens. She's in the kitchen now, sweeping the cracked, brick-patterned linoleum. The thought comes: *I don't trust my feet: they let me down.*

She sits on the back step to rest. In the dimming light, marigolds in Mum's garden glow orange and yellow like lanterns. A rustling catches her attention, as a small animal emerges out of the greenery, snuffling toward her. She stays transfixed as a hedgehog with its bright eyes and twitching little nose sniffs around her feet. Gingerly, Rose explores the pointy bristles: "Did Moggy send you to comfort me?" she asks.

Dad's boots crunch across the yard and Rose calls, "Dad, come and see the hedgehog."

"Look out, girl, here's what we're going to eat." She looks up to see her father holding a chicken by its feet, wings flopping, head and red comb swinging. He lays it on the step beside Rose.

She strokes the feathers, warm to the touch, "Is she still alive?"

"Not since I wrung its neck." Stanley leans to unlace his boots. "Where's this hedgehog you were talking about?"

Rose thinks the wild creature has run away; but there it is, curled in a ball in the flowerbed.

"When I was a boy, we fed them a saucer of milk," Dad says. "But look out for fleas."

Stanley sets up a small table lit by the kitchen window. Rose watches as he methodically plucks the chicken, feathers collecting around his feet.

"Dad, why did you pick her?"

"She was broody. Drove me mad with her squawking. Bring over that torch and hold it."

"We're living on a farm," Mum always says. In other words: no time to be sentimental. If only it were that easy not to visualize the poor hen, hopefully clucking on a clutch of eggs, until seized by her neck. Rose trains the light on her father's hands and the half-plucked breast. "Did you see Mum today?"

"I'm too busy with pigs to feed and accounts piling up. I rang the almoner from the box down the road. She says your mother will be in at least another two weeks. No visitors today, anyway. Saved me a trip."

"Do you think she has . . . cancer?" The word hangs there in the night. "Mr. Jackson's first wife died of it. I remember hearing her crying through the walls."

"Who put that idea into your head?" Stanley roars.

"No one," Rose backpaddles. "Mum told me she was going to have a baby."

"And who's baby would that be?"

The torchlight wavers. "I don't know what you mean . . ."

"Shine the light. You and your mother . . . who knows what you two talk about. There's no baby—never was, so talk about something else before I lose my temper."

Rose sits, her body rigid, knees and thighs squeezed together for fear she'll wet herself. Silently, Stanley pours methylated spirits over the carcass, takes a match and sets light to it, burning off the small, remaining feathers, creating a circle of purplish light that smells of singeing flesh. He blows out the flames and sets about plunging into the bird's cavities, pulling out intestines and saving bluish giblets in a dish.

"Here, go in and turn on the oven. Cook these to make gravy. You know how to do that, don't you?"

Rose has watched her mother. She carries the naked chicken inside and places it breast side up in a roasting pan. The giblets she puts in a pan of water, adding dried spices from the shelf. While the chicken cooks, she sits in the living room with her silent father and tries to concentrate on her history homework. After every few sentences on the Magna Carta, her thoughts return, like a homing pigeon, to her mother. An hour passes. She checks the chicken and find's it still pink in the middle. Her father, who has been staring into the fireplace all evening, says he's too hungry to wait and tells Rose to turn off the oven, and to make tinned baked beans on toast for their supper. They both go to bed early, but Rose doesn't fall sleep until, around midnight, she has formulated a plan for the following day.

$-56-$

ROSE BICYCLES IN THE early morning to the telephone kiosk. She props up her bike on its stand. Dad was up in the dark, long before she was. When he didn't come in for breakfast, she'd gone out to the piggeries and found him at his desk. His eyes were red, as though he hadn't slept. "You'll have to get yourself off to school."

Rose dials for the operator, gives a number she's scribbled on a piece of paper, and feeds coins into the slots. It's all the change she could shake from her money box, plus what was left in Mum's sixpence jar. She hears the distinctive "brrr, brr" of Granny's phone. She pictures the black receiver on the small table, leather prayer book and gloves close by.

"Good morning, Celia Witham here."

The familiar voice makes her gulp. "It's Rose. Mum's in hospital. She was bleeding all over the place on the train. A doctor helped and arranged for an ambulance at the station. Now she's had a hysterectomy. I haven't been able to see her."

Light in the kiosk has a greenish tinge and outside grasses and purple flowers toss wildly in the wind.

"Rose, dear, where are you?"

"In the telephone box down the road. Dad thinks I'm on my way to school, but I thought I should let you know about Mum."

"Of course I want to know; thank you, dear. Sounds like she had a miscarriage."

"The surgeon said there was no baby." Rose looks at the small pile of coins. "Granny, I'm afraid I'm going to run out of minutes. Please tell me what to do."

"How are you and your father managing? Has he seen Alice?"

"Dad says there's too much work on the farm and, anyway, he can't ride his bike because of his back." She adds, "He killed a broody hen for supper. I cooked it, but it was pink in the middle. I don't think the oven's working properly."

"You can still make a nice soup. How's school, now you're back?"

"We're supposed to wear summer uniforms, but nothing fits me from last year."

An operator's voice warns they are almost out of time.

"Don't waste phone money now. As soon as you know anything more about your mother ring me back. You can always reverse charges."

Rose cries, "What should I do?"

"Pray about it. You'll know. I'll put my thinking cap on too. God bless you, dear."

A stiff headwind makes it hard going as Rose pedals back. She hopes Dad doesn't see her. When she'd suggested phoning Granny, he'd said, "She's an old lady and miles away. I don't want you bothering her." Rose is glad she rang but afraid he'll be angry. She lets herself in the front door.

Minutes later, she's hurrying to the gate with a small bag of Mum's things plus her school satchel bulging with books. A few brown chicken feathers blow in the wind.

She almost runs into the postman. "Here's your letters and a parcel for Mrs. Gray." He goes off, whistling, back to his red van. Rose slips the envelopes, mostly bills by the look of it, through the letterbox. She weighs the package in her hands. It's addressed in block capitals, a scribbled return address, and postmarked London. In the midst of strapping the square parcel onto her bike carrier, the front door opens.

"I thought you left an hour ago." Her father holds the sheaf of mail. "What have you been doing?"

"I had homework to finish." She crosses fingers behind her back.

"What's that box?"

"It's a parcel that came for Mum."

Stan steps closer. "What's she doing with a parcel—who sent it?"

"It's from London. There's no name." Rose omits her strong suspicion about who wrote the address.

"Where do you think you're going with it?"

"In case I see Mum." Rose pushes her bike off the stand and heads toward the road.

"Stop, girl, when I tell you."

Rose freezes as Dad grabs the back of her coat, then the handlebars.

"Get off your bike and stand still." He unbinds the parcel, tosses it on the ground, and inspects the small soft bag.

"You really think you're going to see her?"

Rose nods her head.

"You'll be a bother when she needs to rest."

"I'll only stay a few minutes." Rose rejects the idea that Mum would think her a bother. "She'll want her things," she says stubbornly.

"Suit yourself."

Rose interprets the sharp push in her back as permission to leave.

He barks, "Hold still when I tell you." She hears him fastening the bag back in position. "Now put out your arms."

"Dad, I'm going to be late for school."

He roughly forces her arms through the satchel straps, "You'd be sorry if you forgot your books."

Rose arrives at the Carters' house as everyone is about to leave. Annie's mum looks stern. "I'm sorry, Rose: it's out of the question; I can't write you a note excusing you."

George, car key in hand, says, "I could drive her to hospital after taking you to work, Ma. There's probably a bus she could take back."

Mrs. Carter stoops to arrange her hat in the mirror. "Rose has lost too much school as it is—she mustn't miss any more. I've no authority to write notes on her behalf. It's time to go."

Halfway through Latin class, the disturbing memory returns of her father at his office desk. He looked haggard, almost as if he'd been crying. It was where she and Mum found him the night he shot the sow. She tries to remember if the gun was on its rack. The lesson continues. Rose stares out of the classroom window, devising a plan.

At lunchtime, with an air of someone who knows where she's going, she leaves by the main entrance, collects her bicycle, and sets off toward the hospital.

Recalling the railway station map, St. Bede's spire will be her landmark through back streets. Twice she stops for directions. The trip is taking longer than she thought. School lunch must be almost over. Ready to turn around, she sees the tall white structure with its parked ambulances. Rose locks her bicycle outside the main entrance and goes in search of her mother. She follows corridors, dodging past people in wheelchairs, or on crutches, or borne on gurneys in various comatose states. There's a long wait at a lift. Overheated from the bike ride, Rose waits impatiently, sweat dripping from her scarlet face. The lift arrives; a small crowd surges on, pushing Rose to the back.

Mum's ward has a long, double row of beds, some with curtains open, some closed, several with visitors gathered around. Not all the women appear sick but others lie on their backs, mouths open in an O, pale as their sheets. Had she not been counting bed numbers, Rose might have walked right past her mother in a hospital gown, her face shrunken among the pillows. "Mummy, I thought I'd never find you."

"It's my daughter," Alice calls to a woman in the next bed.

"Thank goodness you've come." The woman, her head partially swathed bandages, waves. "She's been longing to see you."

Alice struggles to sit up. "Pull the curtain round and come close. I can't believe you're here. First, hug me . . . gently though; my tummy's sore."

Mum holds on to her hand, squeezing it tightly, especially through waves of pain that come and go. She wants to know everything Rose has been doing.

"Why aren't you at school?"

"I had to see you, Mum."

"But you've missed so much. You mustn't do this again. I'm surprised they gave permission."

"They didn't. I don't care if I get in trouble. Mummy, what's wrong with you? You said you were expecting."

"I'd convinced myself I was pregnant. Now I'm sad. The surgeon said something about fibroids and another name I can't remember, but the bleeding was unusually severe. They had to do the first surgery to stop it. Now I've had a hysterectomy. I overheard him tell the houseman they're waiting for test results."

"Is it cancer, like the first Mrs. Jackson?" Rose asks.

Mum makes Rose look into her eyes. "If it's cancer, we'll face up to it. That poor woman died thinking it was a gallstone. She didn't understand why she kept getting sicker and sicker. Promise you won't let that happen, Rose."

"Oh, Mum . . . what would I do if you died?" Rose can't help the tears.

"Stop it, or I'll cry too. I don't plan on dying any time soon. Matron says whatever they found was probably excised. She's taken away my cigarettes. She says she doesn't want me bursting my stitches from coughing. She scares me, that woman. She was in the air force." Mum laughs, setting off another wave of pain.

Rose adjusts the pillows. She unpacks the small bag and lays out a pretty cotton nightgown, sponge bag with tooth brush and toothpaste, Yardley's lavender soap, Pond's face cream, and Mum's Red Poppy perfume.

Alice dabs a little scent behind each ear. "I feel better already, but I won't wear my good nightie until I stop bleeding." She pats Rose's hand. "Don't look so worried. How are you and Dad getting along?"

Rose tells about the chicken, not her uneasiness about the gun. She makes excuses for her father not visiting—his work on the farm and his bad back.

"He never did like hospitals. Something to do with tonsils out when he was a child."

Rose has noticed purple grapes on the bedside table.

"David Vale brought them yesterday evening. I was woozy from painkillers and scarcely remember. Did he tell you?"

"We haven't seen him since the day you came in." The grapes, a rare treat, are sweet and juicy. Rose chews thoughtfully. Best not to speculate what Dad would say about the vet's visit. Still, it's a comfort to know David's still their friend. She guesses he hasn't told Mum about his possible plans to move away.

Mum soon tires, her face drained of color. Before Rose leaves, there's something her mother needs to know. "A parcel came for you in the post today. I'm almost certain it's from Graham. The postmark's London."

"Did you bring it?"

"Dad made me leave it at home."

"Was there a letter?"

"If there is, it's inside the box."

"What kind of box?"

Rose demonstrates with her hands: "Square, not very heavy."

"And Stanley has it now? You're positive?"

"I have to go. By the way, it's summer uniform at school and I'm still in this one. I'm teased about it. There's no one to take me shopping." Rose can't conceal the resentment in her voice.

"Oh sweetheart, I'm sorry. Maybe Annie's mum would help. Ask Dad for egg money. Try not to say anything that will get him upset. You must go. Kiss me goodbye."

As Rose is walking away, the woman with the bandaged head says, "She's calling you back."

Mum beckons her to lean close. "I promise you, Rose, if I ever get out of here, life is going to be very different. I haven't been the best mother. We'll do better. You'll see."

ROSE REENTERS THE SCHOOL building the way she left: casually, through the front entrance, as though it's a perfectly normal midafternoon. She doesn't get far before Miss Keene, the school secretary, spots her from the open office door.

"Rose Gray, I've been looking for you."

Miss Keene is one of the thinnest people Rose has ever seen and must be well into her sixties. Fiercely loyal to Miss Gordon, many girls suspect her of being a spy to any goings-on or rule infractions. The way Miss Keene looks down her long, slender nose at Rose bears out this theory.

"Miss Gordon wishes me to schedule your Latin tutorial once a week after school. I am looking at Tuesdays. Beginning next week. All right?"

"After school?" Rose sees time she'd looked forward to spending with Annie go up in smoke.

"Yes—may I write it down?" Something about Miss Keene's tone makes Rose nod her head. Who knows what she and Gordy discuss. The proximity to the headmistress's office is double reason not to linger. She's almost out of the door when Miss Keene calls her back.

"Here's a packet of announcements you may have missed. I'm assuming that's one reason you are in the wrong uniform. I'd advise you to read these. Also, in future, private mail via this address will be returned to the sender." Rose reaches to take the envelope from Miss Keene's hand; she holds on to it, fixing Rose with a long, suspicious look. "You're very flushed—what have you been doing? Didn't I see you come through the front door?"

"Miss Cowper gave me special exercises for my weak legs." That much is true. Rose sits down to prove her point and to steady trembling knees. She explains, "I was on my way to the library to meet Mrs. Cave;

she's going to suggest books to read. The last one was Thomas Hardy's *Jude the Obscure*. The ending's gruesome, don't you think?"

Miss Keene relinquishes the envelope and closes the appointment book. "I'm far too busy to listen to your prattle."

Rose waits for the coast to be clear. Clutching the envelope, she darts across the assembly hall. The only person in the library is Miss Browne, the art teacher. She warmly greets Rose. "I heard you were ill—are you better? Everyone is doing sports, but you're probably not up to it yet."

"I'm here to meet Mrs. Cave."

"I saw her in the staffroom; she should be here soon. Meanwhile, look through this gorgeous book of Rembrandt paintings—I'm thinking of using it in my art history class next year."

Rose turns glossy pages, wondering how any one could capture light and dark, and human faces, the way Rembrandt does. In the peaceful book-lined room, the gnawing anxiety she felt earlier lifts—she thinks, *Granny must be praying for me.*

"You look so comfortable," Mrs. Cave breezes in. "I hate to disturb you. This place is going to fill up soon. Let's go for a walk around the tennis courts."

At first they talk about books. Mrs. Cave suggests modern writers: Forster, Auden, and Virginia Wolfe, maybe D. H. Lawrence. The courts echo with the strenuous twang of racquets hitting balls and shouts of "Love thirty . . . Love forty." For a while they watch a game of doubles.

"How does it feel to be back at school?" Mrs. Cave asks.

"Like I'm on the edge of a quicksand." Rose surprises herself with her candor. "I'm hopeless at sports, I can't sing a note, and I'll never catch up with my lessons."

Mrs. Cave laughs her musical laugh. "I'm sorry, Rose. It's not funny. You sound so much like me when I was your age. I've been looking at your report cards. Academically, you are doing quite well. Miss Browne loves the imagination you use in art. The worst thing said about you is that you lack coordination in sports. I spoke to Miss Cowper about that. She admits she's been hard on you. Did you know her mother died recently?"

"No, I didn't know that." Stricken, Rose thinks of Mum.

"Let's walk some more," Mrs. Cave says. "Don't you love this time of year, everything bursting with new growth?" Away from the crowd, she says quietly, "That day I found you hiding in the cloakroom—is the quicksand only about school?"

"My mother's in hospital." Rose gratefully allows herself to be co-cooned in sympathy. As for revealing more, she hovers, wanting to, but conflicted about betraying her family. Mrs. Cave may have interpreted silence as shyness. She says she understands that sometimes it's difficult to talk about things. The tall, graceful teacher walks on, admiring the flowers. Rose follows in her wake.

As they part, Mrs. Cave says, "I find writing things down helps me know what I'm really feeling. Sometimes it's a poem. If there's ever a time you'd like me to read anything you've written, I'd be honored to do that."

School is over and Annie is waiting for Rose at the bike rack. "Mum said this morning you and I could go back to our house if we like, or into town, but no more than a radius of two miles."

It dawns on Rose that Annie has no clue she left the building. Nor did anyone ask questions when she went to collect her satchel from the classroom. She hasn't been missed: a knowledge that leaves her both thankful and overlooked. She contemplates her friend's open, innocent face. "I'm hungry. I vote we check out the new Milk Bar."

"Ma wouldn't let us."

"I don't see why not. I dare you."

Annie still looks doubtful. "We better change out of uniform first."

"You'll have to lend me something to wear."

Rose mounts her bicycle. "We'll go to your house first."

Annie calls, "Rose Gray, wait for me."

Clothes scatter over Annie's bed, most of them hand-me-downs from Carter cousins. In the end, Annie decides on her usual outfit: Aertex shirt, cotton pants, and zip-up jacket. She allows herself to be dissuaded from the woolly hat with its pom-pom. They experiment with lipstick, puckering lips in front of the mirror, blotting most of it off with tissue paper. Rose, in slacks and a pink jersey, unbraids her hair, leaving it wavy and loose. She reminds Annie they'll need cash. A quick raid of George's room yields three shillings and a few pennies. It's the first time Rose has seen George's fleet of balsa wood model airplanes and a gallery of photographs on the wall. Above his bed there's a snapshot of him as a small boy with his father at the seaside.

Annie remarks, "They were very close. Dad would be so proud of him." She turns away. "Come on, let's go. Milk Bar here we come." Annie acts as though the whole idea was hers in the first place.

The Milk Bar is packed, all the high stools taken. A jukebox plays "When You Were Sweet Sixteen."

"Oh help," Annie says. "Who are these people? They must be from Central School. Should we go?"

"Not before I have something to eat."

Annie looks around. "I think we have to go to the counter. What do you want?"

"Surprise me." Rose stands to one side. It's a rowdy crowd but Annie holds her own, laughing off teasing remarks as she elbows forward, her hair sticking out in all directions even though she'd combed it.

A boy makes his way with a plate of chips. "Haven't seen you here before. Want to sit with me and my mate over there?"

"I'm waiting for my friend."

"I know her. She's George Carter's little sister."

Duncan and Jeff combined have given Rose an air of confidence. This doesn't stop her wishing the boy, waving a greasy chip under her nose, would go away.

"How about a foursome—me and my mate are going to the pictures."

"We're going somewhere after this."

"Where's that? Maybe we could tag along."

It's the first thing that comes into her head: "We're going to church."

The boy pops a chip in his mouth. "Never mind, then."

Annie returns holding two vanilla ice cream cones. "What did he want?"

"For us to make a foursome with his mate and go to the pictures."

"George would have a pink fit. He'll kill us if he finds out we were in his room, let alone been seen in a Milk Bar. Let's get out of here."

They sit on a low wall, across the road, licking their cones, catching dribbles down their wrists.

"That place thinks it's so American," Annie says scornfully.

"I'd been thinking more of toasted cheese," Rose says, still hungry. "Face it, Annie, we're square."

Annie's mind is elsewhere. "I'm in the mood for adventure," she says. "We've done nothing with Daring Demons since the water tower. Gordy may call the Milk Bar a sink pool of iniquity, but I think it's overrated."

Rose wipes her hands on the seat of her pants, forgetting they belong to Annie. "Leave your bike here and lock it. We're going to walk."

They half run along narrow cobbled streets. "Where are we going, Rose?"

"To church."

"We're not that square."

Rose doesn't know what made her say "church" to the boy, and now to Annie, or why St. Bede's spire has beckoned all day. "You said you wanted an adventure—we'll climb the tower."

The pews in the big church are empty except for a lone elderly woman, in a headscarf, praying near the front. Rose leads the way to a side chapel with flickering votive candles and kneeler. She takes a taper. "I'm going to pray for my mum."

Annie whispers, "What about the tower?"

"Later." The small, newly lit candle illumines Rose's face.

Annie kneels with her, so their shoulders are touching. "Ma says she stopped believing in God when Dad died. I'm going to pray we won't have to take in a lodger."

"Do you believe in God?" It's a question Rose has not asked her friend before.

Annie's candle joins the dancing lights. She blows out the taper.

"I once dreamt Dad was in heaven. Not all gold and rubies and stuff like that, but trees and green meadows and lakes with white swans drifting by. He looked well and happy. I'd like to think he's with God. I wish Ma had dreams like that."

"Let's just pray quietly for a while," Rose says. At first she feels self-conscious with Annie beside her. She steals a look. Annie's eyes are closed, her lips moving silently. If she'd laughed or moved away, Rose would understand; but Annie's presence in the quiet chapel is like a new, tender shoot in their friendship.

After while, they wander toward the back of the church, past effigies of male figures in their finery, recumbent marble tombs, side by side with their silent wives. In one marble case, a stone pet dog lies at its owner's feet. Rose reflects, *They loved their animals too.* She whispers to Annie, "I came here to church the day Moggy died, though I didn't know he was dead until I got home. There was a man preaching, a bishop. He talked about how muddled everyone is since the war. He said, 'When you can't decide what to do, watch where your feet go.'"

Annie says, "My feet are itching to go up that tower, but look, the sign says 'Guided tours only.'" She tries the door. "It's locked."

"Wait here. There must be someone who'll let us in."

Rose walks down the middle aisle between tall columns and arches. For centuries, people have walked on the same flagstones, some buried right under her feet. Like cracks in the pavement, she steps over inscriptions worn flat over the years. She slips into the pew beside the elderly woman, interrupting her prayer.

"Excuse me, do you know who has the key to the tower door?"

"The verger does but he isn't here."

"Do you know where he is?"

"Went home for his tea, I expect. He'll be back for evening prayer."

Rose wanders away, pretending to admire the carved eagle lectern and, behind that, an ornate dividing screen and ancient choir stalls. She veers off to the side, where she'd watched the altar boy go after lighting the candles.

Annie is waiting by the tower door. Rose turns the heavy iron key in the lock.

"We'll have to hurry."

Annie disappears, climbing the spiraling stone steps. Rose lags behind, holding on to a thick rope fastened to the wall. Every few steps she stops to rest and listens to her friend's steady trudge, round and around, ascending the tower. Her thoughts follow the sounds. Annie has worries too: her mother's job at the cake shop, George leaving, and the thought of a stranger living in their little house. She'd envied her friend's cheerfulness and not imagined she, too, had her secrets. Rose loses count but still the steps go up, and Annie's feet pound above. Then they stop. One last effort on aching legs and Rose sees daylight. Annie pulls her up into the open parapet.

"Come see the view."

They run to all four sides for different vistas of the sprawling town, daring each other to lean over the wall and watch tiny figures below. Between them, they identify shops and public buildings by their red roofs, parks and river, and, in the distance, a plume of smoke from the jam factory chimney. Rose thinks she sees the white hospital building, partly obscured by trees. Annie says, "No, that's the other hospital, where you go if you're crazy."

Several times they stir a white flock of birds that whirl in a flurry of wings and resettle, sounding their low, indignant coos.

"After all," Annie says, "they live here, in their pigeon holes." Rose says no, she thinks they are turtledoves. She describes the scruffy pigeons at Victoria Station. Annie has never been to London.

"I wish I could fly." Annie stretches out her arms. "I dream I'm flying at least once a week."

"Oh, Annie, so do I. Let's pretend we really can."

For a while, they imagine: India, Argentina, China, Bulgaria, Italy, Katmandu, New Zealand, America . . .

"I've already been to Coventry and back," Rose reflects. "Courtesy of Pam Rawlings."

"Wasn't long ago when Coventry city was bombed." Annie says. "Imagine what Lady Godiva would have thought if she'd known what was coming."

"They destroyed the cathedral and thousands were killed. It might've been us."

Annie points north to the main highway leading to London. "Imagine, Hitler marching with his armies right into Woolston. If it hadn't been for people like my dad protecting the country, we'd be dead."

Rose wonders if she'll ever share with Annie her complicated feelings about war. Instead, she points to the spire above. "St. Bede's stayed intact."

"And so have we." Annie's face is serious. "I looked for you today. I don't like that Gordy has separated us."

"I went to see Mum in hospital." Rose pauses. "That's where my feet took me."

"When?" Annie looks incredulous.

"At lunch time. I rode my bike over there."

"I just thought you were . . ."

"Somewhere else? I was. It's all right. Mum's sick, though. She might have cancer. That's why I wanted to come here and pray."

"Why didn't you tell me?"

"I'm glad you know now."

At her side, Annie says, "Promise we'll always be friends."

"Even when we're old?"

"Yes, and funny looking, like old people are; but we'll always find each other, won't we?"

Rose laughs and says yes. She turns away so Annie will not see her despair: how can any heart make a promise that's forever? Hadn't she seen that in her parent's life? Everything will be different, Mum has promised; but supposing she becomes ill again? Rose thinks, *What then will become of us?*

She feels Annie's warm arm across her shoulders. "It's time to go home."

Rose goes first, winding her way down, with Annie on her heels. Rose stops with an idea. "Granny thinks I should be confirmed—would you come here with me to classes?"

"Golly, I never thought of that. I'll ask Ma."

For the last of the steps, bells begin to ring—so loud they stuff fingers in their ears. Rose feels the sound resonate in her chest, happy to be with her friend.

They emerge from the tower door. People are arriving for evening prayer. Music reverberates from the great organ pipes. Leaving the key in the lock, they depart by a side door.

—58—

"YOU'RE GOING TO CATCH it from Ma!" George warns Annie as they wheel up the path. Rose grabs her things and sets off for home.

She walks in the door, worn out. Her father is in the living room, sitting in the dark, his feet soaking in a basin of steaming water. He greets her with barely a nod. Her offer to make soup is met with stony silence. Rose goes to the pantry to retrieve the undercooked chicken when he calls her back. "Sit down," he orders.

"I told you not to involve your grandmother." He tosses a yellow envelope in her direction. "She's sent a telegram—says she's coming on a late train, staying tonight at The King's Arms, and will see Alice tomorrow. Then she thinks she's moving in with us." His words are slow, measured.

Rose reads the message. "I won't need to ring her tonight—I can't believe she's going to be here herself."

"I told you not to bother her."

"She's worried about Mum, of course, but kept saying she was glad I rang."

"So you disobeyed me. Why are you wearing that pink jumper, and your hair all over like that? What happened to your uniform?"

"It's in my bag. Annie lent me some clothes—we rode our bikes into town, to St. Bede's, and climbed the tower. You can see for miles around."

"You're lying. I can tell from your face. You're like your mother."

"I'm not lying." Rose flails against guilt she doesn't even understand. "Don't talk that way about Mum."

She steps back, "Why are looking at me like that?"

Instinctively, she ducks. An object flies past her head. The glass jar of Epsom salts shatters against the wall behind her.

"You do as you're told. Do you get that?"

Rose stays completely still, stunned by how quickly she has stepped in the middle of her father's anger. She quavers, "I didn't do anything, Dad."

"There's something else you and I need to discuss." Stanley points to the dining table: "Recognize that box?"

Rose glances over, without moving her head. "It's the one that came in the post, isn't it?"

"You were going to sneak it to your mother."

"Not sneak, Dad. It's addressed to Mum. I don't know what's in it." That part is true, but her voice shakes.

"Go and look," he orders. "Go on with you."

Rose gingerly steps over broken glass to the table. She lifts the box flaps and removes layers of tissue paper. "Oh, it's Mum's red hat."

"Do you know where it came from and who sent it?"

"Wasn't there a note with it?"

The pupils in her father's eyes are black and huge, nearly eclipsing the blue. "I'm asking you—who sent this? Why's the postmark London?"

"She must have left it at the station café."

Dad leans forward. "It was him, wasn't it?"

"I don't know who you mean." Rose feels so weak she could faint.

"It's that Faire chap, isn't it? I thought he was gone for good—killed in France, with any luck."

"Don't shout. You're frightening me. They had a cup of tea at King's Cross Station while we were waiting for the train. Ask Mum about it."

"To hell with her."

Rose is crying now. "You haven't even seen her in hospital. I went today and she's in pain and she might have cancer."

Stanley sloshes water as he steps out of the basin and hobbles toward the kitchen. On the way he steps on a piece of glass.

Rose follows her father to the back doorstep, where he reaches for his socks and boots. "Where are you going? Your foot's bleeding."

"Out there. Where I spend half my life while you two are off, gallivanting. Not for long, though. We're done for. You mark my words, girl."

"Don't go outside. It's almost dark." Rose envisions the gun missing from its rack. "I'm making soup. Look, you're bleeding. We need to look for glass slivers. I'll find the tweezers." She makes him stand still, wraps a towel around his foot, and coaxes him back to his chair. He leans heavily on her arm.

She kneels, working painstakingly to extract a deeply embedded shard. He speaks to the top of her head. "You don't have to do this."

"I hope I'm not hurting you too much." Hadn't Mum said not to rile him up? It's her job, now, to calm him down. She holds up a long sliver for him to see.

"I'm not your father—you've figured that one out, haven't you?"

Astounded, Rose sits back on her heels. "What do you mean? Of course you're my father."

"I've thought it for a long time. Your mother probably already told you the big secret about Graham Faire—he'd have stopped us getting married if he could. He'll never leave Alice alone. Or you. You'll see. He's your real father, Rose."

She is crying and furious. "How can you say such a thing?" She kicks off her shoes and socks. "Look at our feet: they are identical: same ridiculous high arches, second toe longer the other, and same knobby toes. I inherited them, and a lot of trouble they give me too."

Stanley shakes his head, but looks down all the same. He flexes his toes.

"Like it or not," Rose insists, "I'm your daughter. When did you last look at your old family photos? There's a girl in there that looks a lot like me with her long legs and thick hair. Who is she anyway?"

"Must be Maud, my sister." Dad sounds almost sheepish. "Died when she was twelve, of diphtheria. When you were ill, I thought you'd die on me too."

Rose pushes the hair out of her eyes. "You may not want me as your daughter, but you're stuck with me. As for Mum's friend: he's suffered a lot. I don't think you should hate him for wishing he married Mum. After all, she chose you, and you could be a lot kinder to her."

Stanley inspects their feet, shaking his head. At last he looks up. "Go on, girl, make that soup and be careful you don't step on any glass."

The living room restored to order, they eat their supper. When asked, Stanley agrees the soup is tasty. Otherwise, he's very quiet. To break the silence, she asks about Maud and the grandmother who died before Rose was born. Dad answers in short, terse sentences. Rose visualizes his mind like a great ocean liner slowly turning around. Once or twice, she catches him looking at her, then quickly away. When she rises to clear their plates, a few remaining salt crystals crunch under foot. He swept up most of the mess, wincing with back pain. In the kitchen now, rinsing dishes, she turns off the taps, chilled by the thought of the jar hitting her head; it might've killed her. Her reflection in the darkened window stares back.

She goes into the living room, where Dad sits reading the newspaper. He looks at her over his glasses. "All right, Rose?"

"I have tons of homework to do."

"Better get on with it then."

She settles down with her books. A few minutes later, Stanley says he has things to do in the shed, puts on his cap, and leaves by the back door. Rose, alone in the silent house, opens up her history book. The Jacksons' radio, turned up loud, blares through the walls. She recognizes the theme music for *ITMA* comedy show. She fancies she hears the Jacksons laughing at the jokes. *What a strange boy Keith is,* Rose thinks. She takes a pencil and doodles a head with big ears. Then the thought: *What must it be like to be the* self *who is Keith?* She wishes she'd been nicer. All the while, in the back of her mind, she frets over what Dad could be doing out in the shed.

She hears his slow movements opening the back door. He comes in with her school shoes, newly polished, and sets them by her chair. "Took me a while," he says. "Didn't look like they've been properly cleaned in a long time."

She thanks him, explaining it was river mud that had almost ruined her shoes. She would've gone on about the river, but his mind's elsewhere.

"I want you on the bus with me tomorrow morning," he says firmly. "You'll go to school, I'll pick up Celia at the hotel, and we'll hire a car to see your mother. Don't argue."

— 59 —

IT'S EIGHT O'CLOCK IN the evening and there's a knock on the back door. Dad, who'd been dozing by the fire, wakes with a start. "See who it is."

David Vale stands on the doorstep. "Hello, Rose. That's a pretty pink jumper you're wearing. I was on an emergency call down the road. Thought I'd see how you and your dad are getting along."

"It's Mr. Vale," Rose calls.

"Tell him to come in, and close the bloody door."

David ventures as far as the living room entrance. He repeats what he said to Rose about not stopping.

Stan says, "You might as well, since you've come this far."

Rose offers tea, but her father says she must go back to her homework. "Sit down, sit down," he says to David.

"Well, just for a minute." The small space fills with the two of them face to face across the fireside. Rose moves her books and positions herself to watch proceedings. David undoes his jacket but keeps it on. He inquires about Stan's back, listening carefully to a long list of symptoms. "You need to see a specialist. It could be a herniated disc." Rose observes how cautious he is, approaching Dad as he might a highly strung horse. He asks, "Do you want me to take a look?"

It surprises Rose when her father agrees. David runs his hand along the length of Stanley's spine, asking where it hurts. Next, he tells him to try to touch his toes, but the pain is too great. "You can't be lifting those meal sacks, or your back will never heal."

"It's my own fault," Dad groans.

David sits back in his chair. "What's done is done. God knows, I've made enough wrong calls in my own life."

"I've been off my head. Rose can tell you. I shot her cat. I thought it necessary. Turned out it was a fox after next-door's chickens. She hates me for it, and so does her mother."

"No we don't, Dad."

He seems not to hear. His shoulders shake. "Do you know how my father died?"

"Not in any detail, Stan."

"Shot himself in the head in a Berlin hotel room. He couldn't take it."

"Dad!" Rose recoils at the horror of what had been only a vague, whispered-about event. David glances in her direction, putting his finger to his lips.

Stanley goes on speaking, almost to himself. "Life never turns out the way you thought it would. Look at me. I'll never make a go of it. It's not just my father's dreams that crashed." Dad looks up, his face tear-streaked. "Why's it so bloody cold in here?"

"Temperatures are dropping outside," David says.

"I'll fetch more wood for the fire." Rose jumps to her feet. David nods.

Outside, the night has a chill to it, as though there could be a late frost. Using a torch, Rose gathers split logs from the woodpile into a basket. She turns back toward the lighted house. They're in deep conversation. She feeds the fire and returns to the table.

David says, "All the talk these days is about shell shock for those who've been at the front, and God knows, with good reason. The rest, on the homeland, are expected to get on with it, even if their nerves are shot."

Dad shudders. "That house that was bombed down the street . . . It was on my watch. I hadn't warned them about the lights."

"It wasn't your fault. You need to get away for a time, Stan. You're not well."

Dad keeps coming up with objections. Rose adds her own. "What about Mum?" They've not mentioned her, as if her name is taboo. She informs David that her grandmother will be arriving.

"Well then," David says, "that will be a help." He gives Stanley a long, thoughtful look. "What do you think of me taking that old gun of yours back to my place, until you're better?"

Rose's whole body tenses as a shadow passes over her father's face. He speaks between clenched teeth.

"You simply can't keep your nose out of our family business, can you?"

David Vale, already on his feet, buttons his coat. "I'm off then." He addresses Rose. "It's good your grandma's coming."

Rose looks past David—he hasn't seen Dad's darkening complexion, the way the veins stand out on his forehead. She hurries to usher the vet out, thanking him in a voice that sounds more like Mum's than her own.

David pauses at the door. "Goodbye, Stan."

"I've seen the way you look at my wife."

"I'm trying to help you out. Your wife's in hospital, you're not well, and you have Rose to think about. Where I'm from, people give each other a hand. I'll not disturb you again."

The back door closes. Rose is crying. "Dad, he was our friend. What are we going to do now?"

Stanley stares at her, blankly. "Run out and stop him . . . go on now. Hurry."

Headlights illuminate the barn as she runs in her slippers across the muddy yard, waving for him to stop. She screams his name, "Mr. Vale," afraid he hasn't seen her in the dark. He stops the car and quickly climbs out. "What's wrong?"

"Dad wants to talk to you."

"Over here, Vale." Stanley stands on the back doorstep, his bulky figure outlined against the yellow kitchen light.

"Look!" Rose grabs David's arm. "He has his gun. I'd no idea he had it in the house."

The vet approaches slowly. He calls, "I'm hoping that thing isn't loaded."

Her father waves the old home guard rifle over his head, like a soldier coming over the breach. For a second, Rose thinks it's a really bad joke. She calls, "Don't play around, Dad; you're frightening us."

"Think I'm playing the fool, do you?" He lifts the gun, swinging it in their direction.

The vet's response is rough and immediate. He pushes Rose toward the car. "Duck down, out of sight." She flees to the other side of the Hillman and crouches in the cold, wet grass.

The night sky is clear with a scattering of stars. Behind, in the dark piggery, a brief disturbance: an overturned trough, squeals, a few grunts. In her mind's eye, Rose sees the sow's ruined face. She peers over the car's bonnet. Her father sways in the lighted doorway, the gun erratically aimed at the vet.

Rose strains to listen. She shivers, not knowing what her father is capable of. She must try to stop him. David is only riling him up.

"Are you going to let me have that for safe keeping?" David holds out his hand.

"Arrogant sod, aren't you."

"I've heard variations on that one before. Believe it or not, I'd hate to see you do what your father did to himself."

"You've no idea. Father caused mayhem when he chose his way out. It was easy for him." He raises his voice. "Could I do that to Rose?"

"She's a grand girl, and she's your daughter, Stan."

"I don't give a bugger what you think, Vale. As a matter of fact, there'd be satisfaction in taking you with me, much as that might disappoint my wife." He levels the gun.

"Killing me won't solve anything. You've more than yourself to consider. You have a choice, Stan." David Vale, only a few feet away, stands his ground.

Rose edges around the car, her feet numb from the cold. Mum's bicycle has been propped against the shed. She knows nothing about the scene around her own back door: Dad acting crazy, and David, trampling the flowerbeds, approaching danger, step by step. A bitter wind stirs the shadowy forsythia bush.

She calls from the darkness, "Dad, I know you felt you had to shoot Moggy. If I'd been there, I'd have begged you to find another way. I'm begging you now."

She steps out into the light and stands beside the vet.

"I won't let you kill yourself and you're not going to hurt this kind man who's only trying to help us."

This time she resists David's urgent insistence to get back behind the car. She draws on words spoken by Mum the night of the slain pig. "I won't let you keep frightening us like this."

Stanley surveys them from the higher step. "You two have no idea who I could have been. Women were falling over themselves to marry me. Why do you think Alice ever gave me the time of day? It was for my money. My father could've bought out four of the likes of you, Vale."

Rose pleads, "Mum doesn't care about the money. She loves you. I love you too, but please don't act this way."

"You'd be better off without me." He waves the rifle haphazardly, like a drunkard, mumbling to himself. Rose feels the vet beside her, his body taut, attentive to Dad's every move, like approaching a rabid animal.

Alert as her cat, Rose is long attuned to her father's facial expressions and the movements of his body. His bleak moods are familiar to her, but she fears darkness beyond her reach. She wonders if the vet feels it too, and dreads he'll push Dad too far. An unbearable thought comes of David injured or worse. Rose readies herself to act, frustration rising, like a dam about to burst. She steps so close to David she's almost leaning into him. Stanley abruptly raises the rifle and takes aim at the vet's chest. Rose leaps between them, arms flung out. David roughly pushes her aside and knocks the gun out of Stanley's hand. The two men scuffle together on the ground.

Out of the dark, a squeaky voice shouts, "Rose Gray, what's happening?"

Everyone freezes, caught in a beam of light from the bomb shelter roof.

The boy calls again, "Rose Gray, what are you doing over there?"

— 6 0 —

Rose scrambles to her feet and turns in the direction of the shelter. She calls, "Nothing's happening, Keith, we're just playing a game. Turn off your torch."

Her father, lowering his rifle, hisses, "Get rid of him. I don't want anyone over here asking questions."

"Or calling the police?" David adds, without taking his eyes off Stanley.

"A war game, Rose Gray?"

"Yes, a silly war game."

The light has gone off but they can see his silhouette on the roof. Dad mouths for Rose to deal with the boy. When she hesitates, David nods his head, urging her to go.

She runs to the roof, where Keith is stretched out on his stomach. She reaches for his hand. "I'll play war with you soon if you like. Wouldn't that be fun?"

"And go up the tower?" Keith implores.

"Shush, you promised you wouldn't tell. Don't say anything about this game either. It's top secret. Go home now like a good boy." She waits as he slithers to the other side.

Rose turns toward the house. Her father sits on the back step, the rifle on the ground, close to his feet. David stands over him.

"You look done in, Stan."

"My back's seized up."

"Shift over." David sits. Seeing Rose, he waves for her to stay back.

Rose watches, hugging herself against the cold wind. In the light from the house, Dad looks defeated, his face grimacing with pain.

David is advising Stanley how to release the spasm in his back.

"Try leaning forward as far as possible to stretch your spine." With his hand on Stanley's back, David gently pushes him forward.

Stanley groans, gingerly reaching for the rifle. He relinquishes it to the vet. "You might as well take it. Or my mother-in-law will when she finds out about the cat." He hands it over, like a wounded warrior with his sword.

David empties two bullets and puts them in his pocket.

"One each for you and me," Stanley says. "I'd never touch her."

"You're a cold fish, Stan."

The three of them enter the house. It smells of chicken soup. David helps Stanley into his chair. He suggests Rose makes hot drinks. She spoons Ovaltine into three mugs, while they talk quietly in the next room, with the door closed. Waiting for the milk to heat, she takes off her sopping wet slippers and looks for warm socks. Rubbing her cold toes reminds her of how bound she'd felt to Dad after their talk. She wonders at David's calm attention to him, when her own heart is crushed by how Dad turned on them both.

Setting out the hot drinks on a tray, she joins them in the living room.

David measures out pills for Stanley that he says helps the pain in his own shoulder.

"Why so charitable, Vale? Trying out for sainthood?"

"Hardly sainthood." David rattles the bottle. "Ever read about the suicide rate in veterinarians? We have stronger stuff available than this."

Rose gasps. "Surely, you never . . ."

"It was a long time ago. A dog saved me. I'd put her outside the door but she kept barking and woke the neighbors. With a gun you're not likely to get a second chance. What I found out was people cared. You're a well-educated man, Stanley. You have more choices than you think."

Stanley doesn't reply. His eyes are glazed.

David says it's time for him to go; there's a long day's work ahead of him tomorrow. Rose can tell he's uneasy about leaving. He asks her to walk with him to the car, where he carefully places the rifle in the boot. "I could drive you to the hotel where your grandma's staying," he offers.

Rose says she's promised Mum she'll take care of her dad, but she'll ask Granny to help get him to a doctor.

David says he believes the pills will help Stanley sleep through the night, but cautions her to run next door if she needs help. After he has driven away, Rose goes indoors. Her father sits in his chair.

"I'm going upstairs," she says. "I'm really tired."

He grunts. "Go on with you."

In bed, Rose cries a little, clutching the gold cross. When she was small, she'd listen to enemy bombers circling the countryside and her mother would draw her close. It feels as if ghosts of those death-carrying planes were there tonight, hovering over the house. How far, she wonders, did their shadows reach before they flew away?

"I miss you, Mum," Rose whispers into the darkness. "Please come home soon."

She hears Dad groaning his way to bed. He pauses on the landing. Rose listens until he moves on, closing his bedroom door.

In the dark, she pictures Granny in a four-poster bed at the King's Arms, only a few miles away. She prays, *Dear God, keep us safe.*

—61—

Saturday afternoon, a little over three weeks later, Violet, the old plough horse, stands in the field in the shade of a chestnut tree, swishing flies with her tail. The girls play around the pond, up to their knees in mud: frogs, barely visible except for their eyes, drift on the green surface. The blades of the windmill are still and have been for days. Back at Rose's house, Granny has thrown open front and back doors and all the windows. She's packed Rose and Annie a picnic and sent them off to amuse themselves while she sets about sweeping, dusting, and polishing from top to bottom. Tomorrow, Mum is coming home.

Annie waves a small fishing net. "It's hopeless," she says. "I can hear the frogs plopping all around. They must see me coming."

Rose laughs. "What will you do if you catch one, anyway—kiss it?" She's giddy with joy. Two days ago she and Granny went to visit Mum in hospital. She was sitting in a chair beside her bed, recovering from what had been a worrying wound infection, but looking stronger and at peace. All she needs now are iron pills for anemia, and lots of rest: her doctor swears it's not cancer.

"Let's go to the stream," she says to Annie, "and jump on the rocks— bet you'll be first to fall in."

Predictably, they are both soaked as they spread out the picnic of bread and cheese, hardboiled eggs, and ripe cherry tomatoes.

"I can see your nipples through your wet shirt," Rose says.

"Who cares?" Annie, on her back, tosses a tomato and catches it in her mouth. "Just because your granny insisted on buying you a bra doesn't mean I have to wear one."

"I brought that letter from Duncan to show you. He had the nerve to send it via the school." Rose reaches in her shorts pocket.

"I can't believe Gordy didn't confiscate it." She takes it out. "Oh bother. It's wet through."

They lay bits of sodden paper on the ground.

"The ink's run," Annie says. "What did it say?"

Rose gathers the shreds into a ball and tosses it into the stream. "Silly boy stuff. He's not even a good speller. Now I won't be tempted to answer it."

Annie giggles. "Bye, bye, Duncan." She leans back on her elbows. "Speaking of romance, our George and Dora are breaking up."

"Why, what's happened?" Rose sits up for a better look at Annie's face.

"George's call-up papers came in the post last week. He's deferred them once because of supporting our Mum. Now he says he's going to enlist in the navy."

"I thought he wanted to be a photographer."

"He still does. Ma's having a fit because she's afraid there'll be a war. Dora hasn't stopped crying. I don't want him to go. Now Ma's gone and put an ad for a lodger. George will be off in a month. It's all gloom."

"What about him: is he all gloom?"

"He's excited. I have my suspicions he wasn't all that keen on getting married. Dora wanted him to move the date up, but he refused. She's given him back his ring."

Rose lies back, watching white clouds heap like meringue against a blue sky. "He's doing the right thing. If he's not sure, he shouldn't do it. When else is he going to see the world?" She surprises herself, these days, at how old she sounds.

"I'm never going to get married," Annie says. "Is there any food left?"

After the picnic is packed up, they explore the field, picking wild-flowers and fashioning them into crowns. Grasshoppers tickle their legs as they walk through the long grass. They rest on a rock, legs dangling in the cold stream.

"What will your parents do about the farm?" Annie asks. "I dread the thought you might move away as well."

"They're not making any decisions until Mum comes home. Dad did see a doctor about his back. It's pretty certain he'll have to give up the pigs. Granny's been getting us organized. Dad left yesterday to visit his aunt Bea in the Peak District for a week or two. He says she's fond of him and will give good advice. I promised God that if Mum came out of hospital, I wouldn't complain, no matter what."

Rose moves closer to Annie, putting an arm across her friend's shoulders. "Look at us. We're both in the same boat, helplessly waiting while grown-ups decide what we're going to do." Rose laughs. She adds, more thoughtfully, "Granny says, right now, the future's none of my business."

She's only told Annie bits and pieces. She hasn't said that Dad was admitted to hospital for three days, and it wasn't the one where Mum is. Now he takes tablets every day and has been much nicer. One day he took a taxi to visit Mum and said they'd had a long talk, but nothing about what was discussed.

Granny revealed she'd heard once from Graham Faire. He'd written to apologize for barging into her garden. He hasn't yet returned to France because of his health. Granny thinks he'll stay in touch.

"We are part of each other's past," she said. "John would've been sad to see him so depleted."

Rose remembers Dad's words: "He'll never leave Alice alone, nor you." In a place deep in her heart Rose hopes this is true. She suspects Mr. Baxter, her Sunday school teacher, would say such thoughts are sinful; but she'll never forget Graham's furious wish to protect her from the horrible man at the theatre.

The girls stroll over to feed Violet their leftover apple cores. They tear off twigs to shoo away the horse flies. Annie asks, "Do you ever see the nice vet?"

"Sometimes. He's helping Dad decide which sows to sell for breeding. But he's moving away himself soon, up to the Lake District."

"Golly. You'll miss him, won't you?"

"We all will." Rose sighs. David Vale has been present on the farm on several occasions but he's never mentioned that dreadful night. The next morning Dad had made Rose swear she wouldn't tell a soul about what happened, especially Mum or Granny. Sometimes, she wonders if the whole scene at the back door was a bad dream, except she catches the vet watching her closely. Once, when they were briefly alone, he asked how she was managing, and said he was glad Granny was there to help. He spoke of his plans to move north, saying the countryside where his practice would be was stunningly beautiful. Perhaps, one day, she'd like to come and visit and see for herself? The invitation hovers in Rose's imagination like the tiny yellow butterflies rising as they walk across the field.

Try as she may, it's a future she cannot pin down, any more than she can capture a single butterfly without harming its wings.

"A penny for your thoughts," Annie says.

Rose shrugs off the question. "I want to show you something."

They settle in the shade under an oak tree. The telegram is damp but made of stronger paper than Duncan's letter. Rose's heart beats a little faster as she flattens it out on the ground. Annie reads aloud: "One grief removed. A."

"Who sent this, and who's it to?"

"It's from Mum to a journalist who worked years ago for my grandfather."

"Why a telegram? What does it mean?" Other questions follow, one after another. Rose parries them with vague answers. She should've known that giving Annie a single thread to pull on, she'd start unraveling the whole thing. She explains that Graham is an old friend who'd been in France in the war.

Annie points to the word "grief." "Ma says you never really get over it—she misses Dad every day. Grief can't be removed."

"I've made you sad," Rose says. "Look at you with flowers in your hair, like Ophelia."

Annie clutches her forehead. "Oh, woe is me!" She laughs.

The telegram, spread out in the sun, curls as it dries. In the distance, two cuckoos call to each other from one side of the field to the other.

"Maybe it's in code," Annie muses.

"Graham loves anagrams . . . so does my mum."

"I give up. I'm much better at math problems." Annie picks up her net, and announces she's going fishing, this time for minnows.

The mention of fishing reminds Rose of Jeff, fisherman or priest. On her back, in grasses fragrant with the sun, she offers a prayer. Jeff, by now, would know what became of the swimmer, far out in the rough waves. Did he drown? Did Gracie sell the van to Jeff and his father? The connections are slight, but the idea of seeing the cheeky young man again makes her smile.

"Perchance to dream," Rose quotes to the trees. Then giggles, "More like fat chance . . ." She sits up to examine the telegram and ponders its meaning.

"One grief removed." Had Mum believed not meeting Graham at the station would save him from more grief, especially if she was pregnant? Annie's idea it's in code is uncanny. Rose writes with a stick in a patch of dirt: "devomerfeirgeno." She squints at the reversed letters: "de" could be the beginning of dear, as in "Dear Graham," but she hasn't named him. Besides, there's no "a" for "dear."

She visualizes Graham's teasing face: "Figure it out, Rose," he'd say. Except . . . more likely: "Figure it out, dear one." But wait, Rose thinks, what if she includes Mum's initial, "A"? She crosses off the letters "dearone" and surveys what's left: "vmfeirgeo." It takes two minutes to find the hidden message: "Dear one, forgive me."

"Oh Mum!" Rose cries, holding the folded telegram against her cheek. "What now? What will you do?" For several minutes, she feels immobile, rooted to the ground like the great oak tree overhead. She's unscrambled the anagram but she doubts she'll ever truly solve the puzzle of her mother. A crevice has formed in the ancient trunk, creating a home, over the years, for various small animals. She takes the folded message and pushes it deep into the split.

Rose moves into the sunlight, brushing leaves and dirt from her clothes, determined more than anything to recapture her earlier happy mood.

"Go along you two," Granny had said, sending the two friends off to play. "Make the most of being young."

She finds Annie up to her thighs in pond water, her net full of flopping, silvery minnows. "Let the poor things go," she scolds. Annie lowers the net below the green surface and the tiny, shining fish dart away, free.

They sit side by side on the bank. "You were a long time under the tree," Annie says. "Did you decide the message was coded?"

"I did . . . but it didn't make much sense." One day, she'll say more to Annie about all that's happened, starting with the death of her cat. Right now, her heart's too full.

Annie throws stones into the pond, scaring the frogs. "We have to do something daring for our club."

"There's that old ruined house with the cellar you wrote about in your letter."

"I was thinking about climbing that thing." Annie points with her chin toward the watermill. "While its blades are not moving."

"We'd have to wade through all the muck," Rose objects. "And the bottom ladder rung's too high. Isn't it enough that we climbed the tower that time?"

"Not the whole way."

"Almost."

"You're lily-livered, Rose Gray."

"Not any more than you are, Annie Carter." They wrestle half-heartedly in the mud.

"Oh no," Annie says, "look who's coming." Three boys, bicycles abandoned, are clambering over the cart track fence.

Rose recognizes one of them as the altar boy from St. Bede's. He doesn't look nearly as angelic without his red robe and ruffled white collar. The shortest of the three yells, "What are you girls doing?"

Annie shouts back, "We're the Daring Demons and we're going to climb the watermill."

Rose, quietly dying, says, "No we're not."

It's too late. The third boy, a wiry youth with red hair, leads the way. "We'll give it a try."

Annie and Rose watch from the bank as the three boys wade waist-deep to the mill's cement base. The smallest, hoisted on the redhead's shoulders, grabs the bottom rung, and begins shimmying up the ladder.

"We could've done that," Rose says, dubiously.

Annie smirks. "Of course we could. But we have to let them *think* they're stronger."

Rose prods Annie's arm. "Annie Carter, if we ever let boys into the club, we won't play that game. We're not going to treat them like tin gods."

Annie laughs, "Where'd you get that idea?"

"My cousins."

The boys splash toward them, slapping each other on the back. Rose says, "Should we tell them about the old house and the creepy cellar?"

"What creepy cellar?" the smallest boy asks. "We want to see it."

Annie stands her ground. "No boys allowed."

The boys, talking all at once, say they have their own club, and chime in with adventures further afield than Rose and Annie have ever gone, such as hikes in the woods, a swimming hole in the river, unexplored caves, and a steep climb to a waterfall. The altar boy, whom Rose has long had a crush on, suggests they all plan a bike ride together. His friends enthusiastically agree.

Annie, with arms folded over her chest, shakes her head, but Rose suspects she's relenting. It feels their friendship is on the crest of something new. Adults are planning their fate but other forces are moving them into the future. Perhaps it's the love stories in the books Mrs. Cave has encouraged her to read, or how her dreams are vivid and changing like the sky, or perhaps it's the freedom of having Granny in charge, shooing her outdoors into the fresh air. Mum had hinted she and Gracie quarreled over boys. Rose shakes off the comparison. She and Annie will never allow that to happen to them.

The boys have wandered back to the pond, splashing around after the frogs. The girls watch their easy, boisterous play.

"They're like aliens," Annie grumbles. "It was so peaceful before they came swarming over the fence."

Rose laughs. "You make them sound like hornets."

"I know, but I can't help thinking about George. He used to be like them with his friends, horsing around, and getting in the way of my make-believe games with my dolls. Now he's gone all serious about being in the navy. In a few years those boys will be called up too. They don't have any more control over their future than we do."

Rose resists the sadness, so near the surface, in her friend. She says, "Look, here they come, like lambs to the slaughter. Oh Annie, do let's try to cheer up!"

The three interlopers join them on the bank, wringing out wet socks and putting on their shoes.

Rose assesses the stubborn look on Annie's face and begins to laugh. It's all very well, she thinks, to have had my first kiss on a train and made friends with a boy in a pub, but Annie, with George and his fiancé to spy on, probably knows tons more than I do about boys.

She takes Annie's hand. "Summer is coming up. The swimming pool's closed. Let's give them a chance and do the bike ride. This second we can make a choice that's our very own. Think hard. Where do we want our feet—I mean wheels—to go?"

Annie relaxes and grins, "Okay, you win . . . but shouldn't we first ask them their names?"